Dragon's Justice

Bruce Sentar

All entities in the story are figments of my imagination. Any relation or resemblance to actual events or people is entirely coincidental.

Before you dive into it, this story is fiction geared towards adults and it may contain elements not suitable for people under the age of 18.

There are sexual and harem elements. If that makes you uncomfortable, please turn back now and ask Amazon for a refund.

Contents

Chapter 1

Have you ever felt like there was something inside of you, pushing your actions? A dormant beast so to speak. I know, it sounds crazy.

But, that's the best way I could describe how I've felt for a long time. I thought it was normal, some animal part of the human brain that lingered from evolution. But this is the story of how I learned I wasn't exactly human, and there was a world underneath our own where all the things that go bump in the night live. And that my beast was very real indeed.

It all started one day a few weeks into my junior year of college.

I was shuffling my notes into my bookbag after C302. Organic chemistry was shaping up to be a tough one and I had only covered a week's worth of material at that point.

The fold-up stadium seating was a chorus of noises as they retracted and everyone hurried out of class. Feet pounded on the cheap linoleum tiles that were white with black spatters to hide the scuff marks that so commonly became part of the tiles.

I pushed all the scents and sounds to the background before the herd of students overwhelmed my senses.

My professor didn't seem to understand that computer models took care of all the manual work he was demanding of us. Of course, the fundamentals were important, but that's what C301 covered. I was so ready to move past the rote memorization to actually applying the knowledge.

But I had already half-expected it the first time I had walked into the room and saw the professor. Professor Finstein was a dinosaur, and by the way he struggled with his power point slides, I had a feeling he wasn't really interested in teaching the applications of digital models.

He had that vibe that he might even still use a slide rule to do his math—I'm talking ancient.

As I finished stuffing the last of my things into my bookbag, I stood up, a scent reaching me that once again stirred the beast inside me. At least, that's how I'd come to think about it. A redhead wearing a tight Kappa Phi Alpha shirt walked past my aisle, and the beast pulled my attention to her as he tried to take in her scent.

Taking a breath, making sure to do it through my mouth instead of my nose to help avoid her wonderful cloves and vanilla scent, I made sure to suppress the beast. I'd gotten a full scenting of her last week, and it had taken me half the day to push the beast back down.

This jerk inside of me wasn't going to get another whiff.

I wasn't about to be some asshole that hit on her like all the other guys around. People always talked before class, and I had heard that the few that approached her would get shut down rather hard.

The beast growled, upset at my decision, but I just ignored it, rolling my eyes. It wasn't about to tell me what to do with my life. The need began to weaken, and I shrugged the bag over my shoulder, heading out. I'd gotten used to dealing with the beast.

My friends laughed it off and agreed about wanting to pounce on some hot girl or deck a douche, but I never got the feeling they felt as driven to actually do it as I had since adolescence. The beast didn't control me, but it was hard to ignore.

I had seen a doctor about it once, but they just wanted to put me on meds that would put my whole life into a haze. They didn't seem to acknowledge the real problem, instead just wanting to turn me into a pseudo zombie and call in the next patient.

It was a struggle, one that I kept quiet for the most part. However, the beast, as I affectionately called my urges, didn't like being quiet. So it often left me wrestling it back down into submission to live my life.

And while I controlled it for the most part, I still had to work with it if I was going to finish out my degree and get into med school. It was a balance between me and the beast.

My phone chirped, and I pulled it out.

MAN! Maddie agreed to go to the bar with us tonight. Please tell me you can make it?

Frank, my roommate, and Maddie, our friend since freshman orientation, were close to hitting it off. Frank had been wearing Maddie down one almost-date at a time. They were the strangest of pairs. Frank was a serial skirt chaser, and Maddie was a quiet nerd. Yet he was Ahab and she was his white whale, and he was head over heels for her.

I worried that Frank would move on in a heartbeat after finally getting what he'd been chasing for nearly two years, but I tried to leave my opinions at the door. It was their relationship.

I'd at least gotten better sleep while he'd been pursuing her in this latest push. The walls were thin between our bedrooms.

Sure, Frankie. I just finished my last class for the day. See you at the apartment.

I hit send and made my way through campus on the network of cement sidewalks that cut through open lawns. The campus itself was a verdant gem compared to the rest of Philly. The city skyline loomed in the background, a churning leviathan of industry.

But the city and campus might as well have been two different worlds, separated by nothing more than a street.

Our apartments were on the east side of campus, hugging the business building. Overall, they were some of the newer buildings, making them highly desired, especially by the business students.

It didn't work as well for me since I was a pre-med student, but I liked that it was on the quiet side of campus. The bar street was also a straight shot through the campus on the west side. The science buildings were near those bars. It was a nice perk after a late-night test.

Weaving through the campus, I headed for home. Something about wrapping up for the day and getting to let loose a bit added some power into my stride as I dodged through the masses and hustled downstairs.

The only warning I got was a wobbly shout and the slaps of bicycle tires going down the steps behind me. I spun on one foot, dancing out of the way just in time to get clipped by the handlebars as a bike shot down right through where I'd just been standing.

The girl in front of me wasn't nearly as lucky.

The bike's front tire snapped sideways, with the handlebars catching on me and upending the rider. Both the girl and the rider went down in a tangle as the bike flipped over them and bounced into the grass.

I sprang forward, trying to figure out how to best free them. "Are you two okay?"

"Ugh." The heavyset biker rolled off the girl and looked dazedly at the sky.

Well, that at least told me he was okay enough. But he'd been wearing a helmet; the girl, on the other hand, hadn't dressed for an accident.

I knelt down and tapped her gently. "You okay? I'm going to check you out." It wasn't often I got to use my EMT training for something more than a sprained ankle.

Cloves and vanilla.

Looking at her more carefully, I realized she was that same sorority girl from class. This was around the same time that my beast noticed her as well, her scent reaching me. The beast rattled in my chest, roaring at the opportunity to save her, while I tried to ignore it and focus.

When the girl didn't respond to my touch or words, I started with the basics, trying not to move her. I took her pulse and then put a finger under her nose to make sure she was still breathing. Both of those checked out, so she wasn't in any immediate danger.

A crowd had gathered from the accident, and at least two people were on the phone calling campus security. There were two guys helping up the poor cyclist as he looked around in a daze before noticing his bike. The front tire had warped beyond use.

"My bike!" He came to his senses and dashed to check on it.

"No concern about the people you ran over?" I wasn't sure if it was me or my beast, or maybe both, but I wanted to get up and teach him a lesson with my fists. Clearly, the guy's priorities were in the wrong place.

But I knew it wasn't enough to get me into a fight, despite what my beast was saying. So I shook it off, refocusing my own attention on the girl.

I reached down to do a second set of checks, but before I could do anything else, her eyes snapped open, boring into my own.

Surprised, I said the first thing that came to mind. "Nice contacts."

I hadn't noticed them in class, but she had bright gold eyes, like the kind you'd see on a wild animal. I couldn't help but examine them a little further, trying to see the edge of her contact, but I couldn't. They were just so... real.

She blinked, scrunching her cute face together before opening her eyes again. "What happened?"

"A biker went down the steps. He clipped me and plowed into you."

She started to get up and winced, her arm giving out when she got only a few inches off the ground.

"Hey, careful. People already called the campus security. They'll come and call the EMT. I should know; I'm normally on the other end of those calls." I gave her a reassuring smile.

But instead of relieved, she looked shocked, maybe even a little scared. "No. No hospital. I just need to get back home."

Her shirt was pushed up, and I could already see a heavy bruise forming on her side along with her legs and a few nasty looking scrapes. By the way she could barely get up but wasn't screaming, she very well could have a hairline fracture in that arm.

"I think you might need that arm checked out," I suggested, but my helpful comment only earned me a glare.

"Help me up?" she asked. She was coherent enough that I thought the request reasonable, but she still needed to get that arm checked out.

Holding her under the armpits, I stood and brought her with me.

The crowd cheered, seeing her getting back on her feet. She looked a little roughed up, and she was still leaning on me heavily, but she was able to stay upright.

"Want me to help you back to your place?" I asked. I hoped she would let me check her out again when we got back. Maybe she'd even let me convince her to go to the hospital.

"Yeah. That'd be nice. I don't want to put on a show here." She kept her head down and her bright orange hair shielded some of her face.

"Come on." I wasn't going to leave a girl waiting. I let her lean against me as we shuffled out of the crowd.

She leaned heavily on me but seemed to be getting herself back together remarkably quickly. "This is terrible timing for me. You said you worked at the hospital?"

"Uh, not the hospital. I work for an EMT service they contract with," I clarified. I had been a little bummed when I had figured that out, but it didn't stop me from trying to network with the doctors at the hospital. I hoped I could get some shadowing experience or an internship with one of them next summer.

"Great. Can you help me set my shoulder back in?"

"Wait, your shoulder is dislocated? Let me see."

"No." She pulled away and stumbled. I stepped forward, catching her as carefully as I could, given her injuries. She looked around before nodding her head in the direction of an alley. "Let's go behind the library, and you pop it back in. I don't want to put on another show."

I raised my hands. "Hold up. You should go to the hospital to pop that back in place. There could be complications."

She gave me a hesitant look. "Can't you pop it back into place?"

"Well, yeah. I can try. But the policy is that it should wait until the hospital if possible."

"You aren't working right now..." She paused, her brows pinching for a moment. "I don't even know your name."

"Zach Pendragon." I gave her a small smile.

Her eyes went wide, but I wasn't surprised. It was pretty typical when I gave my full name. "Like King Arthur?" she asked.

"Yep, and spelled just the same. But no relation," I joked. Really, it was the last thing I had of my birth parents, but saying that out loud always brought down the mood of the moment. Humor hid that well enough for me on most occasions.

"Badass name. I'm Scarlett, just transferred over this year. And of course this shit happens the first week. I'm already having trouble fitting in with the girls." At that, she shifted our direction to behind the library.

The change in location seemed to please my beast. I could already feel it coiling up on itself in excitement. I nearly sighed, annoyed that once again I'd have to work to keep my control. But I kept my face in check as we turned the corner into the secluded place.

"The girls aren't the same as where you were before?" Nervous at the idea of popping her shoulder back in, I tried to make small talk as a distraction. I knew the theory of how to pop it back in, but I'd never actually attempted it. Not that I was going to tell her that.

"No, I mean, all sororities are sorta slutty. But this chapter of Kappa is taking it to a whole new level of bitches. Why she has to come here is beyond me."

I lost her then. "Why who has to come here?"

Scarlett made a face like she was cursing internally, then paused, clearly struggling to come up with an answer. "A friend transferred over with me. But she's starting a week late. Actually, she'll be here tomorrow."

"Ah. Friend." I drew the word out.

"No! Not like that." Her cheeks blazed just as scarlet as her name. "Men," she scoffed. "We have just been best friends since we were little, okay? She's transferring over here because her dad arranged this total jerk off for her."

"Arranged, like arranged marriage?" I hadn't heard of one of those in forever. I knew they were common in some areas, but I'd never known anybody to be set up that way.

She winced again, like she'd said something she shouldn't have. "You know what? I think I might have hit my head. Don't mind my rambling." Before I could circle back on that topic, she had turned her shoulder to me, looking over it at me. "Okay, how does this work?"

I paused and looked around. We were totally secluded. No other pedestrians were in sight, and another campus building hid us. We were alone in the cool concrete alley. "Brace yourself up against the wall. This is going to hurt. A lot. You might want to bite on something."

Scoffing, Scarlett rolled up her shirt to her collar, showing off her powder blue bra and ample chest. "Up here. Don't let them distract you too much." She gave me a knowing look before balling up the shirt and putting it in her mouth to bite on.

My cheeks burned, and the beast rattled in my chest. Yeah, he was going nuts over this girl. The best thing I could do was focus on the task at hand. "Okay, let me find the cuff." My fingers probed her shoulder until I had a good idea of where to focus.

"This is the painful part, but we'll do it quickly. Push your back hard against the wall."

Her legs tensed, and I lined her arm up, pushing with the palm of my hand to get it in the socket. But, beyond causing her to wince, nothing happened. It didn't budge.

It was a lot tougher than the movies made it seem. I pushed again, this time throwing my weight into it, and Scarlett let out a muffled cry as it popped back into place.

She let the wadded-up shirt out of her mouth and pulled it back down over her chest and toned stomach, much to my beast's whining dismay and my relief.

"That wasn't too bad," she said, rotating her shoulder.

"Never had it happen to me—they said it's pretty painful."

Scarlett just shrugged. "Meh. I've had worse."

Now that I was looking at her, she didn't look nearly as bad as I thought she'd looked when I'd first given her an assessment. My brows pinched together. It was odd.

She stretched her legs a little and pushed off the wall, looking steady.

"You sure you don't want to take a trip to the hospital?" I tried one more time, though she was looking better.

Scarlett did a small spin. "See? Not too bad. Don't think I'd try tap dancing right now though, if you'll forgive me."

I gave a small snort of laughter. "Don't worry, I couldn't even tap dance if I was in perfect health. You get a grudging pass from me. But I could have sworn you were going to need to go to the hospital."

A small smirk escaped her lips. "Maybe you've just seen too many things go wrong, and you assumed the worst?"

Maybe... but I could have sworn. Either way, I couldn't deny what was in front of me now. "Then in my professional opinion, you just need an icepack on that shoulder and some ointment to keep that abrasion from getting infected."

"Will do, Doc." Scarlett gave me a mock salute as she turned to head down the alley. I couldn't help it; if you were in my situation, you would have looked too. Damn, she had an ass like she destroyed pilates.

When she reached the end, she paused, turning back, totally catching me checking her out. However, that didn't seem to matter to her. "You should say hi in class on Friday. I don't know anyone in chem."

I stumbled over my words. "Yeah, of course. That'd be cool."

She gave me an amused smile, her green eyes glimmering with mirth as she turned, heading north to what I knew was Greek Row.

I turned back towards my apartment from the slight detour. "That'd be cool," I said in a mocking tone. Why did I have to say something so lame?

The beast inside of me grunted, like I'd failed him on multiple counts. It also didn't seem one bit surprised that I'd botched the ending there.

But she'd practically invited me to sit with her in class. That was a win, right?

Yeah, I convinced myself that it was a total win. We'd talk more in class, and I'd see if she wanted to go out to the bars in the upcoming weekend. I could imagine it now, her smile and those green eyes as I asked her. God, I hoped she'd say yes.

I froze mid-step, confusion spreading over me. Her eyes. Weren't they gold when she'd been injured? But I was sure they were green just then.

Rubbing at my temples, I was positive that I was losing it. School all week and working all weekend was clearly wearing me down.

The beast scoffed and curled back up to sleep, clearly done with me.

But that was fine with me. The stupid bastard got in the way too often. Hopefully, he'd be quiet on Friday and maybe I could ask her out after class.

Chapter 2

I walked back into my apartment, still thinking about the prospect of spending more time with Scarlett, but my phone pinged again with a reminder from Frank to go out tonight.

"Yeah, yeah. I won't bail on you. Not like I have anything better to do tonight," I muttered to myself as I put the phone down and looked in the fridge. It was pitifully empty, and I was reminded once again that I needed to do groceries.

The apartment was pretty basic, but there was a nice, open area for the two of us. The landlord had furnished it, so it didn't have much character, but it did the job. Beyond that, we had a shared bathroom and two bedrooms side by side.

My room was my space away from everything. I had my mineral rock collection to one side, built up from a hobby of panning for gold and trying to find and dig up a small vein of metal in the mountains. Somehow, I seemed to have a knack for it.

There were two jars with about an inch of gold flakes in them. I wasn't sure how much it would actually be worth, but they held sentimental value for me.

My adoptive father and I used to go panning. He'd insisted on doing it, and I thought he'd really loved it. It was only later that I found out he did it because it got me to open up when they had first adopted me. When he passed away a few years ago, I'd found his collection of gold flakes sitting alone on a shelf in his closet. Right there at eye level for him.

It meant so much. I knew it had been the first thing he saw every time he opened that closet.

Moisture welled up in my eyes just thinking about it, and I wiped it away. Dammit.

He and my adoptive mother had lived good long lives. They'd adopted me late into their sixties; they said they'd known it was right when they had first laid eyes on me. I was the missing piece to their puzzle.

Trying not to go too deep down memory lane, I picked my phone back up for a distraction. I checked my emails one by one, letting the feeling of loss sweep by.

When I felt more under control again, I took a deep breath and unpacked my bag. I still had some shit to get done before going out with Frank and Maddie. I wouldn't be of any use after that.

***

"Come on. You aren't even dressed to go out yet?" Frank lingered in my doorway.

The two of us were about as opposite as you could get. Frank was a marketing major and fully embraced the work hard, play hard mentality. He'd party and cram, knuckle down and get his stuff done, only to celebrate with multiple bottles of wine.

He must have thought sleep was for the weak, because I had no idea when he actually slept. That party-hard phase often included night long bumping of his bed against the wall.

"It'll be quick." I got up and grabbed a button-down shirt from my closet. Frank had berated me for days after I had worn a t-shirt out to the bars.

"Not-uh. Nope. I thought I told you. No more vertical stripes. You are far too tall and skinny for them." Frank rolled his eyes and barged into my room, taking it upon himself to rifle through my closet. "Really, I don't know how you even dress yourself." He gave an exaggerated sigh.

My roommate and friend. I had at one point mistaken him for gay, but he just cared quite a bit about looks. Personal marketing, as he called it. But it seemed to work for him. He brought home different girls often enough that I had some trust in his fashion sense.

"Here. Try this one." He held out a black button down. My shirt dwarfed him. I wasn't huge by any means, but Frank wasn't very large. He was maybe five nine and very skinny-fit.

"Isn't this a bit plain?" I asked, holding the black shirt up against me.

"Nope, black is in right now. It also is about all you have that is fitted enough not to look like a square block." He then eyed my jeans skeptically.

"Hey, these were fine last year." I felt a defensive lilt creep into my voice as I swapped shirts.

Frank rolled his eyes. "That was last year. Get with the program. But they'll have to do... I've seen some of the other options."

"Better?" I asked as I finished buttoning the shirt and did a little spin for him.

"Roll up the sleeves so you don't look like a nerd."

I resisted rolling my eyes as I rolled up the sleeves. "Happy?" As much as I played the part of being disgruntled, Frank's advice had served me well on more than one occasion.

"You'll do," Frank said with a smile. "Come on. Maddie is meeting us there."

I nodded, pausing to touch on a sensitive subject. "So, Frank, once you get Maddie back to your bed, are you done with her?" Frank went through girls faster than he went through condoms, which was often more than one a night if what I'd heard slip through the walls was right.

Frank gasped and put a hand to his chest. "You wound me, Zach. No, those others were just a distraction. Maddie I plan to date as a serious girlfriend."

I gave him a look full of doubt but put it behind me. What the two of them decided to do was up to them.

"Well, come on. We need to go. The last thing I want to do is start the night off making Maddie wait." Frank grabbed his house keys from the kitchen table and bounded out of the room, with me right behind.

But a knock on our front door made both of us pause. "You said Maddie was going to meet us there?" I asked.

He just shrugged and swung open the door with a smile. Frank was like that. He dove into every situation headfirst without a care in the world.

Standing in the hallway to our apartment was a disgruntled-looking campus security man. "You Zach?"

"Nope, that's the poorly dressed man behind me." Frank hooked a thumb over his shoulder.

The man shifted his attention to me. "I'm following up on an incident reported earlier today. Someone identified you as having helped an injured girl away from a biking accident."

It wasn't exactly a question, but I still answered it. "That would be correct. The girl was a bit banged up, and she asked for some help getting away from the crowd. At the library, she said she could finish the rest of the way home and that was the last I saw of her. She was

Kappa Phi Alpha. I'd bet you could find her at the sorority house if you wanted to check on her."

He pulled out a little leather-bound notebook and pointedly clicked his pen before jotting down the note. "Then I'll do just that. Especially seeing what company you have." His eyes slid back to Frank.

"Oh, so you do recognize me," Frank beamed, but the security guard turned and stormed away. "Rude."

"Please don't antagonize them." The last thing I wanted was more trouble.

Frank shrugged. "He has a cute daughter that goes here."

My mouth fell slack. "You didn't?"

He gave a wicked grin. "A gentleman doesn't kiss and tell. But then again, I'm not a gentleman. Totally banged her in his house and said hello the next morning."

I slapped my forehead. Of course he did. "Anyone else in school I need to be careful about?"

"Never mind that. Who's this girl you went all knight-in-shining-armor on? Is she cute?" Frank asked, heading out the door.

"Hands off her." I nearly growled before reining in the beast and adding in, "I'm calling bro code on this one."

Frank's eyes nearly popped out of his head. "Oh no. Now I need to know everything."

***

Dance music blasted out of the speakers as a DJ made exaggerated flicks on a soundboard, bouncing to the beat of his own music. He was pretty good considering he was playing for a crowd of drunken college students.

It was late enough that the floor had dried beer covering it, causing my feet to stick slightly as Frank and I danced around together like two goofs. Maddie was there with us, but she'd gone off to get another drink. She and Frank were starting to hit it off, and I was feeling like a third wheel.

"Is that her?" Frank pointed out the third redhead of the night. He'd been doing it ever since I'd told him about Scarlett.

"No. She's... shorter, and bigger chested," I answered, feeling a bit like a pig using chest size as a distinguishing quality for women. But I knew Frank's language well enough to know that was how he saw them.

"Blue shirt big, or..." His eyes wandered. "Wow, white pants. Two o'clock."

That was when the hottest woman I'd ever seen walked past. We're talking top tier Hollywood sex appeal. And the beast inside my chest went absolutely nuts. I'm talking crazy, slamming against the cage of my chest, begging for a piece of her. There was a roar in my ears that had nothing to do with the bar.

She had a waterfall of platinum blonde hair, a loose silk shirt that bunched precisely at her impressive chest, and she had the gall to wear the tightest pair of white jeans I'd ever seen. I could have sworn they were painted on.

White pants strolled right past us, heading towards the stage. Men all around the bar noticed her and then got out of her way; she had an almost regal bearing.

"What are you doing?" Frank yelled over the music.

I realized I'd taken a step to follow her, which was just stupid. She was so far out of my league it wasn't even funny.

But the beast in my chest slammed even harder, rattling in its cage, begging me to chase her down. I wanted to too.

"I'll catch up with you later, Frank," I said before I even knew what was coming out of my mouth. The beast was insistent, and I didn't even want to stop it this time. I wasn't sure if my success with Scarlett had bolstered my confidence or the alcohol, but I kept moving towards the captivating woman.

She eventually found an open place and started twisting and dancing on her own, just enjoying the music. I looked around, waiting to see if she was with other people. Women like her didn't usually show up to a bar alone.

But she continued to dance, a slow, sinuous dance that called to me, and my inner beast clawed at me to join. The crowd bumped me forward, and before I could step away, I felt her tight rear push back into me.

She must have felt me nearby, because she shifted back, grinding that ass of her tight white jeans into me. Leaning her head back, she let out the most beautiful voice, just a single note that seemed to reverberate through me.

The beast in my chest, for the first time in a long while, was completely still. It almost seemed happy to just relax in that moment, hearing that single note from her throat.

She reached back, turning her head slightly to take me in, but her eyes went wide as she looked up into my face, followed by horror as she looked over my shoulder.

I followed her line of sight.

Behind me was the college's star quarterback, Chad Brodie, showing off his muscles in the tightest shirt I'd ever seen on a dude. Even Frank refused to wear a shirt that tight, which was saying something. The two plastic drink cups in his hands squished as they formed fists and shot their contents up into his face.

Despite the fact that he'd done that to himself, it seemed to only piss him off more as his eyes dug into me, glowing with anger. It must have been the lights in the bar, but they looked like they actually glowed.

Whoopsie, was this his girl? Fuck, I'd just dug my own grave.

"Run, I'll deal with this," the woman said. Her words took a moment to resonate as I soaked up the tone of her voice, but as she moved away, I processed them.

She turned to Chad this time as another one of those soothing notes came out of her mouth. But as she did it, Chad's eyes dulled.

I turned and left—don't pass go, don't collect two hundred dollars. Just got myself out of there.

There was something strange going on, but I was sure I did not want to get in the middle of it. Chad had a record on campus. Rumors floated around him that seemed to get swept under the rug quickly, supernaturally quick. I wasn't sure if he had connections or what, but it wasn't worth finding out.

If the rumors were true, he'd sent more than one guy to the hospital. Some never came back to school. Some might have not even made it back to their families.

He was also an all-star football player who was rumored to be leaving the school early for the NFL draft next year. He was crazy good and part of our two-year winning streak.

Moving my way through the bar, I focused on the exit. I needed to get the hell out of there. I ended up at a side exit for the bar. The cool fall air hit me all at once as I stepped out of the sweaty dance floor.

Shit, that had been crazy. I took a deep breath, feeling the stress build and leave.

"Ha," I barked out a loud laugh, receiving a few odd looks from drunk passersby in response.

Frank was going to eat up that story tomorrow. It had been completely out of my character to do what I'd just done, but it had felt so damn good.

But, as my phone started buzzing, I knew Frank was not about to wait until the morning.

DUUUUUDDE WTF was that.

He'd clearly been watching the whole thing.

Hell if I know, but I think I'm done for the night.

Zach, we can be out in a few minutes.

I rolled my eyes. It would be good for the two of them to be alone for a while. I'd been feeling vibes that Frank might just get what he'd been hunting for that night. I wasn't going to put a damper on that.

No, you two have fun. Make a move on Maddie. I need to go cool my head, anyway.

The beast inside my chest was furious with me. He wanted to lean into conflict. Luckily, I looked out for my best interest and shoved it down. It was like trying to wrestle a honey badger today. Those bestial instincts of mine wanted to be set loose.

I took one look down the college bar street, considering if I should head to another bar, but I eventually decided just to make the trek back across campus and give myself some time to think and process.

Classes had started up a few weeks before, and it was a typical fall night on campus. The nights were cool and crisp, making the buzzed walk pleasant among the brightly colored leaves. Another school year, I mused, wondering what it had in store for me.

I stuffed my hands in my pockets before continuing down the bar street and through the large stone arch into campus proper.

Evenings on campus could be a bit creepy; all the class buildings were dark, slumbering giants in the night. The campus was abandoned except for a few others like me, that took the fastest route across campus to wherever they were going.

I passed by Wellington Hall, where I had chemistry earlier, my thoughts turning back to Scarlett as I let my mind wander. Friday was both nerve wracking, yet I hadn't been looking forward to something so much in a long while.

"Aaah," a charging yell came from my side, shattering my thoughts into the night. I twisted to face whoever it was, but I hadn't been prepared. I spun, only giving me a moment to recognize Chad before he tackled me to the ground.

My back stung as a stray twig dug into me. Chad was not exactly a lightweight. But that thought was abandoned as my chest burned and I failed to pull new breath into my lungs. I had other priorities right now.

"Fuck you." Chad punctuated his displeasure with a punch to the side of my head that made the sky spin and my ears ring.

In addition to the ringing, however, I could hear my heartbeat beating powerfully. I knew what a heartbeat should sound like, and there was something off about mine. It was almost changing.

A deep growl built up from the beast. But that was usual. What shocked me was that I could feel something inside of me changing this time. The beast wasn't just communicating its displeasure; it felt like it was rising from a lifelong slumber. For the first time, it was getting to its feet. It continued, and it took me a moment to realize that I was giving a deep, loud roar straight into Chad's face.

I tried to think about how much I had to drink, but it was not nearly enough to be yelling in someone's face. For the first time, the beast was well and truly loose. I rolled back and got my feet under Chad before launching him off me with a kick. Even as I stood, there was a deep rumbling growing in my chest.

Chad looked dumb struck as I stood up and squared off against him. He was still growling, but he looked more cautious. There was a hint of satisfaction in his face that this wasn't too easy, but all I could think was how stupid he was for trying to take me.

The beast made me a whole new level of cocky.

I barely registered the movement to his side, my focus so heavily zoned in on Chad, until I realized it was the woman from the bar. She stood panting by his side, giving me an apologetic look.

"Sorry about this. Chad, heel," she demanded. Clearly, Chad wasn't quite as alpha as he acted, as if she was going to whip him like that.

"Go, crawl back to your master. Before you get hurt." My voice was deep and teasing. Part of me winced, knowing it wasn't smart to egg him on, but the other part was highly satisfied with making my dominance known.

Chad howled and... shifted. I stood there as his spine crackled like someone had just stepped on bubble wrap. I thought he was somehow dying at first until his face started taking on a bestial shape and he sprouted fur over his arms. He didn't change beyond gaining another hundred pounds of muscle mass and his arms becoming monstrous. Oh, and his face. He was an ugly sight to see now.

If I wasn't in such a strange head space, I would have been picking up my jaw from the floor. Was Chad a... werewolf?

It was the closest reference I had, even if they weren't supposed to exist. I had definitely stepped into something crazy. Either I had been slipped something at the bar, or the world was a lot weirder than I'd ever given it credit for.

With no idea what to do against a supernatural beast, I gave in to my own beast and let those instincts take over.

"Heel!" the woman demanded, this time punctuating it with a piercing whistle that made me dizzy.

Chad tottered, and I thought it was over for a second, but then he launched himself at me. The smirk on his face transforming into a maw wide with teeth.

Fangs and fur streaked at me. There was a moment where my mind and body were disconnected. My mind screamed to run, but my body roared to fight. I sidestepped in a blink and grabbed one of his out-stretched arms, spinning him in a circle and slamming him down on the concrete hard enough to shatter the sidewalk paver.

I hoped he'd stay down, but the hit only fazed him for a moment. He was back on his feet in seconds, a growling mass of fur and fury. He came quickly after that, his hands—now claws—swiping at my head.

Against my better judgement, I grabbed Chad's arm and stopped him in his tracks, using the other arm to throw a punch that snapped Chad's head back and sent him stumbling away. Holy crap, I was strong.

He paused to recover, but I pressed forward, snapping two more punches against his face, keeping him staggered before I kneed him in the gut and caused him to buckle over. Anybody else would have been down for the count, but apparently werewolves were sturdier.

The beast, not yet satisfied, took his bent head and hit it with the full force of a right hook to the temple.

I could feel a wet crack as I broke my hand, but Chad went down for the count.

Ignoring the pain, I stood over him. "Pathetic pup, you should learn to respect your betters." The words came out growled. Placing my foot on his chest, I pinned him to the ground, pausing for a moment as I wrangled with what to do. My beast wanted to squash the man, but I had regained enough control to try to think it through first.

"Please spare him. I am Princess Jadelyn Scalewright, and my family would compensate you for the damage done here today."

Her name sounded important, even if it meant nothing to me. And this time, her voice didn't seem to calm my beast, who was completely focused on Chad.

"This is retribution. You should both learn your place in the world." I or he... I wasn't sure if I was going crazy just yet... pushed my foot down on Chad's chest. The beast fought for control, ready to finish it completely.

Jadelyn screamed in response, and the air rippled out of her mouth. Her scream became something almost physical as it slammed into my side.

I jumped and rode the wave of sound several yards away from where Chad lay. My ears were ringing, and I felt the warm trickle of blood coming out from one side.

The scream shook me a bit from the primal moment and that loss of control. I knew that scream would have people running from all over to investigate. I did not want to deal with the fallout.

I could feel the beast less than enthused about the idea of leaving, but it didn't try to stop me.

Had I gone nuts, or had the world? I had just fought a freaking werewolf and won. Either way, I needed to get out of here. Something about me was different, I knew that, but I needed to get away and figure things out.

I turned my back to the pair and started walking away. As I moved, it was almost like something clicked in me, and I felt much more in control of my body. I almost stumbled but turned it into a glance behind me.

Princess Jadelyn was staring at me in horror. I seemed to have done something completely out of her expectation, which was saying something given she knew a werewolf and seemed to have abilities of her own. Her eyes tracked me as I stared back at her.

A smirk came across my lips. I just couldn't help it. I felt like a fucking badass.

I almost strutted slightly, which of course was ruined, when all of a sudden, my body was wracked with pain. My head spun and my fist ached. I focused on moving one foot in front of the other and getting out of there. The rest I'd have to figure out later. All I wanted to do was get back home and lock the doors.

The rest of the trip home was blessedly uneventful, but my whole body continued to ache. I couldn't have told you the color of my own shoes. My mind was so addled by the events that had just transpired.

Apparently, that scream of Jadelyn's had been a doozy.

I locked the door behind me and checked to make sure Frank wasn't home before talking to myself.

"Well, that hurt like a bitch." My stomach responded. Gurgling from a pain that wasn't from her.

Now that I focused, that ache in my chest was coming from my gut. I'd thought it might be from getting throttled, but the more I focused on it, the more I realized it was from my stomach painfully reminding me it was about to start digesting itself.

Opening the fridge, I groaned. There wasn't much besides Frank's half a box of pizza from the other night, and condiments. No other real food.

"Sorry, Frank, but I'm starving." I pulled out a slice of the greasy, cheap pizza, but even cold, it tasted better than anything I'd had in a long time.

This left over pizza wasn't going to be enough.

A grocery run this late at night was out, so I pulled out my phone and used an app to order three large pizzas.

I wasn't sure why, but I got the sense that the beast curled in on itself and settled down after that.

"Did you just go to sleep on me?" I asked the empty apartment. When there was no reply, I felt stupid.

The pizza came, and I shocked myself when I had pounded down all three of them and still felt like I had room for more. Somehow my stomach had become a bottomless pit.

I thought about ordering more, but the ridiculousness of that and the waves of exhaustion washing over me won out. I gave up the thought and headed to bed.

Sleep came as soon as I put my head down. I only woke once during the night when Frank came home and drunkenly yelled for me. But he must have brought home Maddie, because it wasn't long before the quiet was broken by a rhythmic pounding beat against his wall.

CHAPTER 3

I woke up as the sun streamed through the window. I stretched, blinking rapidly to try to bring the world back into focus.

Had my contacts fallen out?

I felt for them and ended up pulling one out to look at it, but as I did, everything out of that eye became clear.

Blinking, I pulled the other contact out and stared at my room in awe. Things were clearer, crisper than they had ever been. My eyesight was twenty-twenty, maybe even better. Insane.

Slightly freaked out but also excited, I looked at the clock and groaned. For all that this was interesting, I needed to get going; biology would be starting soon. The mystery of my eyes would have to wait, and I didn't really want to process everything from the night before anyway. Normalcy and biology class sounded weirdly nice.

Scooping up my clothes, I balled them up and hid my nudity as I slipped out into the quiet main room and into the bathroom.

I threw the clothes on the ground, wandering over to the shower to turn it on, but the reflection in the mirror caught my eye as I passed. Stepping back in front of it, I tried to figure out what was different.

I reached up and touched my face. My jawline seemed almost more square than it had been before, and I was definitely a few inches taller? My brows were a bit shaggier, giving me a more rugged look. And I definitely didn't normally have a five o'clock shadow like that in the morning. Apparently, my eyesight wasn't the only part of me that had transformed overnight.

My muscles looked like I'd just finished a month-long workout bootcamp. Doing a quick spin in the mirror, I couldn't help but check myself out. I had always considered myself attractive, but the guy in the mirror was seriously better looking.

Something had changed last night. I wasn't sure what yet, but so far, I was all about it.

Frank's alarm started buzzing across the apartment, and I let out a curse. I needed to get a move on it. I started moving through my normal routine, getting ready for class.

As I ducked into my room after my shower, I ran into a new issue. My clothes didn't fit. I had to rifle through my closet until I came out with a formerly baggy sweatshirt and a pair of old sweatpants.

As I pulled them on, they fit very differently now that my muscles had filled out. Holding out my hand, I remembered the injury from the night before. But it was gone, no sign of the injury.

It all started flooding back. I'd fought a werewolf and outmaneuvered a woman whose scream had physical force. There were creatures I'd had no idea about, and somehow, I seemed to be different now as well. Shaking my head, I tried to push it from my mind. It was a lot to process.

No normal person could have slapped around Were-Chad like that, and it finally gave meaning to the beast besides me being crazy. Giving into the temptation, I talked into my chest, once again feeling stupid. "Beast, are you in there?"

There was a faint sense of a grouchy grumble and the beast turning over deep within me, and then it seemed to go back to sleep.

Stupid... thing.

Whatever it was, it felt powerful. A little smirk turned my lips up. The way I had thrashed Chad the night before had been so satisfying.

Leaving my room, I rifled through the kitchen and got the coffee pot going. The smell of my morning pick-me-up made my stomach growl, as if reminding me I needed more than coffee to survive.

The three pizza boxes from last night were still sitting on the counter. I checked them in the hopes of finding some remaining pizza, but there wasn't even a stray pepperoni left.

"Zach?" Maddie peeked out of Frank's room, wearing one of his button ups.

I decided to ignore her possible nakedness. "Morning, Maddie. How was your night?" I kept my tone even and casual because I knew it had been a big deal for her to finally hook up with Frank. I was hoping it wouldn't affect our friend group very much.

"Uh... good. Is that coffee?"

"Freshly brewed. Grab a cup." I pointed to a cupboard to her right.

"Thanks..." She trailed off. "This is weird."

I smirked. She was so focused on what was going on with her that she didn't even seem to notice I had changed. But I was also hiding it under a pretty baggy hoodie, and she was distracted.

"I hope it's okay. Frank and I, that is…" she continued after I stayed quiet.

I gave her a reassuring smile and grabbed the coffee pot as it finished, pouring her cup first and then my own.

"It has been coming for the last few months. Honestly, I'm surprised it took so long."

Maddie looked surprised. "Oh. I… didn't realize you knew."

"Hah. Yeah, you two didn't hide it very well. Always sneaking off together. And I do live with Frank." I'd have had to have been clueless to miss their interest in each other.

I was happy for Frank. Maddie was certainly attractive, but she'd just never been extra interesting to me. Definitely had never made my beast go wild.

I paused, remembering Jadelyn from last night. Had the beast gone crazy because she wasn't human? No, that couldn't be it. Scarlett seemed normal after all.

"Gosh, you really have it bad. Drifting off with a smile. Frank told me you had a new girl. When do we get to meet her?" Maddie shifted the conversation away from her own awkwardness.

"It isn't like that. We just talked yesterday. We'll see how things go. You know Frank; he's making it out to be like we are going to be married."

She rolled her eyes. "Well, you should get a girlfriend. Maybe it would stop you from trying to take on Chad in a crowded bar. Talk about stupid."

I hid a smile, wondering what she'd think if she knew that I had actually beaten him. Instead, I just shrugged. "Hey, I didn't know. And she was the one that started grinding on me."

"Uh huh." Maddie sounded unconvinced. "That's not the way Frank told the story. It was more like you went on the prowl… which was surprising because you don't ever really go after girls."

"Too busy," I snorted.

Maddie didn't follow that with anything for a moment, and we sat in silence, content to try to sip on our still steamy hot coffees.

She blew at the top of her coffee a few times before taking another tentative sip. "So, do you guys have any food here? Leftover pizza?" She eyed the pizza boxes.

"I think we are in desperate need of a grocery run. Those boxes are old," I fibbed.

She wrinkled her nose. "That's fine. I'll just pick up something on my way home."

I gave my coffee another tentative sip before deciding it wasn't going to scorch my mouth to oblivion, because I needed to get going, and this was what was going to get me there. I downed my cup in a gulp.

It didn't even tingle on the way down.

"Shit, Zach. Are you okay?"

"Yeah, surprisingly. It wasn't that bad."

"This coffee is scalding hot." She gave me the look of a concerned mother.

I held up my hands and an empty cup. "See? No problem. I gotta get running to class. I'll catch you later, Maddie." Scooping up my backpack, I booked it out of the apartment before I had to talk more with my half-naked best friend wearing my other best friend's clothing. I was happy for them, but it was still weird.

As I headed to class, I swung by the dining hall for a bagel.

"Hey, I haven't seen you around before." A cute girl in line gave me an obvious once over.

"Uh, yeah." I had no idea what to do with that. The beast inside of me gave a content rumble at the compliment, telling me to push forward. "See you later, I gotta run."

Well, I definitely failed that one. I just wasn't used to women trying to pick me up in random lines.

Along my way to the biology building, I caught more girls checking me out, and a few even made small talk as they walked alongside me. I hadn't changed that much, had I? Is this what it felt like to be one of the Chads of the world?

The beast grumbled at the missed chances but grew bored and slipped back into sleep.

Ever since last night, the beast had become way more real to me. It certainly felt more real within my body. It was like there was a pressure inside of me, ready to burst out.

But I also felt the best I had ever been in my entire life. My whole body rang with strength. The backpack barely even felt like it was there.

Ducking through the halls, I slipped into biology and looked up at the clock. I'd made it across campus in record time, and I even had a few minutes to kill. I'd been stressed that morning for nothing.

I double checked the time, but it stayed the same. I'd really gotten to class that quickly.

Class settled in. Professor Vandal was playing her typical reggae music, which might make sense if she didn't dress primly in decades-old pantsuits.

The back of my neck prickled. Curious, I turned casually to try to see what might be setting off my senses. And there, entering the room, was none other than the princess from last night herself; only this time, Jadelyn Scalewright was wearing tight leather pants and a green top.

She was staring dead at me, and my turning only seemed to encourage her as she walked down the aisle, turning more than a few heads, only to stop at the seat next to me.

"Mind if I sit here?" she asked in a voice that was both natural yet melodic.

I snorted. "Of course, your majesty. How could I bar one such as you?" My voice dripped with snark.

"At least you know your place today."

I choked on my own tongue at that. "Excuse me?"

She looked genuinely surprised. "Oh. That was a joke." Her brow furrowed in confusion.

"It's not quite as funny when you have to say it's a joke. Sit down, don't make a scene." People were starting to turn and look at us.

"You don't command me," she said, clearly taken aback, but she sat down anyway. "I must apologize again. I'm having Chad reprimanded. It was not how I hoped my first night with him would go."

"You two just started going out?" My beast perked up, but I pushed the nosey bugger down. Scarlett was several times the woman the uppity princess was turning out to be.

She scowled at the question. "More like our families just engaged us. My father wants to further consolidate his power, and I'm a means to that end. And Chad is the alpha of the young pack, one of the largest ones for his generation. It makes sense." A heavy sigh punctuated the end of her statement.

Consolidation of power? Clans? I wanted to look around and see if anyone else was looking at her like she was crazy. But, as I looked at her, I realized she was serious. There was some alternative culture she was a part of, and she seemed to think I should know all about it.

"Um, well. Sorry you're stuck with him; he has a bad rap around here." I realized after I'd said it that insulting her soon-to-be husband may not have been the best move, but I figured she had a right to know.

"Oh? I hadn't heard much before I came yesterday. Besides, after his altercation with you, he seemed alright. Cocky, but that's par for the course with a brand-new alpha wolf."

That seemed like an understatement. The dude had clear problems with aggression, and the night before seemed to only make that clearer. But at least now it made more sense why she was with him if it was an arranged marriage.

I decided to try to fill her in a bit more. Jadelyn deserved to know what she was marrying into. "Supposedly he's hurt a few guys."

But she just waved that away. "As an alpha yourself, you must have broken a few bones, no?"

"I'm not quite sure what you think I am, but I'm not a wolf." I didn't know that for sure, but everything in me told me that wolf didn't fit. It didn't howl, it roared.

"Of course not. The way you trounced Chad, I'd guess something bigger." Jadelyn gave me a small smile. "Chad is going to have to adjust to not being the alpha on campus."

I tried to poke my beast and ask what kind of shifter I was, more curious than ever. What was bigger than a wolf? Maybe a lion or bear? But all I got in return was a derisive snort, and then it went back to sleep. But somehow shifter didn't feel quite right either.

"Not a shifter." I waited, curious what she'd offer up in terms of other supernatural creatures as she guessed.

She squinted at me, as if it would help her figure out what I was. "Troll? No, you're in college. I haven't heard of one of those making it past high school."

Jadelyn drummed her fingers on her pink lips in thought. "Not a vamp either. You don't have that geeky, broody vibe." She hummed again before shrugging. "I give up. Tell me."

I paused, not sure what to say. I hadn't thought she'd ask point blank.

As I hesitated, her eyes scanned mine. Whatever she saw must have made it clear I wasn't holding back, because she gasped. "You don't even know."

Sighing, I ran my hand through my hair, hoping class would start soon and I'd avoid having to have this conversation.

Her eyes darted around before she leaned in and hissed. "Did you even know about the supernatural before last night?"

My dumbfounded look must have been answer enough, because she leaned back and pressed a hand to her forehead. But what came next surprised me most.

"I'm terribly, terribly sorry. Last night was not the introduction you deserved. Had I known you were a lost one..." She sighed. "Please accept my most sincere condolences. It has been over fifty years, but we are still finding lost ones so often."

"Uh. Okay," I said.

She seemed truly distraught and more than a little angry at herself. But then she let out a heavy breath. "Then let me be the first to welcome you back into the fold. Everything that goes bump in the night in the stories is real. We..." She paused for a moment to point between me and her for emphasis. "...are real."

"Alright! Today we are going over mitochondria," Professor Vandal said, overly enthusiastically interrupting our conversation.

"And I'm actually a student and need a degree, so we can talk after class." Jadelyn said, turning back to give the professor her attention.

Shrugging, my opinion of her shifted slightly higher after that brief conversation. I wasn't sure what 'lost one' meant, but it seemed to have made her a bit kinder and more inviting.

Paying attention to the professor after that bomb was nearly impossible. My thoughts kept swirling to all the questions I had for Jadelyn. I started jotting down notes in my notebook, completely ignoring class.

I started with what I knew. Werewolves were real, and so were sirens. I was neither of those, and likely not a troll. And there was some sort of organization or separate culture that the supernaturals were within.

My pen shivered, making the last letter unintelligible as I noted the 'lost ones'. Could I have a family out there? Just like many adopted kids, I'd always had questions about where I came from and who my family was. This might lead me there.

It hit me harder than anything else, even the concept that they were likely supernatural. I'd spent my whole life wondering.

For now, Jadelyn was my only real connection to that world. I hoped she'd be willing to help me. She was my best hope.

I doodled idly, feeling for the beast in my chest, trying to draw it out to see what it looked like. But all I came up with was a vague creature with a big head and a long tail. Maybe next time.

"Did you even pay attention to today's class?" Jadelyn asked, and I was pulled from my thoughts. I heard the familiar sound of paper being shuffled and backpack zippers being closed, realizing class had come to an end.

"Kind of hard to focus when I just learned..." I looked around. "That werewolves are real."

She let out a small tinkling chuckle that reminded me of wind chimes. "Okay, I'll give you a pass for this one. Do you have any more classes today?"

I had two more, but I knew going to them was going to be a waste of time if she was going to offer me answers. "Not that I need to go to. I'm all ears if you could spare the time to tell me more."

"Sure. What do you want to know?" She closed up her own bag and slung it over her shoulder.

"I honestly don't know where to start. I really want to know what I am, but it's probably important for me to understand any rules? I just don't know... anything." It felt like I was stumbling through this.

Jadelyn smiled sympathetically. "You aren't the first lost one I've met, but I've never introduced one to the para world. That's what we call it... I might not know all of what to tell you, but I know someone who does."

"When can I meet them?"

"She's not on campus; we'll have to head into the city, but she's not far," Jadelyn reassured me.

"Cool, let's go. We could meet her for an early lunch?" I knew it was probably a lot to ask, but I was excited to learn more.

"Sure. She runs a bar, so we can eat there if you want."

My stomach growled, as if to agree with her. "I've been starving since last night. I think I grew after yesterday." I offered the information, not sure if it would help her with what I was.

"Interesting. It sounds like something dormant is waking up. There are so many paras out there, it's hard to say just what you might be." She drummed her fingers on her pink lips. It was a movement she seemed to make when she was thinking. It also had the effect of keeping my attention.

"Maybe we start by ruling some things out?" I asked as we left the classroom and started walking across campus.

"Sure. I feel pretty safe saying you're not an elf. No craving for blood?"

"Nope."

"Not a vamp. I assume you have no strange eating disorder? That's one of the clear ways to tell."

I shook my head. "Unless you count eating three pizzas last night and still feeling hungry."

She gave me an appraising look. "And you look like this after eating three pizzas? Damn, I wish I could eat anything I wanted like that. Startlingly good looking and super strong, not a lot to go off of, but we'll see what Morg thinks."

I tried not to blush at her assessment of me and play it cool. Whatever was waking up, I was all for it.

CHAPTER 4

We only walked about fifteen minutes off campus before we came upon the bar that Jadelyn had intended, but it was clearly part of the city and not the campus.

Steam rose from a vent in the sidewalk as the warm subway air clashed with the chilly fall wind. You could hear the SEPTA roaring under our feet. Unlike campus, Philadelphia proper just felt a little grungier, more worn down. Most surfaces were covered in a layer of old coal power plant soot.

But that didn't stop any of the hustle as people moved through the sidewalks, a constantly flowing stream of humanity, and cars packed the streets in the mid-day traffic.

I smiled, always enjoying myself when I was out in the city. I'd moved out of the burbs and into the city when my foster parents had died. It had served as a good distraction from my melancholy mind back then. I'd grown accustomed to the bustle. Never could I imagine a world where I'd go back to the burbs. I had a feeling the deafening silence would drive me crazy.

"That guy up there. Look closely. Do you see his ears?" Jadelyn was gesturing to a guy about to enter the bar.

I paused, taking the man in, and a bit shocked to see what she was referencing. "I see him alright. What's he?"

"Elf. I wanted to warn you about them. They hold the largest bloc on the eastern council and a pretty large bloc on the global council."

She was getting into things I didn't understand. "What's a bloc? Something political from the sound of it?"

"Oh, right. Basics. Okay, so there's three councils in the States: East, West and Central. Philly is the hub of the eastern section."

I had more questions about that, but we were close enough that I could see the sign for the bar. On a simple black awning in white letters, it read 'Bumps in the Night'.

I paused, forgetting our current conversation. "Isn't the name a little on the nose?" I pointed at the sign.

Jadelyn looked up and chuckled. "You'll find that most paras have a little humor about hiding in plain sight. But stop and really think. Before you knew about all of this, how would you take it?"

I opened my mouth and then closed it again. Music, sex, and dancing all came to mind. Not paranormal creatures. I shook my head with a grin on my face.

Yeah, it did have a sort of humor.

"See? You get it. Now come on in." She walked up to the dark black fire-doors, opened them, and waltzed right in.

Over my shoulder, no one paid us any attention, but I felt like I should be more secretive about it.

"Don't dally, just come in. No one goes to a nightclub during the day."

"I thought you said it was a bar." I moved through the doorway, my eyes adjusting to the dark entrance hall.

"You'll see."

We stepped through a pair of curtains, and I squinted as my eyes adjusted from the dark hallway to the warmly lit room.

The place was enormous. Black leather and studded detailing seemed to be the primary decor covering the walls, except for a massive decorative mirror behind the bar, and dark velvet curtains over the stage.

But this was just the first room. It looked like the place sprawled back, going down another level to a dance floor. And beyond that, I was able to make out glimpses of smaller, more intimate rooms.

But my eyes flashed back to the room I was in, which held a rainbow of skin colors. I tried not to stare, but there were so many supernaturals out in the open, I wasn't quite sure what to do.

A Satyr was sitting at the bar as if it was just another day; somehow, the casualness of it struck me. Nearby him was a big, green-skinned guy I assumed was an orc eating with a smaller, brighter green companion that must have been a goblin.

I started to pick out the ears on a number of supernaturals that came in every shade from normal human pink to dark blue. Others had wings and horns adorning them. My brain was spinning as I tried to take it all in.

The way some of them looked at me made me think I was the oddball out.

It wasn't till Jadelyn pulled my hand laughing that I realized I must have been gawking.

"Come on. This place is neutral, so safe for the most part."

"Why Philly?" was the first question that popped out of my mouth.

She shrugged. "Goes back to our history. Well, that and the city is big enough to get lost in, yet so much quieter than New York or DC. But there is a presence of supernaturals in most big cities."

"History?" That caught my attention.

She found a low table in the corner with plush leather chairs and set her bag down, taking a seat. "Okay, I know I'm dropping a lot on you at once. But the simple answer is that, in the 1700s, our secrets started to leak out. We fled all over the world to avoid the church and their hunters."

"Wait, like the church, like the Vatican?" I clarified.

"Sort of. That's what it has become, but back then, the church was much more... brutal. Anyway, many of the paranormal scattered to the States, some went elsewhere. But the end result was that all the paranormal organizations lost touch with each other. Some formed smaller organizations all over the world, some faded into obscurity to protect themselves."

I realized where she was going with this one. "Lost ones."

She nodded, giving me a sympathetic look. "Exactly. It's easy to forget, given we grew up with the budding internet, but before then, communications across large areas weren't possible. Only now in the last twenty years or so have the para groups started to reintegrate into these larger councils, which has been its own political nightmare. So finding lost ones isn't uncommon. Typically, you'd integrate into one of the existing clans."

I nodded along, having a little trouble focusing with all the oddities displayed before me. It wasn't so much that any particular supernatural was making me gawk, but I couldn't stop taking each in and wondering if I was the same type of supernatural they were deep down.

"It sounds like if it's political like that, there are sides?"

"You could say that. There are clans. The three big ones on the east coast are Sirens, Elves and the Faerie," she explained.

"So, what's with Sirens being in charge? No offense, but that's not exactly how media displays paranormal society."

Jadelyn rolled her eyes. "If you think we are a bunch of pretty things that sit on rocks and sing for attention, you'd be dead wrong. We control the sea trade routes and have for hundreds of years."

My mouth made a big O at that. "Like all of them?"

She smirked. "Yes. We own all the big shipping companies now. The way my father describes it, we used to be more like some mixture between pirates and merchants. We'd crash our competition while we controlled which boats got where. Eventually, our competitors gave up, and we owned all the sea bound trading companies. We've kept a tight fist on it all, even if we've broken it up so no one really knows."

I let out a small whistle. If that was true, that was some real old money shit. Enough to make her title of a princess not an exaggeration. "And you're the heir to all of that?"

"Heir to my family, which directly owns much of that."

Before I could ask any more questions, one of the elves strolled over to our table and set down a large bottle of fancy looking whiskey. It was half gone, and it wasn't even noon.

"Well, hello, princess. I thought you'd run off on us."

"Can it, Simon. Even if you want to do this now, I'm going to point out my friend here is a lost one who has just come to us last night. Let's have him see a good side to our culture."

Simon gave me an appraising look while I did the same. He looked like a pretty boy. He was almost too clean and primped, with buttons on his shirt that glittered like they might actually be made of silver.

"What're you?" But he didn't wait for me to answer. "Never mind, doesn't matter. Look, bit of advice man to man? Don't let this little slut lure you into her side with her looks. She's been whored out to the weres by her dear ol' daddy. It's a trick the two of them have pulled a dozen times. Find a strong para, have her lure them into their side, only to pull a bait and switch. If you ask me, I'm rooting for Chad to bend her over before they can pull the switch."

Jadelyn's face had become a cold steely mask of forced neutrality, but there was no doubt there was a volcano of fury just under that cold practiced expression.

So far, she was the one paranormal friend I had, and I had no intention of sitting there and watching this guy rile her up.

"Noted. If that's all, we're in the middle of a conversation." I rose to my feet, hoping to tower over him, but only had a scant inch of height on him. It was the pointy ears.

He ignored me and looked at Jadelyn. "Already got this one wrapped around your little finger, huh? Look at him standing up for you."

"Enough," I growled.

His eyes snapped back to me, and with a quirk of an eyebrow, he reached his hand out an inch from my chest and stated, "Invoketis."

Next thing I knew, I was being launched back, like he'd just hit me with a localized hurricane. My body crashed into a thankfully empty table, shattering it and landing in the prickly mess.

That woke my beast up, and it shook its head out, trying to dispel the daze. Getting it together, I pulled myself out of the wreck of the table, more than a little pissed.

"See, he's fine," the elf pointed out before taking a swig of the whiskey and wiping his mouth.

Jadelyn was standing now, and her eyes had changed into a cool silver. The neutral mask she'd been wearing was gone, replaced by a look of barely contained violence.

In that moment, I didn't feel like containing my violence. I could feel it bubble up inside me, like a volcanic rage was going to come spewing out of my mouth any second.

"Enough," a new voice projected across the room. To punctuate the shout, Simon's whiskey bottle shattered, and a knife quivered where it had found its new spot in the table. "You know better than to start something here."

From a balcony above, another elf stepped out. Her skin was a beautiful azure blue, and her hair was a bundle of silver strands tied up behind her head. She stalked down the stairs so fluidly that it was hard to believe she was in tall black heels with leather pants and a corset.

The whole room was quiet as she glared on her way down.

The silence was only broken by Simon quickly stating, "He started it."

"Ah, of course. Because he stood up? I can see how that would be so intimidating." She gave him a bored look. "I heard it all. He's a lost one, recently found, yet you decided to provoke him and hit first."

There were gasps throughout the bar and looks of disgust were thrown Simon's way.

"I was only trying to educate him about the skank that was luring him into her clan."

"And you'd accept him with open arms. I'm sure." The blue elf rolled her eyes.

Simon still held the neck of the broken bottle and lifted it to his lips before glaring down and remembering it was gone. "Of course. The elves are magnanimous."

"You dare say that to me? Get out," she snapped, and I barely caught the swift motion of her wrist before Simon's clothing tore, and another knife wobbled in the wall behind him.

Turning pale as a sheet, he must not have liked his odds, because he hurried out of the bar after that. His swift exit seemed to only embolden the whispers in the bar, as a number of elves got up and scurried after him.

The leather-clad elf approached me, somehow suddenly in front of us. I looked to where the stairs had been, trying to figure out how she'd crossed the entire floor in the brief time I'd been looking away, but her voice drew me back. "I'm sorry. He likes to antagonize people. Almost more than drinking."

Seeing her up close, I realized she had a pair of fangs protruding from her lips. "I'm Morgana."

I'd been sure she was an elf, but the fangs made me pause.

"Uh. Zach." I did my best not to stare into her cleavage that was pressed up on display.

"Hey, Morg."

"Jade. Sorry about Simon. You know that, when he comes back, I can't bar him from here." Now that she was speaking naturally, she had a clear Swiss accent.

Jadelyn wrinkled her nose. "It's fine. But I don't want to talk about him. I brought you our friend here, brand spanking new to the para world."

Morgana gave me a once over and leaned in, stretching her neck as her nose brushed the soft skin of my neck. She sniffed, then her tongue lapped against my skin, tracing a path along my jaw.

It sent my blood straight south, and I cleared my throat to hide my awkwardness. "What are you doing?"

"Seeing what you might be." She came up and smiled, showing off her fangs.

"Oh. Oh! Sure, go ahead, sorry I just..."

Jadelyn and Morgana giggled like two girls sharing a secret. "Oh, no, it's okay. That was hot," Jadelyn got out. "You just have to get used to Morg. She does everything her own way."

Morgana shrugged. "I like leather, and I like sex. No reason to hide it." She turned back to me. "But unfortunately, I haven't had the pleasure of meeting whatever you are before."

My hopes for an easy answer plummeted.

"I could always take a nibble and see if it's something I've tasted before." Her fangs caught the light a little, and suddenly, I was very aware that I had no idea what she was.

"Sorry, I don't mean to be rude, but what are you?"

She smiled. "Good answer. You should always try to understand not just who but what you are dealing with in the para world." She pulled up another chair to our table and sat down, crossing her legs. "What I am has a little bit of a story to go along with it, so you might as well get comfortable."

I took the cue and sat down, as did Jadelyn.

Morgana snapped a finger, and a server seemed to materialize from behind me. "Two beers and one of my special vintages. He really roused my hunger."

"Of course." The server sped away with unnatural speed.

"Vampire?"

"Him? Yes. Me? Not so simple. I started off as a dark elf but was turned into a vampire." She saw my look of interest and chuckled. "Yeah, sounds great. I get that."

I nodded. "I mean, double immortality, right? Extra strong? Doesn't sound too bad. But guessing there's more to it."

Morgana gave a throaty chuckle. "First of all, elves aren't immortal. They are just long lived. We'll never know if vamps are truly immortal because they kill each other too much. Suffice it to say, though, that both of them hate each other's guts."

I paused, considering that. My guess is the mixing of their para types didn't happen very often. "So neither were a fan of your mixed status?"

Jadelyn swallowed a laugh as Morgana continued. "You could say that. The elves swear they can't be turned into such vile creatures. So, in their minds, the fact that I was a vampire means I never was an elf." She rolled her eyes. "And then the vampires love to get a rise out of the elves, so they love to use me as a prop to prove that the elves aren't as pure as they think they are. It's a mess. But I do tend to get along better with vampires than elves."

She raised her hand just before the server reappeared and placed a champagne glass of bubbling red liquid in her hands. "Cheers to your first toddling steps into the para world."

I took the offered beer and clinked it with her glass, taking a tentative sip of the overly hoppy beer before putting it down. She drank deeply from her glass and set it down.

"Is that blood?"

"Going right for the jugular, I see. Not exactly. It is made with blood, though. We still drink fresh, but long ago, we used the same tactics that humans did and tried to ferment our drink of choice. Technology has only made such dabblings easier."

I nodded, interpreting that it was some sort of champagne-like blood. Not exactly what I expected, but it made sense that they'd find some sort of interesting drink over the years.

"If you're curious, you can take a sip. It won't hurt you."

I paused, initially hesitant. But I wanted to learn more about the world, and to do that, I'd need to experience more. I picked up her glass and barely let it pass my lips. It was like a super sweet champagne, but riding underneath that flavor was a heavy metallic taste that hinted at the blood. The aftertaste wasn't entirely pleasant, but I had a feeling it likely was to her.

"It's an acquired taste, I know. But after you drink blood for centuries, something without that tang just seems empty." She took her flute back and took a small sip before putting it down.

Morgana seemed laid back and in no rush. But I wanted to know more. "So, Jadelyn said you'd be able to give me an introduction to the para world."

"You brought him to me? I thought you'd pick him up quickly." Morgana looked to Jadelyn, surprised.

She shrugged. "I made a very poor first impression of him, and now so have the elves. I'm trying to make it right, I guess you could say."

The drow vampire gave a small snort. "You couldn't have given him that bad an impression."

"I mean, I don't have much of a gauge for bad, but it definitely wasn't pleasant. Sounds like everybody here seems to know who Chad is?" I asked.

Morgana nodded, her eyes showing increased interest. So I continued. "Well, I bumped into Jadelyn at a bar, and Chad didn't seem too pleased. I left, but he chased me down and tried to pick a fight." I took another sip of my beer.

"Oh my. Yet you stand here before me looking healthy. Don't tell me you won the fight with Chad?" Morgana seemed surprised now and gave me her full attention.

The intensity of her attention made me blush; I scratched the back of my head, feeling a braggart saying it out loud. "Yeah. I beat him; my beast helped though."

"You sure you don't want to drag him to your clan for the intro?" Morgana asked.

But Jadelyn shook her head. "I have a feeling trying to force him to do anything is a poor idea, and I know once my father hears that Zach completely trounced Chad, he'll try to sink his claws as deeply as he can into Zach."

Morgana licked her lips. "Then I accept. Zach, I'll be the one teaching you the ropes about the para world. Do you accept?"

I paused. The way she said it had a formal edge to it that set off alarm bells in my head. Something about who taught me seemed important. "What does that mean?"

She nodded, clearly approving of my question. "Well, I'll be responsible for you. And after that incident with Simon, if they want recompense, they have to go through me for it."

"Wait what? He was being an ass."

She sighed. "This is why you need someone to show you around. For what you did, he could very easily request a duel." Morgana paused and looked me in the eye as she elaborated. "To the death."

Chapter 5

"Hold on for a second. I didn't even touch Simon. Why would we fight to the death?"

"You stood up to him, and now his pride is hurt. Elves are very old-fashioned; they hold on to their honor as if it were worth more weight than dragon's gold," Morgana explained. "I should know. I've seen just what they look like when their masks are peeled off, away from the public eye."

I looked at Jadelyn for confirmation. She had calmed down, her eyes once again a chilly blue. "She's right. They will almost certainly come to request a duel, but they'll likely use it as leverage to get you to join their ranks in order to dismiss it. The elves and others will try to get you to join them once they hear that you went toe to toe with Chad."

I sat there, taking it all in. In just a short span of time, everything had changed. And I'd thought getting into med school was difficult enough.

Now they were telling me that I might need to fight in a duel to the death with an elf who just kicked my ass? I wasn't sure this life seemed so desirable after all.

"A werewolf didn't shake you, but the idea of a duel does?" Jadelyn looked at me with barely concealed pity.

I thought about that. But paranormal wasn't a new concept to me, just the reality of it was. Werewolves were somewhat predictable in their attacks. It was brute strength, and that I at least understood. Duels to the death really upped the stakes, and I had no idea how that elf had moved me across the room or what I could have done to stop it.

"I'm not exactly a killer. I'm training to take the Hippocratic oath and save people, not cause death." Snark was my go-to defense mechanism.

Based on the frowns that crossed their faces, neither of the women liked that answer. "Well, you better buck up, because it will happen. Morg, can you delay it a bit?"

"I'll do what I can, but the start of next week is probably the best I can do. Simon is a petty fool, but he's no idiot. He'll know fighting this poor little newbie as soon as he can will be to his advantage." Morgana gave me an appraising look. "Which means we need to teach you a few things, quickly."

Jadelyn stood up, still holding onto the neutral mask that she'd slammed into place when she'd seen Simon. "I'll leave you two to it and go spread word that there's a new lost one under your care, Morg."

Jadelyn didn't look me in the eye as she finished talking. I wasn't sure what to make of that. Was she embarrassed?

Not wanting to end things on an awkward note, I said, "See you in class."

She looked over her shoulder and gave me a polite smile. "Of course." Turning, she held her head high as she walked out of the bar, patrons' eyes following her, and she left.

Now it was just Morgana and me at the table.

"She's a good girl in a very difficult situation."

"What Simon said was true?" I asked, wanting to hear a less biased opinion.

"Jaded, but true. Her father really does use her like a chess piece. Her latest use is to try to bring the new Philly pack under his thumb. They aren't aligned with any of the big three yet, and the pack looks like it'll be a big one. They'd help tip the scales more in his favor."

It sounded far more political than I wanted to entangle myself in. "Politics," I snorted.

"Don't count yourself out. Before I stopped the fight, I could see you gearing up to battle Simon. If you don't mind, I think we should push to see if you can do it again. It might help give clues as to what you are."

"Here?" I asked, looking around at the bar, my eyes lingering on the busted-up table I'd smashed into.

"No, don't damage any more of my furniture. I have a room in the back." She got up and sauntered through the nightclub, seeming to assume I'd follow her. The patrons all seemed to grow quiet in respect as she passed.

I watched the interactions for a moment. The deference she was given and the way Simon had backed off told me that I might have made a very powerful ally. Now I just needed to not screw it up.

Following behind Morgana, we walked down through the bottom level I'd spotted when we had entered. A dance floor spread across the area. It was likely lit by black lights at night, with lights flashing, but at the moment, it was empty.

As we walked deeper and deeper, my brow began to furrow. I didn't get a good look at the building, but I knew the city. Buildings weren't usually that deep. I turned, looking back over my shoulder, confirming that the distance didn't quite add up.

The first bar area and maybe even the dance floor area I could have believed, but as we passed an area for strippers with a main stage and a well of seats, I finally decided to ask the question on my mind.

"Are we underground?"

"Not quite. To answer what you are probably guessing, Bumps in the Night is bigger on the inside than the outside. Also, that's not for strippers. I'm not so distasteful; it's for a burlesque show."

"Bigger on the inside?" Fancy strippers, got it.

"Yes. But since we are going to try and pull out a little of your own magic, I'll give you another incentive. You show me yours..." Morgana paused to give me a suggestive look over her shoulder. "And I'll show you mine."

I swallowed a sudden lump that formed in my throat. When Morgana wanted to, she could turn the sexual energy up to eleven in a heartbeat.

Seeing my reaction, she broke into a chuckle. "Sorry, you're too fun to tease."

That heat that I felt between us dissipated as I realized she wasn't actually interested in me. My libido had shut off when a bit of guilt over her teasing had spread on her face. She had no intention of following through with it.

"You do it well. Just let me get my bearings around here a little more." I caught a bit of her scent as I walked beside her, and it felt like it was committed to memory. Lavender hiding a bitter copper note. I'd just scented her, and instinctively I knew that I'd be able to track her if need be. I stored that away. Maybe it was a clue that would help me figure out what kind of paranormal I was.

"Here it is." Morgana flung open another pair of double doors. Behind it was a room that was largely empty. In the back was a training mat currently occupied by another pair. "Sarah, Tom, can we get the room? This is Zach, a new lost one that I've claimed temporary rights to."

Looking them over, I recognized both as vampires. I felt a moment of satisfaction at starting to understand the world around me. As I locked eyes with them, they were both looking me over like they were trying to memorize my face.

"Understood." They both bowed and left through another door.

Morgana noticed I was eying the door. "Oh, do be careful. You can get a little lost in my home."

"Why do I get the feeling you have a bit of everything in here?" I asked, starting to be certain Morgana wasn't just a simple bar owner. The clans were talked about as powerful, but somehow, she was still able to stand and enforce neutral ground. Simon had left without even arguing with her. I realized there was a lot more to her.

"Starting to understand a few things?" Morgana smiled. "Good. Now let's try to pull a few of your own secrets out." She paused, looking me in the eye. "I'm not going to go easy on you, so be prepared."

As soon as she finished speaking, she shot forward with a right hook to the side of my head. I barely saw her blur forward.

My head snapped to the side, but I stood my ground.

"Strong and durable. But that's common enough." She moved with incredible grace. Grace I might have appreciated more if the world didn't turn upside down, as she used her hip as a lever to uproot and toss me flat on my back on the mat.

Morgana swung her legs around me and straddled my chest. "Is the poor little boy lost?" she taunted.

Her taunt worked, and I felt my anger rise up, the primal part of me revolting at being pinned and taunted. I latched onto her hips and kicked to my feet, still holding her hips as I slammed her to the mat at an awkward angle, a snapping noise coming from her neck. My entire body froze at the sound, and the anger dissipated as I tried to reconcile what I'd just done.

But bones crackled further, and Morgana laughed. "The look on your face. But now we are getting somewhere." Her legs on my torso became a vice, and she grabbed the mat, twisting in impossible ways to lift me off the floor and slam me down. She did it far less dangerously than I had, but it was enough to daze me so she could escape my grasp.

I rubbed my head and stood back up. My fighting instincts rose up in me, like my beast was uncoiling. "You can heal," I said, belatedly understanding what had happened.

"Knowing what your opponent can do is maybe even more important than knowing what you can do," she teased and closed back in.

Knowing there was no need to hold back, I threw a punch with the full force of my supernatural strength.

Morgana caught it in the palm of her hand and twisted it to throw me, but this time, I was a little more prepared. I kicked out my own leg, catching her and sending us both into a tumble, one that she rolled out of with predatory grace.

"Playing dirty, are we? Sometimes you need to ask for a girl's consent."

I ignored the teasing, realizing that flirting was in her nature and a tactic she used to distract. Instead, I waited for her to make her next move.

Rolling to my feet as she came in again with a flurry of jabs, I only managed to get some part of my arm in the way for about half of them, in a move I was telling myself was a block, but I knew that was a generous label for it.

I realized that she was slowly speeding up and hitting harder with each punch. She was testing what I could take.

Sweat pounded down my forehead as I worked to block more and push back at her, but each hit to my side or my chest was like waves pounding down a coastline.

She was wearing me out, and the primordial part of me became angry. The beast could feel myself about to lose, and that was not sitting well with him. I felt a heat in my chest once more, and I decided to let it loose.

Morgana seemed to notice the moment I was about to unleash. There was a flash of something in her eyes, and she jumped back just in time as I let loose a stream of fire that roared to life, growing as it left my mouth.

In front of me, all I could see was the beautiful orange and gold of a bright hot flame. It was like staring into a bonfire at night; everything else was washed out of my vision.

Then it all disappeared, collapsing into something on the other side. As the flames vanished, Morgana was left on the other side, holding a pitch-black orb that sucked in the flames and everything else, including the light, around it.

The little black ball disappeared, and Morgana gave me a smile wide enough to show her fangs all the way to her gums. "Amazing."

Even as I wanted to agree, it felt like all the strength was sapped out of me with that blast of fire. I sagged, and she was there in a moment.

"Absolutely incredible!" She had an excitement on her face that was infectious. "Fire breathing? Completely natural fire breathing. Not some sort of spell mimicry. That's rare; I can only think of a small list of things that can perform such a feat."

I perked up at that information. "Hey, narrowing it down is huge progress."

Her smile was still incredibly wide, but I could tell there was more. "Jadelyn and Simon are going to be so pissed that they didn't get off on the right foot with you."

"Why's that?" I asked, feeling a little of my strength return as she helped me into a chair.

"Look at you. You need food." She frowned. "It took that much out of you?" There was confusion written on her face, as if she was suddenly doubting her assessment.

I paused, not sure how much I should reveal, but she had taken me on to help me, so I decided to trust her. "I... before yesterday, I was pretty normal. I just had this sort of primal instinct, like a beast inside of me. And I guess from time to time I had slightly above average senses. It wasn't until last night that things changed. After the fight with Chad, I ate three pizzas and grew three inches, the strength, the fire... it's all brand new to me."

Morgana studied my face, looking for deception, but she found none. I knew I was telling the truth. "Do you have parents we can ask for more details?"

I looked away. I hated seeing somebody's face when I told them the next part. "No, my parents died when I was less than a year old. And the couple that took me in died a few years back." I gave a tentative look back, and sure enough, Morgana's was the same as everyone else's. I hated that pity.

"Too often," was all she said with a shake of her head. "It sounds like whatever you are is only now coming out. Which means we need to get as much food into you as we can."

Turning away from me, she grabbed a cord I hadn't noticed in the corner and pulled it. Not more than a few seconds later, a vampire sped into the room.

"I'll need a table and chairs brought here. And get the kitchen making as much food as they can and keep bringing it here."

He gave me a look out of the corner of his eye. "Yes, Lady." He disappeared with the same speed that he had appeared.

"My people might be able to rush things around, but good food can't be rushed. I hope you can wait a few minutes."

Another two vampires sped into the room carrying the table and chairs, only to disappear and reappear again with glasses and silverware, setting the table up.

"Really, you have amazing service," I joked.

But she gushed in return. "I know. I do love my employees. Place comes with fantastic perks as well."

I raised an eyebrow, wondering just what those perks were, but she didn't elaborate. "So, the list of what you think I might be?"

"Well, there are a number of things that breathe fire. But that was real fire, and not the magical mimicry that so many of them have. It also wasn't hell fire, so not a demon. Then you said you felt like there was a beast inside of you, so we can rule out an elemental." She ticked off her fingers as she went through her assessment. "Do you like spicy food? Don't mind if something's hot?"

I frowned. There wasn't a particular inclination towards those, but then I remembered drinking the coffee this morning that Maddie thought was boiling hot. "I think I'm still changing, but this morning, my piping hot coffee went down without a problem."

It wasn't much to go on, but Morgana didn't seem to care. "Then I think it's likely you are a salamander, phoenix, or a dragon."

"Those sound intense." I tried to pair each of those up with what I felt dwelled inside of me, and phoenix didn't feel like it fit at all. "I don't think I'm a phoenix—it doesn't feel right."

That only made Morgana grin wider. "Interesting. Well then, this means you need a crash course in what made the para world turn. Magic, or the energy that makes it work: mana."

I nodded, listening with rapt attention.

"We all need energy, but it's not the same as what humans need. Why can I drink blood that has been processed? Why do werewolves go for a run during the full moon? It all comes down to mana and how different paras are able to absorb it and use it in their bodies. Mana is what makes our paranormal halves run; it's what gives us each our abilities."

"How do you get mana?"

"It varies depending on the para, and among each group, it's often more ritual than science. The vamps have made great progress in studying it, but we still don't know everything. What we do know is that there are a limited number of creatures that produce mana, rather than consume it." She gave me a level look that told me what she was about to say was very important. "Mana has been on the decline for decades, for as long as vampires have been able to measure it. We think it began in the 1700s when the mass hunt occurred in Europe."

"What types of paras produce mana?" I asked.

"A phoenix does at every rebirth, and a salamander does if it nests in fire. But what vampires have found to be the largest producers of mana so far is the heartbeat of a dragon. You haven't been in a fire lately? Or died?"

I paused, feeling the weight of the world on me for a moment. "No. Neither of those." So the question remained, how was I powering up? That only left something else, like a heartbeat.

She smirked. "We have more testing to do, so you could still be something else, something new. But given that you seem to be recovering from your mana exhaustion from just sitting here, I'd guess that you might indeed be a dragon." Her eyes lit up at just the thought.

I let that sink in, and then I laughed. Nearly doubled over, losing it a bit at the ridiculousness of that moment. I'd been Pendragon all my life, and that had definitely led to some teasing. And now, I could possibly be a dragon? It was too rich.

"What's so funny?"

I'd clearly not given her the reaction she was expecting. "My name. My last name," I clarified. "Pendragon."

Morgana's eyes went as wide as saucers, and all the sultry humor that surrounded her evaporated in an instant.

"Food." A waiter came in with a platter of four dishes and laid them out. He looked at Morgana's expression and nearly dropped the plates, trying to set them on the table. "Lady?"

"Get me a book from my library. Gaelic text, green binding, with a rosary knot on the spine."

"At once." He vanished only for the platter to clatter to the floor after him.

Her reaction was now catching me off guard. She knew something, or at least suspected something. Her breathing had become heavy.

"What is it?"

"Absolutely nothing. I just need to refresh myself on an old text."

I didn't buy that for a moment, but I could tell she wasn't going to say anymore, at least not till she got that book. Instead, I focused on eating my food and figuring out the mystery later.

Chapter 6

While we waited for the book to come, I dug into the food that had arrived. I couldn't believe the assortment of delicious food in front of me. They'd prepared a medallion of perfectly cooked filet mignon, accompanied by a side of creamy mashed potatoes. Next to it sat a plate of golden-cooked salmon, and next to that was a simple bowl of spaghetti.

I wasn't sure where to begin as I dug in, but the food seemed to vanish in no time. Morgana just watched me, a smile on her face as I devoured the food.

As I was finishing up the salmon, one of the vampires returned, the thick and worn book in his hands. It was more of a tome than a book.

But Morgana didn't handle it delicately. She threw it down on the table, using her finger to leaf through the pages as she traced the words with her free hand.

Peeking over the edge of the book, I couldn't make sense of it. It was a language I didn't recognize in a scrawled hand-written text, small and detailed drawings breaking up the text. Even knowing the language, I was surprised that anybody could read it easily.

Morgana flipped around the book, finding passages that seemed to reference other pages and flipping between them, trying to piece information together.

I was just finishing up the plates that had been brought to me when she closed the book.

"Do you need more?" she asked, seeing my plates scraped clean.

"No, it's fine."

She nodded at that and called for the server. "Bring another round of food for our friend here."

"I said that was enough." I didn't need to keep eating her expensive food; pizza would be fine on the way home.

Apparently, my answer was not satisfactory, because Morgana leveled a stare at me. "No, you said 'it's fine'. Which means you don't want to impose, not that you're done. Don't feel bad. I have plenty, and I'm your host into the new waters of the para world. What kind of host would I be if I let you leave hungry?"

"I feel like I could eat out your entire kitchen," I admitted.

"I'll make you a bet. If you can eat out my entire kitchen, I'll..." She paused. "What do you want?"

I hesitated, not sure how to answer that. So I went with what was most pressing in my mind. "Not to fight Simon to the death?"

"Fine. If you can eat out my entire kitchen, I'll pull some strings that I'd really rather not and get Simon to withdraw. However, if you can't eat my whole kitchen, you come work for me for a few weeks. How does that sound?" She smirked in a way that told me she felt confident in her bet.

But neither really felt like a loss for me. Working for her would be a way to introduce myself to the para world and learn more. "Clarify what working for you entails. Do I get paid?"

"Good. Be careful with what you say to others. And I don't mean you'd work here in the club. I'd get your help with my primary job, which is contract work for the para community. It's quite lucrative, and I'll give you an even split." She surprised me.

"Contract work?" I needed more clarification; the last thing I needed was that to be slang for whoring me out.

"Things people need done that they don't want to ask their clan for help with. Or things they'd rather be kept quiet."

"You don't mean killing people, right?" I wasn't sure where this was going.

She waved that comment away. "No, I don't take a hit very often, and I rarely take work that goes against my morals."

"So you just find things, people?" I clarified.

"Tracking is a big part of it, sometimes quieting people, retrieving lost items... but I do kill often enough, though justified."

"Okay, I'll agree to that. But you need to promise to still teach me all the rules either way."

"Of course, my tutelage is not contingent on this bet."

Her servants placed two more plates in front of me. This time, they served me what looked like a whole casserole dish of lasagna and a lobster.

"Eat up," Morgana said, a bit too cheerily as she clearly waited to win the bet.

***

"How does this all keep coming?" I took another bite of what would be my fifth filet mignon, and I was starting to feel sick of it.

"Because it will never stop coming." She gave me one of her mischievous smiles, or maybe it was the fangs that made it feel like she was up to trouble.

I paused mid-bite, processing what she'd said. Clearly, she'd set herself up to win, but I guess I shouldn't be surprised. She had far more life experience, and I didn't know much about the world I'd stepped into. If it was a real bet, I'd have been mad, but the food had been delicious and was free, so I was taking it as a win.

"Is there magic involved?"

"In the para world, you should assume there's always magic involved. But enough of that. Let me show you what I confirmed." She turned the book around for me to read.

I almost laughed that she thought the gibberish in the book would make sense to me. "You're going to have to help. All I see is this picture of a dragon."

She sighed. "Sorry, sometimes I forget. Old age and all."

I rolled my eyes, but curiosity lingered. I'd figured by that point that she was older than she looked, but it was still weird to think that the leather-clad woman who looked about twenty was significantly older.

She raised a brow at my eye roll. "Thank you. I think I've aged well. But I am quite old; old enough to have been alive when this was written, but just nowhere near where this was happening."

She pointed at the page and read it aloud. "I met one of the unnatural today, a powerfully built man by the name of Uther Pendragon. As we've talked, I've come to believe that his surname is not a surname at all, but a title passed down through their kind. One of great importance."

"Does that mean there's other Pendragons out there? Maybe ones I'd be related to?" I got excited at the prospect of a family I could meet.

Morgana sighed. "I forget how little you know. It's possible, but there are not many dragons remaining. They were hunted in the old days, and nearly disappeared. They weren't built for stealth to hide from hunters, nor did they care to be. They were quite obnoxiously obvious about what they were and made easy targets for the church's cleansing in the 1700s. While the cleansing was happening, many of us fled the area. The dragons stayed, but unlike the vampires, the dragons didn't organize." She shook her head. "Far too many died. By the time they realized their mistake, it was too late."

I tried not to show my disappointment. "So, I could be named after a powerful dragon or descended from one. What do you think that means?"

She paused, chewing on the side of her cheek as she thought. "I'm not sure. Names are powerful things, Zach. But a name means nothing if you don't have power behind it. So far, you seem to be barely a dragon at all, just a tough, strong para. Not much more than a were."

"I beat Chad," I scowled back at her.

"A pup who wasn't even channeling his pack. The strength of the weres doesn't come from individual strength, but strength in numbers. If you marched up to the football field and picked a fight with him right now, it would be a very different story."

I couldn't help but frown.

"Don't worry, I didn't feed you all of that food for nothing. You'll come back here every afternoon. We'll train, and I'll feed you all you can eat. Hopefully, before this weekend when I take you on a job, you'll be able to handle yourself and maybe even survive your fight with Simon."

There was a knock at the door as I went to remind her that the fight hadn't even been set yet. A servant entered holding a scroll, and dread set into my stomach.

"Do you want to bet with me on what is on that scroll?" Morgana gave me a knowing smile.

"No, I'm afraid to tempt fate."

Morgana waved the servant over.

"An elven envoy came with this." He held it out for Morgana. "It is addressed to him, but I informed them that you've taken sponsorship of him.

"Thank you. That'll be all," she dismissed him, and I looked at the scroll in her hand.

It looked like it was an ancient thing, browning at the edges. It was definitely not the clean lines of paper used now. But it definitely didn't look like something that had been written that day, giving me a moment of relief.

"Elves"—she tapped the paper—"are often artisans, or they like to think of themselves as such. They don't like manufactured things." Finishing her explanation, she unrolled the parchment. "You can read it yourself. They want a duel tonight at midnight." She rolled her eyes. "Dramatic."

"Tonight?" I asked, surprised.

"Don't worry, I'll push it off to next week, though they'll push for Monday. That way you have time to at least get your feet wet in a real fight this weekend."

"I have work."

Morgana rolled up the scroll and gave me a dry look. "Cancel it. What's more important to you? Going to whatever normal job that pays you a pittance, or working with me and learning what you need to stay alive?"

What she said made complete sense, but it also meant setting aside my mundane life. I wasn't sure I was ready to do that. The para world was still unfamiliar. "Can't I do both?"

Her responding sigh was so heavy that I knew the answer was not going to be positive. "Try if you must. It won't work out; it never does. At some point, Zach, you are going to have to commit to one of the two lives you now lead. And there's a very strong chance that, if you are in fact a dragon, you won't get much of a choice."

Having choice taken away from me rankled the beast, and it growled in my chest. "Why is that?"

"Because even if you aren't some special dragon, if you can grow and eventually transform, you'll be sought after heavily. While the heartbeat of a dragon produces mana, everything about a dragon is magical and among the most potent reagents. Ground scales of a dragon can cure almost all ailments. Tears of a dragon are capable of waking even those in a coma." A smirk crossed her lips. "The semen of a dragon is part of a very popular beauty potion."

I reared back. "Wait, do people actually sell this stuff?"

"Yes. And they don't wait for you to offer it up. You stood up to an elf, and now they are challenging you to a duel. Imagine what people would do for powerful ingredients like your scales. Heck, if they can get your heart, they could use it for a potion of immortality."

But I needed my heart. That wasn't exactly something I could part with... willingly. I felt a lump in my throat at the thought.

She leveled me with a steady stare. "But you can also use it to your advantage. You could sell your seed once a year and never work another day in your life."

At least there was that. Sperm donor supreme.

Morgana smiled at the look on my face, seeming to enjoy teasing me further. "Don't get me started on what is going to happen when word gets out there's a fifth male dragon around. I wouldn't be surprised if the council steps in and starts arranging women for you and trying to find unattached female dragons for you to meet and ideally procreate with."

"There are more dragons?" I ignored the other parts of what she'd said, focusing on what was most interesting to me.

"Offers of money and numerous women, yet you focus on if there are other dragons?"

I felt a little heat dust my cheeks. "I want to find out more about my birth parents."

"Ah." Her eyes softened, seeming to understand my motivations. "I don't know. And unfortunately, there isn't another dragon in America; the current head of the dragons lives in Dubai."

"Dubai?" I asked.

"Where else can an insanely wealthy, several thousand-year-old creature saturate himself in debauchery? Last I heard, his harem broke triple digits. But he's also provided the world with a dozen daughters, so no one blinks an eye."

"Harem? Daughters?" I didn't understand.

"Yes. Dragons and their ability to produce mana are needed for all paranormal, in an attempt to stop or even reverse the decline of mana in the world. That's how important you just became."

I let that sink in, starting to feel my head spin from all the information I'd been given in one day. "I think I'd like to go home and rest."

Morgana nodded. "Sleep on it. Do your classes if you must but be back here tomorrow afternoon. I've taken you on, so know that I am responsible for you. Running away from this and me is not an option."

I nodded. I wasn't the kind of person to run from a tough situation, but it had crossed my mind. Everything was changing quickly, and it didn't feel like I had much control over it. I'd somehow gone from wanting to save lives to needing to learn how to kill.

I got up and left, but at the door, Morgana called one last thing to me. "Oh, and it should go without saying: you don't tell normals about the para world. After the 1700s, we have worked very hard to quell any knowledge of us, both those that spread it and those that know."

I took her words for what they really meant. I and anyone I told would be killed if I told them about the para world.

Not looking back, I stated, "Understood." And with that, I walked out of the bar and headed back to what was once my life.

CHAPTER 7

The apartment door thumped closed behind me, and I was in such a stupor I tried to lock it twice.

I felt like I was in a daze, but I had grieved enough before to recognize what was happening. I was grieving for the loss of my former life. Even if I was able to keep some of the normalcy, with what I now knew, I wouldn't be able to approach the world the same way again. There was no going back to the way things used to be.

If the change itself wasn't bad, now somehow this new information had led to a duel with an elf in a few days who wanted to kill me and make an example of me. And, to prepare for that, I was going to do some sort of job with Morgana that didn't sound like it would be a walk in the park, either. What had my life become?

I let out a sigh that seemed to last forever.

"That bad of a day?" Frank said from the couch, making me nearly jump out of my skin. I'd been so lost in thought that I hadn't even registered that he was in the room.

He watched me. "Sorry, you look like someone shot your dog. Not about to go on a vengeful quest murdering half of Hollywood's stunt doubles because of it, are you?"

Frank, you watch too many movies. Shaking my head, I couldn't help but wonder what Frank would think of all of this if I told him.

"No, I think that might have been better though." I opened my mouth to tell him more, but I couldn't figure out how to share with him without telling him about the para world. "Something I thought was... well, something turned out to be very different from what I expected."

"Got catfished, huh?"

"What! No. Eww. Why the hell would you think that?" I glared at Frank. He seemed more like the one out of the two of us to have that happen.

"Hey. Never happened to me, Zach. I get my women the organic way." He read my face like a book.

Seeing the segue into a conversation that wouldn't potentially get us both killed and would distract me, I prodded him about Maddie. "So, you and Maddie. Finally got her in your bed."

"Yeah, but then she ran out this morning and hasn't returned my texts." Frank looked down at his phone. "Dammit, it's driving me insane, Zach. Hey, how about you text her?"

"Nope. I'm one hundred percent not getting in between you and her on this one. You officially have a relationship. Work it out between the two of you."

"Maybe her phone is broken?" Frank sounded hopeful. I'd never seen him like this. More often than not, the situation was the other way around. His phone would be blowing up from some woman he'd been with the night before, and he'd just ignore all of them.

Smiling, I wondered if Maddie was doing it on purpose. She knew Frank, and she knew that coming on strong often freaked him. She was probably giving him some space to miss her, maybe keep him chasing her.

"I don't think her phone is broken, bud. I think classes are just more important than you right now."

Frank's jaw dropped at my accusation before he seemed to wizen up. "Here, take my phone and hide it. I know that if she texts back that I'm going to respond immediately, and that's going to seem too needy."

I took the phone and disappeared into my room, putting it right out in the open on top of my desk. In the event that he went looking for it, he'd see it right away.

"Distract me from Maddie. What about you, if you weren't cat-fished? What big revelation has you all down?" Frank had moved to the kitchen and was sitting backwards in one of the chairs.

"What if you suddenly realized that something you'd been told, something important, was a big lie?"

Frank tilted his head. "Why the cryptics? Can't you just tell me what it is?"

"No?" It came out as a question rather than a statement. "Look, someone has it out for me because of something stupid, and now I'm worried that everything I worked for with the goal of being a doctor is about to go down the drain."

"Well, that's bullshit. Fight back. Don't take that shit lying down. Go to the cops if it's too bad." Frank got angry on my behalf. He paused for a moment before coming to a conclusion of his own. "It's

Chad, isn't it? I knew it after seeing him barge out after you that he was going to cause trouble. Good thing that girl was doing everything she could to calm him down."

"No, it's not Chad. But I can't explain it, Frank." I put my head in my hands. "Dammit, this is so messed up."

"Shit, this sounds like some sort of mafia stuff. But we can figure this out. Let's just call them A for asshole, for now. A is after you, why? You're not exactly a troublemaker."

I nodded, figuring we could try his approach. "Because I stood up to him, and he wants to take me down a peg." On second thought, death was more than a peg. "A few pegs. Well, a lot of pegs."

"Okay, so A wants to peg you a lot." Frank started cracking up at his own joke.

I slapped my forehead. "Everything becomes sexual with you."

"What can I say? I always have sex on the brain. Anyway, A wants to peg you. How do you get out of said pegging?"

"Learn to fight," I answered. It was the truth, or at least half the truth. I didn't just need to learn to fight. I needed to learn to kill.

Frank stared at me, still trying to piece things together. "Okay, I've got it. You and A are in some secret fight club. And you don't want to tell me because if you found something that badass and didn't tell me, you know I'd be pissed." Frank nodded along with his theory, clearly also just amusing himself.

I almost argued with him, but it was close enough to the truth to work. "Sure, let's go with that. There's a big fight with A next week. And I think he's going to mess me up, to the point that I might not be a doctor."

"No no. Those things are just about being tough. You'll bounce right back, even if it takes a few weeks."

"He's going to cripple me."

Frank made a face. "Okay, so A was a more appropriate name than I realized. Well, then it sounds like you need to learn to fight. Quickly."

I nodded. "I'm working on that. Made a new friend today who is going to teach me in the afternoons. But it still doesn't solve everything. It will just start a series of additional challenges, people wanting to see how they measure up against me." I decided to roll with the fight club.

"Isn't that the point of a fight club? I've never been in one, but that's at least how it sounds, a club to fight in. Pretty sure that's the main point of a fight club."

Sighing and rolling my eyes, I let it go. That metaphor only served me so long. "It's a little more complicated, but I get you, Frank. One fight at a time."

"Can I join the fight club?" Frank asked. "Got any hot chicks?"

"Frank! You just started dating Maddie."

He held his hands up in defense. "Hold up. I didn't say I was going to do anything with them. Sometimes a man just likes some eye candy."

I held my comments in. Sometimes Frank could be a real nut. But it was also fun to tease him. "Actually, my trainer is ridiculously hot, and she wears these tight, like painted on tight, leather pants."

"Woah, roomy. Now we're talking. Tell me more. And weren't you just all worked up about some redhead? Now you're eyeing your fight club trainer? Don't worry, I'll come join you and take the heat."

"Not a chance. She'd eat you for breakfast," I laughed, imagining Frank and Morgana. It was a total nonstarter between those two, even beyond the obvious para versus human thing.

A loud knock on the door broke our banter, and we both looked towards it.

"Who is it?" I called, not used to visitors.

"Police. Detective Fox," a muffled voice came from the hall.

I scrambled up to open the door. A ginger man with a trim beard stood there with his fist raised to knock again. "May I come in?"

"Sure." I stepped back. We had nothing to hide.

The man did a quick once over of the apartment, but he didn't enter more than he needed to close the door behind him. It was like he just wanted to invade our personal space. Something about him tickled the beast and reminded me of someone.

"Were you involved in an altercation the other night on campus?" he asked, pulling out a notebook and waiting for me to answer.

I suddenly realized that there might have been cameras that had caught Chad and my fight. I'd figured that, if there were, the para world would have wiped them or something. He did shift into a wolf, after all.

I realized I'd already been quiet for too long, and the detective was watching me. "There was a small scuffle with someone over a girl. Nothing too intense. Both walked away fine." Jadelyn hadn't mentioned any permanent issues with Chad, so I assumed he'd healed up fine.

"A small scuffle, you say." He scratched into his notebook far longer than to say 'small scuffle' and I wanted to know what it said.

I decided to give him more but avoided a few of the obvious para details. "I bumped into his girl at the bar and excused myself from the dance floor after. He came and chased me down on campus. We had a small altercation. His girl calmed him down and pulled him away. That was that."

"Uh huh." Detective Fox made a few more notes. "Does this individual have a name?"

"Chad Brodie... the football star."

That made the detective's eyebrows come up. His whole mannerism changed, like he'd just decided to change direction on his line of questioning. I got distracted as over the detective's shoulder Frank just kept mouthing 'fight club' and throwing jabs into empty air. I was glad he was taking this seriously.

"Did anything strange happen, anything you'd like to report?"

I shook my head. "Like I said, it wasn't a big deal. We are both fine. What brought you here to ask about it?"

"You were reported to be heading home last night with a severe limp, clutching your arm."

I nodded. That made sense. A neighbor must have reported it. I was relieved that they didn't have any footage I had to try to explain away. "It wasn't that bad, just a bit tender at the time. A day's rest and I'm right as rain." I did a small circle showing that I was fine.

The detective seemed skeptical, but he closed his notebook and stuffed it into his jacket. "Bit of advice: avoid Brodie. He's a piece of work."

"Will do. I have no plans of antagonizing him further." Truthfully, I had bigger problems on my hands with Simon. Chad was in the rearview, I hoped.

"Then have a good day." The detective let himself out.

"That's how you—" Frank started, and I stopped him by holding a finger to my lips. For all either of us knew, the cop could be right outside listening.

I focused on my hearing, and sure enough, there were no steps in the hallway. He was lurking right outside. Frank and I waited for a moment until the detective's footsteps started down the hall. "He was waiting outside, listening. Yes, it's how I became introduced to the fight club, but it was actually the girl, Jadelyn, who introduced me."

Frank just gave me a big grin. "So there's three girls circling around you now. I can't wait to see which one you pick."

I didn't bother correcting him. Morgana was not really on my radar that way. Sure, she was hot, but she was also hundreds of years older than me and my custodian into the para world. Not to mention she didn't exactly seem the type for commitment.

And Jadelyn wasn't much of an option either, although I had to admit there was some interest there after she'd relaxed and shown me more of herself. But she was a princess and had already been given away. It didn't seem like the best match, but I was still figuring out how the para world worked. Based on Simon's accusations, it was at least complicated, and I had enough complicated things in my life at the moment.

But Scarlett was different. Despite everything going on, I was looking forward to seeing her in class the next day. A bit of normalcy.

Crap. I realized I didn't have any other clothes to wear.

"Frank, I need to go shopping." I grabbed my keys.

"For what?"

"Clothes. Do you want to come with me?"

His eyes lit up like the fourth of July. "Yes, please. I'd love to prevent you from buying more ugly shirts."

***

We ended up at some off-brand store that Frank swore by. There was little in the way of signage, and I didn't even catch the place's name. But the broad front windows full of mannequins covered in bright men's clothing made its purpose clear.

Looking skeptically at the mannequin, I gave Frank a look. I would never be caught wearing something so bright. It had better have clothing that wasn't so obvious and was just using this to draw the attention of those passing by.

"Come on. This place is a closely guarded secret of mine." Frank held open the door.

"It can't be that big of a deal." It was everything I could do to not roll my eyes at his antics.

Frank was a lot of things. Secretive was not one of them.

"Morning." An older man looked up from the counter; I realized we were the only two in the store. "Anything I can help you with today?"

The shop seemed pretty basic. It was decently deep, but it didn't seem like anything extra special for Frank to be secretive about. Racks of men's clothes were laid out in the shop with a half-level further back with the nicer clothing. I tried not to look at the price tags for fear I'd go running for the hills.

"Just getting my friend some clothes."

The man focused on us. "Frank, my best customer." He gave my roommate the sort of smile that said he smelled money. "Was starting to worry you were done looking for clothes."

"I do need to come around again and shop, but today is for the tall one behind me." Frank leaned in conspiratorially. "Todd, if you can help me get him into a few things, maybe I can torch his whole closet."

Todd laughed and nodded along with Frank's joke. "Got it. I'll throw in the fire extinguisher for free."

I found it odd that they both spoke to each other like they were old friends, despite the clear difference in their ages and likely social circles. Frank was odd like that, though. He moved through any social situation with ease.

The front door dinged open behind me and in walked another small group, two girls and two guys. They were idle chattering and stepped up to look at the racks of clothes. The girls pulled items off, holding them up to their man before shaking their heads and putting them back, only to try another. I felt for both of them. It looked like two girls playing with Ken dolls.

"What do you think?" Frank thrust a shirt on a hanger up to my chest.

Given the similarity between our situation and the two couples behind me, I suddenly felt ashamed and snatched the shirt out of Frank's hands. "Cut it out. Just give me a couple of ones you think are decent and I'll go try them on."

Frank raised his hands in a plea for surrender. "Alright, alright. No need to get testy. I'll just go hunt for some things. But if you come out looking uggo, I'm going to be straight with you." My roommate disappeared back into the racks of clothing.

I held up the shirt he'd given me and wandered over to the changing room. It was a nice, dark red shirt. I realized it would hide blood really well, which made my brain screech to a halt. Had I really just looked at a shirt and thought about how well it would hide blood? I looked back at the shirt and frowned. More than the world around me seemed to be changing as I stepped into the para world.

I hung the shirt back on the nearest rack without trying it on. Any shirt would be better than that one. My mind was just revolted at the thought of liking a shirt that would hide blood.

White, I picked another out. White always worked. It matched everything and was simple.

Someone's breath caught my attention, and I turned. One of the men from earlier was hanging over my shoulder. "Can I help you?" I stepped aside and gave him access to the rack I was blocking, but his focus stayed on me.

Out of the corner of my eye, I noticed the other man flanking me. The girls were in similar stances, one girl on one side and the other hanging back, blocking me from the rest of the store. I realized they'd effectively separated me from Frank and the store clerk and cornered me by the dressing room.

That got my attention, and I looked them over more. Both of the men were big, muscle-bound jocks with square jaws. The girls both looked like they could be on the cheerleading squad, complete with immaculate resting bitch faces.

I huffed along with my beast. They smelled like dog. Realization hit me. It wasn't a dog I was smelling, it was wolf. Now it all made more sense "Guessing this is about the other night? You're Chad's friends?"

"Oh look, he's got a brain in that head of his. Kelly, what do you think? He the one?" I thought he looked like he was trying to be Chad a little too much. Amusing myself, I decided I'd think of him as Chad-lite.

The girl sniffed the air and glared at me. Apparently, she was in charge. "Best way to find out is to see what he's made of. But it was his scent on Chad when he came back, tail between his legs."

Soft growls came out of the four of them. They didn't shift, but the muscles under the two men's clothes bulged like they were flexing, only they weren't. They'd done what seemed like some sort of partial transformation.

Chad-lite swung for me.

I'd only had one session with Morgana. It wasn't like I was suddenly a kung-fu expert, but practicing with her did help me understand my strengths.

Knowing I could handle it, I took the hit in the chest. It hurt, but I knew it would be worth it as I caught Chad-lite's arm. My hands turned to vices as I twisted hard and fast. Hearing his elbow crack and pop made me sick to my stomach, but I tried to push that aside.

I ignored that part of myself, letting the aggressiveness of my beast come forward. Sure enough, he reveled in the noise.

Chad-lite winced and growled at me. I had hoped that he'd be more like a puddle of crying muscle on the floor given I'd just mangled his arm. But it seemed werewolves were made of sterner stuff.

The second Ken doll tackled me from the side, and we went down in a heap as he tried to pummel me. Ken doll got a few good hits in before I managed to get ahold of his forearms. My head was starting to feel a little dizzy, but I ignored it.

I wondered why Frank and the shop owner hadn't come running, but I realized we'd been pretty quiet so far, and the racks of clothing were adding additional sound buffering.

I tried to flip Ken, but a boot connected with my head and threw off any maneuver I'd been attempting.

Kelly stood over me, bringing her leg back for another go.

Rolling Ken into her kick pulled her up short. It didn't do much to Ken, but at least I avoided another hit to the head.

As a result of my move, I found myself turned on top of Ken. I quickly gave two quick punches to the side of his chest, feeling the crack of his ribs under my fists.

I didn't keep pounding them, not sure if I'd be able to do enough damage to kill him. I just wanted him down for a while.

"Strong, but stupid," Kelly said behind me, claws prickled at the edge of my throat.

"Careful. I don't know all the rules yet, but I'm pretty sure you could get in deep shit for that." All the bravado I could muster was in those words, figuring it was worth a shot. "I'm a lost one, taken in by Morgana just today. You go that far and there's going to be consequences."

She at least was smart enough to hesitate. "You really are a lost one?"

"Ask Jadelyn. I bumped into her at the bar, and Chad and I fought. She approached me this morning, and it's been a whirlwind of a day for me."

Kelly huffed at the back of my neck and eased up.

"You don't seriously believe him, do you? He's pushing on pack territory." Chad-lite was still cradling his arm, but I noticed it didn't look quite so bent out of shape.

I couldn't see her, but I could feel her shift behind me to focus on Chad-lite. "He's not lying. And Chad put Rick in the hospital today for even looking at his new bitch. Wouldn't surprise me one bit if he went feral on this guy for bumping her at the bars."

"He's got some anger management issues," I added.

Growls sounded around me. "Chad's our pack leader. You got a problem with him, you have a problem with the pack." Kelly got off my back and stepped away enough that I could see her in my peripheral vision.

Getting off Ken seemed like only a fair response. The other girl rushed over and helped Ken get to his feet and limp out of the store. Kelly gave Chad-lite a gesture with her head, and he too headed out.

"Sorry about your rough first day. You are tough. You don't happen to be a shifter?" she asked, her voice sounding a little hopeful.

I had another form, if I was indeed a dragon, but I wasn't sure if I was considered a shifter or something else. I decided just to fib a bit. "Honestly, I don't know what I am. Today's just been one thing after another."

She sniffed, and her ear twitched. "Don't have to tell me what you are if you don't want to. I'm Kelly, head bitch of the new pack forming here at the college." She held out her hand. "Don't think that means I'm a pair with Chad. More like, it's my job to keep him in line, and he's been very out of line lately. Wouldn't mind if there was another big shifter in town to give him some competition."

"Thanks?" I wasn't quite sure if it was a compliment or a threat.

Kelly's eyes roved over me, taking in the damage done and nakedly assessing me. "I bet you're a big son of a bitch, whatever you are. I don't want to pick a fight with you or Morgana." She pulled out a wad of cash from her back pocket and split off a significant amount of money. "Here, buy some new clothes, and next time we meet, there's no beef. Any beef you have is between you and Chad. Keep the pack out of it."

I took the money because I was a little pissed. It was at least a win in a way for me. "And if Chad insists on bringing the pack into it?"

"That gets into what my job is." Kelly stuffed the rest of the cash in her back pocket. "Worst comes and he tries, just challenge Chad. That's how you can force him to fight you without the pack getting involved, but he'll still pull on us and there's nothing we can do to stop that. If you do that, you better be ready to rumble."

Morgana had also warned me that my fight with Chad before wasn't him at full strength. I appreciated that Kelly had at least entrusted me with a bit of information. "I'd rather not mess with your pack business, but if it happens again, I won't hold back."

She cocked a brow at me. "Didn't feel like you were holding back. Better luck next time, tough guy." She patted me on the chest and walked out.

I looked after her just to make sure the group was really going to leave.

The whole affair had been quiet, and clearly, they knew how to organize. They'd known just how to hide the scuffle during the day with a lookout and everything. Their world was clearly more dangerous than the one I was used to.

"What the hell happened to you? Get in a fight with a clothing rack?" Frank asked as he came out from the back, holding an armload of clothes.

CHAPTER 8

Normally I wasn't a clothing guy, but I had to say I felt pretty good as I walked into organic chem wearing some of my purchases from the day before. My new jeans looked better now that I'd put on more muscle mass, and the simple white shirt with my new favorite leather jacket made me feel a bit more armored.

The classroom was the same as it had been for the last few weeks, the same cheap linoleum tiles, white with black splashes to hide scuffs, and cheap stadium seating. But I had changed enough that it no longer felt the same. The massive room seemed smaller now, despite being able to hold two hundred students.

Professor Finstein was up front and struggling to get his computer connected to the wireless projector. I scanned the room, looking for Scarlett, but it didn't look like she had arrived yet.

I stepped all the way down the aisle and got Finstein's attention. "Do you want me to give it a try?"

He scowled briefly before stepping away from his computer in a non-verbal agreement for help. His laptop was a clunky gray brick, and either he was running a ten-year-old operating system, or he was one of those that liked to take the options on the new OS to make it look old.

I almost laughed to myself as I considered that some IT guy had done that to make it easier for him.

"It isn't connecting?" I asked. The blue screen on the projector behind me already told me the answer.

"No. It was there yesterday. Right here." He pulled up the page for connected devices and pointed to a spot that was now truly empty.

"Uh, huh. Let me see what I can do." I hit find new devices, and Finstein bristled behind me.

"I tried that. It can't find the projector." There was a certain tone the older generation took when they were flustered with technology, somewhere between exasperation and denial.

I checked the remote for the projector, and sure enough, there was a 'find me' button that I hit, and a blue blinking light lit up to confirm the action.

It only took a moment for the projector to reappear in his connected devices list again.

"Now I feel stupid," he sighed. "I need to find new devices on the computer and then hit that button on the projector?" He reached for the remote and I gave it to him.

He stared at the remote, muttering to himself. "Find me. I guess that makes sense. Thanks..." He paused. He clearly didn't know my name, although I couldn't blame him with how many students were in the class.

"Zach Pendragon."

His brows went up at my name. "Oh. I remember that name on the roster. Hard to forget a last name like that. Thanks for the help. Now go get seated before that girl gets up and drags you with her." He gave me a knowing smile.

I followed his eyes, finding Scarlett sitting back in the third row at the edge. She blushed when our eyes locked. With both the professor and me staring at her, it was obvious the professor had said something, even if she didn't hear him.

Getting off the lectern, I made my way over to Scarlett. "Is this seat taken?" I asked, seeing her bag in the seat beside her.

"No, it's for you." She lifted the bag and shoved it under her seat without looking.

I could feel a few eyes of other men around me staring as I sat down. I smiled to myself, my beast puffing up as we got to claim the girl next to us as mine. At least for that class.

"Thanks." I got my notebook out as the professor cleared his throat and looked directly at Scarlett and me before he started.

"I hope you are all comfortable, because today we are talking about Huckel's rule of aromaticity. Bonus question." He pointed dead at me. "Zach, does chemical aromaticity have anything to do with our sense of smell?"

I started kicking myself. Finstein clearly didn't know many names in the class, and now I'd just become one of them. I'd made myself a target for when he needed participation. At least I had managed to read the chapter already.

"No, or at least, not broadly. His early research identified the phenomena by smell, but that's only applicable for a small number of the chemicals."

"Correct. That one will be on the test. Easy points if you read and come to class." Finstein emphasized the last part, clearly wanting to make sure people showed up to his class. Turning to his presentation slides, he started rambling more about chemical aromaticity.

"Nice job," Scarlett murmured. "Thought for a second he was going to call on me."

I gave a half-hearted chuckle. "I think my name was just top of mind from helping him with the projector."

"Better you than me, apparently. I couldn't get any reading done last night." She rolled her eyes.

I looked over, specifically interested in what color they would be. They were the same bright emerald as I remembered at the end of our encounter. The adrenaline must have gotten to me when I had almost gotten hit by the cyclist. There's no way she had gold eyes.

"And next we have an example of that in the benzene family, as you can see..." The professor continued class, and I tried to focus on what he was saying and not on the moments when Scarlett's arm would brush against mine.

***

"That's all. I hope you read up through chapter 7 before tomorrow. We won't get through it all, but at least have the first half read or you might be lost." Finstein closed his lecture for the day.

"He's really moving really quickly through the material." Scarlett packed away her things in a small bag with leather straps.

"Yeah, at this rate, he's going to finish the textbook in half the semester. Maybe he'll slow down."

"Or go off book." Scarlett rolled her eyes. "Plus, it's not like we'll use most of this unless we are working on programming the computer models."

Damn, she was so in sync with me. That comment had been on the tip of my tongue. "Exactly." I finished grabbing my stuff and shuffled my bag onto my shoulder. I paused, not wanting to head off my own way, but not sure what to do next.

She saw my hesitation and looked up at me with a bit of hesitation as she swung her own bag over her shoulder. "Hey, do you want to grab a bite to eat? I missed lunch, and I'm starving."

"Sure." I couldn't have sounded more eager, but that earned me a smile, so I didn't feel too weird about it. "I seem to be starving all the time lately."

Her eyes wandered over me, and I was suddenly very happy with my recent transformation. "You look a lot better in those clothes. Either I hit my head pretty hard the other day, or your other outfit really hid your frame."

"Thanks." I stepped out into the aisle and headed out of class, doing everything in my power not to look over my shoulder to check to see that she was behind me.

When she stepped up beside me after we left class, I asked, "Kinsey for lunch?"

"Yes please. They at least serve hot food, unlike the other food courts." She wrinkled her nose. "I'd like to have something more than a preservative ladened muffin."

"Trying to keep away from processed foods?" I asked, making conversation.

"No, I just avoid muffins."

I chuckled, and we shared a laugh. "But really, what did muffins do to you?"

"Besides threatening my waistline? I have a love-hate relationship with muffins." Scarlett blew a raspberry.

I wasn't sure she needed to worry about muffins much. She was a compact little thing. The crest of her bright red hair coming up to my chest, I put her at maybe 5'6". She wasn't crazy skinny, but she was trim with lean muscle that looked like she spent plenty of time at her workout of choice.

"Muffins, is it? Then what's your favorite kind?"

Her face twisted with indecision. "It's too hard to choose. Anything but chocolate chips."

I gasped in fake outrage. "Please tell me you don't have a thing against chocolate."

She laughed. "Please, chocolate is fantastic. Just not in a muffin. It's like a copout. No, you put a little fruit, maybe some vanilla or cinnamon to sweeten them up. Chocolate is like..." She paused, thinking for a good analogy. "Like assuming you have a catalyst in every chemical equation. Totally cheating."

"You just geeked out on me." I didn't hate it, that was for sure. She had looks and brains.

"Better get used to it." She gave me a wide grin.

The more she talked, the more I liked her. The spunk made me happy. She wasn't some sorority girl who would cry about breaking a nail. And we seemed to click. Normally, I was awkward with women, but it was easy with her.

Even the beast was being patient, not wanting to screw this one up. "I think I could get used to it."

Her eyes went wide at that, and I worried I'd gone too far too quickly. As I started to backtrack, she blushed so hard her cheeks nearly blended into her hair. "Thanks," she said quietly.

She was so cute when she blushed. I wanted to pull her into a hug but decided not to push my luck. "No problem, here let me get the door." I stepped forward and snagged the door to the dining hall, flinging it open and nearly smacking myself in the face.

"Careful." She laughed, breaking the tension.

"The retractor must not be working. Normally these things feel like you're trying to move a boulder." We both glanced up at the metal arm. It was connected, but I hoped it didn't seem odd. Clearly, I needed to work on recalibrating to my new strength. I was pretty sure I'd almost torn the door off its hinges.

"Or you might just be too strong." Her eyes squeezed tight with the laughter that followed. I joined her, trying not to show how true that might be.

"Come on. Don't just stand there." Scarlett pulled me back to the present and into the dining hall.

She turned back partially, smiling a bright smile up at me. Her green eyes sparkled, and I found myself caught a bit, just wanting to stare at her longer.

"You're beautiful." It slipped out, but it was also true.

Scarlett blushed all the way to the tips of her ears. "Cut it out. Food, then I'll meet you there." She pointed to a currently abandoned table.

"Sounds good." I was feeling hungry again, so I grabbed anything that sounded good. There were a number of options to choose from. Different types of food lined a wall that went back to a half circle, with more shops before dumping into the main eating area.

The pizza place called to me, but I'd eaten enough pizza lately. So I pivoted and went with Italian. Grabbing a bowl of spaghetti and meatballs and heading to the dining area, I saw Scarlett had beaten me and was digging into a burrito the size of her head.

"I think that thing might try to eat you back," I teased, sitting down and unwrapping my plastic silverware.

"I may be pretty small, but I'm pretty ferocious when I want to be. This burrito doesn't stand a chance." She bit violently into the side of it to prove a point.

I gave her a look of mock horror. "I can see that. Never mind. I feel pity for the burrito."

We settled into eating, and I took a look around. The dining hall was still running even though it was two o'clock, but it was a pretty sparse crowd. There was enough ambient chatter to make it comfortable to have a conversation, but we didn't have to yell to talk to each other. Returning to my food, I saw Scarlett watching me.

"Got a girlfriend I'm not supposed to see?" Scarlett teased, raising an eyebrow.

I pointed my fork at her and shook my head as I said, "No." Wanting to make sure she was comfortable, I added, "Not really many exes even. I normally keep busy between the weekend job and classes."

"EMT, I remember. Can I assume you are pre-med then?"

"Sorta the plan for now. How about you?"

"I'm straight Chem. Lots of opportunities there in just about every manufacturing field."

"Something in particular must call to you," I prodded.

"We all have to start in a lab somewhere. I guess for now I'm assuming I'll end up in Pharma, mostly because it pays some of the best for when I'm starting out."

I nodded. It made sense, but I was a bit bummed she was going after the money and not a passion. I changed the subject. "So, what's your workout routine like?" Based on her toned body, I assumed she must do some sort of workout.

"Oh, just some basics. I do Krav Maga, so be careful, buster." She waggled her brows at me, and I knew she was just teasing. "How about you? Wait, let me guess, you lift." Her lips curled into a smile.

I gave her a little dramatic performance. "How did you know?"

She was working through that burrito quickly, and I realized suddenly that our little stop might end soon, and I really didn't want it to.

I was really starting to like her. Beautiful, fun, and smart. It was hard to believe she wasn't already taken.

"So—" I awkwardly paused, fumbling with what the correct follow up to 'so' was. "Want to have dinner and drinks?" I paused again, clearly not having thought out where I was going very well, so I just went ahead and went for it. "Tonight?"

Her mouth opened to answer, but my phone started blaring in my pocket. I checked it, but I didn't recognize the number and hit to end the call.

"You can answer it. It's fine." She looked at my phone.

"Didn't recognize the number," I explained. "About the—" My phone started ringing again, the same number.

"Go ahead. I'm not running away just yet."

I gave her a smile and answered, "Hello?"

"Zach," Morgana's Swiss accent said hastily. "I need you to come right away. I have a job for you."

"Tonight?" I looked at Scarlett with a frown. "I was just making plans for tonight."

"Cancel them. Isn't learning to live more important?"

It sounded pretty darn important, but I didn't want to cancel on Scarlett. Apparently, the girl in question understood that I was in a tight place.

"Go ahead. She sounds urgent. I should do a sorority activity we have tonight, anyway." She didn't get up and leave after saying that, so I figured I still had a shot.

"Great, sounds like your date just canceled. You should bring her by some night so I can get a look at her. Her voice is lovely." Morgana had switched back to teasing. "I'll expect you in the next hour." Her phone clicked off, almost like she still had one of those old receiver phones.

I hung up and looked back at Scarlett. "Sorry about that."

"No exes?" Her eyebrow cocked in a way that put my answer as something that could sink or swim all of this.

"That was my new boss. She's kind of hot and cold." Given that I was going to work for her, at least temporarily, it was only fair to call her my boss. My very hot, and sometimes overly suggestive, boss, but Scarlett didn't need to know that.

Scarlett's look of doubt cleared up. "Oh. That makes sense. I'm busy tonight and tomorrow, but Sunday?" She seemed as eager as I was to find a time soon, and I took that as a good sign.

"Yes. I'll make it work. Phone number?" I opened the contacts and spun it around on the table for her.

She didn't miss a beat, snatching it up and typing into it far longer than she needed to for just her name and number.

I leaned over to the side, curious, but she smirked and tilted the phone and held it closer.

"No peeking." She deleted something and then typed again before handing it back to me.

'The fabulous and foxy Scarlett' read her name across the top of the contact. I laughed. It looked like she also enjoyed staking her claim. Not like I could have that show up when I was with another girl and still stand a chance.

"Oh, by the way, would you mind if I made it a double date?" She bit her lip, and I could tell she felt bad even asking. I would have preferred just us, but I knew a double date might help her be more comfortable, too.

But before I could answer, she continued on. "My friend, the one that just got here, she is probably going out with her new guy this weekend, and I know she'd feel a lot more comfortable if I was there."

That made me feel better; it was more for her friend's comfort than hers. "Are you sure you aren't just using me as muscle?"

Scarlett waved that away. "We girls can handle ourselves, but I'd love you to meet them. And then maybe once the night is underway, we can slip away together."

I tried not to give away how much I liked that option.

"Sounds good. Well, it seems I need to get going. Duty calls." I grabbed my phone and texted her so that she'd have my number. I started to try to get witty, but in the end kept it a simple 'This is Zach'.

Her phone dinged a second later. "Got it. I'll see you on Sunday. I'll text you where my friend and I decide on going." She gave me a smile that I burned into my mind's eye as we parted. I was going to love Sunday.

I felt triumphant walking away from the late lunch. I had gotten her number and a date. Things were moving in the right direction. Although, the para world had already gotten somewhat in the way, with whatever Morgana needed me for tonight. But it worked. This way, Scarlett could do what she needed to with the sorority, and we didn't go too fast too quickly. I could juggle both worlds, no problem.

I pulled out my phone and shot a quick email to the EMT services, telling them I was very sick and that it would be irresponsible of me to treat people. I felt bad lying, but something had to give. With my schedule cleared, I headed to see what this job Morgana mentioned entailed.

Chapter 9

I strolled into Bumps in the Night. The bar wasn't quite as laid back as it had been the last time I had been there. Vampires and what looked like goblins were busy bustling about on the stage, setting it up for some sort of show. The goblins climbed easily through the stage light frames, testing each one and checking the equipment. Meanwhile, the vampires did the heavy lifting of getting everything into place

Every now and then, one would pull a wrench from their tool belt and adjust something.

"Really amazing what they can all do when they work together, isn't it?" Morgana's voice sounded like it was right behind me, but when I turned, she was leaning against the main bar. It was a dark wooden affair currently lit in warm lights, but I could see the sets of black lights around the outer edge that would probably be the lighting come this evening.

"Does this happen every day?" I asked, seeing all the paranormal races working together. So far, it had felt like the para world was heavily divided by species.

"Friday maintenance. Can't have any issues for Friday and Saturday nights." She sipped a red liquid that I assumed was some sort of processed blood.

Tonight, Morgana had traded out her corset for a tight-fitting dark leather jacket. Her tight leather pants remained. I got the impression they were almost a permanent fixture given how they hugged her legs. Even as covered up as she was, Morgana still had an almost irresistible draw to her.

But completely ruining her dark allure were the pair of curved, short swords that laid on the bar beside her. Even sheathed, the things looked like they might leap up and sever a head before their target could blink. I could almost picture it after sparring with her. I wasn't surprised that a blade was her weapon of choice, given her speed.

"What? It's not like we use magic for everything. Mechanical things are easier with a good goblin or gnome to get into the works and fix it right up." She misinterpreted my stare as disbelief.

I nodded, taking the out. "Still getting used to all of this." I looked back at the blades she had on the counter. "Are we going to be needing those?"

"Decent chance. Why don't we get moving, and I'll tell you about it all on the way?" She took the twin blades off the counter and slipped them into loops on her hips. They were tight up against her hips, sitting at a forty-five-degree angle. I could understand why she'd taken them off when she was relaxing by the counter.

Morgana led me through the maze of the bar that extended far past the building's boundaries. The backroom led into a stairwell. From there, we entered what looked like any other parking garage, the plain concrete slabs a stark contrast to the swanky, leather-draped nightclub above. Although, the cars in front of me were far different from something you'd find in a typical parking garage.

"I know nothing about cars, but I can read all those emblems well enough. Are these all yours?" I saw every famous brand name I recognized and a few I didn't.

"Get a gun." She ignored my question, pointing to a rack fitted with gray foam and a small arsenal. I had completely missed it with the cars on display.

"I don't know how to shoot," I admitted; she looked at me incredulously. "What? I grew up raised by two lovely, but elderly, parents. My father was seventy by the time I could have been taken out to a gun range. I don't even know if his wrists would have held up."

Morgana shook her head, clearly disappointed. "Then stick to the 9mm." She pulled it out of its foam padding and the several duplicates that rested nearby. "This is the safety." She demonstrated, flipping the safety off and back on. "You need to flip that, then point and shoot. Don't even have the safety off until you have it out and are ready to shoot someone."

"Does it have special bullets? Something for paranormals?" I looked at the thing, not even sure I wanted it. I was growing more and more interested in what she was planning to drag me into. But, if she needed the blades, I'd probably end up happy to have the gun.

Morgana was moving next to me, snagging a much larger gun that she carefully placed in a duffel and slung over her shoulder. "Not right now. You can still take down most things with enough bullets, and they can slow almost everything down."

"You seemed to bounce back from when I snapped your neck pretty quickly." I'd been curious on if that was something unique to her or a typical thing for para.

Morgana started strutting out to the spread of cars and didn't look back as she explained, "If you broke my neck a dozen times, I'd start to recover slower. But even then, fixing a broken neck is just realigning what's broken. Try fixing missing pieces of body mass or brain, and it takes a hell of a lot more mana to work."

"Ah." I could understand that. "You can kill almost anything if you keep hurting it till it runs out of mana to heal?"

Now she did turn her head to give me a grin full of fangs. "Yes, which is why, while guns are very useful at range, something more... destructive works better at closer range." She wiggled her hips, making the sheathed blades slap her ass.

Trying to distract myself and get that image out of my head before I had an entirely inappropriate reaction, I focused on what we were about to do. "So, the job? Rogue vampire, mysterious killings or maybe help a kelpie get her cat out of a tree? I'm assuming as I walk around with a gun that we're going after some sort of bad guy and not taking out a decent person."

I gave her a pointed look. I'd only met this woman a day ago, and I didn't quite trust that her morals lined up with mine.

"Drugs. Drugs that, if someone smart got their hands on, would raise a lot of questions the council doesn't want." She partially answered my question, but still didn't give me many details.

"Doesn't the council have people they could send after this problem?" I asked, confused on why they needed Morgana to take care of it.

"It is easier if they don't act directly, and I'm just a mercenary. It means I'm a buffer between their politics and their aggressive actions. But, at the same time, everyone knows I'm just for hire."

She pulled up to a stop at a car that made me frown, and it only deepened when she popped the trunk and threw in her duffel bag.

"You can't be serious." I stared at the ugly thing.

"We are going to a decommissioned coal factory. We'd stick out like a sore thumb if we came up in one of the Jags." She put a loving hand on the beat-up looking minivan that even a soccer mom would refuse to be seen in. One of the sliding panel doors was an ugly brown that might have been a better color than the sort of green that you just knew came with a discount in the car lot.

"This won't stick out?" I had my doubts.

"Nope, just another beat-up, old minivan. But this one has a reinforced frame and enough enchantments that it might as well be a tank." She grinned. "It actually cost more than that Lamborghini."

I held back my cursing and slid into the passenger seat, feeling awkward with the gun, so I just put it in the glove box. "So you dodged the question earlier, what's the drug?"

A frown dusted her face for just a moment before it disappeared. "V-phoria is what they are calling it. It's a derivative of vampire secretions."

"Stupid name," I said.

"Better than 'Molly'. People who come up with drug names aren't exactly known for their brains."

I opened my mouth to argue for a second before snapping it shut. She was right. "So vampires have something in their... fangs?"

"Saliva, and yes. It's potent. It has a few uses, but most vamps use it to addict their favorite feed." The engine started up with a roar that belonged to a muscle car, not a minivan.

"I thought you said this was to be inconspicuous," I noted the noise and tried to ignore the vampire talk. I didn't want to think about it right now. I'd seen enough addicts on my day job; part of me now wondered if any of them had been a vampire's 'favorite feed' once.

"Still need to get away at times. Would suck if this was anything but a custom job."

She turned around to watch the back, and the tires squealed as she spun out of her spot, missing a Porsche by inches. Swinging the minivan around, she threw the minivan into gear, and it kicked forward. It was either a display of skill or recklessness. I chose to believe skill, and that I wasn't about to die with her driving.

She raced down the lanes of nice cars to an exit ramp and bumped us out into traffic, cutting a hard turn east and flooring it into traffic. The sun was still out, but hanging low in the sky, threatening the end of the day and the beginning of the night.

Her windshields were so heavily tinted it might as well have been midnight to me.

I changed my mind. Her driving was terrifying. She bobbed and weaved through traffic like a fish in water, but it still didn't make it any less terrifying.

"So, who was the girl?"

"What?" I focused on her. It seemed best if I didn't watch what was happening on the road.

"I could hear it in how you spoke on the phone earlier. I interrupted a date." It wasn't a question; she had a knowing smirk hanging on her lips.

I paused, not sure what I was supposed to say. I didn't even know what the rules in the para world were around dating. Morgana seemed relaxed, but I didn't want to say anything that would put Scarlett at risk. And it hadn't really been a date. More of a trial run for a date.

"She's a friend, one I'm going on a real first date with on Sunday. It was just a quick bite after class."

"Oh, that sounds like fun. You should bring them to Bumps, we do a nice dinner deal six to eight, and then the club starts pumping a little after nine." She swerved hard enough for me to grab the oh-shit handle and brace myself against the car. I refused to look forward at that point, feeling us bump over a curb.

"I don't know if she's that kind of girl."

"Oh? What kind of girl is she?"

I hesitated. I really knew very little about her. But what I knew so far was she was a sweet sorority girl on the outside, with a tough girl packed inside. Smart too. "The whole package."

Morgana laughed, and with her driving, it came off a little crazed. "That's so cute. You really like her. Good, I want to meet her now. After all, you are my charge, and I want to do my best to look after your best interest."

"Why do I have the feeling I don't want that at all? And it's not like you're my mother."

"No, but I bet you I could be the best wingman you've ever had." She made the statement confidently, her voice dipping back into a sultry tone.

Somehow, I instinctively knew she wasn't just bragging. She was incredibly persuasive and had years of experience. "Well, she's choosing the place, so at least this time it's up to fate."

"Well, you should go for it. I recommend having some fun while you can. It will help take your mind off of things for a while. Is she para?"

"I don't know? Not exactly something you just up and ask. And it's not like there's a dating app for that." I did a double take at Morgana's expression. "Holy crap, there is an app for that, isn't there?"

Morgana's face went hard for a second, ignoring that question and staying on the earlier topic. "Relationships between normies and para rarely work out. Doesn't mean you can't have fun, but be careful, or you'll get her and yourself killed for spilling the beans."

"Can you ever tell them?" I asked once again, blindly poking about for the rules of this new world.

"Yes, but then your relationship is permanent, and you are responsible for them. They leave you, and the council treats it as someone learning our secret. So you need to be absolutely sure about them." She took her hand off the wheel and dragged her thumb across her neck.

So, it wasn't something to take lightly. It sounded more of a commitment than marriage, telling someone a secret that then bound their life to you. At least you could get out of a marriage, this you really couldn't. "The council sounds old school."

"Some of them ARE old school. Elves live thousands of years. You think old people have trouble accepting something simple like civil rights, now imagine the elves on the council who grew up with slaves and servants of every race and creed."

"At least they didn't discriminate?" I tried to joke, but let the smile go when Morgana gave me a glare.

Wanting to change the topic, I shifted to another political question I had. "What did I do to get the duel with Simon?"

"You challenged him, at least physically. Standing up in his face like that was practically a thrown gauntlet. The council is old school, but with new rules, sort of like the casus belli system. You can't fight someone or another clan without being provoked in some way. The elves on the council would have had to approve the duel."

I nodded, still thinking that he'd been extra sensitive. He did insult Jadelyn, which had started the whole affair.

We bumped our way out of what I'd call the city proper and into the industrial area. Gone were the tall apartment buildings and the skyline of corporate offices sprawling to the heavens. Instead, they were replaced by large, squat buildings with smokestacks, puffing away like a smoker on their too short smoke break.

It was a long, quiet drive from there, the sun sinking low on the horizon.

No one was out and about walking around. People didn't have time for leisure around there. It was all tired industrial types. They were there to work and then go home.

As Morgana continued into the industrial area, more and more of the buildings turned into slumbering behemoths, their stacks no longer puffing out exhaust. Peeling paint became more apparent until it became the norm and broken windows became the next sign that we were heading into sketchier territory.

"So, what's the plan?" I asked as the paved road gave way to gravel. The buildings at that point were sparse, and there was only one more structure that could be the old coal plant.

The place was wrapped with a rusting chain-link fence, but there was fresh razor wire running along top. Priorities. I rolled my eyes. However, the brightly polished razor wire was the only thing about the place that looked like it had been updated in the last decade. Between the fence and the building, it was overgrown with enough weeds to make it almost seem tropical. The coal plant itself rose out of the mess, its paint long gone and replaced by the brown of rust stains.

"This is the place." She pulled up to the gate, her minivan having enough momentum that it skidded on the gravel for a foot. "What they are doing is a threat to the secret of the para world. Killing is fully authorized. Once they realize what's happening, I don't think they'll hold back. So don't hesitate."

"Are we just going in and killing them all?" I asked, already feeling my stomach revolt at the idea.

"No, if we can keep some alive, we should. We'll be able to get more answers out of them and cut the head off this thing." Morgana started checking her weapons, and I remembered to pull my gun out of the glove box. I was so not ready for this.

I fumbled with the gun, eventually holding it down with stiff arms and hunched shoulders, doing my best imitation of cops I'd seen on TV. I'm sure the poses were inaccurate and more for show, but I didn't have anything else to go off of.

"Break the chain for me?" Morgana pointed with her chin. That's when I noticed that she had pulled the duffel out of the back and slung the large gun over her shoulder. It hung loosely at her chest while she kept one hand on it.

I stepped up to the rusted gate, noticing the chain was still a rusted piece of junk, but the lock was brand new. Where the lock hung on the chain, the rust had been worn off. It had seen some use recently.

I focused internally. If there was ever a time I needed the beast, this battle was it. I needed its strength and instincts. And I wouldn't mind being able to justify some of what was about to go down as the beast's aggression and not mine.

Thankfully, the beast growled and stirred deep inside of me, and I could feel it, almost like it was coming home to nest inside me once again.

I grabbed the chain and pulled, using my back rather than just my arms to pull it. The links strained as my back ached, and I reset my grip so that I was holding onto two links and I could pull the whole of my strength into the one between them.

Snapping with a small pop, the chain came loose. I did my best to uncoil it quietly. Chains were hard to keep quiet.

A small hoot sounded behind me. And I turned to Morgana, who had her hands cupped in front of her mouth. "Good job. I wasn't sure if you'd pull that off."

I shrugged, not feeling slighted by more testing. While we'd both come to the conclusion I was likely a dragon, I couldn't wait for firm proof to show it to me. I felt like I was missing that piece to accept what was happening to me.

The beast growled deep inside of me, like it was reminding me just how real it was.

"Stick close. That busted window there"—she pointed to one on the side of the building, not far from a conveyor—"would be a great place to peek in and see what is going on."

We crawled around to the conveyor, and I crawled up it on my hands and knees, coming away stained dark from residual dust. I smacked my hands on my pants, but that only seemed to make it worse. Morgana snickered, not missing a beat as she ran up the conveyor.

By the time I caught up to her, she was looking through the scope of her gun into the coal plant. "It certainly isn't abandoned, but not exactly what we believed we would find."

She handed me her gun, and I made sure to keep my hand away from the trigger as I looked down the scope.

Chapter 10

It was hard to make out much through the scope. The inside of the plant was dark, except for an area that had been cleared out and lit with the kind of floor lamps used around construction sites. Between the lamps, clear plastic tents were set up and nearly empty.

Workers hurried about, packing up the last of the paper-wrapped bricks and shoving them into an assortment of bags, from your standard gym bag to a hard-shelled suitcase. There was no uniformity, almost like they'd gone bargain shopping for any kind of mobile container they could get.

It felt rushed as they threw everything into a carrier van. There were about six of them left. It felt incomplete.

"They are moving. Either they were tipped off or someone has really good instincts." Morgana spat.

I lifted my face away from the scope and handed her the gun back. "Then do we bail? If they know we are coming..."

Morgana shook her head with a dark smile. "No, we'll do the job, get paid, and tell them their information was bad. If we can find a lead from one of them, that would be ideal." She rolled off the conveyor, grabbing one of the struts and twisted her way down. She looked intimately familiar with moving on a pole.

I stuffed that thought in the back of my mind and jumped off the conveyor, landing with a thud and no more damage than slightly sore feet. That had been a nearly two-story drop.

"Quiet," Morgana chided me. I thought I had been quiet, but I reminded myself she and many others had significantly better hearing. "We'll circle around and hit the truck first. Best to take out their means of escape."

She crouched slightly and slunk across the side of the building. I followed, keeping my eyes up and looking over my shoulder constantly.

The operation came into sight as we rounded on the open bay door that they had been using to move the truck. Distant shouts came from inside.

"Move! Move! We don't have all night. We need to be gone, now," a rough voice ordered people about. No one complained as they all hurried to pack away the last of the bricks into a plain commercial van.

Now that we were closer, I took another look at the few I could see. None had pointy ears, so hopefully, there was no magic to deal with. But the scent of wolves was in the surrounding air. I couldn't be sure if they were all werewolves.

"Weres," I said quietly to Morgana.

"Humans too." She glowered into the factory. "We go hard and fast. Count to three and come after me."

She slipped into the bay door, her gun up on her shoulder as she stood up and took aim. The tip of her gun flashed as a staccato burst of gunfire destroyed the otherwise quiet night.

One.

Morgana moved quickly, her gun snapping from person to person. A quick burst of fire sounded the second she had someone in her sights.

Two.

Blood sprayed into the air as they went down one after the other.

I saw someone blur around the back side of the truck and come for Morgana. I didn't wait for three, charging from my spot to tackle the vamp into the side of the truck.

The side panel dented as we slammed into it, and the vamp grunted in surprise before she hissed, baring her fangs at me.

Another staccato burst sounded over my shoulder, and the side of her head popped.

"Thanks for the assist," Morgana called, already turning back to the crowd. She'd caught them by surprise, and it would seem that only two of them got back up after her first round of fire.

I went to nod, but something outside the factory caught my eye. There were shapes moving in the dark. "I think we have a problem," I called to her.

Big, bipedal shapes came out of the darkness as a line of werewolves appeared. The wolves appeared in a hybrid form, standing tall on two digitigrade legs, their muscles tight even under the fur, like loaded springs. They weren't that much taller than me, but their perpetual hunch that made them look like they ran as well on four limbs as two was probably misleading.

Then, of course, there were the dozen snarling muzzles baring their teeth at me. Can't forget that.

I heard Morgana's curse over the gunfire. "I need you to stall them." She threw her gun down, and I heard the ring of her two blades before I saw them flash. She blurred forward, cutting into two weres that had shifted after the fight had started.

I wanted to watch, but I had my own problems to deal with, apparently. Stall them, she said. Two days in the paranormal world, and I was going to take on multiple werewolves.

"I don't suppose any of you'd like to call it a day?"

All I got in return were growls, and one of the wolves in the back howled to the moon. After that sound, something strange happened. The wolves up front seemed to grow ever so slightly, and their eyes caught the light of the moon and gave off an eerie glow.

More of the wolves in the back started howling and now it was clear the others were growing stronger. Morgana had mentioned they were stronger as a pack, but I didn't realize till now she meant that literally.

Any hesitation I had burned up in that moment. I couldn't let them continue. It was now or never.

I charged into the wolves, relying more on my beast's instinct than any sort of skill I had with fighting, which was essentially none. Cracking the first wolf's jaw, I sent him flying into a heap, but there were many of them. They quickly closed ranks on me. Good thing I was a whole lot sturdier than a few days ago.

Punches landed on me, and claws raked across my skin as I tried to block anything that I could. It hurt, but I gave as good as I got, slowly taking down a wolf here or there with my swings. Unfortunately, they seemed to get back up as fast as I could take another down. Meanwhile, their claws left deep scratches, my skin tougher than it used to be, but they were still wearing me down.

That frustration built up in my gut, condensing and becoming fiery anger. This time, I knew what was happening in my body. But I couldn't get clear of them to get a good shot, and they were surrounding me, so I did the next best thing and breathed straight down.

Fire washed over my feet harmlessly, but it slammed into the floor, melting the stone under my feet and washing outwards. Look, if fire is hot enough to melt stone on impact, let's just say I was throwing a wolf meat barbeque. The orange and gold flames consumed the wolves and the front half of the van, turning the engine block into shiny playdough.

Yelps and pleading howls mixed with the roar of flames as the night lit up with the few wolves at the edge that tried to escape. I didn't let up—my beast wouldn't let me. It was angry, and nothing these wolves could do was going to stop it. Turning my head towards the runners, I finished the lot of them.

The smell of smoke and char filled the air as I finally let up on the breath, revealing the damage I'd done. One particularly large wolf managed to wobble to its feet. He must have been at the edge of the destruction to have survived, even with their healing. Blackened skin cracked, revealing tender pink flesh beneath it. Even as it glared at me, I could see those cracks closing and it healing.

"You'll pay for that," the wolf said in a guttural tone as it fell to all fours.

The wolf turned and ran, and I couldn't help but notice that his tail had curled under his legs. Either way, it was far faster than I could hope to be.

I scented him, or tried to, but all that filled my nose was the overwhelming smell of barbequed wolf. My throat filled with bile and I braced against the red hot truck and emptied my stomach. It just kept coming as my body took a firm claim on its right to revolt.

If I never smelled a barbequed wolf again, it would be too soon. Next time, I'd need to remember to bring some sauce and spices.

"Well, I guess that's one way to stall them." Morgana flicked her blade and blood spattered on the floor. She regarded the running wolf but didn't give chase.

"Did you know that would happen?" I asked, feeling suddenly like I was strapped with hundred-pound weights. My body sagged.

"Hoped we'd see something. Though..." She looked around at the dozen or so dead wolves that were starting to change back to humans, humans that were just as crispy as their wolf bodies. "I had hoped to take someone alive."

The ground underneath me was already solid again, red hot and warped for its efforts. Sadly, my shoes and the bottom half of my pants didn't make it. Though I'd have ruined them throwing up anyway.

Movement caught my eye, and the vamp that Morgana had shot had her face regrowing. "She looks like she might be healing." I pointed her out. "Should I give her some blood?"

As the action settled down and the adrenaline left my system, I could feel doubt and guilt at what I'd done here start to creep up on me. I wanted to help save the one that might survive tonight.

Morgana's face became a frown. "I don't think that's wise." She sniffed at me. "Your blood smells absolutely delicious. Even I'm having some trouble being around you. That little baby would be stuck on you like a leech if she got a lick. Not to mention that the bite may affect you." She gave me a look over the top of her nose.

Right, vamp bites are addictive. I'd rather not go down that route.

"Got something in the car for her then?" I asked.

"Yeah, under the driver's seat in the van, there should be a case. Go get it. I'll keep watch and do a quick sweep when you get back."

I pulled myself together and hurried out to the minivan. Thankfully, it had been left alone. I pulled out the case Morgana had mentioned. Popping it open, it had five small vials of red liquid. I closed it and hurried back to Morgana, opening it and setting it by the vamp.

Morgana snapped one of the vials and poured it down the vamp's throat. She was still healing, but slowly.

Feeling awkward just standing there, I decided to make myself useful and scope the area, keeping an eye on everything. As I walked through, taking in the scene, a part of me wished I had decided not to. Morgana had mowed down the half a dozen or so people on one side of the van. The two werewolves that she'd taken on with her blades... well, they were entirely unrecognizable. I was just barely able to get a look at the heads. One was a balding man I'd place in his fifties and the other young, maybe not even old enough to drink yet.

Bile started to creep back up my throat and I turned away, wandering back over to Morgana.

"Morgana? Is this operation related to the pack that Chad leads?" I kept my head up trying not to look at the ground.

She looked around at all the dead wolves. "Packs are often of the same age group. The kids from one pack tend to set off on their own and reform a new pack with other weres of a similar age. But these... they are all different ages, all different walks of life." She shook her head in answer to my question.

The vampire below her took a deep breath and looked at the both of us before taking in the scene with wide eyes. "I swear I had nothing to do with this."

"That's pretty hard to believe," I said, crouching but making sure to be far enough away that I might have a chance to react before she got to me.

"I just wanted to escape." She paused before her eyes lit up with an idea. "I know. Let me show you the others. You'll believe me after you see it." She started to get up, and I backed away, throwing Morgana a questioning look.

She nodded at my unasked question. "Go ahead and lead us then."

The vampire got to her feet and wobbled for a moment against the van. I braced, expecting her to dart off, but that never happened. She just pushed herself along the van and over to a large heavy-duty door that was just as rusted as everything else in this damn place.

"Help me with it?" She tugged on the door, and it creaked but didn't budge.

Stepping up and letting Morgana cover my back, I grabbed the handle and placed my foot on the wall next to it and heaved. The door groaned and crackled with flakes of rust but swung out. Inside was too dark for me to see, but Morgana gasped behind me.

"She's telling the truth. Free them." She pushed the vampire forward, who didn't hesitate to dart into the room. Morgana raised her gun, and a light came on, showing me what was beyond the door. Several vampires were chained up, with gags forcing their mouths open.

"What is—" I stopped my question as I already realized the answer. The gags were making the vampires drool into pans. "This is how they were collecting what they needed for the drug?"

The first vampire was already trying to undo their restraints. One of the vampires came free and sniffed at me before licking their lips and lunging. But he was far slower than Morgana, and I managed to catch him around the back of his neck.

There was the brief bestial instinct to snap it, but my humanity won out and I just held him in a vice grip. "What do you want me to do with him?"

"Snap his neck." Morgana shrugged.

I looked at her incredulously. That really felt like overkill.

She raised an eyebrow at my look. "He'll recover in a few minutes, and it'll teach him a lesson."

Right, vampires. I let my beast win out and snapped his neck, dropping him to the floor and stepping away cautiously. The rest of the freed vampires were rubbing where their bindings had chafed them. As they looked us over, I got looks of dread, but they seemed to look at Morgana with a twinge of hope.

"Alright, you stay. The rest of you, get the hell out of here. If I catch any of you doing anything remotely illegal, I'll hunt you down." Morgana jerked her head, but then spoke again before they could get too far. "Grab him and take him with you."

They disappeared into the night without another word.

"Just letting them go?" I asked.

"Don't need nor want a bunch of hungry vampires hanging around you. Let's get our friend back to the club and we can talk." She turned her focus to the vampire. "Got a name?"

"Valerie," the female vampire stated.

"Come on then. I'll drive us back to the club, and we can get you something to drink while you talk."

The vampire bobbed her head excitedly before I saw her nose flare. "What is he?" The way she looked at me was an intensity somewhere between flirting and hunger.

I answered before Morgana. "You don't get to know. And if you try to bite me..." I let my eyes drift over the mess of cooked corpses. "You may not like the results." The beast inside of me let out a smug roar, like it was proud of my assertion. I was too if I was honest.

"Understood." Valerie swallowed and followed after Morgana.

The leather clad drow vampiress was putting a phone to her ear. "Two two four eight Kilbourn. There's a big mess that needs cleaning up. Yes, lots of wolves, humans, and drugs." Even while talking, she pulled one of the bricks from the back of the van and stuffed it in the duffel as she slung her gun into the bag and zipped it up. "Yes, the job is done."

I wanted to argue that the job was not done. We might have performed the narrow scope of the job that Morgana was given, but we did nothing to solve the greater issue of this drug ring. But I was too exhausted to do more than crawl back into the van, and this time, I didn't even care about Morgana's wild driving.

***

We got back to the club and Morgana's helpers appeared to take everything she had, including the vampire Valerie.

"I have some clothes for you. I figured you might need them after we do our jobs." She waved for me to follow her through the maze of her club.

We passed through the club proper. It was dark, lit by blacklights, and the thumping of music and people was in full swing. Even with my ripped and singed clothes, I got more than a few girls staring at me with hungry eyes that begged for me to come introduce myself.

"Not now," Morgana whispered in my ear and pulled me along.

I rolled my eyes but let her lead me through the maze. "Will I ever be able to make my own way through this place?"

"It's purposely built to confuse and hide itself. I spent many, many years building it to do so." There was a wry grin on her face. "Oh, the 20s were a fun time. I loved the looks on the cops' faces when they tried to bust me."

It always threw me when she casually mentioned times far before she should have been alive, given how old she looked. I was curious about her history, but I figured I'd learn more with time.

From what she'd implied earlier, she was even in Europe during the disaster that was the 17th century for the paranormal world. I imagined there were some pretty dark stories from that time period.

Crossing through a doorway, we stepped from the dark thumping bar into a quiet, cozy area in warm wood tones. The contrast from the dark rowdy bar was like a slap in the face. The warm wooden area branched off in dozens of directions.

It was bland yet welcoming. It reminded me of the vibe walking into a family doctor's office.

"This way. If you ever end up back here, that way is the club." She pointed to a door that had the bouncy lights of the club dancing like they were trying to come underneath the door. "This way is my wing, and where I've set up a room for you." She pointed to a stone door that looked like it belonged in some old-world castle capped with gargoyles.

"The rest of them?" I asked, having trouble focusing on just how far the corridor went.

"A service I provide to many. A nexus of sorts. People call it the Atrium."

"The Atrium," I repeated, working to remember it. "And anyone can just walk into your area?"

She smirked and wiped a finger across a cut on my shoulder before putting it in the gargoyle knocker's mouth and puncturing her finger to drip a drop of her own blood.

"No, but you have access now." The knocker's eyes glowed for a moment before she opened the door and walked inside. "Clean up, get dressed, and I'll meet you back here."

Her nose flared in a way that reminded me of the vampires from earlier, and her face struggled for a moment.

"Alright," I said quickly, stepping into the room she had gestured towards.

The room was far more opulent than I'd expected. There were dragon motifs in brass. At least, I hoped it was brass and not gold as the main decoration. Had she set this up for me in just a day? The closet was filled to the brim with an assortment of clothing that would fit me, but with no particular sense of style. I did notice it leaned more towards formal wear; there were more than a few suits hanging.

I shook my head at those and instead went for a t-shirt and jeans with a nice-looking jacket that wasn't quite formal but fitted well enough that it wasn't sloppy.

The place was even fitted with its own private bathroom, the shower head a dragon breathing a spray of water once I turned it on. She'd definitely stuck to a theme.

Undressing, I felt my phone and pulled it out. Curiosity got the better of me and opened my maps. I had a full five bars, but the dot that said where I was kept yo-yoing between Bumps in the Night and drifting off to the east. I waited, but it never settled, moving around continuously.

Putting the phone away, I got cleaned up.

The water ran down my body, quickly becoming dark and grimy from soot and blood by the time it pooled near my feet. I watched it, a bit of a numbness settling over me. I wasn't clean anymore. And not just physically—my soul had blood on it. The beast thrashed in my chest, berating me for looking down on myself for killing.

Despite its protests, I still felt conflicted. I'd been training to save lives, and somehow, I'd gone from that to kill maybe a dozen para that night.

My head hit the shower wall and my body shook. Much of what happened tonight finally catching up to me.

I had skipped right over blood-on-my-hands and gone straight elbow-deep-in-blood. Watching the dark soot rinse from my body down the drain, I wondered if I'd feel clean again. I questioned if I'd just sent my ability to be a doctor and take the Hippocratic oath down the drain as well.

***

Morgana eventually collected my sorry ass from my room and dragged me through another door in the Atrium and into an amphitheater lit with dramatic lighting. High up in the surrounding ring sat dozens of figures. We apparently were the main attraction standing down on the floor of the structure.

Many of them were hidden thanks to how the lighting was set up. Only their silhouette was visible, by design I assumed. No doubt they could see each other, but Morgana and I were in the lower half.

"This is the council," she whispered in my ear.

I nodded, doing my best to pick my mopey self up and square my shoulders. I doubted I wanted to appear weak in front of this powerful group. And I wanted answers for why they hadn't sent more people, and what they were going to do to stop the entire operation.

The beast rallied with me, encouraging that I take over this room.

Chapter 11

"Order, order." An older male elf stood, and the lights from the other side of the ring caught his front, giving me a quick glimpse of him.

For that brief moment, I thought it was a sober Simon, but I realized that the elf before me stood mature and sure of himself, instead of a brat drowning his worries in a bottle. But they easily could be brothers from the resemblance.

"We have a matter of great importance. Weres were found using vampires to produce drugs for humans. Worse yet, humans were involved in the operations. A clear violation of our laws."

"Hold up." A slight man with a southern lilt to his voice stood, also becoming easier to make out. The smaller man didn't look anything like Chad but seemed to speak for the werewolves. "To dump this on the packs is ridiculous. From what we have gathered, it seems like a group of omegas at work."

"Weres leave their homes and form packs in similar age groups," Morgana whispered. "That there was such a varied difference in age suggests they weren't a normal pack. Of course, no one is going to claim them now."

"Your kind has still created this transgression," the older version of Simon stated haughtily. His voice alone made me want to ram my boot up his ass.

"If we are laying the crimes of a single member against their whole race, then we have much to revisit and discuss, Sebastian. Wouldn't we, everyone?" A man stood to speak. Maybe my eyes were adjusting to the light better, but I was starting to see more of the circle of people above me.

The man who had just spoken was flanked by two people I recognized. Jadelyn was there, but scales framed her face, and she wore far too much jewelry. But it seemed almost ceremonial. The other was Detective Fox, but now he had golden eyes and a pair of fox ears matching his red hair sticking out the top of his head. Something moved behind him, but I couldn't make it out.

The man that had spoken looked similar enough that I figured he was Jadelyn's father. Which made him a male siren. I would have guessed male sirens would be lankier, but the man that stood there looked like a marble statue of Poseidon come to life. His outfit was complete with two clunky metal bracers. All he needed was a trident to nail the part. I almost started smirking at the thought but caught myself, not wanting to draw the attention of the council members.

His response made Sebastian wrinkle his face in disgust. But the small man who seemed to be speaking for the weres spoke up first. "Besides, it seems that something other than weres were there, evident by the way everything was cooked. Might that not indicate one of the elven war mages was present?"

Morgana cleared her throat loudly and stepped out into the center. It was outlined as a ring and marked with scuffs and gashes that made it look like more than one fight had occurred on the stage. "I believe I'm here to provide details that would cut through your speculation."

Sebastian the elf latched onto that, seeming to focus in on Morgana for the first time. "Yes, you did fail to report what caused the fire."

"I do not speculate in my reports, but there was one among the fight tonight that used fire. I'm afraid we may have to continue speculating; those burned to a crisp aren't likely to come back and talk."

I paused. She hadn't lied, but she'd directed each of them to believe that one of the dead had used fire. She hid that it was me; then again, that might reveal what I was. Based on Morgana's brief explanation, I needed to be ready to protect myself when that time came.

"Is this what you saw too?" the were asked.

I took Morgana's approach to heart, working not to lie but not to expose myself either. "Yes sir. Unfortunately, my knowledge of the paranormal is very limited. I can't confirm what caused the fire."

"And the weres?" He was still focused on me.

"All wolves. But I witnessed one escape from those that attacked us."

There was a soft whistle somewhere up in the seated members. Apparently, killing so many weres was worth noting.

"I'm surprised your new charge survived," a heavily accented voice spoke, but no one stood for me to put a face to it. I noted no one commented on Morgana's survival.

"He's quite sturdy." Morgana smiled up into a dark corner. "As to what we found, there was a group of vampires held captive, gagged to catch pans for their saliva. The weres were a variety of ages but used pack magic."

"Barbaric." A pale figure stood, baring his fangs.

"I agree." Morgana nodded to him. "The vampires in question have been released. Those that were a part of it tonight and were at the warehouse are dead."

Stepping forward one more step, Morgana spoke clearly. "I completed the task put before me. However, they were packing up tonight when I arrived, and the werewolves ambushed us." Her eyes circled the ring above us. "I do not believe the drug operation was fully taken care of."

I could feel tension in the room as she finished. More than a few of them shifted in their chairs.

"It would seem then that we would still have need of your services," came Sebastian's dry voice. "Your usual rate?"

"Fair. But I'll need access to the packs."

"You'll have access to my pack. However, the fledgling pack on campus..." The werewolf trailed off, hesitation in his voice.

"I'll support them in accessing the pack on campus," Jadelyn's clear voice rang out.

"You do not sit here." Sebastian glared at Jadelyn and her father, who just gave a deep chuckle.

"Then let it be as if I had said it. My daughter will support the investigation into the young pack to clear their name. We will also take care of the matter of the local authorities." The Poseidon imposter shifted for Detective Fox to speak.

"The building is already being staged and set on fire. It will look as if there was a large homeless population squatting and responsible for the fire. Our secret will be maintained."

All the heads around the circle bobbed. One of the first times they seemed to all agree. With that finished, Sebastian stated, "This matter is closed."

Chatter began to flow more freely through the space. Jadelyn caught my eye with a smile and pointed back through the door I had come through, holding up a finger as if she wanted me to wait.

"Let's go. We've accomplished what we came to do. They'll just bicker for the next hour," Morgana spoke, this time not in a whisper.

"We do not bicker," Sebastian spat. "But it would be best if you leave the council to our business."

My mentor only chuckled and swished her hips as she lazily exited the chamber.

As soon as the door closed behind us, I glared at her. "Did you have to antagonize them?"

"It's what he expects. You give people like that what they expect to keep them predictable." She grinned, showing her fangs. "Plus, I didn't want you to have to wait long for your guest."

Jadelyn exited another door in the Atrium and walked to us.

"I'll leave you two alone. I desperately need my beauty sleep before I go with Brent to interrogate his pack. Just go back the same way we came." And with that, Morgana seemed to vanish. I was starting to wonder if it had to do with this all being some sort of construct she'd made or if she was just that fast.

"Hello, you seem to be adjusting well." Jadelyn smiled wide, but it didn't reach her eyes. She seemed a bit exhausted. I had a feeling there was a lot of pressure on her I had yet to understand. She wore a thin, white dress, and her neck was laden down with multiple necklaces to the point they were almost an armored collar. Scales dusted across her cheeks and framed her face. The first time I'd seen her looking anything but human, though I knew her to be a siren.

I scratched the back of my head. "Something like that." I noticed her hands stayed behind her back, her forearms clenched like she was holding something.

"Has Morgana figured out what you are?" she asked. It was an awkward moment. Somehow, Morgana being involved seemed to have shifted our dynamic, and we were still trying to figure out where that left us. I wanted to trust her, but for now, I decided to keep our theories close to my chest.

"Some guesses, but so far she's just pushing me to see if we can't confirm them."

"Like what?" She latched onto the potential topic like a shipwrecked sailor would a piece of driftwood.

I tried not to wince, but I didn't exactly want to have the 'I might be a dragon' conversation with anyone just yet. I wanted proof before I spilled those beans. Even then, Morgana warned me that half the battle was knowing your enemy. Giving up that identity would forfeit that half to many battles that would come.

"Until I know for sure, I'd like to keep myself from speculating too much," I answered, trying to be diplomatic about the situation.

"Oh." She sounded a bit hurt but smoothed it over. "I understand completely. It must be terrible not even knowing what you are."

"Yeah. It's a unique struggle for sure." I shook my head. "Anyway, you said during the council meeting that you'd help us investigate the college pack?"

I was exhausted, and I wanted to move this along. My bed sounded heavenly at that moment.

"Oh, yes." She seemed distracted as she said it, her hands behind her back starting to move. "But before that, I wanted to offer you this." She held up a silver bracer similar in style to the ones her father had been wearing.

"Oh, please, you don't have to—"

"I promised to offer you a reward if you spared Chad that night. You did, and I am in your debt. Please accept this and remove that debt." She held it out to me.

I looked at the item, knowing it was likely magical in nature and worth more than my college degree. "What is it?"

"Shielding enchantment. You hold it with one hand while holding the bracer arm up." She demonstrated with her own arms as if she were wearing it. "It takes both hands, but the shield is strong enough to deflect most spells. I..." She paused. "I heard about the duel that Simon got approved. Thank you for standing up to him, even if it cost you that."

Part of me felt like it was all a flimsy excuse, and she really felt some sort of guilt for it all. But I'd take all the help I could get. I still felt like I was floundering about in the paranormal world.

I took the bracer and gave her my biggest smile I could muster in the moment. "Not a problem. I think Simon is going to have a bad day on Monday."

"Don't underestimate him. Please." She looked up at me through her eyelashes.

"I won't." I knew he'd be formidable, but I had to keep thinking positively.

She nodded along. "Good. Good. Then tomorrow morning, meet up with me at the football field. I'll take you in to see Chad and the pack so you can talk to them."

"Of course. Tomorrow morning. What time?"

"They start at six on Saturdays, but let's let them work off a little energy before we show up. Eight should be okay."

"Sounds like a plan."

***

Dawn was just around the corner as I made it back to my place. Morgana's room was nice, but I just wanted to be home after the night

I had. The only people still out were drunkards stumbling home this late, or a few girls carrying their heels and looking over their shoulders like they were ashamed someone was going to see them.

I wondered if anyone else thought I was doing a walk of shame back home. Not that it mattered.

Bored as I walked, I let my eyes wander over those coming and going. Small details caught my attention. When a girl pulled her hair back over her ear, I checked to make sure they weren't pointed. It was the little details that would mark someone as paranormal.

It wasn't surprising that they could walk among the rest of the world hidden by those small details that others just didn't pay attention to. Part of me wondered who else in my life might be part of the paranormal world.

I idly checked my phone and realized I'd missed a number of messages. Frank wasn't important, though he'd been wondering where I was. Scarlett had texted and confirmed our double date for Sunday night, though where she chose to have it surprised me.

We were going to Bumps in the Night. I nearly groaned. It looked like Morgana was going to get her wish.

The sudden image of Morgana crashing our date flickered through my mind. No, she had more tact than that. At least, I hoped she did.

I shot back an affirmative to Scarlett and headed up to my apartment. As I creaked open the door, I saw Frank and Maddie cuddled on the couch, asleep as the tv continued going.

Smiling, I found myself happy at the simple joy of them being together. If Maddie managed to wrangle Frank into slowing down, that would be good for him.

I tip-toed my way to my own bedroom, making sure not to wake them. Sleep was my top priority. I needed to be on top of my game when I went and saw Chad and his pack in what now wasn't more than a few hours away.

***

I mussed my hair, still wet from the shower. I'd slept in as long as I could. Which meant my hair was still drying as I walked through the football parking lot. I'd only ever been there for an occasional game day, pre-gaming with friends. It was weird being in the area when it was quiet and empty.

Jadelyn waited with her arms behind her back, idly observing the surroundings. She wore a teal shirt today, one that I realized matched the scales she'd presented yesterday. I looked her over, wondering where else she had scales, but I pushed those thoughts out of my head. I shouldn't be noticing so much about a girl that was already taken.

"Morning, Jade," I called as I waved to get her attention.

She startled, clearly having been lost in her own thoughts. "Morning, Zach. But I don't know if Chad would appreciate you giving me a nickname."

I snorted. "Well, Chad is going to have to get used to it. You're allowed to have friends, right?"

"Friends." She spoke the word like she was tasting it. "Yes, I think I'll have to make him understand that I can have friends. Still, he is an alpha of his pack. Territorial comes with the package."

She sounded so resigned to her situation that I felt bad for her. I wanted to help, but the politics of all of it were way beyond anything I understood, and I knew that. She was far savvier about all of it, and she still seemed trapped by whatever arrangement was made.

We walked through the empty security checkpoint and into the stadium. I tried to give her some friendly advice. "You should push him to let you have what you need. A relationship isn't supposed to be so one way."

"How very... human of you, Zach. The para world works differently."

I snorted. "You are human, or at least pass for one most of the time."

She chuckled, but it wasn't a happy laugh. It was a laugh filled with self-deprecation. "My father would make some obscenely racist comment at that. You shouldn't say it too much, no matter how true it might be."

"Oh, good. I'm glad the para world isn't that different from the human one." I nudged her, trying to lighten the mood. But I couldn't help myself from adding, "But regardless, you are powerful in your own right. Make Chad give you what you need."

The rest of the conversation was cut short as we stepped out onto the field. Men were running drills in thick padding while a section of girls lounged nearby, looking tired.

For the first time, I really smelled the football team and cheerleading squad. They all smelled like wolves, with a few indistinct notes that had a bit more spice to them. I knew there were more than wolves that were were-shifters, but I hadn't seen any yet.

Jadelyn and my entrance caught attention as we walked onto the field. A few men jogged over, their faces set in a way that made me feel distinctly unwelcome.

"Get out," number fifty-three barked as twenty-seven and thirty-one backed him up.

"I'm Jade—"

"We know who you are. You aren't pack yet. Get out," fifty-three clarified with a growl.

The play on the field ended, and all the weres were starting to look our way. Even the cheerleaders were sliding off their bench and coming over.

"I'm your alpha's fiancée. I have every right to be here." Jadelyn puffed herself up, and I could see her reach for a bracelet on one of her arms.

"Fiancée," someone snorted behind the three players. "More like a piece to pass around. I can't wait to get a piece of her."

"It's only fair that Chad pass her around, not that she's ever going to be more than a trophy."

I wanted to stand up for her, but what had happened with Simon was still fresh in my mind. She was capable of defending herself. And after seeing her in the council session, I understood that she must have a decently high standing in the Philly paranormal world.

Jadelyn ignored the comments and looked towards the approaching cheerleaders. "Kelly, good morning."

The introduction of the head bitch shut up most of the men who'd been jeering at Jadelyn.

"Morning, Jadelyn." There was hesitation in Kelly's voice. Something was wrong. "What are you doing here on a Saturday?"

"I thought I'd see Chad, as well as talk to him about a council matter that was entrusted to me last night." Jadelyn held her head high through the comments the men made, but I could almost see a crack in her facade. The comments earlier had gotten to her.

Kelly looked around before she leaned closer. "It's Saturday." She spoke it as if it held special meaning, but I was clueless. Her eyes searched Jadelyn's own and didn't find what she was looking for. "Shit. You don't know what he does on Friday nights, do you?" She spoke low enough that a normal person wouldn't have heard.

Unfortunately, we were surrounded by werewolves. "Oh! This is great. She doesn't know that it was Fuck-a-bitch-Friday," number fifty-three shouted, doing a little dance in his pads in cleats. He looked like a clown.

Jadelyn's face twitched. "Excuse me?"

But the players weren't paying her any attention, starting to chant 'Fuck-a-bitch-Friday' and pushing each other around and pumping each other up.

Kelly grabbed Jadelyn and hauled her away. I went to follow, and Kelly threw me a look. "What do you want?"

"I'm working with Morgana, and the council matter we're here for includes something she's working on."

Kelly's face paled after hearing that. "M-mor-morgana is looking for the pack?" Her face paled, like I'd just told her ghosts were coming to kill her.

"Yes?" I felt like I was answering more than just her simple question, and it came out as a question of its own.

"Shit." Kelly pulled Jadelyn out to the bleachers as the players were already putting their helmets back on and starting another play. "Ignore them. They are all freaking boneheads."

Jadelyn swallowed before asking in a soft voice. "What's... fuck-a..." She couldn't quite bring herself to say it.

"You know how packs work, right?" Kelly started, and Jadelyn nodded, dread filling her face. Knowing something and experiencing it first are two different things.

But I didn't know. "Mind sharing for the newly initiated?"

"Right, well, it's a mix of human and wolf, just like we are. Wolves establish a dominant pair, or a breeding pair that then produces all the pups for the pack. The rest of the pack is essentially sterile, but they help raise the breeding pair's pups until they are old enough to go out on their own. The dominant ones then form their own breeding pair and lead a pack one day."

"Okay, so Chad is the alpha male, and Jadelyn will become part of his breeding pair?" I tried to read between the lines, but there was something she wasn't explaining. I had a feeling it wasn't good for Jadelyn.

"No, we are like humans, in that we only have one child at a time. Not to mention, the pack here is almost two hundred strong. No, it's different in werewolves. Like wolves, only the dominant male is fertile... but in order to create enough children to sustain the next generation's pack..." She trailed off, a look of pity thrown at Jadelyn.

The siren swallowed. "Ah, so he's doing his duty to the pack... on Fridays."

I pieced together what they weren't saying. If Chad was the only fertile werewolf among the pack of two hundred, and they needed to produce enough children to create a new generation... then that meant he was going to sleep with all the women. "Wait, I thought that the cheerleaders and the other guys were still pairing up, like the two at the clothing store?"

"They do. They even raise the kid themselves. Like wolves, the pack still supports and raises the kids."

I couldn't help it. It slipped out of my mouth, skipping that oh so handy brain filter. "He cucks all of them?!"

Several of the girls on the bleachers looked up at me with a scowl. Kelly glared at them, and they looked away. "Maybe don't say that out loud." She turned back and scowled at me.

That was confirmation if I'd ever heard it before. I couldn't help but let my vision slide to Jadelyn, whose expression looked like she was going to be sick.

"I'm sorry, Jade," I started, but she waved her hand.

"That's fine. This is what I signed up for." She took a deep breath. "Anyway, if we can't talk to Chad, then I'd like to talk to you about the issue, Kelly."

"Of course, I'm always here for you." She said it in a way that meant far more than the current situation.

"Zach, do you have pictures?" Jadelyn asked, sucking in a deep breath and holding tight to the change in subject.

I pulled out my phone and flipped to some very grotesque photos we'd taken after the fight. I really needed to get these off my phone before someone saw them. "Here. There was a drug bust that Morgana and I did last night. A group of wolves had vampires chained up and drooling into catch pans." I flipped through images of charred bodies.

"I can't recognize any of those; they are all burnt to a crisp. What the hell happened?" Kelly threw me a strange look.

"There was something there last night that caused the fire. Morgana said she didn't know what it was, and I certainly don't know better than she does."

Kelly's very human ear twitched, and she gave me a look that made me wonder if I was a terrible liar. "Okay, do you have any that aren't so... crispy?"

"Hold on." I flipped until I got to some of them that Morgana had killed, and an image of a decapitated head. "Here. Do you recognize him?"

Kelly stared at the image for a moment. "He's old enough to be in my grandparent's pack."

"He's not that old," I commented. The man looked to be in his forties, maybe early fifties.

"They age slower," Jadelyn provided. "After about twenty years old, they start aging at about half pace. That guy is probably around seventy."

I looked back at the photo and did the math. If I put him at forty-five, which seemed about right, he'd be a seventy-year-old werewolf. "Then, what is he doing with this other one that looks like he's not even old enough to drink?" I showed another photo.

"Omegas." Kelly nodded. Seeing my confusion, she added, "Every generation, the children travel and mix to make new packs. Unofficially, college is where we do that. Those that don't go to college, or do but aren't accepted into the pack, become packless Omegas."

"So, this is a pack of outcasts?" I clarified. "It sounds like they don't normally become part of a pack."

"They aren't a pack," Kelly said with confidence.

That didn't make sense with the bits I'd caught at the council chamber. Morgana had clearly stated that they'd used pack magic. I repeated what I'd heard to Kelly. "Sure sounds like you need to be a pack to do that."

She shook her head. "No, that's not how it works. They can't just join up and become a pack." She fidgeted and looked over our shoulder. Something was wrong; she wasn't telling me something.

"Then how do they become a pack?" I took a chance and pushed her, but I must have pushed too hard because she snapped at me.

"They just can't. It's not possible."

I could almost hear the 'but...' on the tip of her tongue, but her mouth snapped shut, and she didn't speak anymore. I decided there was no harm in pushing further. "Kelly, come on. There has to be some way. Clearly it is happening already."

"I said no." She growled the last word, and her eyes became that of a wolf. Several other growls picked up from the bleachers, the pack coming to one another's aid. The players had paused mid-play to watch us.

Holding up my hands, I made a placating pat in the air and stepped back. "Calm down. I thought you didn't want the pack and I to have problems?" I loosened the beast a little and growled myself.

Kelly's eyes changed back, and she looked around, noticing the attention we'd brought. "Everyone, calm down. Go back to practice. Everything is under control." She turned back to me and Jadelyn. "I think it's best you leave."

I nodded and pulled Jadelyn along with me. She didn't put up any resistance and came with me. It wasn't until we were out of the stadium that I realized she was shaking. Sobs bubbled up from her throat and I did the only thing I could think of doing and pulled her close.

"It's okay. It'll all be okay." I stroked from the back of her head down to the small of her back and kept going as she buried her face into my chest and unleashed the waterworks. She smelled like lilies and honeydew. I couldn't help getting a full scent on her this close.

"Why?" she cried into my chest, breaking my heart at the same time. "Why does it have to be someone like Chad?"

I didn't have anything useful to say, so I wisely just kept my mouth shut.

She was grieving. While she might have understood the mechanics of how a pack of werewolves worked, being confronted with him sleeping out on her today must have been too much. Not to mention the antagonizing and talk of sharing her around. It must have felt like she was nothing more than a piece of meat.

"I don't understand why. Fucking father. Fucking Chad." She sobbed into my chest, soaking my shirt thoroughly.

I wasn't sure how long we stood there before Jadelyn started to calm down, wiping at her puffy eyes. "Do I look like a mess?"

"You look great," I lied through my teeth.

"You are a terrible liar." She dabbed at her face. "Shit. I'm so sorry that happened. You didn't need to be there for that."

"It's fine. We're friends, right? This is something that a friend is there for."

She let out a small noise and nodded. "I could use more friends with the way my life is going."

I did my best to give her a cheerful smile. It was clear that she was on a collision course in her life. She'd have to make some tough calls. And I'd be there to support her as best I could. Beyond challenging Chad to a duel, which Morgana had already made clear I wouldn't win with his pack around, there wasn't much I could do.

CHAPTER 12

Jadelyn eventually calmed down, and the calm aristocratic mask fell back on her face. I gave her an extra moment to collect herself before we headed back to Bumps in the Night. I hoped that Morgana had found better luck than we did when she talked with the other pack.

"You know, a vampire owning a nightclub is kind of cliché," I said, going to open the door.

"Do not say that to Morgana's face," Jadelyn warned me with a shake of her head. "Almost like you'd want her to rip your head off."

I held my hand up in defense, while the other held the door for Jadelyn. "Thanks for the tip. I would rather keep my head attached. Unless, wait, are there para like headless horsemen?"

"There are, but I haven't seen one around Philly before."

The club was quiet, and the lights were all on. Morgana's crew seemed to be still cleaning up from the previous night's party. The dark floors were staining mops brown as the workers tried to clean the dance floor.

My phone buzzed, and I fished it out. I couldn't help but smile as I saw it was from Scarlett. I started working on a flirty reply back.

"She must be special to make you smile so much," Jadelyn said coolly. Her expression was a mask that I couldn't quite decipher. But I figured it had to do with her unhappy arrangement with Chad. It probably wasn't fun seeing a happy couple.

"It's just a first date, but... yeah, I think she's going to turn out to be pretty special." I couldn't help but smile even bigger, thinking about all the places it might go. "Speaking of, any tips for dating outside the para world?"

"First date." Jadelyn smiled and looked up into the lights. "Exciting. I'll bet you have all sorts of romantic plans."

I scratched the back of my head. “Just dinner, maybe some dancing afterwards.”

“Nothing?” Jadelyn asked, sounding surprised. “You at least have to know what her favorite food is.”

I thought about it for a second. Based on our conversation, I guess I’d go with muffins? At least, she’d seemed to like them. They could be her favorite. “I do, but it's breakfast food.”

“Doesn’t matter. Just remember it. It always helps to show you remember what she likes; make sure you have some at your place.” Jadelyn coached me as we found a table. “Besides that, just be a gentleman, but not a doormat.”

I raised an eyebrow. “I can do that, but sometimes my beast likes to get a little pushy.”

“Beast?” Jadelyn asked, her brows pinching down. “Right, why I thought you might be a were. Is it causing trouble?”

“Sort of,” I answered. At the moment, my beast was drooling over Jadelyn. “It’s like holding a part of myself back at times.”

She smiled and leaned close, her lips brushing just past my cheek. It was intimate in a way that should make me uncomfortable, but then a soft clear note rang in my ear. Jadelyn sang a quiet song just for me and my beast. There were no words, simply a lapping of vocals that washed through me and the beast, imparting both of us with a sense of peace and tranquility.

The beast was satisfied, but I could also feel it dig its claws in. It was calmer, but it was also more focused than ever on Jadelyn, like it wanted to possess her. But when she finished, I did feel more aligned with my beast.

“That’s amazing,” I spoke after the song ended. Not only did the beast and I feel less distinct, but I felt like I had gotten a far better night’s rest than the pitiful three hours I had managed.

Jadelyn sat back in her seat, a blush dusting her cheeks. “Don’t tell anyone I did that. A siren’s song is typically a very personal thing. Chad wouldn’t be happy I did that, but damn him.”

I couldn’t help a smirk quirk up at the corner of my lips. “Do what you want. I’ll support you however you want to proceed.” My words only made her blush deepen, a warm smile dancing across her own lips. I had meant to be supportive, but she’d seemed to have taken it as something deeper.

The moment grew strained and awkward for a moment, so I tried to push past it. “So what else can sirens do?”

She startled, and her eyes focused back on me. “Sorry, what did you ask?”

"Thinking of something?" I asked.

Jadelyn muttered something under her breath so low that I couldn't pick out what she said. "Anyway, you were asking about sirens." She seemed to focus back on the present. "We can do a wide variety of mental magics, using our voices as a medium. It's powerful magic, but out of water, it has its limitations. We can do some simple cantrips of other things such as evocation, but it is very limited."

"Strength or speed?" I asked.

"Outside the water? Still within the human range, but in the water we are incredible. Not much wants to tangle with a siren in the water. It's why we spend so much on enchanted items." She brushed the pendants hanging from her neck. "They keep us safe outside the water, too. After all, it's pretty hard to do much if you keep yourself in the water. We need to be able to operate on land as well."

"Most of the world is water," I added helpfully. But she didn't seem to think it was quite so helpful, her face set into an unamused glare.

"Look at you two. So cute together," Morgana's Swiss accent spoke up behind me. "How did your investigation go? I hope it went better than mine." She swung around a chair and mounted it backwards, her leather pants crinkling against the chair's own leather padding.

"Not so great." My eyes darted to Jadelyn, whose eyes dipped down. I avoided the parts that were less than flattering to the siren and gave Morgana the rundown. "I think Kelly knew something that she wasn't telling us. It seems to revolve around these omegas that shouldn't be able to have pack magic."

Morgana nodded along, her blue, pointy ears bouncing slightly with the motion. "Brent had much of the same concern, but without hiding anything. He's convinced there's no way they have pack magic, insisting it must be something else mimicking it."

I shrugged; this was clearly out of my depth.

"I can ask around, but I think that, if it was common knowledge, it would have come up at the council." Jadelyn bowed slightly. "I'll take my leave; I'm quite tired."

Morgana waved her away and watched her go before turning back to me. "Going to challenge Chad for her?"

"What?! No. God, Morgana, where did that come from?"

She shrugged. "It's in the air."

There wasn't time for this. "No. I have enough problems with Simon coming up. Even if I was interested, I don't have the capacity to deal with another problem."

Morgana's lips curled into a smile that showed off her fangs. "So you are interested. Then we better get you prepared for your duel with Simon. It is only two days away."

I frowned at her as I stood. "Do not meddle with this. Besides, I have a date on Sunday with an incredible woman."

She swung her leg off the chair in a way that was controlled, almost like a ballet. "Do not forget what you are. Like many paranormals, you will not be constrained by your human thoughts on relationships."

I flashed to what I'd learned of Chad and the pack. A shudder ran through me. "I don't know if I want to have anything but a normal relationship."

The beast would have smacked me if it could, growling in my chest after Morgana as well. Greedy little thing.

"I think you'll find that your ability to resist what you are will be harder than you give credit for. Your 'beast' as you call it is a part of you that you'll need to come to terms with."

"You make it sound like it's holding me back."

Morgana arched a brow at me as she opened the door and looked back. "I think that is exactly part of your problem. It's why you cannot access what you are; you've separated it from yourself, thinking you have to abide by all these social rules." She stepped through the door into another area.

I rushed behind her. "It's not like I can go do whatever I want. There are laws, rules everyone has to abide by." I realized we were already in the training room with the sparring mats almost a moment too late.

Morgana's foot lashed by my head as I rolled to the side. "You don't have to become a murderer or a rapist to be true to yourself. But you must embrace what you are. Holding back your nature is only going to cause headaches for you."

"What do you know? You hide down here completely separated from the rest of the world." I came up swinging, but Morgana leaned back and swayed around my fists.

"I know far more than you, little whelp." Her legs went to sweep me, but I dropped my center of gravity and weathered her strike as firm as a mountain. "You are a dragon, a creature of such great lineage that your heart beats with mana and your blood dances with dominance and power. To pretend to be human is a disservice to yourself, to who you are, and who your parents made you to be."

She hit me deep with that last statement. I let myself get angry and joined my beast in charging her, tackling her into the wall. I could hear several of her bones crackle as my full strength crushed her to the wall.

"Yes." She smiled as her legs wrapped around me and wedged one of my knees to buckle. The slight shift in my stance was enough for her to throw her own weight into it and roll against the wall, bringing me with her.

Unable to gain my balance, I couldn't stop her. She had far more experience in wrestling than I'd have in several lifetimes. The room tumbled, and I felt my back smack on the mat as Morgana stood up, using my chest as a step. That only made the anger burn brighter.

"You want to find out who your parents were?" She gave me a cocky smile as she stepped away for me to get up for another round.

I glared at her, standing up. "You know the answer to that. Of course I do."

"Then you must be stronger, and you need to be a proper dragon. If I took you today to Dubai and introduced you to the head of the dragon clan, he'd see you as a weak whelp and tear you apart. Dragons are not humans; the whole of the para world is not human. So stop holding yourself to human standards."

Frustrated with her, I was ready to let loose, and based on the growl rumbling in my chest, my beast was in full agreement. What she was saying wasn't untrue, but I refused to think about it. It brought up things I'd struggled and already figured out how to deal with my entire life.

I charged again. Morgana shifted to roll me, but I pulled up short and snapped a kick into her leg. It cracked in half, and she bent over with a hiss. I knew by now that she could handle it. She was tough, and I wasn't going to hold back.

For the first time, I wanted to breathe fire, and it came, more controlled than any of the previous times. A rumble in my chest like jet engines starting up before I blasted fire over her.

Only seconds after I released the jet, my logic returned to me, and I realized I might have gone too far. Cutting off the flames just after I started, Morgana was suddenly not there.

"Careful," Morgana said just as her heels hit me in the side of the head. "If you want to play with magic, we can do that."

I punched, but it seemed to stretch on forever, like I was throwing a punch from a mile away. Even worse, I'd thrown my whole body into the move, and it wasn't ending.

Morgana swerved unnaturally to my side, and it was like she barely had to move her arms before jabs cracked into my side like machine guns.

I pulled my punch, preferring to end it rather than be trapped in Morgana's magic. It still made me wobble as I came out of it off balance. "Why not use your magic last night? I saw you absorb my fire breath before; this time you teleported."

"My magic, though great, comes at a great cost. Why should I make a small pocket of void to kill people when I can just connect the space between my bullet and their skulls? Every bit of mana I use had to come from something living. It isn't something to be wasted on extravagant shows of magic." She glared at me; somehow, I'd touched a sore spot.

I squared off again. I could feel the heat in my chest, ready and at my beck and call. Jadelyn's song and my anger had somehow brought the beast closer than ever before, and for now, he was willing to help me how he could.

"Your magic changed when you became a vampire, didn't it? You lost something." I tried to anger her just as she had done me.

She came at me again, her heels snapping at my head. I dodged back, but even then, they still connected with my temple. I was as disoriented by the hit as I was by the logistics of how it had connected.

"Like my magic? It is very rare, almost unique."

Another kick connected when it shouldn't have. This time the side of my leg.

"When a vampire bites someone, it changes them. Infests them with a greedy little magical parasite that does everything it can to strengthen the host so it can get more mana. It often gives rudimentary magic to a human, but to an elf, a drow sorceress..." She punctuated the statement with another kick. Even as I raised my arm, space bent and my arm shifted back, opening me up to another kick in the side of the head.

"It warps their magic into something different. Greater, some might say, but all at the cost of perpetual hunger." She let out a cry of rage, and I could see the strength of this next kick. Even through those tight leather pants, I could see the flex of her muscles.

I could see so much. The air around my head warped and shifted with dark particles of her magic. I realized I was actually seeing the magic she was using. So this time, instead of blocking her leg, I slammed my fist with the same anger that I used to breathe fire straight through her magic.

It bent and cracked just as her leg used it to try to bypass my guard again. But instead of hitting me, my fist disrupted her magic and connected with her shin, shattering it and putting another joint in her leg.

Morgana rolled out of her kick, clutching her leg as she let out a cry of surprise. "How?" She looked up at me and her eyes only grew wider. "Zach, your eye." The smile on her face grew until it threatened to split her face in half. "Zach, look at your eye!"

CHAPTER 13

"What's wrong with my eye?" I pulled my phone out of my pocket and flipped the camera around to see myself.

"Your eye is a slitted pupil," she said, but I barely heard her as I looked at the phone. Staring back at me was exactly what she had said. My eye looked like a serpent's eye. It was a dark, nearly black iris, with a faint gold outline that pulsed in time with my heartbeat.

"No way."

"Way," She chuckled behind me. It was a strange sound mixed with her bones healing back together with clicks.

"Do magic again," I insisted.

Morgana gave me a brief glare at the commanding tone I'd taken with her. She took her sweet time, clearly wanting me to understand she was doing it of her own free choice and in no way because I'd told her to do it.

Eventually, she held her hand up, and the little black motes of magic swam around it. But they were only there for a moment before they faded.

"Huh? It stopped working."

She nodded. "Your eye has gone back to normal. It would seem that while a partial success, you still need far more practice to control it."

"I can see magic though." Excitement bubbled out of me. This was progress. I had a feeling that could come in handy in the para world.

"Yes, and it would be wonderful if you could control it. So far, it just seems that angering you is the best way to draw out aspects of your dragon."

I wanted to tell her she was wrong, but even as the fight ended and the excitement of combat faded, I could feel myself slipping further away from the beast. "Damn it."

"It's okay. It takes a vampire years to learn to control it all." Morgana got to her feet, her injury already healed. There was an understanding look on her face. "We'll keep drawing out your anger if that's what it takes for you to learn control."

"All that was just to make me angry?"

"Of course not. I wouldn't lie to you. If you went to Dubai today, he'd tear you apart and curse your parents for raising such a weak whelpling. You aren't human, Zach Pendragon. I do hope today's events help you convince yourself that you are a dragon. I can see that part of you rejects it."

"You don't understand," I started, before wishing I'd never said that. In truth, I knew little about Morgana and her past. She had lifetimes of experiences.

"I think I understand plenty of rejecting yourself. My transformation into a vampire was not a willing nor pleasant experience. As many of my fellow elves disbelieve that it is possible, I too clung to that idea like a drowning rat." She scowled with a mixture of disgust, but I knew it wasn't meant for me.

"How'd it happen?" I asked gently, not wanting to push her but interested in learning more.

"Old story. To summarize, I was young and stupid, believing I could weather the church's inquisition in the 18th century." She narrowed her eyes at me. "But the bigger story is a topic for another day. For now, we need to be focused on making you stronger and solving our problem with the drug ring. Thoughts on what we do next?"

I wanted to ask more, but Morgana had made it clear it wasn't something she wanted to talk about, at least not now. I decided to let her get away with changing the topic. Maybe I'd be able to pull more out of her next time we sparred.

"We both ran up short, so I guess we wait for them to step out of line again." I wasn't exactly a private investigator. "Maybe we figure out what they need next?"

She sighed. "I put out some of my people and a general warning in the local vampire community. If these guys want to make more of this, they'll need vampires. We took away their supply."

That... that made perfect sense. "But the next question becomes who is doing this and why?" I tried to get ahead of the direct problem and dig into the source. "Money is always a reason, but they could deal with normal drugs to get that. Hell, that pack of omega wolves could just crush the local drug dealers if they wanted. Why make this new V-phoria?"

Morgana smiled. "That is an excellent question. Why indeed did they start dabbling with vampire saliva to make this drug?"

"Is it different from a bite?" I asked, not exactly wanting to try the drug.

She stood up, and I noticed in the corner was her duffel bag from last night. She pulled out a brick of the white powder. "Do you want to try the two?" She smiled, showing off her fangs.

"I think I'll pass." I shuddered slightly, knowing the warning she'd given me about a vampire bite before.

"Correct answer. Though, once you master your... beast... you should be able to shrug off most poisons. Vamp bites and drugs included." She stabbed the brick with her nail and pulled out a dollop of the powder, raising it to her nose.

I watched wide-eyed as she snorted the drug. Her eyes rolled back momentarily, and her blue lips hung open, like she was having the best orgasm of her life. But the drugs quickly faded in less than a few seconds, and she came back down to earth looking at the brick.

"Yes, this is interesting. It is similar to a bite, but people have tried to preserve their saliva and dole it out to their favorite feed in the past. This is a powder and far more stable than those attempts." She put the brick down and tapped at her lip for a moment in thought.

"That means you have someone with the smarts to make the drug. And funds to be able to support the research to create it. There wasn't much research or chemistry equipment in the warehouse, so either they moved it, they made it somewhere else, or it's a simple process. But it still leaves the question of why," I tried to work through it.

"Someone could have been an addict of the bite, and tried to make the drug to wean themselves off?" Morgana worked out the question aloud.

"Fair thought, but that doesn't give reason to mass produce and sell it like a drug. There's something we are missing." I shook my head. I couldn't puzzle through it here. We needed more information.

Seeing my look, Morgana nodded. We were stuck until we got a new lead.

"Then let us hope someone bags a vampire that we can follow." Morgana grinned and threw the brick back in the duffel bag. "Before more people get hurt."

I nodded. As we headed to the door, I decided to pick her brain on a new topic. "Morgana, how do I get more in tune with my beast? You said vampires go through something similar?"

She looked over, nodding. "We practice meditation, learning to control our urges at times and become them at others." She paused, checking the time. "We still have a bit of time left. Sit, we'll work through some practices that I was taught."

***

"Man, you have been in this aisle for like the whole trip. Decide already." Frank leaned over the shopping cart, giving me a look of pure exasperation.

"Blueberry, or cinnamon raisin?" I held up the two boxes of muffin mix. "Blueberry is just so boring, but I know breakfast isn't supposed to be dessert."

"Blueberry," Frank said as soon as the options left my mouth. He was ready to move on.

Ah, screw it. I threw both into the cart.

Frank rolled his eyes but wheeled the shopping cart out of the aisle. When I'd gotten home, Maddie was making her feelings on no food in the apartment clear to Frank. She was threatening to not stay over, and he'd given in.

So, Frank and I quickly found ourselves out grocery shopping soon after. And Jadelyn had given me an idea, and I wasn't really a bake from scratch man, so muffin mix it was. Well, and a bunch of frozen pizzas.

Morgana's buffet the other day had put my stomach's strike on hold, but I could feel it creeping back up, and I needed to have some emergency supplies on hand.

I snatched a big box of crackers off the shelf as we passed and threw it in the cart.

"How much are you going to eat this week?" Frank stared at the cart in shock.

"A lot. I feel like I'm putting on some muscle mass; I've got to eat to satisfy that." It was an easy excuse. I had bulked up in the past few days.

"If that was how getting buff worked, do you realize how many ripped people there would be in our country." But he ended that comment with a squint at my body. "But I swear you are filling out."

I paused a bit, hoping he wouldn't ask too many questions, but he seemed to shrug it off.

"Eating all this and looking more fit. Not fair," he muttered, picking out his items and throwing them on the conveyor belt for the overworked lady to scan.

The blips of items running over the scanner faded into the background as I felt another text from Scarlett. I felt a twinge of guilt as I texted her back another witty reply. I'd been spending so much time with others like Jadelyn when I should be spending more time with Scarlett.

"Hey, Frank, I met this girl. She's taken by an asshole and doesn't want to be in the relationship. What do I do?"

Frank looked shocked that I'd actually asked for dating advice. "This isn't Scarlett, is it?"

"No, we are going out tomorrow night. This is another girl."

Frank's gasp of shock might have been genuine; I couldn't tell. "Another girl? Zach, are you dying? Has an alien taken over your brain? Come here. Let me check for a fever."

I chuckled. "Calm down. She's just a new friend in a tight situation."

"Friend. Right. Is she hot?"

My look must have given away the answer, because Frank's smile grew.

"Perfect. Solution is just to bang her." Frank shrugged, stepping forward to pay for his portion of the food.

I rolled my eyes at his oh so subtle solution. "Her guy would kill me. And not in a kidding way. I'd be dead in a ditch somewhere." Though, the beast grumbled in my chest in disagreement. It seemed to think the other guy would be dead in the ditch.

"Don't make things too complicated. First, go on your date with the lovely Scarlett. Then, talk to this other girl, see if she's really interested. If she is, you should be selfish. Let's be honest, nice guys really do finish last. You need to be a bit of an ass here. It would be good for you to get out and date more." Frank started bagging the groceries and unceremoniously dropping his bags back into the cart.

I winced when he started with the eggs on bottom. Poor eggs, it was nice knowing you.

"So just go for it?"

"Why not? You and Scarlett aren't exclusive yet, are you? Play the field, man."

I pulled Frank's eggs out of the bottom of the cart and laid them on top while I put some of the heavier items in the cart. "I don't know. What if that messes things up with Scarlett? I'd hate to do that."

"You only live once, Zach. Live a little. And you haven't even been on a first date with Scarlett; it's not like you're in some deep relationship."

I paused at his statement; I guess I was getting a bit ahead of myself, but I really felt connected to Scarlett.

Frank had continued on while I was thinking. "Ask the second one out on a date for Monday. No girl asks for a second date the next day. That makes them seem desperate. So your schedule should be clear to pursue this other girl then. Do I get a name to go with her yet?"

"No," I answered, maybe a little too quickly. Frank grinned and pushed the cart out of the store. "I want to meet them both. Just not at the same time, preferably. I may not be able to wingman you out of that."

"No duh, sherlock. I'm not that big of an idiot," I said, but then I remembered some of what Morgana had told me about other dragons. Though part of being a dragon apparently was being with two or more women at the same time, I still hadn't wrapped my head around how juggling multiple women was supposed to work.

Scarlett texted again, and I pulled out the phone, only for it still to keep ringing. "Hello, this is Zach."

"They took the bait. I'll come snag you. Where are you?"

I paused, trying to figure out how to explain this to Frank. Noticing me pausing, he turned halfway to the car. "What's up, man?"

I squeezed my eyes closed. "I'll be at my apartment in fifteen minutes."

"No, where are you now?" Morgana repeated while Frank eyed me and started loading the groceries into his car.

"The grocery at 5th and Meadow," I said, feeling odd with Morgana coming to get me. She would stick out like a sore thumb.

"What's going on?" Frank asked, and I started to help him load up the car.

I fumbled for a moment on how to explain it. "A friend says she needs me, wants to pick me up right now."

"Holy shit, do you have a magic cock now or something? Midday booty call..." Frank trailed off, shaking his head.

"That is not what it is. It's... work." It was the closest I could come to telling him the truth.

"No problem, man. I owe you for wingmanning all those times with Maddie. I'll put the groceries away. So, is this number 2?"

Before I could answer, a silver jaguar flew into the parking lot and spun in front of us. I could only see the outline of Morgana through the heavily tinted front window as she spun, tires screeching.

"Get in," her Swiss accent shouted as the passenger door opened. The car was low enough that I had to bend over to see more than her leather pants from where I stood.

Frank just whistled. "No way this is number 2, this is definitely number 3." He chuckled and started to bend down to look in the car, but I couldn't have that. He'd definitely notice she wasn't exactly human looking and ask more questions.

I grabbed my roommate in a hug to stop him from bending down. It was the most awkward hug of my life, but I still tried to play it off. "Thanks for getting the groceries! I'll see you later." I slipped into the car and Morgana gassed it, the door slamming shut from the momentum of her acceleration.

"What's the nine-alarm fire? Couldn't it have waited fifteen minutes?" I was a little miffed at how abrupt Morgana was being. It was going to be hard to keep a normal life and keep my friends out of the para world if she kept making me drop everything at a moment's notice.

But Morgana didn't even turn to look at me, keeping her eyes forward as we went over curbs and scraped the bottom of her beautiful car. Her face was set in a serious line, and I realized it must be serious.

"Two vampires were bagged in the last half an hour, only a couple of blocks from each other. White painted van with a red dripping faucet on the side. If we get over there now and it is still circling, looking for more, we can follow it. This is serious, Zach."

I pushed down any annoyance I had. She was right. There were vamp lives at stake and many more human lives if this drug kept getting pumped into the city.

Morgana's phone vibrated in the center console. "Can you get that?"

Given how she drove, I was surprised that was where she drew the line. Recklessness seemed like her norm. "This is Morgana's phone," I answered.

"Ah, you must be the young man that was with her. Are you able to accept a job on her behalf?" The voice was a boisterous male voice. It reminded me a bit of Jadelyn's father's voice the other night, but phones could make voices murky.

Morgana nodded, her pointy ears twitching and reminding me she could probably hear him.

"Yes, I can. What do you need?"

"My daughter has been kidnapped. A white panel van with a red symbol, and blue letters on the side."

That sounded super familiar. "A red leaking faucet?"

There was a muffled conversation on the other side of the line, like he was covering the receiver while he confirmed with someone else. "That could very well be what the image was. Dare I ask why you knew that?"

"We are currently on the trail of a van matching that description that had kidnapped a vampire. We believe it to be in connection to the drug bust last night."

The other end of the line was silent.

"Hello? Did I lose you?"

"No, you did not. I'll offer Morgana double her normal rate to ensure the safety of my daughter on top of her job to flush out this new drug and its makers."

I looked at Morgana, and based on the giant smile that spread across her face, the job had just become ridiculously lucrative.

I was curious as to what her rates were. Given her garage, they were pretty darn good. "She agrees to that."

"Good. Then good day..." He paused, not knowing my name to finish his sentence.

"Zach." I left off my last name.

"Good day, Zach. Get my daughter back in one piece and I'll owe you a debt." He hung up as soon as he finished, not waiting for a reply.

Morgana spoke after I hung up. "A debt from him is valuable. Don't waste it while we rescue your princess."

I felt my cheeks burn. "She's not my princess. Wait! Is that the truck?" I pointed down a street we just passed.

Chapter 14

"You may want to hold on."

The jag's engine revved as Morgana spun the wheel. We bumped up on the sidewalk, scattering pedestrians as she made the turn late and shot down what I belatedly realized was a one-way street. And we were going the wrong way.

Horns blared as Morgana swerved through the traffic, her tires blazed black rubber against the ground as she took the turn, following where I'd just seen the van. But, as I scanned for it, it was nowhere to be seen.

She didn't pause, pressing the accelerator down to the floor as the jag roared like its namesake and shot down the street. Her head was on a swivel, looking down each street as she went.

I spotted the van, but it registered too late to turn again. "Next street. Take a left."

She spun the car down the next street. "Where?"

"One street over, heading parallel to us." I looked down the alleys as we passed. "There."

Rubber screamed underneath us as Morgana pitched such a fast turn that the car went on two wheels. She flew down a too tight alley, her mirrors sparking against the bricks on either side.

I held tightly to the oh-shit handle and braced myself for something to go wrong and my seatbelt to come in handy. But she made it out of the alley with the car largely in one piece, her bumper sending up a shower of sparks behind us as it hit the curb and she spun out into the street.

"Get me the gun in the back seat," she barked, switching gears and getting the car going again. The white panel van was ahead of us.

I didn't hesitate, unbuckling my seatbelt and trusting her. Fumbling around in the back seat, I came back up with a short, stocky machine gun. I did re-buckle my seatbelt as soon as I was back in my seat, though. I wasn't an idiot. Have you seen how she drives?

"Want me to?"

Morgana didn't answer, instead grabbing the gun and using the butt of the gun to roll down the window. She stuck the gun out the side and sprayed lead at the van, a few stray bullets scratching the hood of her jag, sending up more sparks adding to the mayhem.

The van's tires blew out. I breathed a sigh of relief. Thank god it wasn't like car chases in the movies, where they could never seem to hit what they were aiming at. That, or none of them had Morgana's skills.

As the van swerved, it lost control and flipped. My heart sank as I realized there wasn't a red faucet on the side. Instead, it was red letters that I didn't even bother reading. What had I done?

"Zach, that's the wrong van," Morgana's voice was cold and disappointed. She set down her gun on the dash. Her jag was slowing down, and sirens were kicking up in the distance. There was no way this wouldn't bring down the hammer on us.

Another van came flying around the corner, quickly dodging the downed van. It jackknifed just long enough to see the logo on its side.

"That—"

"I see it." Morgana's expression turned back into a feral grin as she slammed down the accelerator and shifted into gear. The jag's tires smoked up behind us as she gave chase.

Feeling like I needed to make up for the prior van, I snatched the gun off the dash and rolled down my own window, leaning out and doing my best to sight down the short barrel before spraying the back of the van with bullets.

Unfortunately, it was not as easy as Morgana had made it look. The gun soon clicked empty, and the van was still hurtling ahead of us. Just its back looked like Swiss cheese for my efforts.

"What are you doing?" Morgana hissed. "Jadelyn could be in there."

I started to argue, but then snapped my mouth shut. Her point was fair. "What then?"

"We follow it." Morgana's hands creaked against the leather steering wheel.

I could hear sirens in the distance, and I just knew they were coming for us. We'd shot up a van and were driving a clearly beat up jaguar. We weren't exactly inconspicuous. Someone was going to put out our description, and they would arrest us.

Morgana took a hard right and raced to a parallel street, keeping pace with the van. "They are leaving the area. I need you to ditch the car."

"Wait, what?" I asked as she unbuckled her seat belt. The car was still moving.

She let go of the steering wheel, using her knee to hold it where she wanted it, and put a hand on the door handle. "I'll call you when they get to a stopping point."

I grabbed the steering wheel as she released it with her knee. "Wait, can't we pull over?"

Morgana's answer was a click of the driver's side door, followed by her tumbling out of it. I couldn't believe what I'd just seen. I looked back to find her, but she was gone.

Working on not freaking out, I tried to focus. Steering the car as best I could, I worked to try to piece together what I was supposed to do with the police chasing me down. Morgana really needed to teach me more spy moves if she was going to ask me to do this kind of thing.

The car was at least slowing down, and I was able to steer it straight through an open lane as I unbuckled my own seatbelt and wiggled into the driver's seat. I got settled in just in time to see the good ol' blue and red lights in the mirror.

I clicked on my seat belt and slammed my foot down on the gas. The car fishtailed with the sudden acceleration, but it was only for a moment. Then the back wheels caught traction, and the car tore forward. Holy shit, it felt amazing. A little whoop of excitement escaped me.

I was starting to understand why Morgana drove like she did, but I also recognized she had more experience. I was far from a professional driver. That was only reinforced as I started needing to swerve through traffic with half a dozen small heart attacks as people slammed on their brakes or changed lanes.

These other drivers clearly didn't understand my pressing need to get through them. Did they not see I was running from the cops? My foot touched the floor as the pedal did. Soon, the speedometer climbed over a hundred and the engine roared as it broke one twenty.

Hitting the turn signal—because some habits just couldn't be broken—I took the on ramp for I95, running a poor little, white economy car off the road.

Behind me, the flashing lights seemed to multiply, as patrol cars poured onto the highway on my tail. It was still a little before rush hour, and I was thankful for that as I changed lanes far too often as the jag's engine gave me its all. I teetered at the edge of one thirty on the highway, moving like a bat out of hell. I could feel the adrenaline pumping through my veins.

The flashing lights behind me fell back further and further away.

"Phew." I blew out a breath. I was still working on dodging cars, but I was grateful for the break in distance between me and the cops.

A rhythmic whomping sound came overhead, and I looked up through the tinted sunroof. A helicopter was in the air above me, keeping pace. I was officially in deep shit, and if I made it through this, Morgana was going to hear about it. You don't just jump out of a car and tell me to escape the cops.

A heavy engine roar caught my attention. I checked my rear-view mirror and saw a Charger with its lights on, racing up behind me. Shit.

"Come on, little Jag. You can beat the stupid Charger, right?" I pushed my foot down even harder, though it was already to the floor. The Charger was gaining on me, built for the highway pursuit.

"Pull over," a megaphone blared as the Charger tried to come up on my side.

Right. Like I did everything up to that moment, not realizing they were behind me and wanted me to pull over. Not going to do it now that you asked not-so-politely.

I bobbed and wove, but the highway had cleared out, and the Charger rode up on the shoulder to come even with me. Thankfully, Morgana's windows were one hundred percent illegally tinted. There was no way he could see me.

My blood was pumping, and I could feel that familiar heat in my chest.

The Charger's window rolled down, and an arm came out with a gun. This guy really wasn't messing around.

Out of most of my options, I did the only thing I could think of doing. I rolled down my own window and belched enough fire to smoke his ride. Praying that the moment I was exposed that no cameras caught my face.

Bright orange flame exploded out of my mouth. The flames engulfed the Charger, and a few lingering in my open window. Several loud pops sounded as the Charger spun and flipped. In the rear-view mirror, I could see just how badly I had cooked that car.

Its side door was literally dripping down onto the pavement, and the fire wrapped around it continued raging. Apparently, my dragon fire was pretty hot.

I smacked at the fires at the edge of my window and rolled it back up. It was just a little toasted... ah who was I kidding? Morgana was going to notice that.

The road was clear for the moment, but I suspected there would be cops lining up ahead to form a blockade, and I had no current way to get rid of the helicopter.

I needed another way out.

As the highway bent back towards the Delaware River, I felt my stomach drop. Sure enough, blue sirens were laid out ahead of me in a barricade. And a few hundred feet ahead of it, they were trying to clear out the construction vehicles.

"Ah shit," I muttered to myself as I spotted possibly my stupidest decision yet: a semi bed with a ramp you'd use to load up a backhoe. Maybe I had watched one too many action movies at this point because that seemed like my best option.

Screw it. I veered away from the highway, the suspension bouncing as I left the well paved road and gunned it for the ramp, the jag giving me everything it had.

The bottom of the jag scraped against the metal as it flew up the ramp and I launched myself into the air. Everything seemed to slow down as my heart hammered my chest, adrenaline pouring through my bloodstream.

I got a good look at the cops, not two hundred feet away, their heads all turning together to follow me. The looks were a mix of awe and skepticism. We were on the same page. I had no idea if this was going to work.

I made it. Almost. Yeah, we'll count it.

The jag clipped the concrete side wall, and the car tilted, throwing me against the driver's side door. A door that happened to still be smoldering from my earlier torching.

The fire must have screwed with the lock, because when I slammed against it, the door flapped open and the only thing holding me in my seat was the seatbelt. I felt like I was going to float away as the car spun midair.

There was a brief moment of weightlessness before gravity started doing its job. The car plummeted down. Hard.

I was thrown forward just as the airbag deployed and socked me in the face, like a pillowcase full of bricks. I thought it was supposed to be softer than that. It hit harder than a tackling werewolf.

I took quick stock of my body. At least I was still alive, slumped around the deflating airbag. But I was pressed to the seat and moving was a little difficult till the air bag lost a little more air.

A wet stream hit the side of my head, and I realized I was still moving. Disoriented, I looked around to figure out how.

I realized the car was moving downward, slowly. The door to my left wasn't sealed and was rapidly taking on water. My side of the car was tipping down, and I struggled with my seat belt to free myself. It finally clicked open.

The jag was sinking into the Delaware River. "Good thing I know how to swim." My tired, beat-up body protested as I tried to move.

Taking a deep breath, I tried to galvanize myself into action. I moved towards the pocket of air forming on the other side of the car and took deep breaths. Eventually, the car was going to hit the bottom of the Delaware, and the cops were likely already calling a diving crew. At least it would take them a bit to organize. Maybe that would count for something with Morgana.

But it wouldn't matter if I disappointed her if I were dead. It was time to see if dragons could swim.

The cabin was filling, and I was running out of time. Taking one last big gulp of breath, I swam out the driver's side door, the car still sinking as it was being carried by the river.

Deciding that going with the river was a much better option than going against it, given my current energy reserves, I held my breath and let the river carry me. Trying to remain streamlined, the river carried me past the car and further down, towards the south end of Philly.

My lungs burned with the need to surface, but I kept telling myself not yet. If I could hold out longer, then maybe the cops wouldn't see me surface. I don't know how many times I told myself that, but eventually, my body defied my mind and I kicked up to the surface, gasping for air that seared my lungs.

I was happy to see that the river had been faster than I'd realized. The helicopter was circling a few miles upriver, and I hoped they couldn't spot me. After taking another deep breath, I ducked back under water and continued to let the river carry me. Every time I came up, the helicopter was further in the distance. Finally, on one of my breaths, I saw that it had circled back to where I'd gone into the river. It hadn't spotted me.

A laugh bubbled up and escaped as I leaned back in the water, a mix of hysteria and joy. Each pump of my lungs made everything hurt, but I was alive.

After another few minutes, I started paddling over to the side, hoping to come out under a bridge in what looked like Queen Village. People were jogging along the riverside wearing bright workout clothes.

"Oh my god. Did you fall in?" A jogger stopped and helped pull me out of the river.

"Something like that. Thanks, man."

"Do you need to go to the hospital?" he asked, helping me to my feet. I looked down, noticing that I still had my shoes on. I'd count that as a win for the day, given how it was going.

"No. Just shaken up."

The jogger was joined by another. "You should go to the hospital; you have a big cut on your forehead."

I resisted the urge to reach up and touch it, but now that the second jogger mentioned it, I could feel the sting of raw skin meeting air. "Thanks. I'll call someone here in a minute."

"Here, have some of my water." The first jogger pulled a water bottle off his belt. I took it and sprayed warm water in my mouth. Relaxing against a concrete wall, I handed it back.

"Are you sure we can't take you to the hospital?"

"Fine. I'll be alright. Just need to get back home." I realized my phone wasn't likely to be any good now. I stuck my hands in my pocket and pulled it out on the slim chance it worked.

No luck. The black brick was just that now.

"You can put that in some rice, and it'll work again," the jogger eagerly provided a solution.

"Thanks." I stumbled up the steps to the street, giving them a thumbs up to try to alleviate the concern on their faces. Both joggers hesitated for a moment before continuing on their riverside run.

Up at the street level, there was a gas station only a few blocks down the way. It quickly became my next target. People stared at me as I walked along the side of the road sopping wet, but I did my best to not pay attention and act normal.

Which was a complete joke, because the day had been anything but normal. I had been involved in a car chase where Morgana blew out a van's tires. Then I had been on my own for a police chase where I had taken out one car by breathing fire and somehow survived a plunge into the Delaware River.

Just a few days before, I had been a nerd trying to keep my grades up so I could apply to med school at the end of the year.

The door to the gas station chimed as I opened it. The teller looked away from his small TV with a bored glance before going back to watching the game. I was glad that gas stations saw some crazy things and me being sopping wet didn't even register on his radar.

Going through the aisles, I found that awkward grocery-like isle and grabbed a cup of instant fried rice. It would have to do.

"Breaking news. A high-speed chase ends with the driver running into the river. Our sources say they have no identity for the driver, but it is suspected he died in the accident. Work is underway to find the body." Overhead, video that must have been taken from the helicopter became the main picture while the news anchor slid into the bottom right.

"As you can see, the police almost apprehended him during the chase, but he used an incendiary device detonated from the side of his car to throw off the police." The frame froze. Morgana's car was too tinted in any of the images to see inside the car. But, in the frozen frame, fire was spewing out the side.

I was glad that they hadn't come up with a better image. If they had had one of me breathing said fire, I'm not quite sure where that would land me. But based on Morgana's warning, it would have likely been the end of my time in the para world and life.

"At this time, both officers have been admitted to the hospital, and we wish them a speedy recovery. Next up, we have a story about—"

I tuned them out and breathed a sigh of relief. I was glad I hadn't killed the cops in the Charger. They'd only been doing their jobs.

"Is that it, sir?" the teller asked as I approached; I gave him my card and was already ripping open the cup and stuffing my phone in it. "Works better if you pour a second one in; they aren't very full."

The look on his face and the way he said it in such a bored tone hit a chord with me. There was no doubt in my mind that he was absolutely correct and that he saw the strangest things working at a gas station.

Chapter 15

I was on my third Snickers, sitting outside the gas station waiting for my clothes and my phone to dry out. At this point, the sun was setting, and I'd seen the same report on my high-speed chase cycle through the news feed two more times. No image of me or an indication that they were looking for me was present. They were still working to find a corpse at the bottom of the river.

Checking the phone again, I nearly knocked the cup of rice off the bench. It actually started up.

It also had half a dozen texts from Morgana, and a few phone calls. I decided now might be a good time to call her back.

"Zach! Where have you been?" she hissed.

"Oh, you know. Dodging cops on the highway after you ditched me, setting cop cars on fire, and lounging in the Delaware."

There was a stretched moment of pause on the other side of the phone. I thought maybe I'd lost her and checked my phone; it was still on.

"What happened to my car?"

"Gone. Well, not gone. It's at the bottom of the river, and the cops are probably trying to pull it out now."

Another pause before she sighed. "Fine. Get here ASAP. I have already texted you the address." The phone beeped, indicating the end of the call. She might have been upset about the car, but then again, she had put me in that situation, and I didn't feel an ounce of remorse. Except for the jag, poor thing.

I took a look and copied the address into a rideshare app. It only took a few minutes for the ride to show up. The driver eyed me in my still damp state, giving me a judgmental look before getting out, grabbing a towel out of the trunk and throwing it along the backseat of his car.

Ignoring his unhappiness, I plopped onto the towel.

The driver got back in his seat and drove off, leaving the pleasant neighborhood of Queen Village behind and heading south along the river to another industrial area. I was starting to think maybe abandoned factories attracted criminals.

"You can stop here. I'll walk the rest of the way," I said, not actually wanting him to drop me off at the building.

"You sure?" he asked, meeting my eyes in the rearview as he took in the surrounding area cautiously.

"Positive."

The driver shrugged and pulled to a stop just long enough for me to get out before he booked it out of the sketchy industrial park.

Someone came up behind me and I jumped, putting my fists up.

"Don't make a fuss. Come with me." Morgana lurked in the shadows and crept along the buildings as we went. "Recognize this place?" she asked.

"Should I?" It looked like every other industrial park I'd ever seen. It was just a large number of big squat buildings. With the setting sun, it was difficult to pick up details.

She pointed west. "Three blocks over is where we raided the other night."

"You're kidding me..." I felt stupid for not checking for nearby factories. They moved right in under our noses.

"Don't feel stupid. The police did a sweep of the area after Detective Fox set fire to the last factory. They didn't catch it either, so these guys might have stepped away temporarily, only to come right back." She shook her head as she crouched in the growing shadows of dusk.

I had questions about how the detective fit into everything. "I saw the detective with Jadelyn's father when the council questioned us. Do the para control the cops?"

"No, not like you're thinking. But we do have people in most of the emergency services. Helps us cover things when someone gets stupid. Like, you know, when someone breathes fire during a police car chase." She gave me a knowing look.

A nervous chuckle slipped out of me. "You saw that?"

"Wasn't hard to look it up after you told me. You need to be more careful. You got lucky with that one."

She rounded a corner, and the factory ahead of us had boarded-up windows. A new van was pulling up to the building. Two men jumped out of the van, throwing open the back doors and quickly taking a look around before they moved to pull something out of the van.

"Let me go," a woman yelled. Two more men came out of the warehouse, and together the four of them held Kelly down as she tried to shift. I could see her body swell just before one of them cracked a bat over her head; she slumped down to the ground.

Morgana and I watched it happen. I was itching to leap forward and help her, but Morgana put a hand on my arm. "Not yet."

"Why are they kidnapping other paras?" They needed the vampires for the drug, but what were Jadelyn and Kelly for?

"Hostages. Kelly is Brent's daughter, the one he raised with his wife. You remember Brent from the council meeting, right?" She turned to look at me.

I nodded. They'd taken two of the council members' kids. That move wasn't for a drug; it was for their own protection. "They had to know the leaders wouldn't stand still if their kids were kidnapped. Does that mean we are going to have more?"

"Play stupid games, win stupid prizes. All hell is going to break loose if we don't get them back tonight. Brent won't be as... tactful as Rupert."

I filed Jadelyn's father's name away for later.

"As for others, I'm not sure. Simon would be a good target, but I hear he's been locked up until your duel on Monday. If they took someone from the Faerie, then we should just back up and let them handle it."

"The Faeries are that terrifying?" I asked.

"Sirens and Elves have money and numbers. The Faerie? They have raw power, and some heavy hitters that demand respect." She looked me up and down again. "You might actually fit in best with them if you ever decide to take a side."

I'd have to learn more about them later. "And here I thought I was on your side." I nudged her side.

Morgana snorted, a smile curling up at the edge of her lips. "You wish."

The men successfully dragged Kelly into the warehouse, and Morgana waved forward, darting across the last street and hugging the factory's exterior wall. This place reminded me a lot of the past factory, although they all seemed a bit cookie cutter—big concrete, boxy buildings with high windows.

Morgana snuck around to a side door at the docks and pulled out her blades. In one clean swipe, she cut the lock. "Keep your big head down. This is different from our last job. We didn't know there were hostages then. We need to secure the hostages before they realize we are here. Once we do that, you'll stay with the hostages to protect them; I'll clean out the operation."

"Don't want me setting this one on fire?" I smirked. Guard duty on Jadelyn and Kelly was perfectly fine with me. My beast agreed that we should protect them.

Morgana didn't respond to my joke, already in motion. Slipping into a small opening in the doorway, her soft blue skin and her dark leather attire made her practically a ghost in the dark warehouse. Tall metal racks covered the inside of the building from floor to ceiling. Their contents seemed abandoned to collect dust. Further past the racks, I could see a light and an open space full of machinery.

We skirted around the lit area, scouting for where they were keeping the hostages. Between two factory lines, there was a setup similar to what we'd seen at the last factory, with a clear plastic tent. But this time, there was activity within the tent. People looked to be packaging the drug, wearing white masks over their faces while they did so.

One piece of equipment was running; a large, slanted drum bigger than a car spun, depositing out a thin line of white powder at the end.

Up in front of the drum, I watched a shifted werewolf lift a large blue drum and pour the contents in. It made me wonder where that drum was made.

Morgana patted me on the shoulder and pointed to her eyes before pointing further off, away from the light. Kelly was being dragged by two men into another area of the factory. We slipped around the central area of the facility, avoiding detection, and heading towards where they'd been. As my eyes adjusted from staring at the lit area, I realized they had opened a set of heavy freezer doors and pulled Kelly inside.

I scanned around. I'd expected to find guards like the previous factory, where a small pack of wolves was guarding it. But I hadn't spotted any yet. It made me uneasy.

Morgana moved quickly, grabbing the freezer door before it closed and motioning me in. Crouching in the shadows, I followed the werewolves hauling Kelly.

As we stepped inside, I was happy to find that the freezer had been left off. I could likely generate heat, but regardless, I did not want to freeze my butt off in a freezer.

The door clicked closed behind us, and the men started talking. They seemed to have been waiting until they were alone in the thick, likely soundproof room.

"You sure we can't fuck this bitch? I hear she's a big dog in the pack."

"Shut up. Our alpha said she and the other bitch are important. If we want the pack to grow stronger, we need her and the drug."

Why did they need her? I wondered.

Chains rattled as they hauled Kelly up and started wrapping chains around her, securing her to the racks in the freezer. She was right next to Jadelyn, who hung from her own rack, her blonde hair hanging down and matted with blood. She'd clearly put up a fight.

I winced, imagining the headache she was going to have when she woke up. I looked to Morgana, communicating my need to do something. It only took the subtlest nod from her before I lunged out of the darkness and grabbed both of the werewolves, squeezing tight with my hands and crushing their windpipes.

Both of them immediately tried to shift, but Morgana jumped in. With two quick stabs, she'd stopped their shift and kept them human as their bodies focused on healing.

"I get that talking is probably difficult right now. So, raise your hand if you'd like to have a moment to breathe as you tell us why you need Kelly?" I looked between the two werewolves expectantly.

Instead, they both started struggling; I only saw the flash of Morgana's blade before they stopped. I tried again. "Okay, I'll make you a deal. The one that talks doesn't get gutted by my drow friend here in the next few seconds."

Both hands shot up, and I picked the one that had spoken more intelligently earlier. I pulled him away from Morgana.

The other was suddenly gurgling his own blood as Morgana finished him, leaving the other one looking even more talkative.

"Speak." I shook him to get his attention, which had been drawn to his bleeding friend.

"If you let me go for a second, I can show you. I got it in my pocket." He held one hand up and reached down with the other.

I stayed cautious, not knowing if he was going to pull out a gun. But instead, he pulled out a ziplock baggie of white powder. It looked like what had been coming out of the machine in the factory. "The drug? What does that have to do with Kelly?"

He lifted it slightly, but then moved quickly, tearing the bag open and shoving the powder in his face, snorting heavily. It was so sudden that I didn't have time to react before the man came away with a powder covered face, kind of like a kid after they eat a powdered donut. At the same time, a deranged look filled his face, and his eyes began to glow with what I'd come to realize as pack magic.

The shift happened so quickly that I barely had time to squeeze his neck before a massive paw slammed into my chest and shoved me off him. Morgana flashed past me, and I heard the ring of her blades hitting something hard before she reappeared to my right.

The wolf stood on his back legs, its tongue lolling out in a dopey look for a dog. I'd seen werewolves before, and this didn't look normal. One of its arms was larger than the other, and lumps were rising under its skin. I could feel the wrongness of it in my bones as I looked at the wolf, which was now crouched low to avoid brushing its head against the ceiling.

It didn't make any noise. There was no howling, no growling. It was bizarre.

The werewolf moved forward, slamming into me and driving me further into the crumpled racks. The hit drove the wind out of my lungs, but Morgana followed behind, using her blades to carve off chunks of its flesh.

The wounds only lasted so long, healing unnaturally quickly. Her blades weren't able to keep up with its healing, but I knew she was at least wearing the beast's mana down.

I grabbed the werewolf's wrists and tried to hold it still, but the thing's large, warped arm was strong enough that my weight meant nothing. It didn't matter how strong I was if the weight difference was so big.

The wolf thrashed me into the wall and ceiling, even as I held both of its wrists in a vice-like grip. I was not about to let it have range of motion in its arms again, but I also wasn't too pleased with getting smashed around like some sort of comedic moment in a superhero movie.

"Just cut its head off, Morgana. Let's be done with this," I grunted as I made a new dent in the ceiling.

"Can't." She hacked with her blade, and that metal ringing sounded out again as it got stuck. "Shit." Morgana shifted her stance, starting to use her magic instead of her blades.

I realized my eye must have shifted, because I could see her magic again. I looked at the werewolf and could see his magic, too. It was a dark orange, but it had a sickly oily sheen to it. The magic seemed to be connected to something else further off. I followed the connection and could see it connected to a whole network—it was his pack. There were less than a dozen in the facility, but more elsewhere to the west. They all connected to a single point, one that was coming closer.

I focused back on Morgana and her magic. Even in the dark freezer, there was a new level of darkness that started at her fingertip before she drove it right into the wolf's skull.

It dropped like a rotten sack of potatoes.

"Phew." Morgana let out a huff. "Running around all day in the sun, and now this. I do hope there aren't more of them."

Something pounded on the freezer door, and we both went still. I didn't see pack magic on whatever was out there.

"Mark, you okay? If you and George want to start a fight, do it elsewhere."

I pulled myself out of the wire racking I'd landed in and wrinkled my nose at the smell. The dead wolf smelled absolutely terrible, but I pushed that aside.

Instead, I strode up to the door and threw it open, catching whoever was on the other side with a heavy thud. Stepping around the door, I grabbed the man by the throat and hauled him into the freezer. We didn't have much time; someone else would come looking, eventually.

"Speak, what's going on here. Why kidnap these two?"

The man instantly began shaking. "I'm just human—I swear. They just sell me drugs. This stuff is taking over the market. Huge demand." He raised his hands, but there was a small spark of magic in his eyes.

I didn't want another problem on my hands, so I squeezed as hard as I could and jerked my arm. His neck made a satisfying click and his eyes glazed over.

"What was that for?" Morgana asked, scowling at the dead man she could no longer question.

"I felt something start to stir in him and I didn't want another of those." I pointed to the dead wolf with my chin. The wolf was shifting back to human, like the others I'd seen, only he still had those grotesque proportions.

"He was human though." Morgana frowned, and I just shrugged. I didn't know what to tell her. "Fine, stick to the plan. Post up next to the freezer. I'll do my best to clear out these wolves before they become a problem."

"Step out with me." I opened the freezer door and looked around; no one else had come to check yet. "There are two wolves further out in the office. I figure you can take those two down quietly. One outside." I pointed, following the trace of pack magic. "Then you have another five in the center operation. There's obviously the one hauling the barrels, but also three girls in the tent and the guy putting the drugs in the truck."

"You can see them all?" she asked, but her eyes focused on my right eye. "Ah. I see. You seem to be better when you get thrashed around. I'll remember that for the next time we spar." There was a faint smirk that vanished in a moment as she slipped away towards the office to take care of the first two, leaving me to guard the two unconscious girls.

"Bart, what the hell is taking you so long?" the wolf who was placing bricks in the truck stood up and barked my way. I tried to step to the side into deeper shadows, but the wolf wasn't satisfied when he didn't get an answer. He shaded his eyes from the light and started heading my way.

I waited, letting him get closer. The longer Morgana had to take out the ones away from the main operation, the fewer surprises we'd have to deal with.

But it didn't take him long to spot me. As he stepped away from the light and into the darkness, his eyes glowed orange like a wolf's, and his head snapped to me.

Guess the jig was up. I burst from my hiding spot, making sure to be as quiet as possible as I tackled him before he could shout.

I was able to take him down, but he shifted in the process. At that point, I wasn't entirely sure who had who. I was stronger than him, but he definitely had mass on his side in his wolf form.

Each time we rolled, my body reminded me that I was covered in bruises from being knocked around by the last werewolf.

"Intruders!" someone yelled behind me, and I cringed. Now it was going to get messier.

I saw the workers in the center tearing up the bricks and throwing them into the air. White clouds of V-phoria filled the air. The workers that were human were immediately evident as they fell down, writhing on the floor. I wasn't sure why they would overdose themselves like that.

But the wolves in the room seemed to be shifting into grotesque werewolves, like the one in the freezer.

I watched in horror as the white cloud of drug continued to expand, threatening to smother both myself and the wolf I was struggling to keep down.

Chapter 16

It looked like a snowy Christmas morning as the air filled with falling puffs of the dangerous, addictive drug. Everything seemed to freeze for a moment as everybody watched the massive cloud spread across the warehouse.

There wasn't anywhere to outrun it. Despite my effort to hold my breath, I soon was forced to breathe in the drug, and my body started to feel really good. Maybe even great.

Enjoying the wave of happiness, I inhaled deeply, but my breath was cut off as I was launched into the air. My body came tumbling down onto my hip with a sharp pain that made everything clear again for a moment. Shaking off the momentary high, I tried to focus harder, but I could already feel myself slipping back into the euphoria.

The damn thing had clearly gone straight from my mucus membranes to my bloodstream and there was a ton of it in the air.

"Zach." Morgana's blue face came into view.

"You're pretty. I bet you're a good kisser." I smiled up at her, wondering what her lips would feel like. My head rocked to the side and my face stung.

"Snap out of it. Focus, Zach, or you're dead."

I tried. I really did. But I could feel my focus slipping away, even as I put all my energy into it. It was like trying to catch a greased-up pig, not that I really knew what that was like.

Mmmm pork sounded really good. I licked my lips, surprised when they tasted bitter.

Smack.

"Focus, Zach. I need you. Jadelyn and Kelly need you to get the fuck up and fight."

The mention of Jadelyn and Kelly helped. They were depending on me. I had to figure this thing out. I dug my nails into my hands, working to use the pain to help orient me. Rolling, I got up, my head spinning in fun ways with the movement.

"Up," I pronounced proudly to the world.

Something hit me in a flying tackle. It hurt almost as much as an airbag to the face, and it was fuzzy. Wait, not fuzzy. It was fluffy in a mangey way. It took a bit, but my mind registered it as a werewolf.

"You need to work on your hugs, man." I pushed the wolf off of me.

It looked confused and came swinging again. I'd like to say that I dodged with the skill and grace of a fighter, but I'm pretty sure I just swayed and stumbled out of the way.

I did manage to grab his paw, taking a moment to marvel at just how fuzzy it was while twisting and bringing my shoulder up into his elbow. It snapped and crackled. Now it just needed a pop. That came after, as I managed to continue twisting and dislocated the wolf's elbow.

It howled in pain right in my ear. It was loud enough to make me even more dizzy than I was already. But what distracted me most was the sickly pack magic that danced around the wolf, a kaleidoscope of orange motes.

I tried to pull my anger into my chest. But it slipped away, and I couldn't gather up the heat that I'd felt before to breathe fire.

The wolf's arm clicked back into place, and I went for another rough tumble with him. I ended up on my back with him over me.

Only one idea made it through my fuzzy brain, so I went with it. I used both hands and grabbed onto the bracer Jadelyn had given me like she'd shown me. As I held it tight, magic came to life in front of me like a big round shield.

The wolf pounded against it, but the shield absorbed the blows. Unfortunately, that still left me feeling a bit like a nail being pounded into the concrete floor.

At some point during the nail and hammer byplay, I saw another magic, one I hadn't seen before, race into the factory.

It was a small man, and one I recognized. Brent shifted as he came into view. His pack magic was far cleaner than these other wolves. It blazed orange like a fire as he became the largest werepuppy I'd ever seen. I was sure he was at least ten feet tall, and that was hunched over.

Brent flew into a rage in the middle of the factory.

Seeing him reminded me of Jadelyn and Kelly, and I refocused on my role, moving my body back in front of the freezer. The wolf that had been attacking me was now torn to shreds, and the fight was focused on Brent.

It wasn't long before other wolves came charging into the factory, but I could see their pack magic tie back to Brent. Reinforcements had arrived.

I relaxed a bit, considering sitting down on the floor, when their magic caught my attention. Something was wrong.

"Zach, are you okay?" Morgana grabbed me by the collar.

"Their magic fireflies are going bad," I said, pointing to the wolves that had come with Brent. They had flooded in among the airborne drug, quickly outnumbered the remaining grotesque looking wolves. It didn't matter that the drug had made the enemy pack stronger, Brent's pack tore them apart with greater numbers.

Morgana frowned at the scene that was unfolding in the warehouse. "What do you mean?"

"The ugly wolves had dirty pack magic. I think it was the drug; now Brent's wolves are being exposed." I tried my best to focus while I spoke, but I could feel my focus slipping in and out. My adrenaline was wearing off.

"Hold on." Morgana disappeared, coming back with one of the masks and wrapping it around my face. "Hopefully, we can keep you from getting any more in your system."

Behind her, the last of the grotesque wolves was killed, and Brent and his pack started closing in on us. When I looked at them now, I no longer saw their magic. My eye must have returned to normal now that the fighting was done.

Looking up, I noticed Jadelyn's father entering the warehouse, with Chad next to him. He waved to Morgana, who pointed both groups at the freezer. Brent tore open the door and one of his packmates came out a second later carrying Kelly.

His big wolf head turned and sniffed me before he marched out.

Chad hurried in and collected Jadelyn, carrying her like a princess. Something about it rankled me. "Coming in at the last second and pretending to be the knight?" I said, skipping that oh so important filter between the brain and my mouth.

I blamed the drugs.

"Excuse me?" Chad asked, turned slowly with a scowl on his face.

"Ha. Boys. Why don't we get Jadelyn out of here before there is more trouble," Rupert said, trying to cut the tension.

His statement didn't seem to cut any of the tension in Chad, who walked over, clearly intending to kick me while I was down. As he made his move, I caught his foot, but I didn't use it against him while he was holding Jadelyn. We stayed like that for a moment, staring each other down, before I let it go with a bit of an extra shove.

Morgana moved quickly, her blades hovering in the air at Chad's neck. "Get out. Now."

Rupert grabbed Chad by the shoulder and hauled him away with an apologetic look at Morgana. "He's riled up from Jadelyn getting kidnapped. Let's not spill any more blood tonight. Take your charge and see to him, Morgana. We'll get people to come and clean this mess up."

The drow vampiress turned back and lifted me off the floor, using her shoulder to support me. I was impressed she was able to hold my weight. Everything hurt, but at least the drugs made focusing on that pain difficult. It all slipped through me like sand through a sieve.

"Come on. Let's go before I have to kill that puppy alpha," she said.

I snorted. "Puppy alpha." I hoped I'd remember that when I came to.

***

"I feel like shit," were the first words out of my mouth when I woke up. It felt like my throat was full of tar, and I was sure there were elephants taking turns sitting on my head.

"The drug seems to be out of your system." Morgana sat on a chair a few feet away from my bed, an IV bag hooked up next to her.

Scattered thoughts went through my head as I tried to piece together what had happened. I could put together most of it, although the memories were a bit addled here or there. "We got the girls out okay?"

"Yes, both of them made it out okay. I wanted to ask what you remember about 'their fireflies were going bad'," she said with a smirk.

I looked around, realizing I was in the room that Morgana had said was mine in the Atrium. Gold dragon motifs were everywhere. The lamp between me and Morgana was a dragon winding around a mountain and holding the lightbulb in its mouth. "Where did you find all these dragon decorations?"

She shook her head. "Not important. The bad fireflies?"

I struggled to remember what I'd seen. "Their magic. That's the fireflies. To me, magic looks like a collection of little balls, kind of like bubbles or a tightly clustered group of fireflies. I saw Brent and his pack's—it was different from the omega wolves'. It looked healthy when they had first entered, but when they were tearing the others apart, it..." I struggled with how to describe it. "Their pack magic became dirty, oily almost."

Morgana nodded. "The wolf in the freezer. Did you get a good look at his magic?"

"Yeah. His was very dirty, more like sludge once I had Brent's to compare it to."

"What about Chad's?"

"Didn't get a look at his magic. Oh! But I did notice something else. When I was looking at the wolf in the freezer, I saw the link between all of the wolves moving, coming towards the factory. I think it must have been the omega's alpha. It was tied to him like Brent's wolves were to him. Did he show? Did we get him?"

Morgana shook her head, her silver ponytail thrashing with the motion. "No, just the wolves you identified before the fighting started. Given what we saw with the wolves, the council is taking this more seriously. Rupert and Brent are throwing considerable manpower into having this drug ring tracked down and stamped out."

I nodded. The threat was clearly real after everything that had happened the past few days. It was no longer a small problem of a few rogue wolves and a drug that would make humans ask questions. Something very wrong was going on. Something that was powerful enough to believe they could take the council's children and get away with it. There was going to be more blood.

I startled as a new thought crossed my mind. "Wait, what time is it?" I had a date I needed to get to; I hoped I hadn't already stood Scarlett up.

"It's four in the afternoon. You slept through the morning."

I searched around for my phone, realizing that I was naked under the covers. "Morgana, did you undress me?" Heat dusted my cheeks.

She smirked at my embarrassment. "Yes. I also bandaged you and set up an IV. You heal quickly. Not vampire or werewolf quick, but something that would take weeks only takes a day. You should stay in bed."

I shook my head. "I have a date. Tonight."

"Oh, would this happen to be The Fabulous and Foxy Scarlett?" Her eyebrow arched and she pulled a phone out of her pocket. Clearly, Morgana had been looking at my phone while I was out if she knew what Scarlett had put her name in as in my phone.

"In fairness, she put that down."

Morgana just gave me a chuckle and handed me the phone. "It's fine. Go on your date tonight but take it easy. I'm sure there are nice enough clothes in your closet here. I happened to see some of those texts. You can meet her here at the club. Promise I won't intervene...

much." She gave me a pat on my leg and stood to leave. "Glad you are feeling better. Let me know if there are any side effects from the drug."

She spun around before she left. "Oh, and before I forget. There's your payment for the last two jobs."

A gold brick bigger than my hand sat on the side table next to me. I wasn't quite sure what to do with it. "Is that really gold?"

"Four hundred ounces. I only accept payment in gold. That's your half of four payments."

I did the math quickly. "You are getting half a bar per job. Rupert offered you an entire gold brick to save Jadelyn." Holy crap, no wonder she had a garage full of expensive cars. I didn't know what this brick was worth, but it was far more than I'd make in a year even if I was an expensive specialist. "What do I do with it?"

"If you'd like, you can sell it to me. I'll handle everything and convert it into cash. I just thought that you being a dragon and all that you might like the gold."

The metal did call to me, but it was nothing like the gold I'd dug up with my father. "Take it and cash it in for me. I wouldn't know what to do with it."

"Can do. I'll get your information from you later. Rest up." She left with the gold brick, leaving me alone with my phone buzzing again. It was another text from Scarlett. Rather than text back, I decided to call.

"Hey, is this the Fabulous and Foxy Scarlett?" I asked. She laughed, and I could have sworn there were other voices in the background.

The phone clicked, and I could hear it shifting. "You did not just call me saying that." I could practically hear her blushing.

"Was I on speaker?"

"Yes... It's a sorority thing. God, that was embarrassing, but sweet."

"Good." I swung my legs off the bed and suppressed a groan. "I wanted to apologize. I worked late last night into the morning. I actually just woke up."

"Oh." There was a mixture of surprise and relief in her tone. "Now I feel stupid. Don't read those texts."

"It's fine. Consider them forgotten. We still on for the date tonight at Bumps in the Night?" I pulled out a casual suit from the closet and held it up to my chest. It was simple, just a black suit with a white shirt. It might be overdressed, but I could always take the jacket off. And, if I left a few buttons loose, it should read casual enough.

"Yeah. My friend and her date are excited to go. What are you going to be wearing?"

"I was just looking at my closet. The place seems pretty nice. I hear they do a decently fancy dinner before the club starts. I was thinking a suit with no tie?"

There was that background noise again; was I still on speaker?

"Do that. Please?" she asked, a slight pitch to her voice made me think she had a big smile plastered on her face.

"Your wish is my command." I smiled into the phone. I was smitten just talking with her. "Okay, we should hang up before I run out of my limited conversation topics. I'll meet you at the club at seven?"

"How about eight? I couldn't get a reservation before then."

"What if I told you I could get you a reservation there any time of the day you wanted?"

She snorted. "Do you have some secret I need to know about?"

My gut dropped and felt like it had been punted back up into my throat. I did have a secret. Shit, what was I doing?

"Zach?"

"Yeah, sorry. No big secrets. I just know someone."

"Sure, then we'll do seven."

There was an awkward pause. Wrapping up calls was always awkward, and of course, I panicked.

"I look forward to seeing the Fabulous and Foxy Scarlett tonight. Talk to you later." I reused the same joke, but at least she laughed before she hung up.

The beast coiled in my gut, snorting at my awkward send off. "Well a lot of help you are," I chided the beast and started to get ready for my date.

***

A quick ask of Morgana had gotten someone's reservation 'lost' and ours bumped up to seven. But it had also given her even more details on the date to nose her way into.

"Oh come on. You look great, stop fussing with your cuffs."

I tugged at my shirt sleeve again. They kept disappearing under the cuff of the jacket when I moved. "I know. Just a little nervous."

"Your Fabulous and Foxy friend will no doubt be coming. I'm as excited to see her as you are. You'll stay for the party portion of the night, right?" She grinned wide enough to show off her fangs.

At the moment, Bumps in the Night was warmly lit up, showcasing the large wooden bar and illuminating the tables under soft warm light. Each of the tables had their own candle to add to the ambiance. People had started filling the tables, and the air smelled of steak and expensive wine.

At the moment, it looked like a five-star restaurant, with prices that put a single person's meal in the triple digits. But I also knew that it would transform faster than a werewolf when the clock hit nine, and a speakeasy club in the back would begin to take center stage.

I was kind of interested to see the transformation.

"Is that her?" Morgana asked from our vantage up on the balcony. We had stayed out of sight while the lights were on full blast. Morgana apparently waited until the club was darker to walk around, but I still didn't understand how her blue skin wasn't noticed.

"Shit, it is." I checked my phone. She was fifteen minutes early.

"She showed up early. She must be eager," Morgana whispered into my ear, but when I turned, she was gone. I wondered if she was trying to be so spooky, but my focus was entirely on Scarlett.

Hustling down the stairs, I came up behind her. "I see I'm not the only one who showed up early."

"Zach." Scarlett's face split into a blinding smile as she came up to my side, having to look up to make eye contact. "My friend and her date ended up a little delayed, but I guess that gives us a little time to ourselves?"

Scarlett looked absolutely stunning. I'd been in such a rush that I hadn't taken the chance to really look at her. She wore a short green dress that was tastefully long enough for the nice dinner we were about to have, but enough of a dipping neckline that I knew I'd have to work on keeping my eyes on her face during the night.

She laughed, clearly seeing where my eyes had gone. "You approve of the dress?" She was biting her pink lips and the little sparkle of mischief in her eyes said she was enjoying the attention.

"You look absolutely lovely." I looked her in the eye, wanting her to see how much I meant it.

She blushed heavily, tucking her hair behind her ear as she looked around. "Let's see if our table is ready?" Her voice squeaked a little, clearly still feeling a bit nervous.

I offered my arm, and she hooked hers through mine as we walked up to the hostess' podium. Scarlett had styled her hair from wavy to full on curly tonight and it bounced against my arm as she leaned against me.

The hostess looked up from her podium and gave us a genuine smile as her eyes opened wide. "Mister Pendragon." She stepped around the podium and snapped up two menus. "It's our honor that you are here tonight. Please come with me."

Scarlett gave me a cocked eyebrow in question.

Damnit Morgana. I looked up towards the balcony, swearing I spotted her for a brief second. I had no doubt she was amusing herself.

"This will be your table. Best seat in the house." The server led us to a four-person table that would have a fantastic view of the rest of the establishment and a window if we wanted to people watch those going by.

The hostess pulled out Scarlett's seat and handed us menus. "Please, ignore the prices for tonight for yourselves and your guests. We are so pleased to have you tonight, Mister Pendragon. The owner has said everything is on the house. I'll bring you two some of our best wine, a 1963 Chateau D'Yuvore, in a moment. Please feel free to wave me or any of the servers down should you need anything."

I wasn't a wine snob, but if the brand required her to say it in a French accent, it was probably way over my normal budget. Since Morgana was going this far, I wasn't going to turn it down. But, as I looked across the table, I had Scarlett's full attention.

"Spill." Scarlett pushed down her menu and hissed across the table. "That's a five-hundred-dollar bottle!"

I could have sworn I heard Morgana's throaty Swiss chuckle from somewhere deeper in the club.

Chapter 17

Scarlett was staring at me. An eyebrow quirked as she waited for an answer for our lavish dinner.

"I swear, one of my friends is just messing with me," I answered, spreading my hands out defensively. "I'm honestly not a big deal at all."

Scarlett's eyes narrowed further conspiratorially. "Who?"

"The owner of this place and I... have a work arrangement. And I guess we are kind of friends now?" It felt weird saying it, but in the few days I'd known her, Morgana had become a friend. She was my sponsor into the para world and part of my safety, but we also had each other's backs in a less mentor and mentee way.

"Friend or *friend*." Scarlett's tone grew more defensive.

"She's ancient Scarlett. I'm sure she looks at me and sees a little twerp barely out of diapers." I figured it was all accurate enough, although I wondered that, at Morgana's age, if it played as much of a role anymore.

Scarlett nodded and looked at her menu again. "Alright. At least I get to pig out. She's really going to pick up the bill?"

"If she doesn't after this, I'll drag her around by her ears." I picked up my menu and scanned it, looking for the most expensive steak just to spite Morgana. She was having too much fun at my expense.

"It's fine. Sorry for all the questions—I'm just being cautious. Suddenly, my date is a lot more mysterious. I thought he was just a normal student at school, then suddenly the fancy restaurant gushes over you. Makes a girl wonder." She shrugged but didn't seem too put off.

I did my best to push down my annoyance at Morgana, looking out at the people passing by the window. A woman hurried by, clearly late for something. Another man was strolling, but subtly ducked into a darker area of the street. Curious, I watched him closer.

Leaning next to the wall next to a man that had been standing nearby, he slipped a wad of cash to the side, passing it to the other. In return, he received a small baggie of what looked like white powder, although it was a bit hard to make out from a distance.

My gut spun. It looked a lot like V-phoria. Were these guys dealers? I wanted to go after them, but I was on a date, and we needed to move further up the chain than the low-level distributors.

Committing their faces to my memory, I tried to make sure that, if I spotted them again, I'd be able to do something more about it.

"You're cute when you're thinking, you know that?" Scarlett's eyes were fixed on me when I looked back from the window. Her statement had the immediate effect of warming my cheeks.

"Thanks, but really? Only when I'm thinking? Hurts a little." I winked at her. "And here I am trying to keep up with you, who seems to look stunning in about anything."

She blushed, leaning forward as she put her arms crossed on the table, raising her breasts higher and pushing them forward. Based on the look on her face, she knew exactly what she was doing as I tried to keep my eyes level with hers.

"Flattery will get you everywhere. But I need to let you know, even though sororities have a reputation, I have a rule that I don't sleep with a guy on the first date."

I choked and nearly spit my water out at her bluntness, and she burst out laughing. I recovered and wiped at the corner of my mouth, where a few dribbles had escaped. "Fine with me, but I'd still love to have you over to my place after, if you're up for it."

Her hand slipped across the table to grab mine, our eyes locking. "I'd love that."

The sudden lump in my throat stopped me from responding. She was gorgeous. How had I gotten so lucky?

"Hush. We aren't that late," a voice I could have sworn was Chad, came up from around the corner. Looking over, I groaned internally. It was Chad's voice. He was led over by the hostess, with Jadelyn at his side.

"Zach?" Jadelyn stopped just short of the table while the hostess guided Chad to sit next to me.

"Jadelyn?"

"Fucker." Chad glowered at me, not taking the offered seat. "Jadelyn, you didn't tell me this guy was going to be here." He shot her an accusatory glare, but Jadelyn was too startled, staring at me to make any comment back.

Scarlett's voice cut through the tension like a sharp knife. "You all know each other?" Her confusion was evident.

Not wanting her to feel awkward, I tried to push aside my desire for Chad to be anywhere but at our table. "Please, sit down."

The hostess walked away while Jadelyn and Chad got seated and I turned to Scarlett. "Yes, I met them the other night." I tried to keep it vague, not sure how to explain our relationship without giving away the para world.

Jadelyn's face grew more puzzled, looking between us. Suddenly, she burst out laughing. "Neither of you know, do you?"

"Know what?" I asked. Scarlett's eyes were narrowed at her friend.

"You can stop with the subtleties. Both of you are para." Jadelyn dropped it suddenly, and my mind spun for a moment.

I turned, staring at Scarlett, who was looking at me with the same surprise. Her eyes flashed for a moment to gold, reminding me of when I'd seen them after the bike accident. I'd been such an idiot; of course, they really were able to turn. And she'd healed so quickly.

"I think you broke him." Chad barked in laughter.

"Hush, or we are going home." Jadelyn shot across the table. "You said you'd be civil tonight."

Chad raised his hands in defense. "I didn't know it would be him. But I'll behave." He put his hands down on the table and started to ignore me while he looked through the menu.

Across the table from me, Scarlett's mouth was still open in a flat 'o'. She might have frozen in place, but now that she had my attention again, she realized it and snapped her mouth closed. "What are you?"

"I actually don't know." I rubbed the back of my neck. "Jadelyn calls me a lost one. And since you know about the para world, I guess I can explain this dinner better. I know the owner of this bar because the owner is mentoring me into the para world."

Jadelyn turned to Scarlett and added a detail I didn't know she was missing. "Morgana is sponsoring him. This is her bar."

Scarlett softly smacked her forehead. "I feel like such an idiot."

"Please don't. When the whole bike thing happened, I didn't even know. It wasn't till that night that I got in a fight with Chad and my abilities showed themselves." I made a small explosion gesture with my hands.

"Wait, you were the one that fought with Chad on Friday? But then—" She paused as Chad started growling low.

"Don't you say it." The threat was clear in his voice, and I immediately bristled. I didn't like him talking to Scarlett that way.

Jadelyn jumped in first, though, using her most calming voice. "Chad, you need to calm down. We all know you are an alpha. There's no need to push your dominance right now."

He turned to her, clearly calmer but still flustered. "You don't understand. The pack bond and pack magic are still forming. I have to push all contenders down or I could lose my position." There was an undertone of almost fear in how he said it. It was hard to feel sorry for the guy, but I could imagine the immense pressure getting and maintaining that sort of position would cause.

Jadelyn wasn't happy with that answer, and she frowned. "None of us here are going to fight you for your alpha position."

His head shifted slightly to me, looking out of the corner of his eye. "You sure about that?"

I spoke up for myself. "Look, I'm not a shifter. I have no interest in your pack." It was true that I had no desire to join Chad's pack, but they were still of interest in my investigation. Now didn't seem like the right time to push that topic, though.

He continued bristling next to me, but he at least stopped growling. Not wanting him to ruin my date, I shifted my focus back to Scarlett, wanting to make sure we were still okay. "Is it rude to ask what you are when I can't tell you what I am?"

"I'll show you later." She beamed back at me, clearly doubling down on our plan to go back to my place after. A tension in me that I hadn't realized I was holding was released. We were still good, even with the secret out in the open. I couldn't help but grin back at her like a love-struck fool.

It took only a few more seconds before I realized the full impact of her knowing. I didn't have to hide my paranormal life from her; I could even talk to her about it. Our relationship had a much better shot at working out now.

"Hello, here is the Chateau D'Yuvore." The server broke the tension at the table as he poured me a small sample. Chad's eyebrows rose at the wine, but he didn't say anything.

I didn't know much about wine, but it wasn't spoiled, so I gave her a nod and she poured each of us a portion before setting it down in the bucket next to the table.

"I do hope you enjoy the wine, but I'm afraid that before I take your orders, I have one unpleasant reminder I must voice on behalf of the owner." She fixed her focus on Chad. "The owner would like to remind you that violence in her establishment will be met harshly." Our server bared her fangs for a moment before the polite server facade slipped back over her face. "Now that that unpleasantness is settled, what can I get for all of you?"

We took turns ordering, and Scarlett jabbed at Jadelyn to whisper something in her ear while I was ordering. Chad ordered a porterhouse while Scarlett ordered a filet and Jadelyn the halibut. I joined Scarlett with another filet with blue cheese on top. It was hard to pass that up.

"So, has Morgana narrowed down what you are yet?" Jadelyn started the conversation back up after the server left.

"Sort of. She has a guess, but it is a little embarrassing." I took a sip of wine to try to hide the awkwardness.

"Oh, come on. I'll tell you if you tell me?" Scarlett's added excitement made me almost want to spill right there, but I wasn't sure I wanted to tell Chad and Jadelyn yet.

"Later, when we are alone." I deepened my voice on the alone, enjoying the small shiver that spread across her body. The corner of her lips quirked up as she offered me her hand across the table again. I took it and let my rough thumb run over her soft knuckles.

Jadelyn smiled at the two of us. "You two are just too cute together. Scar has been gushing about her new guy. I just didn't realize it was you."

"Jade." Scarlett batted at her friend. "Girl talk stays in the house."

I didn't mind. It was nice to know that Scarlett was as into me as I was her. But the mention of the house told me they were also sorority sisters.

"What good are friends for if you can't tease them?" Jadelyn smiled, taking a sip of her wine.

I looked over at Chad, who had his phone out and was texting at the table. My smile faltered for a second, and Jadelyn noticed. She went to chastise him, but I gave her a small kick under the table. If he wanted to exclude himself from the conversation, I didn't mind. He never seemed to have much to contribute anyway.

She got the message, suppressing a chuckle as we continued chatting.

"So, how is it working for Morgana?" Scarlett asked. "I've heard a lot about her, but there are a lot of rumors." There was an interest in Scarlett's eyes that almost seemed like she looked up to the vampiress.

"Don't know what you've heard. She's been great so far. Although, I'd say that even if it wasn't true. I'm fairly certain she can hear just about anything said in this bar, or at least it seems like it." I looked over my shoulder at the balcony again, but I didn't see even a hint of her this time.

The girls followed where I was looking, but both came away as empty-handed as I had. "She's pretty badass."

"I got to drive her jag yesterday." I remembered the harrowing drive in a positive light after surviving.

"Yeah?" Scarlett leaned forward. "That sounds amazing. I bet it felt like you had a monster under you."

"Something like that. We were tracking down the vans..." I paused, my eyes trailing over to Jadelyn to see if she was okay with me telling this story.

Jadelyn waved away my concern. "I'm not offended." She looked over at Scarlett. "They were the vans that had kidnapped Kelly and me. We would have been so screwed if Chad hadn't been able to get to us." Her face softened slightly as she looked over at the werewolf, who was engrossed in his phone.

I paused, not sure what to do with that. If it helped their relationship, I didn't want to blow it up. But I also didn't like that Chad was taking credit for more than was his due. Unfortunately, I wasn't able to slip the look off my face fast enough, Jadelyn catching it.

Her head pivoted slightly, a question in her eyes. I tried to cover it up and wave it away, taking a sip of my wine to avoid having to say anything, but she didn't let it go.

"What, Zach?" Based on the look on her face as she said it, Jadelyn was going to wait until I spilled.

Sighing, I looked over at Chad, who still didn't seem to have a clue about what was going on in our conversation. As I played with the decision to tell her, I ultimately decided she had a right to know, especially when she wasn't yet actually tied down to him.

"Well, like I was saying, we were chasing after you both. And we found you at the factory. We took down the men keeping you in the fridge, and then I guarded you both while Morgana did her thing, slaying the drug workers. She got a lot of them. Brent and the pack took care of the rest when they arrived."

I waited as she processed that information. When she looked up again, I finished it off. "But"—I nodded towards Chad to avoid getting his attention—"just arrived at the very end, after it was all settled. He took you from the freezer and carried you away."

A small gasp from Scarlett indicated that my news would not go over well. I looked at Jadelyn, who looked completely pissed. Her eyes pulsed silver for just a second.

"I see." Her voice was level and cold.

"Look, I'm sorry. You two seem to be in a better place, and I didn't want to mess that up. But you deserve to know."

Jadelyn shook her head. "Never feel like telling the truth is trouble."

Chad put down his phone as another jock came up to the table and put down a little baggie of white powder. Just seeing it, even if it wasn't V-phoria, gave me the chills. One unpleasant night had been enough. I had no desire to be anywhere near it, and I had a feeling Morgana would be massively pissed if she knew this was going down in her club.

The jock jerked his head up in greeting and walked away.

"What the hell was that?" Jadelyn whisper-hissed at Chad, who seemed to notice her again. I had no idea how a guy could spend his time on the phone when he was across from such a beauty.

Chad and Jadelyn broke their brief stare off, and he held the baggie up. "New drug. It is supposed to be a fantastic time. Really enhances how IT feels." He bobbed his brow suggestively.

Jadelyn's face actually curled with disgust. "Don't even try it. You know my family's rules. If you think you can have me before marriage, you can also expect my father to have you hunted down and killed."

His nostrils flared, and Scarlett's nails dug into my palm, causing me to look up at her. She looked ready to fight.

But Chad calmed down and turned to me, like I was going to be his lifeline. He didn't know that I was holding back my own anger that he'd take a drug that could cause so much trouble for the para and human worlds.

"Have you tried this stuff? It's supposed to be amazing. Supposed to pump up shifters." He dangled the bag between us in an offering.

"No interest. That's V-phoria, right?"

He nodded, a cold grin spreading across his face. "You've heard of it." His tone took on that salesman quality.

"Yeah, no thanks. You shouldn't do that either. I saw what it did to some wolves in the factory we busted; it made them into freaks." The images of the grotesque transformations of the wolves the night before came to mind. I was half-tempted to grab the bag and flush it.

But Chad just chuckled, arrogance in the tone. "You saw pussy omegas use it. A real wolf is nothing like them."

"The council put out warnings about this stuff, Chad. You should reconsider." Jadelyn pushed a deep frown on her forehead.

"The council does what the council thinks is in their best interests. I bet they'd say the same thing if the drug gave wolves an advantage too." He gave the rest of the table a toothy grin that would have looked more appropriate as a wolf, baring their fangs.

I had to wonder if he'd been hit in the head, or if he always made wolfen gestures when he wasn't shifted. Remembering how the drug had messed with the pack magic I'd seen before, I tried to focus on my right eye. I was curious if I could push it into shifting to see his pack magic. But it didn't come. Instead, I just felt Scarlett's hand squeeze my own.

Lost in my own world for a moment, I realized she was trying to get my attention. The other two at the table were glaring at each other, the tension thick enough to cut with a knife.

"Hello. Which of you ordered the halibut?" A server kicked out a collapsible stand and set down a platter with four steaming dishes. They smelled fantastic, and the tension at our table broke.

"I'm the halibut." Jadelyn raised her hand.

"Filets here." I pointed between me and Scarlett.

"That just leaves the porterhouse here." The server put the last plate down in front of Chad. "Now, the plates are very hot, please be careful and enjoy." The server collapsed their stand and made their way back to the kitchen.

Scarlett's eyes were wide as she looked over at me. "Zach, you are going to burn yourself."

I realized I'd rested my hands on the edge of the plate, but it actually felt pretty good. "Oh. Whoops, guess it isn't really that hot." I lifted my wrists to show her that I hadn't burnt myself and dug in.

Conversation died down as our silverware clicked against plates. The filet was absolutely to die for and seemed to have only needed seasoning with salt and pepper. Cooked perfectly, the meat was so flavorful on its own that it needed little else.

I thought for a moment about that room in the Atrium that Morgana had given me. If I stayed here, would I get to eat this every night?

"This is amazing." Scarlett leaned back, chewing with her eyes closed, enjoying the filet.

"It would be so much better with a little pick-me-up." He dangled the bag over the center of the table again, trying to offer it to Scarlett.

"Chad. I said no. Scarlett, don't touch that." Jadelyn sounded like she was ordering Scarlett, and I found it bothered me.

"Wasn't going to. I don't think that's going to make the night better," Scarlett agreed. "Chad, maybe it's time you left."

"I think so too," Jadelyn agreed.

"Fine. Let's go." Chad pushed himself back from the table and stuffed the baggie of powder in his pocket with one hand while he extended the other to Jadelyn.

"No, I think you should spend a night on your own." She stayed seated, rooted to the seat by her posture. She hadn't even hesitated. I was glad she was starting to stand up for herself.

Chad's fist clenched tight, the veins on the back of his hand bulging with the promise of violence. My eyes narrowed. If he hit her, I was going to have to act.

"So be it. I'll remind you of this moment later. Maybe I'll have you tag along to my next fuck-a-bitch Friday." He said it in such a way that it made my blood curdle. I had to work hard to stay seated, focusing on my breathing.

"Right this way, sir." The server was there by our table immediately, gesturing for Chad to leave. I felt like I saw a glimmer of a blade tucked away in her apron, but I wasn't sure. Either way, Chad took the out he was offered and stormed away.

"Now, is there anything I can bring to help you three have a more pleasant evening?" As we shook our heads, the server bowed and drifted back to their job.

I let out a breath in a huff that I hadn't realized I'd been holding.

"Sorry. He's such an... alpha." Jadelyn gave us a fragile smile. I could see she still was bothered by his Friday night activities. He must have found out that she'd been told about them. I couldn't believe he'd brought it up just to bother her further.

"I don't want to ruin your date. I'll get going." Jadelyn stood to go, but Scarlett reached out and grabbed her arm.

"Wait a while? At least till we are confident that he's gone. Then you can call a driver to take you home." Scarlett coached her, and Jadelyn nodded with a small thanks and got back to her meal.

"I'm sorry again for ruining your date."

I waved it off. The last thing she needed was any more guilt. "Don't worry about it. I'm sorry your situation isn't turning out well."

"I knew he was an alpha, but hearing about it and... being part of it are just two different things." Her mouth twisted, and I could see her eyes water with unshed tears before she used her napkin to dab at her face. "Gosh, I'm being such a downer. Let's talk about happier things."

A bit of mischief entered her watering eyes as Jadelyn asked, "So, Zach, what's your favorite position?"

I nearly choked on my next piece of filet. "Uh, what?"

Jadelyn and Scarlett's giggles filled the room as they watched my face. The conversation eased back into something more comfortable after that, and we dug into our dinners.

CHAPTER 18

After dinner, I took Scarlett down to the lower levels of Bumps in the Night. Jadelyn had bowed out at that point, saying she needed to go do homework. I knew it was a lie, but I was thankful for the time alone with Scarlett.

The club had shifted around the time that we had wrapped up dinner. Downstairs, the club's other areas had come alive with bass beats bumping in the night. The warm lights had been dimmed, with the only dim lights illuminating the bars and the wall of alcohol a neutral white. Further into the club, cool black lights added mystery and darkened corners while the band kicked off some music.

I could see how it might be a safe space for the paranormal. Under the black lights, it was almost impossible to tell if you had pale, tan, or blue skin.

Scarlett eagerly led me out onto the dance floor with a smile, quickly shifting herself against me and dancing in my arms. It felt so good to hold her close, leaning into her and enjoying the smell of her cloves and vanilla perfume.

She rocked against me as I ran my hands along her body. Time seemed to float away as we forgot where we were or anybody who surrounded us. We moved our bodies to the beat of the music, enjoying the moment with each other.

I wasn't sure how much time had passed before she leaned in and whispered into my ear, "Take me home."

Quickly coming to full attention, I gave her a smile. Holding her arm, I took the brunt of the surrounding mob, pushing my way through the crowd towards the exit while she followed behind. I made sure to clear a path big enough for her to get through without issue.

Once we were through the dancing mob, it got easier to move. She looped her arm into mine, leaning against me slightly as we wove our way back out the front of the club. We exited into the night, the smells of the city greeting us once again.

A number of patrons were standing in line behind the velvet rope to the side, waiting for their turn to go in. Girls stood dressed together in skimpy clubwear, but what held my attention was the way the rainbow lights coming out of the club lit up Scarlett's skin, playing along the shadows of her curves. She was stunning, and she was mine for the night.

I was still smiling so wide when we got back to my place that I was worried I might get permanent wrinkles.

"You know, I expected worse," Scarlett said, looking around as she stepped into my apartment.

"I seem like a slob?" I teased.

She shrugged. "Not that. It's just, normally, college guys have super simple apartments. This one at least has some character." She slipped off her heels and put them by the door.

"Drink?" I asked, opening the fridge.

"Water if you have it. That wine was pretty dry."

"But it was nice, right? At least say it, so I can tell Morgana that you loved it." We both chuckled, knowing we didn't necessarily know the difference between it and a twelve-dollar bottle from the store.

I poured us both a glass and casually moved over to the couch, but Scarlett gave me a questioning look. "Is your roommate going to interrupt us?"

"Probably," I admitted. It didn't seem like Frank was around at the moment, but I figured he'd likely come back. He and Maddie seemed to like to spend their time at our place.

"Which room?" She danced through the apartment, poking about.

"This one." I opened my door and gave her an exaggerated gesture inward.

She dipped in a small curtsy. "Thank you, Mister Pendragon." She drawled out my last name in an English accent.

"Oh please. I've gotten enough jokes about my name." I paused, realizing that if I told Scarlett what Morgana and I thought I was, she'd be the first I had ever told. "Actually. About my name..."

"What about it?" She went over to my little collection of gold and looked at it before checking out my closet.

"Do you have to be so nosey?" I rolled my eyes and sat down on the bed, not minding so much that I got a chance to watch her from behind while she snooped around in her dress.

She ignored my comment, continuing to open random drawers. "My father is a detective, and in case you haven't picked up on it, I work for Jadelyn. I help with security around her most of the time. So, yes. I'm not going to pass this opportunity up and scope you out."

"Really?"

"Which part?"

"All of it, I guess. Mostly the security for Jadelyn." I hadn't really been expecting that, but it explained why the two of them were close. I had a feeling Jadelyn would be around quite a bit if I continued things with Scarlett.

Scarlett nodded, her hair bouncing with the motion. "My family has worked for hers for generations. And what I am has an ability that is very useful for scouting."

"And what would that be?" I asked, taking a sip to hide my curiosity.

Scarlett looked over her shoulder with a smoldering look. "Promise to tell me what you think you are?"

I nodded in agreement. In response, two fox ears that matched her hair popped up on her head. Little white tufts accented the tips. But what got my attention even more was when two tails swirled around her back with tips like they'd been dipped in black ink.

"Fox?" I asked, the two tails throwing me off.

"That's my last name, but my family are Kitsune," she answered, her tails swirling in a pattern that was particularly entrancing.

I said the only thing I could remember about them. "I thought they were Asian?" I wanted to take it back the second it came out of my mouth, but it was already done.

An exasperated huff told me that it was indeed the wrong thing to say. "No. My family is Irish." She bounced her hair in her hands for emphasis.

"Huh, so what's the ability?" I asked.

She smirked, and her tails made shapes behind. Soon, she blurred and there were suddenly three Scarletts in my room. They spoke one word after the other but changed which one was speaking with each word. "We can make very real illusions. Limited to the number of tails we have."

Ah, so one of them was real, while the other two were illusions.

"Woah. I can see how that comes in handy."

One of the Scarletts disappeared, and on my bed was a giant chest of glittering gold.

"Touch it."

I did, hefting the gold. It felt real in my hand. However, when I grabbed the chest and tried to heft it, there was no weight, and the illusion shattered in a puff.

The two Scarletts sat on either side of me on the bed. "It's tricky. You can confuse sight, sound, and even smell. But touch is super tricky. The illusions can trick you into holding it, thinking you feel something small, but there's never any weight."

The Scarlett to my right leaned in for a kiss, but when I went to lift her into my lap, she disappeared in a puff. The other Scarlett tittered at my side as her tails flicked around, brushing against my back. She let out a small giggle. "Sorry. It was too tempting."

"You are amazing. And here I thought I was something cool. After seeing that, just being strong and durable doesn't seem so impressive. Oh, and I can breathe fire, which is probably my coolest ability."

Her eyebrows bounced up to her hairline. "Breathe fire?"

Taking a deep breath, I braced for her reaction. "Morgana thinks I'm a dragon. All the signs point there too." I expected some doubt, but I got none.

Instead, her mouth dropped open and her tails went completely still, like a critter before a greater predator. Finally, she spoke in a hushed whisper. "Please tell me that's a joke."

I shook my head, wishing I could do something right now to prove it. "How do you absorb mana?"

"My tails. It's why they swish around most of the time. I run them through the air to collect more."

Reaching out to touch one of her tails, I waited for permission. She nodded, and I brought it to my chest. I had no idea if it would work, but based on what Morgana had said about dragons generating mana, it seemed like a possibility. I hoped that my heartbeat gave out enough mana that maybe she could sense it.

Scarlett gasped, and her second tail came over and rubbed against my chest. "I can feel it. It's coming off of you in waves. Zach, do you know what this means?!" Her voice grew louder with each word.

"Probably not fully at this point," I chuckled. "But Morgana has told me some. I know that my kind is rare and looked after for the mana we pump into the world."

"And sought after or even hunted! Your body is a magical treasure trove capable of making the most profound magical items." Her tails rested against my chest, rubbing slowly. I guessed that the mana coming off of me felt good, but there was worry on her face.

I nodded with her. "I know. Don't worry, I'm being careful. And I still have a lot further to go to figure this all out."

When she paused, I figured I might as well hit her with the other big event happening to me. "There's something else I should tell you, too. I have a duel with Simon in the morning."

"The douchey elf?" She barked a laugh, her cute button nose wrinkling. "Are you kidding me? What a freaking idiot. He picked a fight with a dragon!" At least she was far more confident than I was. "Holy crap, the peak of stupidity."

"Scarlett, I might be a dragon, but I'm not much of one. Morgana is working with me, but besides doing a few things when I get upset. I can't control it at all."

Her laughter cut off sharply. "Then cancel the duel."

I shook my head. I knew Morgana would have done that if she could. "Can't. I offended him apparently enough for him to get the council to agree."

"Do they know you are a dragon?" Concern was etched on her face.

"No. Only Morgana, and now you know." I smiled, stroking her tails and wanting to comfort her, but I found them comforting myself.

Scarlett's face was cute as she tried to puzzle through options. "Parents? If a full-grown dragon shows up, that'll really make it hard for them."

"Died when I was a kid."

She gave me that familiar pitying look. "Oh, I didn't know. I'm so sorry for bringing it up."

I played with her tail, stroking it. "I was too little to remember anything. The people that raised me were great."

As I did a particular stroke on her tail, Scarlett bit her lip. "Mmm, that feels good. I'm really questioning this no sex on the first date nonsense I said earlier."

I laughed. "What? No confidence in me? I've been training with Morgana. If I have anything to say, there will be a second date." I pulled her into my lap and looked her in the eyes. "There's no way I'm missing out on more of this." The conviction in my own voice was powerful enough to give me more confidence.

Scarlett smirked, and her eyes shone with mischief before she kissed me on the cheek and leaned past me to whisper in my ear. "For the record, there's no rule on the second date."

The beast slipped loose for a moment, and I growled, pulling her tightly against me and kissing her. I had watched her lips all night long, and they felt as good as I could have hoped. Her pillowy lips parted, and we locked together, crushing our bodies as we let out all the pent-up sexual tension from the night of dinner and dancing. Our sexual chemistry exploded in a torrent as we tried to smother each other with our lips.

I ended up pushing her down on the bed and rolling on top of her. She broke the kiss first, her hands on my chest and her tails battering me playfully.

"First date rule," she said.

A growl escaped my chest in response, and she laughed, her face blushing. "Growl for me more. It's kind of hot."

We went back to making out on my bed, tumbling about a bit in frustration that we were both remaining clothed. After a long while, we both laid next to each other, staring into each other's eyes as we breathed heavily from our tumble.

"So, dragon," she said again, like she couldn't believe it. "Do you have a horde? Oh, my gosh. You are going to have so many women. Do you have other women?"

I chuckled. "Hold up. So many questions. No, I don't have a horde." Then my eyes flicked over to the jars of gold flakes and the several lumps of rare metal sitting on my shelves.

"Wait, is that real gold?" Her eyes shined with a smile. "You have the start of a horde."

I paused, realizing I did. I'd never thought of it like that before. But the idea of putting mine and my father's vial of gold together in a pile of other metals appealed to me and the beast. "Okay, maybe I do. I just never realized it. Next question."

"Other women?"

"None. I've been studying for medical school and working on the weekends. I haven't had time to date."

She traced my chest with a finger. "And yet you had time this weekend?"

"Of course. For you, I made time. I decided it was about time to use those sick days." I kissed her again, but it was full of adoration rather than the raw passion that had consumed us earlier.

Her tails picked up the pace at which they batted me; it was a small tell that she was getting excited. "Careful, dragon, you might just sweep me off my feet. Will there be other women?"

I opened my mouth to say 'no,' but the way the beast thrashed in my chest and the words Morgana had said before came back to me. "Honestly, I don't know. Morgana speaks of it like it is an inevitability, and the beast in my chest wants it. So I can't promise you'll be the only one, but you have my full focus right now."

She nodded, smiling up at me. "Thanks for not lying. I'd rather know the truth. It's not that uncommon in the para world. There're different types of relationships. What is 'the beast'?"

I paused, not really sure how to touch on that topic. "So, as a preface, I didn't have any paranormal attributes before a few days ago. Morgana thinks something held the dragon part of me back. Along with that, my dragon instincts feel like something separate from me. They are there." My eyes drifted back to the gold on the shelf. "Present in small ways, but I call them 'the beast'. It almost feels like a physical thing at times."

There was a flicker of concern in her eyes. "Some paras talk about their 'other halves', so it isn't that strange. But I don't know what that's like. Everything comes naturally for me, even peeking about in my date's closet for used condom wrappers."

I put a palm to my face. "Please tell me that's not what you were looking for."

She put on a practiced face of pure innocence and shrugged into the bed. "I blame having a detective for a father."

I paused, putting two and two together. "Detective Fox?"

"Yeah." She took in my face. "Oh no. Please tell me he didn't come pester you. Wait, no, he doesn't know about you yet. There's no way."

I held up my hand to forestall anything else. "No, after Chad attacked me on campus, he came around asking if there was anything to report."

"Oh. Okay. Yeah, he does that. Works to quell any rumors of paranormal activity." She blew out a breath of relief. "But he will probably snoop around you at some point as we keep dating. I'm just warning you now: he's nosey."

"Says the girl who looked for condom wrappers in my closet?"

She laughed and rolled over onto her back. "I can't believe I'm dating a dragon."

"You can't believe it? I can't believe I am a dragon, much less dating such a cute kitsune."

Scarlett narrowed her eyes at me before batting them. "Mmm, I love when you compliment me."

We devolved into some more kissing before finally I drifted off to sleep with my clothes still on and her tails brushing against my chest.

***

I woke up to an empty bed and felt the spot next to me. It was cool; she'd been out of the bed for some time.

Disappointment crept in. I had been looking forward to seeing her again in the morning, but I still had the happy butterflies of the night before swirling in my stomach. Even Chad hadn't been able to ruin our incredible first date.

And today I had other problems. I'd need to dig deep to try to get through the duel.

I came out of my room in my previous night's clothes, my brain still a bit groggy. As I headed to get some coffee from the kitchen, I realized I was hearing two girls giggling in it.

"Morning, Zach. I was just getting to know Scarlett." Maddie sat in the kitchen, next to Scarlett, who was wearing one of my sweatshirts like a dress. A bit of flour smudged her on her nose.

"Hope you don't mind me borrowing your clothes." Scarlett smiled, and I felt my emotions buoy up, like a balloon filling up and lifting off.

The carton of blueberry muffin mix was to her side, opened up. I smiled. "No problem at all. I see you sniffed out the muffin mix."

"Funny you had that on hand." She tapped at her lip in play. "Maddie, do they normally keep muffin mix on hand?"

"I've never seen either of them use the oven besides to make a pizza." Maddie joined in on the act. "Why? Do you like muffins?"

"Love them. I think I mentioned it the other day. Huh. Odd." They both enjoyed my discomfort as they continued the byplay.

I grumbled past both of them, heading over to the coffee machine before Scarlett's hand caught my arm, giving a soft tug towards her. "Come here and give me a good morning kiss. The muffins will be done soon."

Stepping around Maddie, I collected Scarlett and gave her a long kiss, inhaling her scent of vanilla and cloves. The beast curled around the smell, satisfied with itself, calming down. I wondered for a second what the beast would do if I let something happen to this relationship.

"You two are too cute," Maddie said, pouring out coffee into another cup for me.

I didn't even test to see how hot it was, drinking my morning pick-me-up as quickly as I could.

"Zach, be careful. That's hot," Maddie reminded me, but Scarlett just looked curiously with a smile before nodding at something to herself.

"It isn't that bad." Scarlett helped cover, sipping her own coffee far more carefully.

I looked around, but my roommate was nowhere to be seen. "Is Frank here?"

"Still sleeping. The lazy bones stays up all night with sex and then can't be bothered to get up."

It was everything I could do to not snort into my coffee. "Please. No details. I don't want to think about Frank naked." It was terribly amusing that Frank was the one that ended up all tired out. Apparently, Maddie could keep up with Frank.

Maddie started to open her mouth, but she was interrupted by the oven timer dinging. I was thankful for the distraction. Maddie was definitely going to give more details just to mess with me.

"Move, move. Muffins take priority." Scarlett shooed both of us away and took out the baking pan. We must have had it in the apartment, but I couldn't think of a single time we'd used one in the two years I'd lived with Frank.

"Here, try one." She stabbed into one and cut off a piece with the knife before handing it to me.

I popped it in my mouth, suppressing a small groan. It was amazing. Fluffy and moist, almost as good as a piece of cake. "This is great," I said with the food still in my mouth.

Maddie got a piece too. "That came from a box?"

"Not exactly. Luckily, you had the secret ingredient for muffins: soda."

Maddie shook her head. "They are really good. Sorry I doubted you."

Scarlett whirled on Maddie and pointed at her, waiting until she had both of our attention before she spoke. "Never doubt me when it comes to my muffins."

Chapter 19

Scarlett walked next to me, her arm looped into mine as she peered up. "You've got this."

She'd been repeating encouragements throughout our walk to Bumps in the Night. I wasn't sure if it was for me or herself, but it was nice to hear, regardless.

As we walked up, I was struck by how different it looked in the light of day from the night. All the scuffs and imperfections were easier to see, worn and showing the building's history.

In the strobe lights and darkness, it hid the imperfections at night, just like the paranormals that frequented the bar at night. As we walked in, they were all sitting around in plain sight, playing cards or eating a meal. You'd think that was dangerous, but who would go into a nightclub during the day?

"Hello, Zach. And you must be Scarlett! I do hope you enjoyed last night." Morgana came down from her balcony with a little teasing smile on her face. She gave Scarlett a kind smile before her focus shifted to me, her face becoming serious. "Ready for the fight?"

"You talk about it as if it isn't a big deal. It's a fight to the death, Morgana." I met her at the bottom of the stairs. Scarlett followed close to my side.

"Maybe I wouldn't mind either outcome after you sunk my jag in the Delaware River." She shrugged and managed to say it with a straight face. A part of me paused as she held it, but then she broke into a big smile. "Though maybe I did have some involvement in that cop chase before I ditched you with the car. Really, it's hard to say who is fully to blame." I gave her a look, letting her know just who I thought was to blame.

Scarlett looked between the two of us. "Wait, I saw that on the news. That was you?"

I sighed. "Yes. Morgana and I were chasing after the pack that had kidnapped Jadelyn. Morgana jumped out of the car and told me to lose the cops. But she did not say anything about needing to return the car in one piece, so I think I was totally within the bounds of my instructions." I gave Morgana a look, waiting to see if she took the bait.

"Semantics. But it's true. That's why I didn't take it out of your cut. Cost of doing business, I suppose. At least that one wasn't a rare model."

I tried not to think too deeply about the fact that Morgana talked about losing the expensive car like I would talk about ruining a shirt.

"So, what do I need to know about this duel? I'm not feeling totally prepared." I started making my way to the back of the club. I had a feeling the Atrium would be our means to get to wherever the duel was taking place.

"Right. Do you want to help, Scarlett?" I appreciated that Morgana made the effort to include her in the conversation.

Scarlett hesitated before seeming to decide. "Here are the basic rules. Each participant gets to choose their own weapon. You have to take off your shirt to show you aren't wearing any armor, but you can wear enchanted items. And that's really about it. From there, you fight to the death, and anything goes really." She looked to Morgana for more information. "I've only seen one. I'm not really an expert."

"Simon is over a hundred years old. So he's skilled enough that you have no hope of winning in the skill department. Imagine fighting me with a sword if I was really trying to kill you. That's what you're going up against."

That did not paint a pretty picture. Was I screwed? "What weapon should I choose?"

"He'll choose a sword. Almost every elf is trained in the sword as part of our early education. You don't happen to have any hidden skills with a weapon?"

I shook my head, trying to stay optimistic, but the ability to do that was fading by the moment.

"Grab the mace then. The spikey end should go into his skull if you can manage it."

A snort came from Scarlett over my shoulder. "Sorry," she added sheepishly.

"It's okay. I think I can handle that. Spikey mace to the face."

"Simon won't be a pushover. If you have the chance to grapple with him, that's your best bet. Throw down your weapon if you have a chance to grab him and pull him to the ground. Once you are grappling, he'll still have skill, but your strength has a much better chance of overpowering him."

We had continued our way through Bumps in the Night, reaching the Atrium. Morgana opened a door we'd gone through before, and I found myself back in the council chamber in the lower circle that was scuffed and burnt.

Jadelyn was there already, smiling and coming to give me a hug. "Thank you for standing up for me; I'm sorry that you got tangled in this duel. Don't forget that bracer if it can protect you." She put her hand to my arm where the metal bracer sat under my suit jacket.

I nodded in thanks, and she turned to Scarlett. "Did you give him a good time before he goes off to battle?"

Scarlett rolled her eyes, swatting Jadelyn away. Pausing before they headed off, Scarlett walked up and wrapped her arms around me, pressing her body against me as she gave me a deep kiss. It was a little awkward with the others around, but I savored it anyway, not sure if we'd get more dates.

When she finished, Jadelyn gave a little whistle, earning herself another half-glare from Scarlett. Both girls dissolved into whispers and giggles as they walked away to where the council sat along the top.

I looked around. It seemed like we'd gotten to the site a bit early. Not everybody was there yet. We waited for a bit down at the floor level before a member came over, giving me a brief greeting as they headed up to their seat. It felt more like a spectator sport as they all jostled for front row seats.

Unlike last time, more than the council was showing up; it seemed like it must be open to the public.

I was more than a little nervous, which only increased when I saw the next two people who came through the doors. "Hello, Rupert, Detective Fox."

Rupert gave me a slow nod and then looked up to his daughter and Scarlett. "I hear Scarlett was with you last night."

The detective beside him narrowed his eyes at me in a way that only a protective father could.

"I want you to understand that the Fox family works for us, and our safety will always take priority for them," Rupert said.

Detective Fox nodded in agreement, eyeing me for a moment before he spoke. "I have no reason to object to you dating my daughter. And as long as it stays that way, you are welcome to pursue her. But you will always be second to Jadelyn. Always."

It felt like they were trying to chase me off. They were likely used to Chad and other alpha types that couldn't handle not being first in everything. I'd definitely had her full attention the night before, and her whispers of even more attention on our second date. They wouldn't chase me away from her so easily. She already felt like mine.

Up on the balcony, Scarlett was glaring at her father as he walked up. She looked between her father and me, clearly curious about what we'd talked about. Jadelyn nudged her, and they went back to whispering back and forth. Jadelyn seemed more like her best friend than anything else from the way they interacted.

"Do not worry about that right now. They were in very poor form to talk to a combatant like that. I do hope they remember those words when they discover what you are," Morgana said from my side. "Just think about everyone's face when you win. I cannot wait. I haven't been this excited in a long time. It's difficult to get one over on the elves."

I nodded absently, my mind wandering all over as I greeted a few more people. I paused, realizing one face I hadn't seen. "Is Brent or someone from his pack coming?"

Morgana shook her head slowly. "It would seem not, because here comes Simon."

Simon came up, wearing something like a martial arts gi, but it was too long. It was more like a gi mixed with a wizard's robe. With him were several elves who looked past their prime, which meant they were old as dirt.

"Greetings, challenged. Both of you may enter the arena," one of the older elves spoke. His face twisted in disgust as he noticed Morgana. "Morgana, please join us to watch the duel."

"Of course." She nodded before giving me one last look. "Just remember."

"Yep. Mace to the face." I laughed, but it showed my nerves.

Morgana didn't laugh, instead looking me in the eye and saying, "You can do this. I didn't put all this work and food into you for nothing." She winked as she turned to head up with the rest to view.

In that moment, I felt truly on my own for the first time since entering the para world. It was a surreal moment. The training wheels had fallen off, and I was hurtling down a hill. I was about to find out if I could stay upright or crash down into the asphalt.

"Inside." Simon jerked his head. His punchable elven face was neutral. He was taking it seriously, and I needed to too.

"Participants. Today we have a duel to settle an altercation that started with one Zach, a lost one new to our world, who physically challenged Simon Greenleaf." Apparently, Jadelyn's father was hosting this duel, as his voice continued to ring out across the arena.

"Our traditions are what keep us from descending into barbarism, and they must be upheld. A duel to the death has been issued in response to the altercation." He looked back at his daughter, who nodded firmly. "Given that the offender was new to our culture, I would like to offer one last time to withdraw from this situation and work it out through other means."

Rupert surprised me with that. I hadn't thought he'd try to help me get out of the duel at the last moment. I had a feeling Jadelyn and Scarlett, who were on the edges of their seats, had some influence in that decision.

"We of the elven council have considered the matter, and we can certainly be reasonable within the circumstances. If the offender removes his own arm, we will consider this behind us." The elf nodded, while murmurs of agreement sounded around him from the other elves.

"What?" It burst out of me before I could hold the exclamation in check. By the stares I got, it was in poor form, but I didn't care. I'd literally stood up in front of another para, and they thought a fair punishment would be to remove an arm?

"I will not cut off my arm. All I did was to stand as he spewed insults. Offer declined." A growl entered the last bit of my statement, my beast beginning to rise.

The elves glared daggers down at me. I had a feeling that, if looks could kill, I'd be coughing blood. But there were a few murmurs in the crowd from the non-elves that seemed more on my side. I caught one person close by murmuring. 'Heavy handed even for them.'

Morgana had chosen not to sit in a seat, instead sitting on the lip of the raised platform, her legs dangling down. Her voice projected out as she smiled up at the audience. "I'll give the elves a counteroffer. If you kill Simon's father for teaching him so poorly, we'll voluntarily withdraw. I think when this is done, you'll be surprised."

Damn, Morgana could bluff.

"Ludicrous!" the elves shouted, their eyes raging. "This duel goes on. And on a personal note, I hope you soon crawl back into whatever demon hole you came out of, Morgana. Your entire family should be dug up from their root tree for their impurities."

Morgana was still, but it was as if the room had just plunged into a polar vortex. I didn't get the whole meaning of what he'd said without knowing the importance of the root tree, but it was clear that it was something that went deep in elven heritage.

Rupert slammed down on the stone lip, getting everyone's attention. "It would seem no concessions are to be made here today. I see

Simon has a weapon already. Zach, would you like a weapon of your choice?"

"A mace," I said, remembering Morgana's last-minute advice. I guess it was time. I shucked off my shirt and folded it in the corner, hoping I'd be back for it.

Someone I didn't recognize approached and tossed the weapon down. It bounced off the stone floor, and I scooped it up, hefting it in one hand.

"This is a fight to the death, but mercy may be granted at surrender. Attempting to climb out of the ring or use the exit will be considered forfeit, and your life surrendered. Bow to each other, for you should always respect your opponent, lest they get the better of you."

Turning back, Simon had his robe off his shoulders and hanging from his waist right there, along with a gleaming sword. Simon did a flourish and bowed at the waist quickly, while I just did a quick bob like one of Morgana's servants.

"Fight."

At that single word, Simon flowed across the arena, not wasting a second. His sword flashed dangerously towards my chest. There was no doubt, no hesitation as he struck to take my life.

I stumbled backwards, trying to get enough room for the mace to be effective, swinging up hard.

His sword dinged as the two weapons struck, but the sound was so soft, so light, that it didn't even surprise me as it danced around my mace and swept towards me again.

Simon held one hand behind his back in a fencer's stance as his sword continued to weave forward. I remembered Jadelyn's bracer, and while still holding my mace, I grabbed my other wrist, bringing up the magical shield in time for his sword to scrape the edge.

I pushed forward, using the shield like a battering ram.

For the first time, Simon had to go on the defensive and stepped back, rapidly trying to circle around me. I continued using the shield to batter him away.

"I see," was all Simon said as he made space between the two of us. I was glad to find that he wasn't quite as fast as Morgana, but he still moved with a quick grace and a speed that would be beyond the top of human capability.

He reminded me the next moment of what made elves supernatural. "Invoktis." He swished his sword and a small whirlwind sprung up between us and engulfed me.

Once again, I cursed at my lack of mass as the wind picked me up and spun me for just a second. The moment was long enough to feel a sting creep along my back with a new cut as Simon struck in my moment of disorientation.

I landed, growling at him. The beast hadn't appreciated the dizzying spell or the cut. It was angry, and it was ready for blood.

"What are you?" Simon asked, looking at me growl. "Some kind of animal? Be civil or I'll sever your head right here."

Something wasn't quite right, though. He had made every effort to end this quickly from the start. It didn't fit with the shallow wound I felt in my back. He had had a chance to end me.

I saw the slightest glimpse of uncertainty on his face now. "You couldn't cut that deep," I said aloud, realizing it in that moment. He didn't have the same strength as Morgana or a werewolf.

"Your blood isn't limitless," he snorted. "Invoktis."

I expected another whirlwind, but I was shot backwards by the same spell he had hit me with that day in the club. Slamming against the back wall of the arena, I could smell my own blood. I stood up, guessing I'd left behind a smear of blood on the wall, but I ignored it.

Once again, I raised the magical shield in time to deflect his next attack. Pushing off the wall, I charged him, scooping him up on the shield and plowing forward.

He rolled off my shield at a strange angle and came down on his feet to my side, his sword flashing dangerously before it tore at my ribs. I felt pain, but I could confirm my suspicions. His blade wasn't able to sink more than skin deep. He did, however, manage a foot-long cut along my ribs.

My body clarified that, while not deep, the cut was not pleasant, as pain lanced up my side, and I was slow to bring the mace up for the next attack. As a result, the hit caught dangerously close to my fingers.

I could feel the beast prowling in my chest, but something was wrong. It was holding back, almost like it had decided to sit this one out. That was not okay with me, and the last thing I needed was my beast to throw some sort of fit. I tried to channel it and focus on my draconic instincts, but it did nothing.

It watched the fight angrily as I took small losses again and again. I was slowly being worn down. Simon's skill, plus his ability to disorient and toss me around with his magic, was a lot to keep up against.

My toughness was all that kept me on my feet as he expertly carved my torso with dozens of cuts. It didn't matter that I was several times stronger than Simon. It meant nothing if every strike I managed to get in was expertly parried.

The crowd was quiet up in the stands, and I couldn't bear to look up and see Scarlett. I couldn't see the loss in her eyes. I knew I looked like a mess, and everything was pointing in Simon's favor.

I tried to draw up the heat I'd felt before in my own gut. The only move I had remaining was to cook him alive, as I'd done to so many of my enemies up to this point. I desperately wanted to surprise him with a gout of fire to the face, but my breath was only warm with my own exertion. The dragon had failed me. For whatever reason, the beast had abandoned me.

Still, I was strong and durable to where Simon was panting and looking like he might just wear himself out if this kept up. That would be just fine with me.

Simon stepped back, and I expected another spell. But he drew out a flute from his pocket and breathed deep before putting it up to his mouth. There was no warning before the circle filled with fire.

Orange flames wrapped around me, cutting off everything else. But the heat almost called to me. Morgana had always said that one of the most important things was knowing what you were fighting. And Simon hadn't a clue of what I was. Even if I couldn't breathe fire, it was still a part of what I was.

As those flames wrapped around me, my clothes burnt and my nostrils filled with smoke, but I felt like I was in a comfortable sauna. The flames didn't bother me one bit.

This was my chance. I knew I'd be hard to see in the flames and smoke. Summoning all the vigor I had left, I charged him one last time, reaching towards the source of the fire. I couldn't see him, but I knew the source must be coming from him and that damned flute.

When my hand caught something, I latched on with all my strength and squeezed. The crackle of bones under my hand was all that told me of success, my target still hard to make out within the flames.

The fire winked out, and I could see what I'd caught. Unfortunately, I hadn't gotten his throat, but I had crushed the bottom of his jaw.

I kept my momentum in the battle, reaching forward with my other arm and grabbing his shoulder, pulling him to me. I had confidence that, once I got him in a grapple, he was done for.

"Itotssss" His words came out a slur and only a scant breeze welled up around me, but it was nothing.

Pulling him down to the ground, I manhandled the elf who had caused me so much trouble. His sword clattered to the floor as I tossed him down on the stone floor. Showing my dominance in front of the arena of people made my beast sing in praise.

"STOP!" someone in the stands screamed just as I pulled him down and put my weight on him. I was seconds away from dismantling Simon, limb by limb.

The scream made me hesitate for just a moment. I went back to lifting his arm to pull it off as the wail continued.

"You will unhand my nephew! You will be fairly compensated for your win." Panic filled the elf's voice as the elf that had walked in with Simon stood, gripping the edge of the arena. Their face was bulging with tension veins.

I paused, not sure what would be the right move. My beast thrashed in my chest, angry at my hesitation.

But the distraction was enough to get my fiery blood to cool so that my brain was mine again. The beast had sat out during the fight, and now it had to deal with my decision.

"Zach," Morgana's voice came from the edge of the arena. "I'll support you in whatever decision you make, but know that, if you let him go, they won't miss or hurt from the money they owe you. This world is harsher than the one you know; you will need to show your resolve to keep it from wearing you down."

"Shut up, you stupid whore," the elf screamed, spittle flying from his mouth.

They clearly hated each other, and that only added to the complexity. Was I stepping deeper into a conflict I didn't belong in?

My eyes drifted up to Jadelyn, who smiled, but they quickly moved to Scarlett. Her opinion meant the most to me. I didn't want her to think me brutal if I finished this. But my beautiful woman just looked at me, drawing her thumb to her throat and slashing it across. Her message was clear, and I turned back to the task at hand.

Looking back down at Simon, making sure I didn't underestimate him at the moment, I decided it was high time to have a quick internal chat with my beast and see if we couldn't come to an understanding.

I felt crazy, but I talked to myself, to my beast. I... I need you, need you if I'm to survive here. I'll do my best to be more dragon-like, but if you ever abandon me like this again, I'm going to find a way to fucking lock you away. We are a team.

The beast in me seemed to consider for a moment before I felt what seemed to be like a nod of agreement.

That settled, I let my dragon instincts win. My fingers pinched into Simon's throat hard enough to tear flesh as I savagely ripped his throat out and roared up at the council. I put all the weight of my dragon heritage into my roar.

Everyone up in the council took a step back as the smell of fear washed heavily down from them. Whatever had just happened had struck a chord; not only physically, but there was something more to it. Like I had symbolically accepted more of myself. It definitely felt like a step forward towards my draconic heritage.

The beast settled, and I could feel it come more in tune with me. It was like a mantle was settling down over my shoulder and back.

A yell of rage came from the council above, and the elf who had spoken out raised his arms as a spell came to life in his hands. Before we could find out what he was casting, Morgana was there, cutting him across his face just before he released it.

"What a disgrace, moving against the clear victor in a council-sanctioned duel. I should challenge you and your family. Dig them up from their root tree for the disgrace you just displayed." Extra vehemence entered her tone as she spat a similar insult right back at him.

He clutched at his face, a mask of rage in the moment. "How dare you."

"Silence." Sebastian, who had spoken up at the council before, glared at both of them. "The duel is over. But as for you, you will regret making an enemy of the elves." The man spat at me and turned to leave, pulling Simon's uncle as he clutched his bleeding face.

Morgana turned down to me with a smile and a thumbs up.

I smiled back, pulling myself to my feet unsteadily. There was a blur of orange hair before Scarlett jumped down into the arena and wrapped a towel around me, kissing my cheek. She had dried tears on her face from where they must have been streaming down her face.

"I knew you'd pull through."

I rubbed away the tears, not liking them on her face. "I didn't mean to scare you. We can talk about it later. I was having... issues."

She shook her head hard, scattering her orange locks into my face before pulling my head down and kissing me again. "No, I should have trusted you."

We had a moment of quiet before others were around us, and it all became a bit of a blur. Congratulations were given by those who passed by me. Some were genuine, some were clearly faked, but all seemed more wary of me than they had when they'd entered. I was joining Morgana in my excitement at what their faces would look like if they knew I was a dragon.

As they left, my injuries began catching up with me, the pain growing as my adrenaline decreased, but I stayed standing as everybody left, barely.

Morgana kept watch, ensuring no other attackers came for me. Once the arena was empty, she walked over to me. "That was a very different man down there than the one that arrived at my bar only a few days ago."

I let that sink in.

I was changing. No longer was the top thing on my mind studying for the next exam. Whether by fate or chance, I had stepped into something completely out of the norm. It was a part of me, and it felt more natural than I would have expected.

Putting my arm around Scarlett, I started heading out with Morgana. A nagging thought circled in the back of my head as I remembered the few people I had expected to see that hadn't shown.

"Morgana, I think we should check on Brent. After what we saw those drugs do to the omega pack, I just have a terrible feeling."

She looked at me and gave a slow nod. "Of course. It sounds like you are starting to trust your instincts. Let's see if we can't get you patched up first and fed. I'll get someone to tell us where Brent is, and we can make a house call."

CHAPTER 20

Morgana paced behind the well-lit bar. Colored lights lit up the hundreds of liquor bottles from underneath, coloring them into a vivid red and attention pulling display. Even under the bright lights during the day, the bar was still the centerpiece of the bar.

I gnawed on a bone from the latest rack of ribs that had appeared in front of me. I was sitting up at the bar, watching Morgana as she hung up from yet another phone call. She turned and saw my expectant look.

"You know you can just get another portion. Gnawing hungrily on a bone will not help your hunger."

Putting the bone down, I paused, realizing that she was wrong. Gnawing on the bone had been pretty satisfying, though it had been more of a solution to boredom than hunger. I decided not to analyze that too deeply. "Any news on Brent's pack?"

"No. And that's the weirdest part. It is like they dropped off the map."

That concerned me. "Do you think something happened to them? Do packs have hideaways?"

I scratched at the scars on my back. Morgana had used some old school medicine, poultices made of crushed herbs. Most of my wounds had healed between my natural ability and her extra concoctions, but they were still crazy itchy. The only wound remaining was the deepest along my right ribs.

"Most of the paranormal have a bolt hole or two. But why would they have gone to ground?"

I thought back to what I'd seen when the drug had hit all of them. Their pack magic had fizzled, dimming. I wasn't sure what effect it had, but I had a feeling that it was tainted somehow. It wouldn't be crazy for Brent to take his pack and bring them together, trying to work to clean it up. If he was in danger, he might even bring his daughter with him. She would have been free from the drug locked up in the freezer till it had settled back down.

"I have an idea." I pulled out my phone and dialed Scarlett.

"Didn't I just see you? Miss me already?" she teased over the line.

"I'm far from getting enough of you." I saw Morgana roll her eyes, but I ignored her. "And I was a bit messed up the last time I saw you. I wanted to let you know that I'm feeling better."

Scarlett cut me off before I could say any more. "Good. So look, about what Jadelyn's father said before the duel..." She hesitated.

I smiled. She was worried I'd bail out. It was cute. She clearly cared about us. "Sounds like something to talk about on our second date." I tried to give her a bit more certainty that I was still interested, but I was also in a hurry to move on to the reason I'd called.

I could almost hear the smile spread across her face, a relieved breath coming out over the line. "I'd love that. But you should also know that I've been strapped down to Jadelyn for the next couple of days. My father says it's not him meddling in my relationship or trying to prove a point, but I'm not buying it for one minute." She let out an exasperated sigh.

"But they're using her kidnapping as justification for her to be under twenty-four-seven surveillance. Which will make it hard for me to see you. But if you could swing by the sorority party tomorrow night, you might just find me there with Jadelyn. We could get a bit of time together while I stay close enough to her and fulfill my duty." She trailed off on the last words, uncertainty filling her voice.

"Sounds perfect. I'll be at KPA tomorrow night, at seven? What should I wear?"

"Swimsuit and a t-shirt. Bring a spare pair of clothes. There's a fair chance you'll get wet." Based on her voice, she might just be a part of it. I chuckled. It would be just like Scarlett to push me in. There was a mischievous nature in her. But that probably came with dating a kitsune.

"Sounds great! I'm looking forward to it." I paused, trying to figure out how to pivot the conversation. "But hey, I had another reason for calling, actually. Do you or Jadelyn have Kelly's number?"

There was a pause. "Moving that fast, eh?"

Morgana must have been able to listen to the phone even from where she stood several feet away, because she burst into laughter.

"Who's that?" Now Scarlett sounded hurt.

"Morgana. It's impossible to hide anything I do from her with those pointy, blue ears of hers." I enjoyed the well-earned glare I got from the drow.

"Hi, Morgana, don't hit on my man too much," Scarlett said loudly into the phone. Morgana reeled back like she'd been slapped, shock on her face.

I ignored both of them, instead moving forward in the conversation with Scarlett. "I'm looking for Brent. After what went down at the warehouse, we wanted to check up on him and his pack. We're having trouble getting in touch with him, so we thought Kelly might be reachable."

"Oh, got it. Hold on." The line went quiet as she likely talked to somebody else. A few seconds later, the background sound came back. "I have Jadelyn here."

"Scarlett said you were looking for Kelly?"

"Yeah. Technically looking for Brent, but I figured Kelly might be our best bet to get in touch with him."

"Alright. Got something to write it down with?" Jadelyn asked. Morgana was already grabbing her phone out to take down the number.

"Go ahead," I confirmed, and Jadelyn read off a number. Morgana nodded along. "Alright, thank you, ladies."

"No, I wanted to apologize," Jadelyn cut in. "I mean, I wanted formally to apologize for the duel. It was my fault that you were in that mess, and I didn't do enough to get you out of it. Not only that, but it seems like I keep dragging Chad around you and making things unpleasant, like dinner. If you need anything, know that I owe you a big favor. Anything," she repeated.

Scarlett snickered in the background.

"What are you laughing at?" There was something I was missing, not being there in person.

She jumped to respond. "I swear. I haven't told her what you are."

I frowned, wondering why she would feel the need to reassure me of that. However, I just rolled with it. "Okay. I'll see you two tomorrow. We have a pack to find."

"Good luck," they both said, and there was a bit of fuss before the phone clicked off.

I hung up the phone and looked up to find a smiling Morgana. "She likes you."

"Of course, she's my..." I pulled back before I said girlfriend. "We are going out," I corrected myself, but Morgana held her smile with a knowing smirk, like I was missing something.

Then it clicked. "You mean Jadelyn?"

"Yes, I think our little siren princess is quite smitten with you. She just can't show it, given her situation."

"You're nuts. I didn't know vampires were such romantics. There's nothing between me and Jadelyn. And it needs to stay that way. I don't need more werewolves to worry about." She and I were just friends. That's all we could ever be with her being engaged to Chad.

Morgana's eyes bore through me like I was in denial, and maybe I was, but I really didn't want to process any of that at the moment.

Wanting to change direction from the current conversation, I focused us back on the pack. "Read me off Kelly's number?" I held my phone ready and dialed the head bitch of Chad's pack as she read it off.

It rang five times before finally Kelly picked up breathless, likely from sprinting to the phone. "Hello?"

"Hey, Kelly. This is Zach." But before I could introduce myself further, there was snarling in the distance that sounded like there might be a fight happening. "Kelly, is everything okay?"

"Great." She sounded anything but convincing.

She was in trouble. "We are looking for your father, Kelly. After seeing what the drug did to the other wolves, I wanted to check up on him."

The moment stretched out. I knew she hadn't hung up because I could still hear the snarling in the background. But she didn't say a word for a long time. After a deep breath, she finally spoke. "My dad isn't well. His pack is keeping him contained though."

"Kelly, about the other wolves I saw taking this drug... their pack magic looked like it was sick. I don't know if containing him is going to make it better. Can you tell us where you are?" If he was still being affected by the drug, it was more than just a drug. Given his power and werewolves' ability to heal, he should have had it all out of his system by now.

Kelly's voice was a bit bristlier when she spoke again. "Look, I appreciate you wanting to help, Zach, but this is pack business."

Morgana had come around the table and pressed her head up to the other side of the phone. "Kelly, this is Morgana. We are handling council business in checking up on your father."

I heard Kelly's hesitation given that new information, and for a brief moment, I thought she might tell us where they were, but then there was a loud bang and the sound of metal falling in the background. The snarling I'd heard before doubled in volume.

"Shit. Shit. Shit," Kelly cursed. "I have to go."

"Kelly, where are you?" I made one final pass, knowing she was likely about to hang up.

"Shit. This is such shit!" More clanging rang in the background. "Fine. Here's the address." She rambled off the address of a warehouse outside of the city limits. Morgana entered it into her phone as Kelly talked, and in no time, I heard the app chirp and start giving directions.

"Thank you. We are on our way," I told Kelly and hung up.

Morgana's face was scrunched up in worry but shifted to neutral resolve. "Let's go."

I went with her down to the parking lot and pulled out a handgun from the foam rack, checking the chamber and magazine before grabbing two spare ones that looked the same. I turned to head to the car, wondering which we'd take this time.

"Really? The van?" I saw her opening the ugly thing's car door.

Morgana only shrugged as she unzipped, checked, and rezipped several bags. "I already had it packed. Plus, you wrecked the jag." She turned to narrow her eyes at me. I had a feeling she wasn't going to let me forget that for a while.

"Fine. But I need to start packing puke bags in this thing," I joked. I'd been fine, but her driving was insane.

She was less than amused. "You puke in one of my babies and I'll never forgive you."

I held back my comment about how her driving could improve to lessen those chances, but she was about to be behind the wheel. The last thing I needed was for her to be annoyed with me and take it out on the road.

Sliding into the passenger seat, I buckled in and tugged it a few times to make sure it was working. "Let's get out there."

***

We pulled up to the warehouse an hour later. During the drive, I realized that I'd missed three classes in the chaos of the day, but I'd just have to make them up later. My professors might not understand my absence, but I was pretty confident that making sure a local pack of werewolves didn't go crazy was more important. School had become trivial by comparison.

The warehouse was a newer building, made entirely of concrete slabs painted white. It was odd seeing them try to pretty up a warehouse. It was still a big concrete cube in the end.

Paw prints covered the surrounding area, and minor details didn't make sense. Flood lights sat on the corner, and it had a few too many cameras. The docks were too clean, too fresh looking.

"This isn't really a warehouse," I said as Morgana came to a full stop.

Her eyes scanned over the structure. "No, it's a bunker. Those doors are reinforced." She pointed to the dock doors. "And they are missing the chains to pull them up; they might not even be real."

Now that she pointed it out, I saw what she meant. The dock doors were a façade.

"Think the front door still works?" I was already getting out of the van, my shoes disturbing the paw prints in the dirt.

My leather jacket had the two spare magazines in it, and Morgana had even insisted I carry a grenade from her bag. She said it wouldn't explode, just create a bunch of acrid smoke. Apparently, they did wonders against werewolves.

I'd use my strength where I could, but I was glad to have a handgun tucked into my belt. I was learning the savageness of the para world. It wasn't about the beauty of how you fought or killed; it was about winning and using what you had at your disposal. At least I knew enough now to check the gun again and make sure the safety was on.

Feeling prepared, I looked up at the door. I was only going to crash a party with an alpha wolf needing containment in a bunker. What could go wrong?

"When there is a lack of options, often simplicity is the answer." Morgana took the lead and walked up to the one door we believed was real. I waited to see what badassery she was about to unleash. But my mouth fell open as she simply reached up and pushed the buzzer.

"Who's this?" a voice on the other end barked. "We aren't expecting any deliveries today."

"We are here to see Brent, on council business," Morgana added the second half like an afterthought.

I looked up at one of the cameras, feeling like somebody was watching us.

"Come in." The speaker clicked off, and the door buzzed as a heavy bolt smacked open.

"They really haven't skimped on security." I pulled the door open and let Morgana lead. She could survive having her neck snapped, so it seemed only fair that she took the lead.

Following in after her, I entered a small room with a second reinforced door. I took back what I'd said before. They'd definitely gone overboard with security. What were they so afraid of?

To the side of this room was a room with bars and plexiglass separating us from a man that looked like he'd come from a typical office job. "Welcome. IDs, please."

Morgana pulled out a plastic card and slapped it against the barrier for him to see.

I was more than a little curious about what she was holding. It looked like a driver's license, but there was no way Morgana had one of those. She's blue!

"Alright, Miss Morgana. Please head in. Someone will come see you. I'm afraid that you may not be able to talk to Brent, but we'll let you see him." The second door was just like the first.

"Come with me." A woman in a cardigan and a short skirt stood on the other side, turning and immediately moving before we responded. She headed down a set of stairs to the side. She was more petite than I'd expected, and her outfit looked like she'd just come off a tennis court. She did not scream werewolf.

Looking over her shoulder, she commented, "Welcome to the pack's den."

"Den?" I asked.

"Because we age slower than most humans, we often 'leave' wherever we were living every five or ten years. Most of the time, we come to the den and hang out for a few years. After all, the pack sticks relatively close. Then we reinvent ourselves and come back a few years later. But the den also doubles as a safe place for the pack. Many of us are back here today because of Brent." Her voice dipped as she talked about her alpha.

"I saw what that drug did to the omega wolves; it made their pack magic dirty."

"You can see it?" She turned with a look of shock.

"Zach is a unique para." Morgana smiled at the woman and nodded for her to keep going.

"Right." She spun on her heels and kept forward. "He's not well. Having spats of rage. The pack pulled back and are hoping to help him while this gets out of his system. After all, he's our connected Alpha. If something were to happen to him..."

I had been hoping to get more information. "What would happen?"

She sighed. "We'd become omegas. The pack would dissolve without Brent."

They'd be in a similar position to the other wolves. A few more dots began to connect. If I had a pack of omegas, it would be in my favor to have more candidates to join my pack.

Despite Kelly's claims before that omegas couldn't be part of a pack, the ones I had seen clearly had formed a pack. I still wasn't sure how they were doing it, but it seemed plausible that it had been intended that the drug affect Brent like it was.

"The wolves that fought Brent were omegas, but they had pack magic. Do you know how that is possible?"

"No. That's impossible. We leave our parent's packs in our teens and form packs in the new generation in our early twenties. It takes a few years for the pack magic to settle over and the alpha to establish dominance, but once the pack magic settles, the bond is forever. Once broken, it is like a severed arm, or so I've been told."

I winced at the comparison. "Can you feel your bond with Brent? Has it changed?"

A pained look flashed across our host's face. "Yes. We can feel him across the bond. I think your description of dirty is correct. It's like a rage is muddled in my bond with him. It makes me want to lash out, claw someone." Her voice got quiet. "It is another reason we are all here, to protect us from doing something we'd regret."

She led us down a spiral stairwell that emptied into a large open space. It was simple painted concrete walls and bland linoleum flooring. Long tables with benches like cafeteria tables filled most of the room. It felt almost militant.

Down below, it looked like the aftermath of a battle. Blood was everywhere and wounded werewolves were being patched up, and scraps of what I guess used to be a table were being cleaned up. Deep under the bunker, there was a cell block, each equipped with large iron chains.

What caught my attention was a cell that looked utterly destroyed, like something had exploded out. And in one of the other cells was a naked and unconscious Brent.

Nearby, several wolves were hauling a chain big enough to be the anchor line for a barge.

"What happened?"

"He got out."

I looked at the carnage. Three dozen wolves were heavily injured. "He did all this by himself?" I'd gotten a glimpse of him in action at the drug operation, but this was violence to a substantial degree worse.

There was pride in her voice as she spoke next. "Of course. He's our alpha. We are a decent sized pack, and we've been around for almost fifty years. Brent is amazingly strong."

The subject in question was being wrapped in more of that anchor line. They were using heavy looking fasteners to clamp it to itself and around the bars of his cell. That anything could break out of that was mind boggling.

"Zach, is there anything you can do?"

I wanted to look at what was going on with his pack magic, but I wasn't able to summon it at will. I needed to get riled up, get my blood pumping. At least, that's all that had worked so far.

As I thought about asking for a few of the wolves to fight me, I felt my dragon stir, this time more helpful than when I had battled Simon.

The world grew into perfect clarity as the lights became almost painfully bright and details exploded around the bottom of the bunker. So much information came at me at once that my head felt like someone had stabbed my head with an ice pick.

Morgana put a hand on my shoulder to steady me.

"Is he going to be okay?" our host asked.

"Oh, he's doing great."

I didn't even need to turn around to know Morgana was smiling enough to show her fangs.

It felt like I could see everything. Reflections off of the metal were in such perfect clarity that I could see all around the room. Strangely, my spatial sense was several times what it had ever been before, and I just knew where things were around me. It was like being in a familiar room in the dark; I knew what to expect. But most importantly, I could see Brent's magic.

CHAPTER 21

It was easier to see Brent's pack magic now that I was clear-headed and not looped up with drugs. His magic wasn't as dirty as the pack magic the wolves in the factory had been, but it had the same oily darkness mixed into what was once bright, gleaming orange. The part that concerned me, though, was that it was like he was the center of a spider web. The pack magic flowed out from him, and it was the dirty pack magic that was flowing.

He had time for it to have gotten better, but from what I could guess, it hadn't changed at all. The isolation and his healing abilities hadn't been able to fix it. If anything, it seemed like it had gotten worse as it poured out and collected from the other wolves.

I watched it a moment longer, and a bigger puzzle emerged. Where the links were dirty, they seemed more flexible. It was almost like something was pushing on Brent's magic, pulling and tugging at the pack bonds.

"Zach, what do you see?"

I didn't feel the need to turn to her, wanting to keep watching the magic. "His magic is still dirty, and it is flowing out to the rest of his pack. And like a feedback loop, the same dirty magic is coming back to him."

"The alpha is the source of our magic, and we all support him. But you are saying that it is getting worse?" our host asked.

"Slowly, yes. But I'm not even sure that's the biggest problem. There is something external putting pressure on all of your pack bonds. Pushing and pulling them, trying to realign them." Then it hit me. "If this drug is making your pack magic flexible, could it do the same for the omegas? Make it flexible enough to make a new pack?"

She shrugged. "You tell me. It sounds like you have a better view of all of this. But this pressure is what is causing our alpha to lose control?"

I wasn't sure of anything, but logically and instinctually, it felt right. I had a feeling the side effect on the human population was just a happenstance and way of earning extra revenue. This drug seemed to best loosen pack bonds, and it was allowing the omegas to reforge the bonds under a new alpha.

"Morgana, I think this drug is allowing someone to reform pack bonds and create a pack out of omegas. Now that it's affecting Brent and his pack, I think it could break his bonds or reform them."

"Could it take his pack from him and give it to this other alpha?" Morgana asked, eliciting a gasp from our host.

"I... yes. Yes, I think that's exactly what is happening."

Our host's gasp turned into a ragged sob. "No. No, no." She pulled at her hair, and I realized the mania in her eyes. Even considering such a thing was agonizing for her.

"Calm down. Please, calm down." I turned to her and grabbed her by the shoulders.

She whimpered as she bit the inside of her cheek and shuddered. Just the idea of their pack bonds being broken or repurposed was sending her into a fit. What would the same pressure do to their alpha? I looked up at all the bloody and injured wolves and got my answer.

Brent was being driven insane by whoever made the drug and was exerting pressure. That also meant there was an expedient solution of removing said person. If only we knew who it was.

"Okay, we have at least a rough understanding of what's going on, but I have absolutely no idea how to fix it. I'm way out of my depth here, Morgana. How can we stop the drug from pressuring this pack?" I let go of our host, who took the opportunity to go sit down. She put her head in her hands as she tried to put herself back together.

"Well, I guess it isn't so much a drug as a potion now. If it is playing with magic, it's a potion. So, we need to solve it with the same; we need a potion to counteract it. Elves in the past used some simple tinctures to cleanse their magic. We could start there and see if there is anything stronger out there."

I could feel my eye shift back, and my vision became normal once again. "Okay, that sounds like a decent start."

Kelly waved as she came over, worry evident in her eyes. "Sorry to listen in, but I couldn't help my curiosity. You think you can help him?" She pointed with her chin towards the man wrapped now in an anchor chain, her father.

"Maybe. We at least have a working theory and a plan. Are you noticing any differences? Any effects from this?"

"Eww." Kelly made a face. "I'm not in the same pack as my father. No, the newly formed pack hasn't had any issues."

I thought about Chad and his baggie of white powder. If she wasn't feeling anything, maybe Chad never ended up doing the drug last night. "Good, I saw Chad hocking V-phoria. I was worried he might make a dumb decision and end up spreading this into his pack as well."

The face Kelly made next should have gone down in the dictionary, next to disappointment. "I really wish there was another big shifter in town to push Chad out." She looked up at me, hope clear in her face.

"Not a werewolf unfortunately." I did my best to hide my wince as she nicked the big cut on my side. "But back to your father. Morgana says there is something the elves used to use to cleanse their mana. We'll do some research and see if something like that could help your father. We need to remove what the drug did to his pack magic before any of this will get better."

I avoided talking about reforming pack bonds for fear of setting her off like I had our host.

Kelly nodded, her face pensive at best. "Sounds like it is worth a shot. Any chance we can solve this by killing someone? That would make the pack happy."

"Maybe, if you could find the alpha who was leading this drug ring. The drug is warping their pack magic, and the pressure on their bonds is coming from him. If he was gone, I think that pressure would disappear."

Whispers picked up, and what I said was being repeated around the bottom of the bunker. It seemed to spread like a wildfire after a drought.

Kelly gave me a snort, her ears twitching, following the growing conversations. "Oh, boy. You really shouldn't have said that."

Growls picked up around us as several of the wolves of Brent's pack started to shift. Bandages tore as their bodies bulged and warped.

"You need to get out. Now." Kelly pushed us towards the spiral staircase in time for the first wolf to come charging through. "Back." Kelly snarled and partially transformed. Her hands turned into paws, and her ears popped out on the top of her head.

More and more of them shifted, with barely contained violence in their eyes.

"What's happening?"

"You just gave them a target for their aggression. They are going to find this other alpha and tear him apart." Kelly snapped at a wolf that got close, but more and more of them were shifting and prowling forward as we made our way upstairs.

Howls picked up at the back of the pack, and the rattling of chains caught my attention. Brent was waking up and starting to thrash about. More than a few wolves shifted over to check on Brent, but dozens were pressing us up the stairs while Kelly held our rear, warding off the eager ones.

I had thought it smelled like wolves before, but now it was overpowering. The bottom of the bunker filled with werewolves shifting and howling. They followed Kelly up the stairs, keeping a good distance, but they stacked in shoulder to shoulder, crowding each other up the stairs.

One got bold and snapped at Kelly only for her to swipe at his nose and send him reeling back with a whimper.

"Up. Move it," Kelly yelled.

I stopped looking at the wolves below us and started up the long spiral staircase as fast as I could manage. But each time I rounded another bend, it was like a stop motion film. The wolves crept forward.

Morgana flung open the door at the top of the stairs and was met with a growling wolf.

Shit.

I threw myself forward just as the werewolf lunged. I grabbed the scruff around its neck and brought it down with me, its maw snapping dangerously close to my face.

"A little help here?" I called out. Sure enough, Morgana was there, putting two rounds into its back. The wolf's body went still, but there was still intelligence in its eyes as it snapped at me. I pushed it off me.

"That should keep it down for a bit."

"What did you do?"

"Shot its spine. It's a werewolf; it'll recover in about a day. Plenty of time for us to get out of here."

Kelly was right behind us. The wolves charged her, trying to get through the door. She swatted at them as they got close, but it wasn't enough to deter them now. While they might act like wild animals at times, they were as intelligent as any person. They knew that, once that door closed, they would be trapped.

I pulled my gun and squeezed off three rounds, aiming for center mass in the two closest wolves, before grabbing the door and helping Kelly pull it closed.

"Does it lock?" I braced myself by putting a foot against the wall next to the door so I could hold it closed.

"From the inside—this is a shelter, not a prison," Kelly snapped.

She was clearly upset. Worry for her father had already exhausted her, and now she was holding off his pack.

I looked around for a solution. Spotting a few aluminum hanging fixtures with tube lights above us, I got an idea. "Kelly, can you rip that off?" I pointed with my chin. My hands were too busy bracing against the door.

The peeling of the thin aluminum sounded above me, but I was distracted watching through the little square port in the door. Werewolves were throwing themselves against the door, their claws scraping loudly against the metal, and occasionally one of them would catch the handle on the other side and jerk at the door.

"Got it. What do you want with it?" Kelly asked, holding a bent and torn piece of aluminum with shattered glass all over the floor.

"Twist it up to make it more solid, and then we'll use it to bar the door."

Kelly's big dangerous looking paws started to crunch the metal. More than once she hissed in the process, but she managed to create what looked like a wadded-up straw wrapper dotted with blood.

I made room between myself and the door to jam it in. "That isn't going to hold them long."

"We just need a head start. Morgana, do you have any backup you can call?" That question was punctuated with a deep bestial roar greater than anything I'd heard before.

"Shit. Dad's up. We need to be gone, now."

The sound of metal being ripped to shreds was coming from beyond the door, and I had to agree.

Turning, we ran as the door continued to pound with werewolves, trying to tear it down.

We rounded the corner on our way out and the security guard that let us in was shifted, raising himself up to glare at us. Something between a bestial scream of rage and a howl ripped from his lungs before he charged.

Three flashes went off next to my head. I heard the first one, but after that all I could hear was my ear ringing. Morgana had just fired a number of shots at the security guard. I was less pleased that she'd decided to do it right next to my head.

She yelled something at me, but it sounded like a million miles away. Luckily, I didn't need instructions to know what happened next; it was time to get out as quickly as we could.

I ran to the door, but it boomed as I came to a screeching halt.

Kelly was on my other side, which was ringing slightly less. "It's a door meant to keep out the paranormal; you aren't going to be able to brute force it."

I'd heard what she had said, but somehow it only translated into a challenge. Unlike some of my other physical feats, I didn't have to worry about mass. I was far stronger than a werewolf; here where I could wedge myself between two objects, I could put that strength to use. Grabbing the locking bar, I pulled up, throwing my whole body into the motion for leverage. It was solid, but I could feel it give just a little, and that was all the encouragement I needed, rooting my feet on the ground.

The metal groaned as it warped and bent enough to pull the bar out of the lock.

"Holy shit," Kelly said behind me. "I've seen my father try that; it didn't even budge."

"I'm strong, but your father would destroy me in the mass department." I kicked open the door and the bright sunlight suddenly felt like heaven after being down in the bunker.

Morgana was already on her phone as she ran to the van. I was right behind her, but Kelly paused in the doorway.

"Kelly, we need to go."

But she shook her head. "You need to go. I'll be fine."

There was a loud bang deeper in the building. They must have finally gotten the door to the stairwell open, because howls echoed out from there.

"I'll try to stall them. Go," Kelly repeated and shifted fully into a werewolf, tearing her own clothes and heading back in.

I got to the van and had one foot inside the car when Morgana gunned it. Nearly falling out, I swung myself in and slammed the car door.

"Yes, Rupert, this isn't a joke. Brent's pack is going wild, and they are going to be loose soon. We need all the help we can get to contain this."

Rupert, who I assumed was on the other end of the line, started saying something, but she hung up and started dialing another number.

I braced myself in my seat and clicked on my seatbelt because Morgana's driving terrified me as she hit one hundred. And she wasn't even looking at the road this time.

"Claire. Tell your asshole of a brother it is an emergency. Council session now. Get your people ready. A pack is going crazy and on the loose. We need all hands on deck to contain it."

It continued like that as Morgana went through her mental rolodex, calling everybody she could think of.

"You're calling everyone to arms. Where do we go to get these potions you mentioned?"

Morgana paused between calls. "Zach, I think that's out of the question now. A crazed werewolf pack is about to run loose in the city. The council is going to call open season and start doing damage control."

"So? If we don't figure out how to stop this, it is just going to happen again and again. Let's see if we can't save at least one of them."

It was clear Morgana wasn't convinced. Killing those that caused trouble seemed like an easier solution to most problems, and likely the approach they'd been taking for centuries. It was like they were still using medieval logic.

Maybe it was the future doctor in me, but I had to believe there was a way to cure it. It was going to keep happening, and I wanted to help those that were affected by it.

But the drug also seemed to have the potential of continuing to make the alpha behind all of it even stronger. If we didn't cut it off somehow, they might become too powerful to stop. My options were to find a cure or allow the deaths the council was planning for. I opted for a cure.

Ridding the harm from their pack magic could be the first big win in pushing back the damage that had been done. So far, all we've been able to do was slow them down.

"Shit, Morgana. If they are doing what we think and trying to disrupt the other werewolf packs, then that means any other pack around Philly is at risk."

Morgana cursed along with me and pulled her phone back out, shooting off texts. "Fine. We are going to see one of my old friends." She banked a hard right as howls sounded loud enough behind us that I almost thought it was a weather siren going off.

Unfortunately, it was the sound of a crazed werewolf pack on the loose.

Chapter 22

I watched Morgana turn the van into a parking lot, convinced we must have missed a turn and needed to turn around. But, when the van flew into a parking spot and came to a stop, I realized we had hit our destination.

"An old person's home?" I asked. I'd expected some sort of elven tree house, not something so... mundane. This was just an old, nondescript one story building with a simple sign out front designating it as Pleasant Hollows.

"Yeah. Paras get old too." Morgana rolled her eyes. "Plus, he isn't exactly welcome back home."

I tilted my head, waiting for a better explanation, but one never came. Morgana hopped out of the car, her heels clicking on the pavement.

"Morgana, someone is going to see you."

She shrugged. "I think you overestimate people's concern. They have a desire to explain away the unexplainable. It isn't like they think vampires exist, much less a drow. So, what do you think they think when they see me?"

I paused, not quite sure how to answer.

"They think it's makeup or a wig. Here, the workers might not even look up from their stations." Morgana strode through the automatic doors. I noticed that the doors locked behind us with a keypad to exit, making it feel more like a prison than a nursing home.

Morgana put on a big smile as she approached the woman at the desk and picked up a pen to sign in.

The woman looked up, taking in Morgana. "Is there a convention in town or something?"

The drow vampire just rolled with it. "You like? I think I did a pretty good job this year."

The nurse just shook her head. "Fantastic. I have a friend who likes to cosplay; she'd shit herself if she saw how good yours was."

Morgana did a little bow and thanked the nurse before moving deeper into the place.

I was still baffled by the interaction. "What the hell?"

"I told you. They don't believe it could be real. That is one of the best defenses we have. Since there is no way in hell it could be real to them, they make up their own excuses. If you ever get caught, just roll with whatever they say."

Still baffled by the casualness of it all, I took in the sleepy nursing home. For a moment, I thought I had somehow gotten the ability to slow down time, but as I watched, I realized things just moved slowly there.

Most of the inhabitants didn't even seem to notice the world around them. Their focus was either fully on moving what little they could or on the TV playing in the main room. I felt creepy watching them, knowing that they were once lively people with busy lives.

Morgana guided us through the bland halls that reeked of cleaning supplies until we got to room thirteen. She stopped and rapped on the door before she just opened it and went through. More like the knock was a notice rather than a request for entry.

She must have known its occupant well enough because a... something sat hunched over in robes in the corner of the room muttering to themselves. I couldn't believe this was the wise elf we had come to see.

"Tee, good to see you," Morgana practically yelled as she slammed the door behind her.

"Huh?" The robed form turned and stood. He was a tall, thin elf, like a needle pointing to the sky. He was wrapped in thick robes that probably had more volume than his body. His patchy hair was thin and gray, reminding me of cobwebs. I counted five bags under his eyes; his skin drooped so much I was worried it was going to sag and fall off all on its own while we stood here.

"Ah. Morgy. Long time no see."

I would have said his eyes filled with intelligence by the way they shot up, but they were opaque white with cataracts, so bad the guy must have been blind.

"Oh. What is this?" He turned to me. "You brought me a dragon? Fantastic, I could use his heart for so many things. Oh, and his teeth. I'll reward you so well for this gift, Morgy."

"Shut up, old coot. The dragon is my charge. Don't you dare even think about harming him," Morgana snapped.

The old man continued on as if Morgana hadn't spoken. "Yes. I could brew a potion of immortality with his heart, even as young as it is." Tee licked his dry, wrinkled lips in a way that made my blood curdle.

What had Morgana brought me to?

But my alarm settled as Morgana moved right in front of Tee's face, close enough that even with those cataracts, he could read her lips. "Do not touch him."

"I don't know what you want today, Morgana, but bringing that here has just raised the price of anything you ask for. You can't expect me to let such a treasure trove walk away. At least let me carve out one of his eyes. I bet the sight of a dragon is magnificent."

"Excuse me. Do I get to roast him?" I wasn't about to stand there totally defenseless against this guy.

"Please, Zach. Tee is from a far older generation."

"No argument here. He looks older than dirt," I snorted. Didn't make it okay to be an ass, though.

Tee turned to me, showing that maybe his hearing hadn't gone with old age. His pointed ears dropped in a way that almost made him look sad. "Dirt is far older than me. I don't yet have that respectable of a longevity. The younger generation these days, no respect."

"Tee. I just need a simple cleansing potion," Morgana stated.

"You could go get one from any root tree." He waved his hands.

"No, Tee, I can't. They all stopped making them, and I need the best. You always were the best." She circled the old elf, trying to stay in front of him as he meandered around the room.

"What part of the dragon do I get?"

"None. Damnit, Tee, don't make me do this." Morgana's scowl became less playful and more intense.

Tee sneered. "You must have pissed those fools off if I'm the one you came to for something so simple."

"Tee. I'm here because we are friends. I've held the secret of your daughter from all of them; you must know they've pressed me." With Morgana's words, the old elf's posture and countenance shifted. Gone was the old, feeble man. The ancient elf in front of us made it feel like we were standing in the room with a magical lighting rod in a storm.

"Don't you dare bring her into this. If they were so set on finding her, they'd try to get it out of me."

"No. They let you live in hopes that, when you die, she'll surface. Don't think they don't watch this place night and day." Morgana glared at the ancient elf, who seemed to deflate at her words.

"If I make you these, will you get a letter to her and bring one back to me?" His voice was so full of both hope and loss that I forgot for a moment that he'd been just discussing taking pieces of my body. Tee and Morgana clearly had a complex history. No doubt, they'd been through a lot together.

Morgana shook her head. "Even if you don't do this, I'll do that for you. For two friends both slighted by those snoots."

Tee huffed, and his hands came out of his robes. The skin over his hands was thin, clearly showing each of the veins in his hand.

Walking over, he grabbed a letter set on the top of a shelf on the bookcase. Everything else on the bookcase was covered in dust, but that letter was pristine. "Take this to her."

"Of course." Morgana took it and started to head out. I almost thought we were going to leave.

"Wait," Tee grumbled. "Damn you, Morgana. Let's get this done."

Morgana was facing away from the old elf, but by the way she flashed a victorious smirk, I felt this wasn't the first time that she'd had a similar exchange with Tee.

"Whelp. Got anything you can spare me?"

"I need to clip my nails. Want some of those?"

"YES!" he said excitedly.

Morgana shook her head at me, but I just shrugged. I wasn't going to miss my nail clippings.

"This way." He grabbed something else off the shelf and stuffed it in his pocket before he grabbed his cane and started out of the room. The elf was so tall his head almost brushed the ceiling.

I leaned to Morgana and whispered as low as I could. "What's his deal?"

He cleared his throat, and Morgana threw me a narrow-eyed look, telling me that we could talk later.

The halls were mostly empty, and I was wondering where we were going until he ducked through a swaying door that led into a commercial kitchen.

"Mister, you aren't supposed to be here." Three employees looked up from boiling pots.

Tee pulled out a fist full of yellow dust from his pocket and blew it into their faces. Instantaneously, all three of them dropped like sacks of potatoes. "Make yourself useful and drag them out of the way. We have potions to make."

I paused, re-evaluating the space. He was serious. He was really going to make magical potions in a nursing home kitchen.

Going straight to work, he opened a cabinet and stepped fully into it. I realized it was large enough inside that it was almost a walk-in closet. Inside were all sorts of oddities, floating in pickle jars.

"Help me, will you, Zach? It helps if they don't have such a crick in their neck when they wake up." Morgana was already moving one of the kitchen staff.

"That cabinet... it's like Bumps in the Night." It wasn't a question. The depth was far more than it should have been.

She nodded. "I made that cabinet for Tee. He keeps quite the collection there. Oh! Watch that one; it looks like they pissed themselves."

I stepped around the yellow puddle and hauled the staff over into the corner. "He just does this?"

She shrugged. "None of the elven clans could get him to talk. You expect nursing staff to be able to control him? Tee's too old to learn new habits."

"I am still young enough to hear you just fine, Morgy." Tee came out of the cabinet looking at what was already on the stove. "This'll do."

He focused on one stove, so I went around and started turning everything else off so we didn't have a fire on our hands.

Tee muttered in a language I didn't understand as he pinched in ingredients and pulled items out of jars. "Who is using this? I know it isn't the whelp."

I spoke up. "Werewolves. There is a drug going around tainting their pack magic."

Tee made a noise of disgust. "Of course their magic is dirty; they are filthy mutts."

"Now, Tee, this is serious. Someone is spreading a drug that is driving werewolves mad. It's warping their magic." Morgana went on to explain everything we had learned and what we hypothesized. Tee nodded as she went, going back into his cabinet for different ingredients based on what she was saying.

At times I offered details from what I'd seen until Tee came out on one trip with an empty jar and a pair of nail clippers. I shrugged and clipped a few nails, dropping them in the jar. When I'd finished, Tee moved faster than I could have expected and whisked away the jar like a new prized jewel.

"You really shouldn't have given him so much." Morgana shook her head.

"Is it really worth that much?"

"To most, it might even be worthless. But to Tee? He's a freaking genius. Exiled because he knew too much. He dabbled too deep in things that elves don't like to talk about." Morgana's face became serious, but there was a sadness to it I'd seen before on her face. A reminder of her own exile.

I realized why the two got along. They both shared a love for a place that hated them.

"Thank you, whelp. I'll use those carefully." Tee came out of his cabinet. "And while Morgana is sharing stories about me, why don't I give you some delightful stories about her. You see, my granddaughter and her were as thick as thieves. Why, I remember when they played naked in the pools at the bottom of our root tree."

Morgana's blade happened to come loose and find its way close to Tee. "Are you sure you want to rehash dusty stories, old man?"

He looked at her like she was a petulant child. "I didn't realize you were so sensitive, Morgana. Now that I know, I definitely won't talk about the two elves who played tag naked in the pools, one of them falling into a trapper's noose and hanging naked for almost half a day refusing to utter a peep and admit they'd been so foolish."

The way Morgana's cheeks darkened and her blade hand twitched, it was clear who the two elves had been. "Of course you wouldn't say such things. Some things are better forgotten."

"Indeed," Tee agreed as Morgana put away her blade. "Although it would be a shame. It would also mean not thinking about how when the same elf passed out from hanging upside down, I cut her down and gave her remedies for her ails. And then, out of sheer happenstance the next moon, a dressed deer showed up at my doorstep without a whisper of the elf who brought it. Those are fond memories."

Morgana snorted and turned, her cheeks turning a darker blue. "I think your potion needs attention."

"So it does." Tee leaned over the pot and stirred it idly while an uncomfortable silence descended in the kitchen.

The two of them clearly had a serious history. I wondered what it would be like to be that old, have that much history. And then I realized I might one day.

Morgana had mentioned that the dragon leader in Dubai was over a thousand years old. Did that mean that I could grow that old? If my heart was part of a potion for immortality, did that make me immortal?

Before I could properly freak out over the new thoughts, a grating alarm sounded outside the kitchen. I looked through the window out to a serving area that was like the college dining halls and lounging area.

Warnings were going across the TV, and their standard show had cut out to a news anchor. Red banners scrolled across the bottom of the screen. "Everyone, please get somewhere safe and lock your doors. This is an emergency broadcast to warn the city. Several gangs have started an all-out turf war over the drug trade in Philadelphia. We advise everyone who can to stay home and lock your doors. The city's police force will be out in force tonight. Governor Mair has even called in the national guard to help. The best thing you can do is stay home and out of the way."

The council had worked quickly. There was no doubt in my mind that this broadcast was the start of the council's cover up. But it made me wonder how deeply they'd woven themselves into the inner workings of the city.

"Seems you have an enormous problem on your hands," Tee said, having heard the broadcast.

I nodded. "The pack affected by the drug is on the loose. I'm hoping this'll help save some of them."

"Noble," he grunted as he went back to stirring. "But you'll need them to drink this. And even then, I can't guarantee it'll work. This is something that young elves used to use to cleanse their magic and help them grow closer to nature. I modified it in hopes it'll work on your werewolves, but I offer no promise beyond the best of my ability to help."

"Tee is the best. If his potion doesn't work, we don't have any other options," Morgana said stiffly, clearly worried about the news broadcast. But as she turned to look at Tee, her confidence in him was clear.

Tee grunted and pulled out several small flasks. He ladled them full of a dark green liquid that reminded me of the time I had thought a juice cleanse was a good idea. Spoiler, it was not.

"You'll need to get them to drink this. It won't take much, so start with just a mouthful."

I almost laughed, picturing myself spoon feeding the werewolves. Somehow, I had a feeling they weren't going to sit still for me as I administered the dose. But I hoped I could keep my head from getting ripped off as I did it.

Tee turned to Morgana. "Will you need more than this?"

She looked hesitantly at me for a moment before turning back to Tee. "We don't know, but more wouldn't hurt."

Tee shuffled around and started making another batch. At this point, we had four vials of the potion. I hoped it would be enough to save those currently affected.

"Thanks, Tee." I snatched them up and awkwardly filled my coat pockets, now bulging with glassware.

Morgana got the hint and waved the envelope at Tee, getting his attention. "I'll get this to your daughter. Have no worries."

"Thanks, Morgy. Good luck to you and the whelp. If he dies of natural causes, you could always bring what's left here. I'll give you a good price."

I tried not to bristle at the man once again wishing for my body parts.

"Fat chance. He's not going anywhere anytime soon if I have anything to say about it." Morgana gave Tee a look to emphasize her statement before she turned, and we headed out of the kitchen.

Chapter 23

The car doors clicked closed and Morgana's tires were already burning rubber as she peeled out of the nursing home.

I was taking the vials out of my pockets and trying to find a way to secure them so they wouldn't rattle and break during her driving. "So, Tee was pleasant." It came out like sarcasm, no matter how hard I tried.

Morgana barked a laugh. "It's okay. He's an old ass. But he's dependable, and we get along because we both hate the elves."

"What's his deal?"

Morgana got quiet for a moment, the only noise was the sound of the tires on the road and a few drivers honking at Morgana for cutting them off.

"Elves get their mana from their root tree. Every family has and protects one. It is sacred to that family, and there are many rituals and communion rights that involve the family's root tree. Tee dabbled in some magic related to his root tree and doing so is strictly forbidden. I don't know for sure what it was he did, but he's been exiled from elven communities and is watched. They haven't killed him, so I get the feeling there's information in his head that they want. Something that must be powerful. But I'm not sure what it is."

She swerved into another lane, and I worked to make sure the bottles remained secure. I went to grumble at her to be careful, but she just continued on. "Like I said, they tried for a bit to get information, eventually leaving him to his life in the nursing home. There's very little that could break him, but his daughter is one of those exceptions. She's been in the wind for decades."

"And you know where she is, or at least can get in contact with her?"

Morgana sighed. "I'll get the letter to her. But I'll have to be careful. They will know that I visited him."

She bumped over a curb and turned back forward, facing the road. "Where are we going?" Morgana asked.

Flipping open my phone, I quickly googled to see where the supposed gang wars were most prevalent at that moment. "Head to Nicetown. Shit," I cursed reading the post.

People had been torn to shreds in the street. I quickly moved through the images, not wanting to see the outcome.

"Of course." Morgana swerved onto an exit ramp. "They think some drug dealer is involved, so they'd go to the rough parts."

***

By the time that we rolled up through Nicetown, it looked like a war zone.

"Morgana, how are they going to cover this up?" My eyes grew wide at the two nearby bodies, if you could call them that, torn up at the corner of the street.

"Make up a story and broadcast it widely. Then quickly move onto the next news cycle. People forget easily. You tell the other story enough, and they start to change their own memories. Hell, politicians have been doing it for years. They are the real monsters."

I didn't comment, still occupied by the sights on the street, but then movement caught my eye. "That way. I thought I saw something."

Morgana took a left at a red light, but it didn't matter. The streets had cleared out, the battle here already fought. She might have said they could cover this up, but I'd never seen an area of the city so deserted like this before.

I wasn't sure you could just keep pumping the same story for this and make it all go away. But that was for the council to figure out. My job was simple. We needed to find the werewolves and hope that Tee's potion worked.

"Stop. Stop the car." My head came inches away from the dash as Morgana plowed to a stop. I gave her a quick glare, but she only smiled and shrugged in response.

Jumping out of the car, I saw a werewolf bent over in the alley. Spent rounds littered the ground, as did several more corpses further into the alley.

The werewolf turned to me and growled. Holes in its chest were still healing from what looked like an interrupted drug deal.

One hand slid into my pocket for the vial of liquid, but the werewolf surprised me.

"Zach?" The wolf shifted back, and I realized it was Kelly.

"What the fuck! Did you kill them?" I found myself suddenly outraged; she wasn't under the drug's influence.

"No! God, no. I was running with the pack, trying to stop them. But these idiots slowed me down. It was the pack that tore them to shreds. The gunfire brought them here," Kelly explained rapidly, her hands held up in the universal sign of innocence, and completely failing to cover her naked body.

I cleared my throat as I felt heat dust my cheeks. "Here, have my coat." Slinging it off my back, I held it out to her, looking away.

"Oh, right. Sorry, this is sort of usual for us. What a gentleman."

I felt the weight leave my hands and turned back. She wore it like a baggy dress, but it would have to do.

"I like that jacket, so don't shift in it." I tried to lighten the mood, but all the gore around us made that difficult. "I need to find your father. The potion in one of the pockets of that coat might help him."

Kelly froze; like if she moved another step, she'd ruin it. Her hand dipped into the right pocket that was weighed down and pulled out the vial. "This?"

"Yep. He needs to drink it. The batty old elf who made it said to start with a mouthful, but I think we are going to have to be less delicate than that."

Kelly snorted a small laugh, her lip curling at the edge. "Yeah, better just throw the whole thing in his mouth. He can live with indigestion for a few days."

The idea of glass tearing up someone's insides while they rapidly healed from it sent shivers down my spine.

"Get in the car. Any idea where the pack is?"

Kelly's ears twitched before I heard anything. Then, off in the distance, the rapid staccato of gunfire went off. Some large automatic rifle was firing a few blocks over.

"I'll bet you everything I have that they are or will be there shortly."

I hurried back into the car. Morgana didn't need any guidance, already hitting the gas and turning around towards the gunfire. I reflected for just a moment about the fact that I'd become a person charging headfirst into where gunfire was coming from, but Morgana's driving quickly shook me from my thoughts.

We peeled around the corner, and the less than respectable citizens of the area were lined up in the street making a blockade. The gangsters' faces were set with grim determination to defend their territory. I had to give them some credit. The werewolves were not an easy enemy to stand against.

The gangsters lined up against the pack of wolves, firing every gun they had and holding the line. None were fleeing and ditching their gangmates. Unfortunately, for all the effort they were putting in, it wasn't very effective. The pack was slowed, but not by much.

As we reached them, the pack fell on them. There wasn't a hope of a chance for them, and they knew it based on the looks on their face. But they still stood their ground, firing as long as they could hold out.

One of the gangsters was tossed into the air by the large werewolf up front, only for several wolves to leap up like a dog catching a frisbee and tear him into pieces, shaking each body part and spraying blood everywhere.

"We're supposed to interrupt that?" I said, hesitation in my voice. This level of violence was a whole new stage, one I wasn't sure I was ready for.

"We might be able to peel one off," Kelly said, but she didn't sound very confident.

Luckily, we weren't the only ones out hunting the wolves. I had almost forgotten that the council had put out the kill order. If we had found them, so had others.

Two military Jeeps roared into view behind the pack. Mounted on their backs were the biggest guns I'd ever seen in my life. They were also the loudest, as I learned, when the firing began. The muzzle flash lit up the faces of the men as they swung them back and forth into the mass of werewolves.

I could see scales peppering their cheeks under their helmets. These were the sirens. No doubt Jadelyn and her father had the money for this equipment.

The gangsters and their handguns might not have worked well, but that Jeep mounted gun tore through the wolves. I watched one werewolf jerk as it caught the brunt of the gun's hit, blood spraying into the air repeatedly like a kid splashing in a pool.

That got the pack's attention, and they turned on the Jeeps, seeing the larger threat and abandoning the gangsters. Howls filled the air, and I could almost taste the bloodlust coming off the pack as they charged at their new target.

But the Jeeps had the advantage, and they continued to use it. Soon half a dozen wolves lay on the ground, too injured to keep up with the pack. The gangsters closed in, but Morgana was already hitting the gas again and sliding to a stop between them and the downed wolves.

"Be quick," she said.

I was out the door, grabbing the first wolf I could reach. He was healing from... I wasn't sure how many bullet holes. But that didn't stop him from thrashing, so I grabbed him by the scruff of his neck.

"Hold still idiot, I'm trying to help." Popping the cork, I pushed the vial deep enough in his muzzle that he couldn't spit it out.

My eye shifted, and I could see their magic. I waited.

"Is it working?" Kelly asked. She was administering her potion to another werewolf.

"Who da' fuk do youse think youse is doing?" came a rough voice from around the van. "Kill dem fucks."

I heard several guns cock and realized that while this had been an opportunity; it had also been fraught with danger. The gangsters only saw themselves as friends; we were foe.

Not even turning to them, I yelled out, "I'm an EMT. These guys are very sick. I'm trying to help them." I pulled the vial away; I'd given this wolf more than enough to work.

The man walked forward, his tattoos peeking out from under his shirt and crawling up his face. As he looked at me, his eyes went wide. I'd seen it before, and normally, it was followed with a 'how can I help'. Most people reacted that way when I said I was an EMT.

But this time, his face shifted from that to a hard browed look that didn't promise help. "I don't know what youse are, but that eye is freaky. These guys killed my uncle. Ain't no way they live." He dangled his handgun sideways, pointing it at me.

"I'm something far worse than them. I wouldn't recommend messing with me." My voice came out nearly a growl.

"Biggy, cap their asses," a hoot came up behind me, but I didn't turn to look. My eyes locked on Biggy as we both struggled to be the dominant one in this situation.

But neither of us got the chance, as an arrow suddenly appeared in Biggy's throat. His eyes went wide, and his gun started popping off as he stumbled back. Sparks flew off the concrete next to me and another off of Morgana's van before he fell over.

They were sudden and without warning. Arrows started blooming in the throats and faces of the gangsters.

Two elves descended into the group, their blades flashed, cutting the remaining gangsters to pieces before they even realized what was happening.

Morgana was out of the van, her hands hovering over her own blades. "That was unnecessary."

"They saw the para world," one of the elves sneered, spinning his weapon idly.

"Or you are just angry you missed your chance at the pack."

The other elf smiled. "No, our chance is right here. We are cleanup." He swung his sword lazily as he approached, but Morgana shifted in front of them.

"We have a cure for their madness we would like to try first." Her words reminded me of what I'd been doing before we'd been interrupted.

Turning back to the wolf I'd given the potion to, I looked at his magic. The dark oily mixture in his magic was receding slowly. "It's working," I announced, giving more weight to Morgana's words.

"Does not matter. Too little too late. They should be put down for the exposure they have brought upon us."

I didn't look up as metal on metal rang out and then continued like a snare drum as Morgana no doubt fought the two elves. Instead, I worked my way through the wolves along with Kelly, giving them each a dose of the potion. This time, I was a bit more judicious with the dosing. By the time we got all six of them, my vial was a little less than half full, and so was Kelly's.

The math didn't look good. Even with all four vials, we were looking at saving maybe twenty-five wolves.

Kelly must have been having the same thoughts because she wilted.

"Don't worry, we'll save some for your father. Maybe curing him will help the rest through the pack magic." I tried to say it like I meant it. There was no proof of that, but it made enough sense to cheer her up.

"Thanks," Kelly said before she looked behind me.

I already knew what was happening; I trusted Morgana enough that I didn't need to get involved.

"Ugh. Where am I?" The first wolf I had treated came to his senses enough to talk.

"Your pack was infected with foul magic," Kelly supplied. "You all shifted and are going on a rampage through Nicetown.

He smirked. "Couldn't have happened to a better place."

Kelly's glare shut him down, and he got that special kind of quiet when you knew your comment wasn't welcome. "There is a kill order out on the whole pack. All of you are within the kill order. The whole para community in the city is getting in on it."

He clutched his chest. "That explains the bullet holes."

A few more groans sounded as the others started to similarly get their senses back. It was fascinating to watch, but we needed to get moving. "You guys can handle yourselves? Get some clothes and get off the streets," I said, standing up and dusting off my knees.

Morgana and the two elves had entered a stalemate as the wolves started to get up. The elves paused for a moment, uncertain if they were about to be outnumbered.

"Morgana, we are going. Kelly, get in the car. You two, these wolves are cleared by me. If you so much as touch them while they leave the area, I'll come kill you and burn your root tree."

I didn't know exactly what I was saying, but I knew enough to threaten them. Not to mention, I felt like I might actually follow through on it. These were my patients, and they were on their way to recovery. If they killed them, I wasn't sure what exactly I'd do. But it wouldn't be good for them.

The two elves looked at me, then each other in confusion before hurrying away.

"I'm surprised that worked," Kelly commented, sliding into the car. Morgana was slower, keeping her eyes on the two elves as she moved.

"They could not have won," Morgana explained. "And Zach has an aura of power around him. Not to mention they've seen enough to be wary of him from his battle with Simon." Her foot hit the gas, and I lurched back against the seat.

"You never said that before."

"You didn't have it before. It was subtle after your duel with Simon, but it has been growing steadily since."

I frowned. The only real change since the duel with Simon was my beast and I coming to more of an understanding. Would I keep changing as time went on?

I scanned the road, using my dragon eye to follow the magic. "That way, Morgana; I can see the connection of the pack magic."

Kelly turned in her seat to get a good look at my eye. "That is a wicked eye. I haven't heard of anything that can literally see magic. Most of it is in more of a sixth sense."

"Zach is a very unique para," Morgana supplied a vague explanation.

Kelly smiled. "Whatever you are, thank you for your help."

"We still have more to do. But thank you." I clicked on my seat belt as Morgana tore around another corner. Even without my sight, it would have been obvious at that point to know the pack had been there. Several wounded werewolves were struggling to their feet in the street.

"Do we stop to help them, or do we try to focus on Brent?" I asked both girls in the car.

They shared a glance before Kelly spoke. "Selfishly, I'd like to try and use it on my father. Even if the rest of the pack isn't cured, he should be able to exert some influence on them and hopefully stop this."

I nodded; it made enough sense that I was on board. "Then that begs the question, how do we separate him from the pack?"

"Leave that to me," Morgana said. "Can you get to the duffel in the back?"

I reached over the backseat and pulled a heavy duffel bag filled with lumps at the bottom over it to me. Curiosity got the better of me, and I unzipped it to look inside. "Morgana, you have to be kidding me."

"What's—" Kelly leaned over to look in the bag. "Shit. Yeah, that'll get his attention."

"Are you sure it won't kill him?" I looked at the gun that looked like a revolver for a giant and the large shells in the bottom of the bag. "This seems like a little overkill." It was a freaking grenade launcher.

"Say that after you fight him. I'm just going to try and take him down." Morgana kept her eyes forward. "Be a dear and load that puppy up, then give it to me."

I looked at the grenade launcher and shook my head, grabbing the shells out one by one and loading the thing's six chambers.

CHAPTER 24

And just like that, I found myself riding in a beat-up minivan, driving parallel to a raging wolf pack while Morgana leveled a grenade launcher out the window and Kelly reached across, holding the steering wheel stable.

I was really starting to question what life decisions had led me down my current path. I'd gone from pre-med student to... whatever this was with Morgana, in just a few days.

But I also wasn't sure I was entirely sorry. I felt like I'd been able to do far more good in the past few days than I'd ever been able to while learning in college. It was like I'd sped straight to developing life skills. Keeping werewolves from rampaging the city would save far more than my EMT job.

Morgana's grenade launcher made a plunking noise as it shot. I'd been ready to have my ears blasted out as it sounded, but I watched the grenade soar out of the car, following the slight plunk. I had to admit; it was anticlimactic. You'd think such a big gun would make a big boom.

The explosion came a moment later as the grenade hit the mass of the pack. Two wolves flew up into the air only to come down behind the pack as the group kept charging the siren's two Jeeps.

Morgana adjusted in the car, then continued sending grenades out with multiple plunks in a row. The first exploded as she fired off her last shot. It was like popcorn in the microwave; four of the five exploded directly on Brent, taking the alpha down. How she had managed to keep readjusting to aim at him with each quick firing was beyond what I could understand.

I heard a cheer come up from the sirens ahead. The majority of the pack continued on their quest towards the Jeeps, but a few peeled off and turned to protect their alpha.

Brent struggled to get back up; one of his arms was missing most of its muscle, which made standing a tall task. Yet the massive werewolf was regenerating. I had a new respect for just how powerful an alpha could be when it was with its pack.

All three of us bailed as soon as the car stopped. Morgana sped forward, a rifle at her shoulder as she shot into the wolves that had stayed behind to protect Brent. As soon as she was spent, she tossed the rifle to the side, pulling on her blades and carving enough away to keep them busy.

"I'll try to keep my father busy." Kelly threw down my jacket, thankfully, before she shifted and dove on Brent, wrestling with the huge werewolf. He had to have been almost twice her size. She jumped on his back and strained to get his head in a position where she'd have the leverage to hold him.

With Morgana keeping the pack at bay and Kelly working to hold her father, that left me with the fun job. I just needed to feed a giant, angry werewolf a potion without losing any of my fingers.

"Good boy." I couldn't help it as those words slipped out of my mouth as I got up next to Brent.

"Shut up and feed it to him." Kelly's voice came out guttural and strained.

I popped the cork and went to pour it in Brent's mouth before he could recover, but a wolf that I'd thought was down lurched to life and grabbed my leg, pulling itself up. Its maw snapped at my leg to hamstring me.

I didn't think, I just reacted, pulling my leg away from him. What surprised us both was when his large wolf body was pulled with it. As his body moved forward, I tried to use my other foot to kick him off and ended up cracking him hard enough in the head that I heard the breaking of bone.

We were both a bit stunned, but the hard kick had at least distracted him from biting me and loosened his grip. I quickly turned back to Brent before Kelly lost control of him.

Just as I turned, Brent bucked and tossed Kelly up over his head. She still had a hold of his head, but her weight was already carrying her over and off the giant werewolf.

"Zach!" she yelled, crashing into me.

I caught Kelly juggling the potion in my hand, sloshing some out.

My eye must have shifted, because suddenly I could see the pack magic around me. And it told me the second alpha, the one that led the drug ring, was closing in. Its magic was pressing down on Brent's more than ever before, and the leader was drawing closer.

Brent was already pushing off the ground, howling into the air, trying to call his pack to fight. He must have sensed the other alpha too now.

"Kelly, the alpha leading the drug ring is almost here. Fuck. Your dad can sense it."

"Zach, we have to stop him. There's no way he wins a fight with those injuries." Her pleading tone plucked at my heartstrings, and I did something stupid.

Setting her down, I charged Brent. "Here, puppy puppy," I yelled as I tried to tackle Brent. But my mass once again wasn't anywhere close to what was needed to take down a werewolf.

Instead, I found myself clinging onto his back like a tick as he staggered two steps and then shook like a wet dog, trying to shake me. My finger found the opening for the flask and pressed down onto it, hoping to keep as much of the potion inside as possible while he flung me around.

When he settled down, I started climbing his back as his clawed hands tried to reach around and get a good hold of me. They scraped at my clothes, and I found myself pressing my body as close to him as possible to avoid them as I got my arms around his neck, squeezing hard. Luckily, it was strength and not mass I needed for that move; his throat closed like I had it in a vice.

He thrashed, his claws raking across my arm and causing me to wince in pain as he tore my skin. But I also noticed that in trying to get a breath, his mouth was wide open. I had what might be the only opportunity I'd get; I had to take it.

Working to ignore the pointed teeth and treat it more like dunking a basketball, I shoved my arm into his mouth with the potion, trying to pull it back as quickly as I could before his mouth instinctively closed, like it did. It was a natural reflex, like when a fly goes into your mouth.

So I didn't blame Brent, too much, when his teeth skinned the back of my hand as it exited his mouth. I did, however, blame him when he decided to step up his attempts to get rid of me by flopping backwards, crushing my body against the pavement.

Brent rolled away after that, leaving me in a me-sized hole in the pavement.

I gasped, but my lungs refused to pull in air. My chest hurt, almost like I was just body slammed by a half ton werewolf.

Kelly flew onto Brent, her claws raking over the already terrible looking werewolf. He was preoccupied for a moment, trying to get Kelly off, giving me a moment to recover. Flickers of confusion ghosted over his lupine face as he danced away from my hole, and I lost sight of him.

I managed to sit up slightly, wanting to watch his magic. My body protested, but I pushed through it for the moment.

As I got a good look, I could see his magic shifting. The darkness was receding. "Kelly, it's working. We just need to stall him."

"Try—ing." Her voice hitched and started to fade away. I looked over at her to see her be flung off into a crowd of oncoming werewolves.

"No," I wheezed; they'd tear her apart. Struggling, I pulled myself out of the hole one painful inch at a time.

Brent now was staggering, shaking his head, like he was trying to get something off it. "No. No. NO!!!!" he howled as he started shifting back into a short, naked man. The rest of the pack became a mess and started shifting back.

The sirens pulled up at the edge of the area, their guns aimed but not firing. "What's happening?" the gunner shouted.

"I think we have it under control," I tried to yell, but it came out with less wind than I intended. Either way, the siren nodded, holding his mounted gun steady on the pack.

Morgana stood to the side covered in blood, but okay. She'd done her part of stalling those wolves.

"Chad? It's fine, we have this under control." I picked Kelly's voice out of the mess as she went to try and comfort her father, despite the nasty wound on her side.

I paused at her comment. Had Chad been running with Brent's pack? Had the drugs somehow tied him into this mess?

But then I got distracted as I saw the pack magic flutter and flex. The other alpha had arrived.

I looked around, trying to spot the alpha and warn everybody. As a few wolves shifted, the picture became clear, and I felt like I'd been hit by a ton of bricks. Chad was the other alpha, the one connected to the omegas making the drug. His pack magic didn't have a hint of the orange glow the rest of the wolves had; his was completely tainted, pitch black.

"Kelly, it's him!" I shouted, trying to warn her, but Chad stepped past her, swiftly grabbing Brent. The young alpha shoved his fist into Brent's body, pulling out his still beating heart as the spark of life left Brent. Chad pushed him off, holding the heart in his hands.

Shock. That was the only way to describe the moment. Everyone was frozen, trying to process what they had just seen. Even for a pack of werewolves, it was unbelievably savage.

Chad took that moment to pull out an obsidian blade with a carved bone handle. It looked like it belonged in some exhibit for Native Americans, not in a college football star's hands. A tassel of horsehair stuck out the butt of the handle and it just felt completely incongruous with everything. Like it was just wrong.

He stabbed the heart and tore a slit in it.

Everyone came back to their senses at that moment. Screams of outrage and howls of mourning filled the air as they rushed Chad. I wanted to get up and move, to fight him, but even standing was beyond my capabilities at the moment. Brent had wrecked my body pretty heavily when he'd slammed me to the ground.

Chad ignored the charging werewolves, lifting the heart to his face and drinking from it with a wide smile on his face. I could see the magic now. The pack magic branched from Brent's heart to all the other wolves present except Kelly. There was a faint bond between Kelly and Chad, but it was a whisper compared to the rest of the bonds present.

As Chad drank from Brent's heart, the bonds flowed with the blood and switched from Brent to Chad.

Chaos descended on the scene as the werewolves felt the bond to Chad forming. They were torn between their hate for what he'd done and the emotional tie they now felt. Chad smiled, seeming to recognize their dilemma.

Chad chose that moment to shift. He grew and didn't seem to stop for several seconds until he was even a head taller than Brent had been.

But he wasn't a majestic beast as Brent had been. There was something sickly about him, his proportions just slightly off. His mouth seemed too big for his head, which seemed too big for his body. It was almost like a caricature.

Chad's oversized head lifted into the air, but he didn't howl. Instead, he let out a deafening roar, his mouth stretching so wide that his skin tore at the edges of his jaw. It was just unnatural.

I could see the bonds between Chad and the pack pulling tighter. Like he was leading a hundred dogs for a walk, Chad broke into a lope, pulling each of the wolves with him. As I watched, he took control of the pack.

Some tried to root themselves to the ground in protest, but it didn't work. His pull as the alpha was stronger. Soon, the entire pack was off in a full run.

That was when I noticed the sirens, standing at their guns and seeming to stare dumbfounded at the scene. "Shoot him," I yelled at them, pointing at Chad.

That seemed to pull them to attention. They brought their guns around, firing into him, but Chad just plowed past their two Jeeps, pulling his new pack of werewolves with him. I could see his pack magic solidifying as they ran together.

Kelly's sobbing brought me back to the present. I tried to get up again, only to stumble and fall. Morgana came and helped me up, shaking her head at the situation. I didn't blame her for not taking on Chad and his new pack, but part of me wanted to be angry with someone or something about this.

"Morgana, I could see his magic. He's the one that was behind the drugs; all the omegas had a pack bond with him. I never saw his magic before, I didn't think to check him. I should have known." My fists clenched until my knuckles popped.

"Yes, it's clear now. But don't beat yourself up for not seeing it sooner. He was a jerk, but no one suspected this level of treachery from him. I didn't see it. Jadelyn and her father didn't see it. Knowing Rupert, he had that boy investigated by Detective Fox before he sent his daughter anywhere near him. All that, and they missed this. You are not at fault." Morgana did her best to console me.

It helped some, but I couldn't help but still feel guilt. It had been right in front of me. I clenched my teeth so hard I was afraid they were going to crack.

The other wolves started to stir from where they lay in the street. A few had been pushed past their regenerative abilities and were dying in the street, but some were regaining consciousness and awareness. They had been too beat up to follow Chad, but as they recovered, it seemed they were being pulled like the others to run with him.

Kelly looked at me, and I nodded. They were the best use of the potion now. Kelly ran back to the van and gathered what potion we had left, going around and distributing it to the recovering wolves. At least she didn't seem affected, I noticed that the bond between her and Chad was fading, almost gone. Had he broken her trust so much that she left the still forming pack?

"Morgana. The boss wants to speak with you." One siren handed a brick of a phone off to her.

Morgana held it up to her ear, and I could hear unintelligible squawking on the other end. Whoever that was, they weren't happy. The tirade continued for a moment, Morgana's face an impassive mask, but finally it stopped.

"Rupert. I don't know what they told you, but it was Chad. All the drug business, all the omega wolves, and now this." She looked over at me as she continued.

"Somehow, he stole Brent's pack bond. He dirtied Brent's magic and then used that to steal all of his pack bonds. It was the same dirty magic as the wolves that worked the drugs; it all led back to Chad."

There was a pause on the other end, and Morgana's face hardened. "Did you get that Rupert? My charge can see magic. I have no doubt what he saw was accurate. You need to put a kill order out on Chad. Now."

More squawking sounded, but Morgana cut him off. "I don't care. Look, I know he was supposed to be your future son-in-law, but this isn't something you forgive and forget. You didn't see this, Rupert. He tore out another alpha's heart and stole his pack. This isn't just werewolves fighting for dominance; this is dark and forbidden magic."

Her anger was barely restrained at that point. "Don't test my patience. This isn't the time for games," Morgana hissed before hanging up on Rupert and talking to me as she handed the sirens the phone. "Sometimes I wish he'd dispense with the politics."

"What do you mean?" I asked, worried about the answer.

"It almost sounded like he wanted to discuss a truce with Chad and to deescalate the situation. Idiot. I've seen people this power hungry before. They've thrown off the guise of civility and given the chance, they would tear everything apart before they give up any power."

"Are they at least looking for him?" I asked.

"They are, but he isn't a wild pack of werewolves this time. It seemed like he was in control. He'll be harder to track."

I had a feeling that was why they ran. It hadn't felt like he was fearful for his life. He must have been using it to exert control. Based on the way the pack magic had solidified further, it must have somehow strengthened the bonds. I explained what I'd seen to Morgana, but it was Kelly that finally spoke up. She'd been standing nearby, listening with her enhanced hearing.

"Packs run during the full moon to restore their mana and to reinforce the pack bond. I have no doubt you're right; he ran because that was how he would finish stealing my father's pack." Her eyes watered, tears threatening to fall. But she squeezed her eyes shut and wiped her face with the back of her hand, spreading a smear of blood across her face.

"Zach, it's time to go home and rest," Morgana urged me.

I wanted to keep chasing, keep fighting, but I knew she was right. My body wouldn't put up with any more of that. I needed to heal before I'd be of any use in hunting Chad down.

Chapter 25

Shots continued to pepper into the paper target, which had more holes than paper at this point. I held my hand out for more, but unlike before, Morgana didn't hand me a filled magazine.

"You're done, Zach. I thought you were going to rest after just a few." There was a knowing smirk on her face. I had said that, but I had so much unused tension filling my body, and it wasn't like I could run it off. My body needed to heal.

When I'd found out she had a shooting range, I wasn't even surprised. She had a bit of everything in the odd twisting building. And after the day we had, I was starting to recognize the need to have better aim.

"I'll be fine. Just a few more."

Morgana gave me a look and didn't produce a loaded magazine. "You have shot enough. Let your body heal; take time away from the range for the work you've done today to settle in. If you keep firing, you are just going to learn bad habits. Resting is part of training."

I went to grab my own, but her face made it clear that she wasn't budging. I let out a sigh and put the gun down. Staying active had been helping me avoid thinking about what had happened.

"Besides, you have a visitor," Morgana said cryptically, stepping away and opening the door. Jadelyn was on the other side, her hand raised to knock.

"Oh. Hi. I had one of your people bring me in, Morgana. I was hoping to hire you. Both of you." She fumbled around with her words. She looked tired and more than a little frazzled.

"You know my rates?" Morgana smiled.

"Yes. Happy to pay them. I'd like some extra guards on me tonight. There's a party at my sorority house and..." she trailed off.

She didn't need to say more. She was scared of Chad, or more specifically, what he might do.

"No luck finding Chad?" I asked.

Jadelyn shook her head, sending her platinum blonde hair into the air around her. "No. He disappeared after he left Nicetown. They haven't been able to find him yet." Her eyes searched mine, looking for hope.

I had told the council everything that had happened. After way more questions than it should have taken, the elves had begun mass producing the type of potion Tee had made. We were hopeful we could stop a future incident and reduce the need for slaughter.

Although the elves didn't seem too concerned about the lives of the werewolves, they agreed to help. It was in everybody's best interest. Even if the elves were snoots, they could put it down from time to time for the greater good.

The council believed Chad would make a move to gain more power, using his growing pack. There were differences of opinion on if he'd focus on taking down high value targets or work to amass a larger army by absorbing more packs, but either wasn't a good outcome for the council.

They had no other obvious solution besides reaching out and trying to locate other packs in the area. Brent would have known where they were off hand, but with him gone, the council was having to do some hunting to pick up those connections to other packs.

Morgana and I were on call as a result. If they located a nearby pack, and they were in trouble, we'd be sent out. This time, I promised myself that I'd do more. I still hated how feeble I'd felt laying on the ground while the battle played out.

"So, about the protection detail?" As Jadelyn spoke, I realized there'd been a long pause after her question, and Morgana seemed to be waiting for me to decide.

"This is the same party on Tuesday that Scarlett invited me to?" I asked.

Jadelyn nodded. "The same. And it's already Tuesday, Zach. Bring your swimsuit. You can hang out with Scarlett; that would make a perfect cover."

"I guess that leaves me hanging in the shadows. Always in the shadows," Morgana said overly dramatically, but I could see the twinkle in her eye. I wasn't so foolish to think she really had a problem with it.

"You just blend in with the shadows better than my pale ass," I teased back before returning my focus to Jadelyn. "We'll be there. Sounds like I'm missing classes again today to get some rest." A part of me groaned at all the work I had to catch up on, but this was more important.

Jadelyn gave me a weak smile. "Things have been crazy the last few days. It is a rough introduction to the para world, but I swear it isn't always this crazy. Thank you both. I need to get back." She bowed slightly and left.

"So I get to spy on your date tonight?" Morgana's smile was one of wicked delight. I remembered feeling her eyes on us when we had dinner at Bumps in the Night. Creeper. Though I didn't hate the idea of her looking out for me, and even more importantly, Scarlett and Jadelyn.

"I guess, but keep your eyes out for Chad. It sounds like I'm going to be in the middle of a sorority party." How I was going to keep my eyes out during that, I wasn't sure. I knew Scarlett was going to be one hell of a distraction.

"Don't worry so much. Her father no doubt has a small army watching out as well. We are mostly there in case they don't have enough firepower to deal with what comes. If Chad comes, he might be more than guns and enchantments can handle."

I swallowed at the thought of a werewolf pack crashing the party. It was not a pleasant image. "Okay, so I just head to a date at a sorority party. To protect a girl I like from the potential of being ripped to shreds by werewolves. Just a regular Tuesday night." I ran my hand through my hair.

Morgana slapped me on the shoulder. "That's the spirit! I'm sure you'll find a way to enjoy yourself. I hear there's a pretty kitsune there that might have a thing for you."

***

"Hey, Zach. Come on in," Scarlett greeted me at the door to the sorority house. It fit the mold of what you'd picture, a large Greek-styled manor with grand columns.

Looking past Scarlett, I could see girls giggling and pointing at the interaction. Scarlett noticed my attention. "Sorry, there really aren't any secrets in the house. Just ignore them."

She rolled her eyes, which looked extra bright at that moment. But she also seemed to be wearing a bit more makeup, making her features even more stunning than normal. I smiled that she'd gone to the extra effort.

Scarlett wore a tight tube top and a dangerously short skirt that liked to swish as she led me into the house.

Her sorority sisters gawked, and I felt a little like a zoo animal on display. "Have somewhere a little less..." I struggled for an apt word, my mind re-centering on the zoo analogy.

"Public?" Scarlett offered, smiling. "That's kind of how a sorority house works. We mostly have large public spaces. We even all sleep in the same cold room. But Jadelyn and I share a study room. I'll take you up there." She gave a dramatic wave to the girls that were gawking and took my hand, pulling me up the stairs.

As we walked away, I heard a fresh wave of eager gossip trailing behind us.

When we got to her study room, she pushed me inside and closed the door, leaning against it with a blush that made her look adorable. Her ears and tails popped out. "Sometimes they can be pretty embarrassing."

"What's to be embarrassed about?" I teased, walking over and running my finger along her ear. "This is business, after all. We are here to protect Jadelyn tonight, right?" She gave a little shiver as I stroked her ear.

"Right." The way she stretched out the word wasn't convincing.

I smiled, leaning in to kiss her soft lips, my body pressing hers against the door. As it thumped with our weight, I could hear voices in the hall laughing, but they really didn't matter to me at that moment.

Scarlett wrapped her arms around my head to prevent me from pulling back, and her tongue came out to play. Nobody else existed as I focused on Scarlett and her lovely lips.

By the time we broke apart, we were both breathing heavily. "Best guard duty ever."

Scarlett beamed up at me in response. "We should probably get the business talk out of the way, huh?" Scarlett bit her lip, clearly not happy with herself for saying it.

I nodded. "Get the important things done in case we get distracted. Because right now I find myself incredibly distracted." I let her watch as I ran my eyes up and down her body. She was stunning, and I was feeling like a lucky man. The electricity between the two of us at that moment was intense. I had to remind myself that we were still early in the relationship and I shouldn't get too carried away.

The beast snorted inside of me. He wanted to get carried away.

Scarlett cracked the door, making sure the eavesdroppers were gone. She seemed satisfied, so they must have just wanted confirmation of what I was to Scarlett.

"Okay. So her father finally got on board with a protection detail tonight. We have two paramilitary teams out there watching. They are focusing on the entrances, and we have two working the main entrance as bouncers."

Pushing down my desire to continue where we'd paused, I focused on what she was saying. "Can they take down a werewolf?"

I pulled her over to the couch and sat down, pulling her into my lap. But I hadn't missed that there was a pull-out daybed under the couch.

The room was simple. It had two desks next to each other in the corner, which clearly showed how close they must be, and a single seating area that was the daybed we were on. It wasn't set up to do much other than study and relax.

"A few, sure. If a whole pack comes? Not a chance. They're more detection than anything. If the pack comes, I'm on extraction while you and Morgana deal with any heavy hitters to buy us time."

Keeping up with her, I nodded, but I wasn't sure where my limits were. "Uh, thoughts on how destructive I should be? I could accidentally torch this whole place if I breathe fire."

Scarlett paused, her eyes wide. "Can you control it? I know you said you were having"—she giggled—"performance issues."

I frowned, not loving the choice of her words. But the glee she clearly felt at getting that reaction made it worth it. "It's gotten better, but not completely clear. I can do one ability on command now." My eye shifted, and I saw Scarlett along with her magic.

This time, I could see the magic in her tails as they swished around. Her magic was a ghostly blue and came off of her like fire. "Your magic looks awesome. Like blue fire."

Now it was Scarlett's turn to be surprised. "You can see it? What does this look like?" She made an illusionary Scarlett next to me. With my dragon eye out, it was plainly obvious that it wasn't real. It was made up entirely of magic.

I smiled, pleased I could see the difference. "Nice. This'll be useful if you try to play too many tricks."

"No fun," Scarlett pouted. "But that's a pretty neat trick." The illusion puffed away like a cloud of spent smoke. "If there really is a problem tonight and you want to breathe fire, just try not to kill anyone but the wolves."

"I'll do my best. So far, I've melted a car and concrete flooring, so I can't promise furniture and landscaping won't be harmed in the process."

"Damn," Scarlett breathed. "I hope you know that you packing that kind of firepower is stupid sexy. Also, it is painfully hard not to brag to Jadelyn that I'm dating a *mother fucking dragon*." She whispered the last part.

At the same time, the door to her study room opened. "What about me? I hope you aren't spreading anything embarrassing." Jadelyn closed the door behind her and slapped down a pile of books.

"Never." Scarlett spun around with a mischievous grin as her tails swished behind her and bumped against my chest. I shifted my eye back before Jadelyn looked up.

Jadelyn was in her signature form-fitting white jeans and a hoodie for the cool fall weather. "The girls are getting everything set up poolside. Do you want to help or stay hermited up here with him for now?"

The siren didn't look like she was in the mood to party. There were bags under her eyes that spoke of a restless night last night. I wanted to collect her and give her a comforting hug, but that would be inappropriate. I was here to be with Scarlett.

But it didn't stop me from trying to cheer her up. "So, Jade, tell me some dirt on Scarlett."

That brought a smile to her face. "So her first boyfriend—" A second Scarlett appeared behind Jadelyn, wrapping her hands over her mouth, but apparently Jadelyn was used to that, because she bit the illusion hand and popped it, continuing her story. "He was a guy in college when she was in high school. He came home for the first time in biking leathers that looked like he belonged to a biker gang. Her father was absolutely apoplectic." She laughed.

Scarlett grabbed her ears and pulled them down while she covered her eyes with her wrists. "It was a prank on my father. He told me to get my own ride. I wanted a bike, so I just dated him that one time, to go for a ride."

"You guys have quite the history. Did you live together?" It sounded like Jadelyn was there when Scarlett had brought him home.

"Okay, this is going to sound insensitive," Jadelyn started. I waited, my interest piqued. I couldn't wait to hear what was going to follow that statement.

"She was literally born for me." As Jadelyn finished saying it, she looked slightly sheepish.

My eyebrows climbed into my hairline. "What?"

Scarlett stopped hiding behind her hands and sighed, starting with an explanation. "When they found out Jadelyn's mother was pregnant, my father purposefully had a kid. We were raised together. I was trained to be an assassin to protect her. It's how our two families have always been."

Jadelyn waved her hands, like she wanted to stop before this got too far. "It's not like I had any say in it. I love Scarlett like a sister. We just have our own roles to play. I'd never impede her life too much."

I remembered what their fathers had said. Given that they literally viewed Scarlett as made to protect Jadelyn, it made even more sense. I let out a sigh. They were bound to keep interfering, as they thought I had a strong pull on Scarlett.

Both of their faces fell at my sigh, and Scarlett wiggled into me, clearly distraught. Jadelyn started babbling quickly. "I promise not to get between you two, Zach. I think you're fantastic for Scarlett. And I'm really excited for you both. Our dads don't get to control our whole lives, despite how much they try..."

I held up my hand to stop her. "No. It's fine." Collecting Scarlett's hands in mine, I pulled her attention to me. "I understand your obligation. No, that's a lie. I don't really, but I can conceptualize it. I'm screwing this up. What I want to say is that it's okay. I don't scare that easily. I am a d—" I cut myself off, realizing Jadelyn was still there.

Scarlett's ears perked back up. They were really quite expressive. "Really? I'm going to have to do things for her constantly. It'll mess up dates or plans we have."

"You already do that. Besides, that is just more reason for me to make sure you have time to be happy," Jadelyn tried again. "There will be family matters, but I'll work with you the best I can." It was a plea not only to Scarlett, but to me too.

"Besides, Zach and I are friends. I can hire him and Morg, and send you all away on the same missions."

Scarlett snorted. "Their rates will break even your bank."

"You'd be surprised. I think it can rival a dragon's horde now." Jadelyn smiled, seeing her best friend perk back up.

I froze a little at the reference to the dragon's horde. Scarlett and I shared a look at it and burst out laughing.

"What?" Jadelyn looked between the two of us, confused.

"Nothing," I supplied between chuckles. "Just a joke between us about dragons."

Jadelyn nodded slowly. She didn't understand, but that was okay.

Scarlett pushed herself off my lap. "I think I should go check on our friend hiding in the shadows. I'll come back with drinks, then we party?"

"Don't make them too strong. We might have work tonight," I called after her, feeling a little at a loss.

"She just wants a little alone time," Jadelyn said quietly after Scarlett had left. I nodded; Jadelyn knew her well.

Jadelyn looked down at her hands. "She had plans for tonight, and I'm afraid I may have just spoiled them."

That got my attention. "Plans?"

Jadelyn smirked and shook her head. "Sworn to keep her secrets. You aren't getting a thing out of me." She stopped standing in the middle of the room and came to join me on the couch, keeping a friendly distance. "I'm a little jealous of you both. Something like you have would be nice."

I wanted to console her, but apparently my brain and mouth weren't working well together at that moment as I tried to console her by saying, "Well, I might end up killing Chad."

The look on her face was priceless. Surprise was followed by hope, fear, and longing so quickly that I nearly missed them before she slammed down her neutral mask.

"You don't have to hide all that from me. Friends, right?" I nudged her.

She sighed and let go of the mask, her expression still a swirl of emotions. "It's been a hard day. Honestly? Getting the engagement with Chad broken is something I'm completely okay with, but there's fear too."

"We'll get him," I offered and pulled her close to comfort her.

"No— eh yeah," she started to object, but seemed to decide just to go with what I'd said. I could tell I had misunderstood, but I couldn't figure out how. If she wasn't afraid of Chad, then what was it?

With Chad out of the picture, she'd be free to be with who she wanted.

But then it hit me. That wasn't true. Her father controlled her life to the point that he had a bodyguard created for her. He would just arrange the next-best engagement for his own advantage. "Your father is going to engage you again."

She nodded weakly and leaned against my shoulder. "Yeah. But I have a lot of feelings about that now. With Chad, I just didn't care. I knew it was going to happen, and it was my duty. But now..."

Scarlett barged into the room, squeezing three cups together to carry them. Her mood seemed much improved. "Hey, quit trying to steal my man," she teased, seeing Jadelyn's head laying against my shoulder.

"No!" Jadelyn nearly jumped out of her skin as she tried to get away. "I'd never."

We both looked at her funny, but Scarlett supplied our thoughts. "It was just a joke, Jade. And don't worry about earlier, I'm over it. Now, who wants a drink?"

Chapter 26

The party was in full swing by the time we made it downstairs. Girls were dancing around in bikinis covered by white shirts that I had no doubt were going to get wet at some point. Music pumped out of a tower of black speakers as people went around with red plastic cups, filling the sorority's backyard around the pool.

I had changed into my mandated swim trunks and t-shirt. I blended right in with the rest of the party.

Based on the guys around me moving a little more leisurely than usual with glazed over expressions, Scarlett had gone easier on my drink than whatever they were drinking. I was glad to be able to keep my wits about me; I needed to make sure Scarlett and Jadelyn stayed safe.

The area was an odd mismatch of elegant, permanent fixtures like sculpted bushes and the ornate stone wall around the backyard, and very cheap looking and cracked plastic lawn chairs, fold out tables and red solo cups already starting to litter the lawn.

"Stop staring," Scarlett chided me, taking a sip of her own drink as we meandered around.

"Keeping my eyes open. We have a job to do."

Her eyes narrowed at my comment. "I could have sworn I put enough alcohol in that drink to make you at least buzzed by now."

I looked at the cup as if it had betrayed me. "Wait. Could I have a different tolerance now?"

"Very possible." Scarlett shrugged, but my eyes drifted to the top of her head. I'd already grown used to using her ears to read her better, but because we were in public, they were tucked away once more.

I reached out, touching where they should have been to see if it was part of her illusion ability.

"What are you—? Oh, no, they aren't there right now." She understood after a moment. A smile curled up on the corner of her lips. "Here, watch this. Hold my drink."

Only after I took her drink did I realize two things. One, she had that look on her face that seemed to appear right before she caused trouble. And two, I was standing precariously close to the pool given the look on her face.

Sure enough, Scarlett threw herself at me, trying to push me into the pool. If it had been a week ago, it might have worked, but I was at least twice her weight now. And, with Morgana's training and the battles I'd been in, I was getting better at reacting.

I stepped back as she overextended. She must have grabbed my shirt because she was tugged forward with my movement. I dropped the drinks to try to grab her, but I was too slow. She curled in on herself and turned it into a dive at the last second.

Scarlett went a few feet out into the pool before surfacing, her bright orange hair wet and dark as she gasped for air. Her white shirt was plastered to her skin.

Not wanting her to be alone in the pool, I picked up and put the cups on a nearby table and jumped in with her, cannon balling to the crowd's great amusement.

"Idiot." She splashed me as people cheered us on.

"Didn't want you to look silly. Come on, let's get out." I swam over to the ladder and pulled myself out, turning back to give her a hand.

Scarlett got another one of those looks as she got to the ladder and started climbing out slowly, keeping eye contact with me.

My eyes were glued to her as she made her movie-worthy exit from the pool. Her eyes were smoldering, and I was mesmerized. It wasn't until she grabbed my hand and started pulling me through the crowd that the spell broke.

We got a few whistles and catcalls as the two of us found our way from the party to the house, still dripping wet. "Where are we going?"

"I have some towels in the study room. Come on."

"What about watching over Jadelyn?" I asked, feeling stupid for bringing up another girl, but we had responsibilities tonight.

"Morgana is out there and so are several teams of her father's men. It'll be fine." She kept pulling me along through the house. I felt a little guilty for dripping on the floors, but I knew the place well enough that I could scoop her up before we went up the stairs to carry her up.

Scarlett let out a small squeak of surprise before she turned and gave me a long, lingering kiss.

"Get a room," a passing guy teased, clearly a little jealous.

I was still a bit confused about why we'd change out of wet clothes when we were at a pool party. They'd dry if given a bit more time. But Scarlett seemed intent on drying off.

But as we walked through the empty hallways, I started to have a feeling there was more to Scarlett's plan than just changing.

The door closed, but there was no lock. So instead, I plopped Scarlett on the daybed and picked up one of the desks, pushing it in front of the door.

"Now why would you do that?" Scarlett asked, leaning back with her wet chest stretching the white fabric that offered little barrier showing off the bikini underneath.

"Wouldn't want anyone coming in—while we are changing, of course." I stepped forward, pulling her up to stand in front of me. I kissed her again; she was already feeling warm again after being dipped in the pool

She nodded. "Of course, just changing. Why don't you slip out of your wet clothes?"

I shucked my shirt and tossed it to the side, letting it land in a wet wad. It was quickly followed by my wet trunks, which I pushed to my ankles and tossed to the same area.

Scarlett licked her lips as she took in my body, holding two towels in her hands. But as I reached, she held them just out of reach.

I raised an eyebrow, taking in her still clothed body. "Are you going to get out of your wet clothes?"

"Not yet. Let me help you." She took one towel and stepped forward, hunger in her eyes as she started rubbing my chest before moving slowly outwards, tracing every muscle of mine with the towel. She was being thorough as she dried my upper body, then began moving south, taking my semi-erect member between two fistfuls of towel and fluffing it.

It didn't take long before it hardened under her work.

"Doesn't look like you have any performance issues in this regard." She looked up at me through wet eyelashes.

"I do not," I confirmed, my voice coming out rougher than I'd meant it to. It was closer to a growl. My beast felt like he was perched on the edge of a cliff, waiting for more. It was still and silent, like it was afraid that any movement would throw everything off.

Feeling a little pent up after all the teasing, I reached forward, tugging her hips up against me until our bodies were pressed together. Sliding my hands along her waist, I caught the bottom edge of her shirt, sliding it up over her body.

She lifted her arms and let me pull it over her head. "What's got you all excited?" She slid to her knees, continuing her work on my member, drying it thoroughly as she looked up at me.

I snatched the other towel and pulled her to her feet again, pushing her against the wall and kissing her lips, nipping at them as I used the towel to dry her off.

Eventually, she dropped the towel she'd been holding and reached back to undo her bikini top. It fell to the floor and her breasts sprang free, and I made sure to dry them well, eventually letting the towel slip down to massage them while I kissed her neck. Her moans grew as I worked her breasts, flicking over her nipples playfully.

Still kissing her neck, I slid my hands down her body, tracing just along the top of her bikini bottoms. Her body gave a small shake as her hips thrust forward, clearly wanting more. I ran my hand along the front of the bikini bottoms, slipping lightly into her folds, using the material to help tease her further.

A frustrated moan came out of Scarlett as she reached down, quickly dropping the bikini bottoms to the floor and spreading her legs slightly. I couldn't help but chuckle at her eagerness.

Scarlett's eyes met mine, lust filling them as she pushed me back, panting. Her hand came down and wrapped around my erection, pumping it and letting out a satisfied sigh. "You're really above average in most things, huh?"

I smiled, not minding the ego stroke. I picked her up and brought her over to the daybed, catching the handle with my foot and dragging the mattress out from under the couch. It was only a twin mattress, so there wasn't that much room, but all I needed was a soft surface.

I laid her down and crawled over her, kissing her tender neck and trailing kisses down to her nipples. I cupped her soft mounds, feeling their softness and letting my fingers sink into them. "You are so damn beautiful."

Scarlett lay under me, her bright orange hair splayed out and already regaining its wavy quality as it dried. Her emerald eyes watched me as she bit her plump lips and raised her arms, exposing herself to me. Something about the motion and her eyes screamed of submission. The beast in my chest roaring with delight.

It ignited an extra fire in me. I wanted to satisfy every inch of her.

Kissing her nipples one last time, I kissed my way further south as her fingers threaded themselves through my hair and I confirmed that the carpet did indeed match the drapes. My mouth and tongue elicited gasps as I got to work, making her body writhe.

Her scent of vanilla and cloves filled my nose, but with it, a deeper scent. There was something about it that sent the primal part of my mind into overdrive, the need to claim her more fully driving me.

I wiped away some of her lubrication from my nose and lips. "Yes?" I made sure she understood the question.

"Yes, please! Take me, my dragon." Her eyes twinkled with mischief that vanished as soon as I pushed in. She bit her lip and tensed up.

"I can slow down," I offered with as much sincerity as I could. In reality, every instinct and hormone in my body was screaming at me to speed up. But I held my body rigid, using my control to wait until she was ready.

"No, just tight. Not used to being with somebody so large. Keep going."

I pushed her shoulders into the bed and feathered her neck with kisses as I slowly worked myself deeper. As I leaned back up, I realized something felt just slightly off about all of it. "Bring out your tails. I want to be with you fully, as you really are. All parts of you."

Emotion swelled in her face, and I felt her sex clench around me like a vice before she revealed her full kitsune glory. She looked up into my eyes, searching for something.

She must have liked what she found, because her sex eased and opened up, allowing me to slide to the hilt as her tails tried to wiggle themselves out from under her and get back to swatting my chest. "You don't mind?"

"Of course not. I like it. It's who you are, Scarlett. And I happen to like the whole package." I smiled, rocking back before slamming deep into her, eliciting a small gasp.

Smiling, I leaned down and gave her a slower kiss before I started moving my hips to a rhythm again, her tight, wet sex squeezing me with each movement.

"Then it's the whole package you get." The mischievous look entered her eyes again. She held her arms out, clearly wanting me snug against her. Taking the cue, I leaned down, but then I felt somebody else pressing their soft chest into my back. And another set of hands ran over my chest.

"What?" I looked up quickly, almost pulling out, but then I spotted two more Scarletts, dressed in sexy lingerie. They were pressed around me, covering me with soft touches of their own tails and adding to the fluffy battering of soft sensual pleasure.

My beast declared that we do whatever we needed to keep this one. I found myself agreeing and trying not to forget myself in her illusions, making sure the real Scarlett got my focus.

She was clinging to my shoulders, raising and lowering her hips in time with my thrusts, helping me to reach deeper into her.

I kissed her, holding her close as we let our bodies tangle over and over, savoring the feeling of each other. The two illusions twisted around the two of us, adding to the moment without distracting from what we were doing.

The only noises in the room were our heavy breaths and the wet slap of flesh in time to an unheard beat.

"This is lovely, but I think I'm going to need something a bit faster," Scarlett admitted, her tails picking up their tempo. I smiled, taking the cue. I started thrusting to her beat.

The moan she gave me only encouraged me further. Grabbing her hips to hold them still, I started swinging my hips into her, pulling her down onto me again and again. I chased my own pleasure in her silken vice.

"Fuck. You feel amazing, Scarlett," I groaned as I lifted her hips slightly, constantly adjusting them, trying to get at a better angle. She was a heaven of soft flesh as I kept pounding into her.

I realized through the haze that I'd half-lifted her body off the bed by that point as I pounded into her. My body was different now, and I had forgotten just how strong I'd become. I was glad I hadn't accidentally hurt her or been too rough as a result, but something told me my subconscious would not let that happen.

Knowing that, I decided to experiment a bit with what my strength could do. I hooked an arm around her hips and lifted her off the bed, shifting myself so I was standing on my knees.

"Ah! What are you—" she asked in surprise as I changed the angle completely. Only her shoulder blades were still on the daybed as I held the rest of her weight and pumped my hips into her. It seemed like she tried to speak several more times, but each was cut off with a gasp of pleasure, her thighs squeezing my hips before she pulled herself up to face me.

We kissed as both of us thrust and writhed our hips together in a delicious, discordant beat filled with nothing but raw lust for each other. I wasn't sure how long we continued like that, but soon I felt my balls tighten and my body build with tension.

Letting myself slip over the edge, I grabbed her hips and squeezed her to me as I emptied myself into her.

The immense satisfaction of pumping my seed into her did something that I wasn't sure how to describe. Letting out a satisfied grunt, I reveled in the moment's bliss.

As soon as I released, I felt her sex clench down and quiver around my erection, like it was sucking out the last of my orgasm with her own.

I sagged and pressed her back to the bed before wiggling to the side and propping myself up next to her. "That was... I don't even know how to describe that."

"Amazing works." She gave a full bellied laugh that made her tits jiggle in my face. "I just fucked a dragon." Her fingers went down to and came up with a smear of my seed. "Do you know how much this is worth?"

I paused. I hadn't really thought about it. "Morgana had said everything about me was valuable. But she never put a price to it." She had also mentioned every part of me, dead or alive, would have enough value to kill me. But that seemed like a post-sex buzz kill.

"Hundreds of thousands of dollars for what you just pumped into me."

"Will it help you like that?" I asked, suddenly realizing I hadn't asked a very important question. "Oh shit, are you on the pill?"

Scarlett started laughing even harder. "Your face. Yes, I am. If not, I would kick your ass right now. As for this? It feels amazing. It's so full of mana, it's like firecrackers going off inside me constantly right now." She blushed to match her hair. "They say sex with a dragon is different. I think I get it now. Just feeling your seed inside me sent me over the edge."

I kissed her softly. "You're welcome to it anytime you want. As far as I'm concerned, it's your personal pump if you want it."

"Careful, I could go make millions off you and run away." Her hand wandered down my pelvis and tickled my softened member.

It felt nice, but then I felt it hardening again. I sat up a bit, staring down at it in shock. "What?"

Scarlett giggled. "It isn't uncommon among the paranormal that heal quickly; they recover quickly too. Plus, how would dragons always have so many wives if they didn't have the equipment to keep them all happy?"

Recovering from my own shock, I just grinned and pushed Scarlett back down on the bed. "Careful what you wish for."

"Let's switch." Scarlett pushed me back, and we rotated so she was at my side while I lay on my back. The two illusions came over and started feathering my cock with kisses and soft touches while Scarlett stayed up by my head. We fell into a flurry of kisses, but she pulled back slightly.

"Kitsune don't heal that much faster than a human. You're going to break me if I let you."

I nodded, not wanting to push her body too far. If she needed a break, I was happy to just tumble around the bed for a bit. I was pretty sure the illusions couldn't offer enough substance to get me off, but they were a very pleasant distraction.

CHAPTER 27

I felt refreshed and more than a little smug as Scarlett walked, tucked under my arm. The way she leaned against me felt like I was bigger than I was and sparked something in me that made me want to protect her.

After the second round, we'd taken a break. I'd been happy to just feel her lying against me; it was a high of its own. My beast and I were experiencing a new level of contentment just getting to touch her.

I knew from my studies that there was a cocktail of hormones at work in my body right now, making both of us connect on a different level.

"The party seems unnecessarily rowdy now," I commented.

We could hear the music and the boisterous laughter mixing together out by the poolside, followed by shouts as people tried to talk above the music. The party had split, though. Part of the party had moved into the sorority house, and we got more than a few looks as we came down the stairs.

The party inside the house was calmer. It seemed to be a place for people to talk and apparently play games that involved dares. I watched a group that included Jadelyn cheering on a couple to make out. Based on how awkwardly the two people were looking at each other, they were not already a couple.

My phone pinged. I reached down, checking it. Morgana had sent me a text with a thumbs up, a nice hand sign, and a message that read, 'glad you got a much-deserved break, all good out here.'

I held the phone up so Scarlett could see it and rolled my eyes. There was another ping as I did that, and Scarlett burst out into a fit of giggles.

There was a meme now of an old man telling a knight, 'I told you to slay the dragon, not lay it!' In the image, a dragon girl stood by his side with hearts drifting off her.

"Funny Morgana," I snorted and stuffed the phone back in my pocket before she could send something else.

I looked back to the game that was underway, noticing that Jadelyn was the new target of some dare. She turned, spotting us and seeming relieved.

Jadelyn fumbled her way over. "Scar, can I borrow him for a second?"

"Sure?" It came out more as a question than an answer, but Jadelyn took it, grabbing my head and pulling me down for a kiss.

I let the peck happen more out of surprise than anything and tried to pull back, but her hands wrapped around the back of my head, and she pulled herself into the kiss deeper. There was passion behind her side of it, but I was conflicted. I hadn't expected it.

The crowd cheered and hollered, egging her to keep going.

She didn't belabor it past my failure to return it and let me go with a smiling blush that was spreading down to her chest.

Scarlett cleared her throat and gave Jadelyn a glare. Jadelyn looked bashful, giving Scarlett a weak smile before she scurried off.

"I—" I wasn't sure what to say.

"I'm only a little mad with you right now. Mostly, I'm pissed at her. You tried to pull away."

My mouth opened and closed several times before I found the right words. "I'm sorry. Won't happen again; I just didn't expect that."

"Me neither, and technically, I told her she could borrow you. But you aren't some rag doll that she can just play with." Scarlett's nose was flaring as she talked.

It was cute seeing her get jealous, but I hated that she was so angry with her close friend. I didn't want to be a wedge between the two girls. Thinking back on some of Jadelyn's comments, I realized that she was crushing on me.

I'd been so focused on Scarlett that I'd thought it was all pretty harmless when she was with Chad, but now that she was free of his engagement, it looked like she might want more.

I thought about what Frank would say. He'd tell me to be selfish. That sounded like a terrible idea right at this moment.

"You're thinking about it," Scarlett said, a bit of hurt in her voice.

I pulled her closer. "Not like you're thinking. I'm just replaying things she's said before and seeing it a bit differently now. Jadelyn is great, but you're my priority, Scarlett."

My phone dinged several times urgently. Morgana was messaging me. 'Trouble in paradise? I have eyes on your princess. She's taking a call. It sounds urgent.'

"Morgana?" Scarlett asked.

I nodded. "She confirmed she is keeping an eye on Jadelyn. Asked what happened."

"Well, not like I can avoid her. Let's go have a chat." The way Scarlett said it sounded like she was going to chat with her fists, or maybe her nails. I wasn't sure how the two of them would fight.

The party faded behind us as Scarlett led us out the side door. She must have known where Jadelyn would have gone to be alone, because despite being an isolated alley, there Jadelyn was, pacing back and forth as she talked on the phone.

"—know where? Uh huh. Are you sure just those two?"

I paused at the exit, waiting to see what happened. I was happy to stay out of what was going to go down between the two friends. They had more history than I could understand in the short time I'd known them.

Jadelyn looked up to see Scarlett coming towards her and hurried up with whoever was on the other end of the phone. "Yeah, yeah. Text me them both. I gotta go." She hung up on whoever it was and squared herself off against Scarlett, who stopped just at arm's reach.

It felt like I was watching a Mexican standoff.

Jadelyn broke the silence first. "Sorry. I had too much to drink tonight. That wasn't okay." Her head dipped ever so slightly.

Scarlett wasn't about to let her off the hook that easily; her hand flashed out and slapped Jadelyn hard enough to pitch her head. "That sober you up?"

My phone buzzed with what I knew was Morgana's by-play of the situation. I did not need to burst out laughing reading it right now, so I kept my phone in my pocket.

Jadelyn turned her face back to Scarlett, her eyes going silver. I almost took a small step forward, thinking it would escalate into a fight I'd need to break up, but then Jadelyn's head hung in defeat. "How can I make it up to you?"

"Dammit, Jade." Scarlett stomped her foot. "You don't get to just do that and 'make it up'. I'm pissed and... and confused..." She turned to me for help, but I wasn't sure what she wanted. "Jade there's something you don't know, and I can't tell you." Scarlett gave me a meaningful look, a question in her eyes.

I realized she meant that I was a dragon. She'd said she understood that I'd normally have more than one lover. I wondered if the illusions were her way of trying to satisfy that need on her own.

"If I don't know, I can't help," Jadelyn said, looking up and seeing the looks pass between the two of us.

"I can't say. Not yet," I answered the unspoken question, also clueing in Jadelyn that it was my secret that Scarlett couldn't talk about. "Scarlett knows what I am. Morgana knows as well. But that's all, and I'd like to keep it that way for now."

"You two don't trust me?" Jadelyn asked, sounding hurt.

"I don't trust your father," I clarified. Part of me wanted to tell Jadelyn, but once her father knew, it was going to make my life a headache. There was no way he wouldn't rope me in and use me as a prop. It was telling how much he used his own daughter for his purposes.

Her face twisted. "He doesn't have to know."

"Let's let things cool down from tonight and see where things are. Maybe then we can have a conversation. I think Scarlett and I need a chance to talk first, about her confusion." I lowered a stare at the vixen.

Scarlett gave me a curt nod. "I think that we should have that conversation first."

"You come first, Scarlett. Anything after that, you get a say in." I kissed the top of Scarlett's head. She melted into me in response.

"Jade, I'm pissed. But we have a job to do, and I don't want this to impede that for now. Can you head back in the house?" Scarlett asked from the comfort of my arms.

The siren in question's phone pinged several times, and she let out a sigh of relief. "Then I have better news. Your father thinks they know where Chad might be going."

"Really?" I pulled out my phone and called Morgana. "Hey, they think they know where Chad is going."

"Give me the address. Let's finish this nonsense." Morgana sounded angry.

Jadelyn hesitated for a moment. "Uh. Sorry. It isn't one place. It's two. Detective Fox's department has been trying to track down the drug movement, and he's gotten leads. But they're two different directions."

"How far apart?" Morgana asked.

"Several hours? Both areas are known to have werewolf packs."

"Shit," I cursed, and everyone turned to me. "We will have to split up. It's the only way we get rid of Chad before he amasses a bigger army."

I could hear Morgana's stillness on the other side of the phone. "Are you sure, Zach?"

Jadelyn was perhaps the most surprised. "You can't take Chad on alone."

"First off, he won't be alone." Scarlett glared up at me before looking at Jadelyn. "I want to— scratch that, I need to go with him."

"Of course. Sending you to go take care of Chad now that we don't think he's coming here is the best use of your time," Jadelyn thought on her feet, twisting Scarlett's request into a logical reason to send her. I wondered if she needed that sort of reasoning to use later when their fathers questioned them.

"Then we don't have any time to waste," Morgana said. "Send me one address and send them the other. Zach, meet me at the van."

Scarlett patted me on the chest and left my embrace. "Let me get dressed. We can take my bike." She bolted off as Jadelyn stood, clearly torn with what she should do next.

"The council is sending their people. You'll both have backup to help with the packs."

I took that piece of information with me as I headed over to the van, knowing Morgana had a full kit waiting for me.

Morgana's van sat in a dark spot in the corner of the street where a streetlamp wasn't working. I wondered briefly if that was Morgana's doing or if the light had already been out.

Morgana was already at the van, throwing open the trunk and stashing the large sniper rifle she'd been planning to use. "Feel comfortable with something bigger tonight?" she asked over her shoulder.

"Jadelyn says the council's people will be there again. I don't think I'm going to have anything near as big as what they had on those Jeeps. And despite being huge, those shots didn't seem to do much to either of the alphas." I smacked my chest. "I'm hoping to bring my own big gun to bear."

If those Jeep mounted guns hadn't worked, I hoped that my fire would be enough to take down Chad.

"Think it's going to come when you need it? You've changed a lot and gotten some more control, but will your fire come?"

I paused, replaying my last week. I definitely had changed. A week ago, I wouldn't have made the move on Scarlett, or even considered pursuing more than one woman. I'd gained more alignment with my beast, letting some of the primal urges guide my decisions. And it felt right. I still felt like I was doing good for the world, but it was a different path than I'd once planned to take. This one was a bit more gruesome, and there was blood on my hands now, but I'd also made the world a lot safer and saved wolves' lives.

"It'll come." The confidence in my tone satisfied her, and she handed me a pistol and a grenade.

"This is so you can save it for when it really counts."

Putting the gun in my pants and throwing on my jacket I'd left in the car, I looked back at her. "Thanks for everything, Morgana."

It seemed to catch her by surprise. She stopped to turn and give me a once over. "You are very welcome. But don't think this is all over after this. That room is still yours, and you can keep working with me."

I let out a sigh. In my mind, I'd already accepted that I was embracing my paranormal life. "I'll call the EMT service tomorrow and quit. Seems stupid to keep doing that now."

Morgana's lips curled up in a smile. "And school?"

"Who knows?" I shrugged. "The real world didn't just vanish. I think I'll finish if I can." A weight lifted off my shoulders that I hadn't realized was there. But it seemed like the obvious answer. I was a dragon about to go chase down a killer werewolf with my kitsune girlfriend. It was ridiculous to think I could pretend to live a normal life after all that.

"Good. I'm glad you finally made up your mind. Now go, before I have a dangerous little kitsune mad at me." Morgana shooed me away.

The thought of Scarlett made me smile, and I turned back towards the house. The garage started groaning as it opened.

The first thing I saw was a pair of leather boots that capped off just below the knees. As the garage continued to rise, I spotted dark leather pants tucked into the boots, followed by an open biker jacket with a fitted bodysuit underneath. I already knew that body better than any other.

When the garage finally finished raising, Scarlett was pulling her hair back, a hair tie dangling from her mouth as she wrangled her hair. Her eyes found mine, and she smiled before jerking her head for me to follow her.

The garage had several nice, yet several-years-old, cars. In the back, there was a big black and chrome bike that looked like it was made for speed.

"That's your bike?"

"Yep. Bought it with the money from the first few jobs." She caressed the bike and threw me a helmet. "Wear that. It's Jadelyn's, but we'll get one of your own later."

"What exactly is your job again?" I asked as I squeezed the helmet over my head and got a nose full of Jadelyn's lily-like scent.

"We protect the Scalewright family. But the best way to stop an assassin is to think like one. Or rather, to be one," she clarified, a wicked smile spreading across her face. "There are times like tonight where it's better to go out and eliminate a problem rather than to wait for it to come."

"Badass."

"Glad you think so." I could hear the blush even through her helmet. Swinging her leg over the bike, Scarlett straddled it. "Hop on and please lean with me."

"I've only ridden a few times, but it's like riding a bicycle, right?" I joked.

She wasn't amused and flipped up her visor to glare at me. "If you wreck my baby, I am going to wreck you."

I gave her a sharp salute and got in place behind her, having to talk loudly around the helmet. "Roger, no joking about the bike. Jadelyn, bike, boyfriend." I made steps in the air to clarify where they all stood.

"Boyfriend?" she asked, kicking up the kickstand.

I paused, and before I could answer, she throttled the bike and peeled out of the garage. I noticed the phone she had mounted on her bike bars. Curious, I looked to see where we were headed, but my mouth dried up as I got my answer.

We were on our way to the neighborhood I had grown up in.

Chapter 28

Scarlett's bike slowed down as we got off the highway. We had spoken little during the drive; I made a mental note to get us Bluetooth earpieces if we made it a regular thing.

We had traveled into the suburbs, the very same ones that I had grown up in. Things were nostalgically familiar as we drove. I spotted a shop that was still around on old, familiar roads.

Memories flooded back. Happy ones, that included my foster parents, my heart aching with the reminder of what I'd lost. I breathed deeply, trying to push them aside to focus on the job we needed to do.

Scarlett rolled to a stop at a light, and I fished out my phone. Morgana had already texted from her location. Everything was quiet on her side, and I replied ours was the same. No sign of a rampaging werewolf pack. After Nicetown, that was something I wanted to prevent.

The loss of life had been unacceptable. And it would be regardless of where we were, but something about being back in my hometown made it extra powerful. I wouldn't let Chad rip this town apart.

I stuck my phone back in my pocket as the light turned green, wrapping my arms around Scarlett as we continued through the streets, scanning for any signs of trouble.

The area became more and more familiar as we got closer to the neighborhood where I'd grown up. A chill was creeping up my spine as I wondered if it was all just a big coincidence.

Knowing the area, I called out, "Take a right here, Scarlett."

She trusted me, instantly turning down the less direct route. "You know this area?" she shouted back.

"Yeah, I grew up in a house on this street." We rolled on by the house, which looked similar to how I'd remembered it, although a few changes had been made.

It was sitting quietly, the residents already asleep tonight. A blue sedan sat parked in the driveway near a plastic basketball hoop. A discarded children's bike sat off to the side, tipped over in the grass. It was a young family's home now.

Memories welled up, threatening to overwhelm me, but I squeezed Scarlett's side, indicating to keep moving, and she did it without question. The house moved past behind me, and I let out the breath I had been holding.

Scarlett continued following her directions, pulling up to one of the larger houses in the back of the neighborhood. Mr. Ziggler had lived here, if I remembered correctly. His property butted up against the woods that served as a buffer between the neighborhood addition and the highway. He had been known for often throwing enormous parties at this house, and it seemed like tonight might be another one. The street was lined with cars.

I took off the stuffy helmet and hung it on Scarlett's handlebars. "Let me go first. I might know these guys."

"And you never knew they were wolves, huh?" she said, taking off her own helmet. "Strange how small the world is sometimes."

"Yeah," I said absently, going up the steps and ringing the doorbell. We waited a few minutes, but there was no answer. I tried again, but still got no answer.

"Let's look around back and see if there's even anyone home." The lights were on and music played, but it didn't seem like anyone was actually in the house.

The woods loomed off in his backyard, familiar yet oddly strange tonight as if they were filled with mystery. I'd even played in those woods as a kid, yet tonight they hid secrets that I felt I should have known back then. Could they have been hiding a wolf pack the entire time without me knowing? I felt like I would have spotted them at some point.

We stepped around back, and someone came out of the woods. "What are you doing? Get off my property."

I squinted, peering through the moonlight and spotting Mr. Ziggler. "Hi, Mr. Ziggler, you probably don't remember me, but I'm Zach Pendragon. I used to live with the Richards."

"I remember you." Mr. Ziggler squinted. "Why are you sneaking around my house?"

I decided to go straight to being direct. "Are you a werewolf?"

He laughed good-naturedly. "Oh, that's a good one. But it's late, Zach. Go mess with somebody else; I'm too tired for games."

"We are on business from the council. There has been trouble with the packs lately. Brent is dead," I clarified.

That brought Mr. Ziggler up short. "Brent? He was a powerful alpha."

"A new drug went through his pack, and they all succumbed to rage after it. They ran as werewolves through the city and were hunted down." Everything I said was true, but I purposefully left out that Chad had taken his pack. I worried the wolf would just see it as a simple challenge and underestimate Chad. Or worse, it could rile up the pack and cause another incident.

"This drug what... uh, what is it like?" It was hard to see his face in the moonlight, half of it cast in shadow, but from what I could tell, Mr. Ziggler was worried.

"White powder," I said, feeling unhelpful. "In addition to the side effects directly felt, it messes with pack magic." I shifted my eye, taking in Mr. Ziggler's magic. It had the same oily taint as the wolves of Brent's pack.

But what surprised me was that his bond flowed off to an alpha. I had assumed with his big parties that he would be the alpha of the woods. But, based on the connection spreading into the woods, that person was somewhere behind him.

"There's something wrong with your pack, isn't there?" Scarlett spoke for the first time; she must not have needed the confirmation I had.

"No. Things are fine," he began but was cut off as a howl split the night behind him, joined by several more. "Shit, they aren't supposed to howl out there."

"Why not?"

"Because that sounds like a great way to get someone calling animal control or somebody saying there are wolves out in the woods. We run in them; some of the pack lives in the old fort. It's best to keep it all on the down-low."

I remembered the old fort; it was a popular play spot for the neighborhood kids. "It's just an old-ruined building."

Mr. Ziggler gave me a look that made me rethink that. "Exactly what we wanted all the kids like you to think. There's a bunker under it. The pack used to own all this land, but we sold most of it off to developers in the 40s."

I nodded, realizing that, while Mr. Ziggler looked in his late fifties, he must be a hundred years old as a werewolf.

"Take us to your alpha. We need to talk and prepare. The council can bring potions to help with the side effects of the drug and fix your pack magic. The bigger concern is the ones spreading the drug. We think they are coming here tonight to mount an attack while you are weak." I pointedly didn't tell him that it was to take over the pack; I remembered the woman's reaction when I'd told her.

Right now, I had to keep Mr. Ziggler focused and hope the council's forces would be right behind us to help us deal with Chad and his warped pack when they arrived.

"Come on. I'll show you." Mr. Ziggler waved over his shoulder, turning around. "Sorry about what happened to your parents."

"It's been a few years. The time and the distance have helped," I admitted.

"They were good people, normals though. I would have never guessed you were para. Must have been a shock." He made conversation as we picked through the woods.

I was half-listening at that point, keeping my eyes up and looking through the woods. My shifted eye was able to see in the dark far better than my human one. "It was a shock, a recent one too."

"Oh, that's too bad. I thought your biological parents would have reached out and told you."

I missed a step. "Excuse me?"

"You didn't know? They came around once in a while when you were young, maybe just out of diapers. They made a big stink, and the Richards called the cops on them; your parents really rattled them, apparently. I only know because we pay attention when the police show up this close to the pack."

It felt like a hole in the ground threatened to yawn open and devour me, but Scarlett was there at my side, holding me from falling in. "We can check it out later," she promised in a whisper.

"Do you remember anything else?" I asked him.

"No, but you might still be able to get the police report from back then."

Scarlett nodded quickly. "My father can get you that. I'll make sure it happens."

Pushing all the emotions that began welling up inside of me to the side, I peered through the dark towards the old fort. "There it is. Where's the door to the bunker?" I couldn't believe I hadn't found it when I was playing with my friends.

"Past it. No one ever wants to climb down into the sewers. Plus, it makes a great bottleneck."

I nodded, remembering that there was an old, exposed sewer pipe out there. Dammit. We used to use that as a meetup point.

"I can see it on your face; you feel stupid for not knowing. But how could you? We spend quite a bit of effort hiding the pack out here."

More howls in the distance rose up. It sounded like arguing.

"That's almost the entire pack." Mr. Ziggler's brow furrowed.

"We need to hurry." I ran through the woods, roughly remembering where the old sewer hole cover was. Sure enough, the rusted metal jutted a few feet out of the ground and the cover was tossed aside haphazardly. Not the best hiding.

Above the access hole, Scarlett stopped, and her fox ears twitched. "There's plenty of people down there. I think we might have company."

"Company?" Mr. Ziggler said, more and more howls joined the night until it sounded like an entire army was there. It was far more than just his small pack.

"You said this entrance makes a good choke point? I think you'll need it tonight. They are coming for you and your pack."

Mr. Ziggler's nostrils flared, and he squared his shoulders. "I dare them."

"Get down there, and fight smart. If I'm right, there's nearly two hundred wolves out there." I grabbed the older man and physically lifted him into the sewer hole.

His eyes popped out of his head as he wriggled in my grasp, not happy about the sudden change in dynamics. Scarlett wasn't having any of this. "Go, get your pack ready. We'll be right behind you."

"What are we going to do?" I asked, seeing Scarlett summon two illusions and run them into the night.

"Calling for backup." She had her phone out, texting rapidly.

"Get in the bunker. We'll fight with them down alongside Mr. Ziggler's pack." I pushed her towards the entrance. She finished her text, jumping in.

The howling was getting closer, and I knew that, if Chad was there, he'd be able to sense the pack underground. He'd be coming for them, and we had little time to prepare.

The access hole led into a long concrete shaft barely wide enough for a single person, equipped with a metal ladder that went to the bottom.

Scarlett slid down the ladder, and I followed her example, burning my hands and squeezing with my feet to maintain a steady speed until my feet hit the ground and I was surrounded by a dozen shifted wolves. Their magic was inky with the corruption from the drug.

"Not much time. A wild pack is about to come attack you. They've already killed another pack's alpha. Do not underestimate them. The council should be on their way, but we need to hold out. Where's your alpha?"

There were looks between the wolves before Mr. Ziggler spoke up. "That's Zach, the boy the Richards adopted. And his heartbeat says he's telling the truth. Prepare for the other pack. I'll bring him to Stewart."

The wolves parted, and I got a better look at the room we were in. It was like a blast from the past. Thick colorful shag carpeting blanketed the floor, and the bright colors clashed in that style that was popular in the 1940s and 1950s.

"Your interior decorating could use an update," I commented as we moved through the rooms.

Mr. Ziggler was not amused. "Can it," he growled, pushing through a set of curtains.

We entered a room that smelled like a hospital, the scent of harsh cleaners hitting my nose. In the middle of the room was a dying man, hooked up to several machines. It didn't seem like he could be the alpha, but with my dragon's eye, I could see all the other wolves connected to him. But his system was only slightly darkened by the drug.

"Did you really give this man the drug?" I looked at Mr. Ziggler accusingly. It didn't look like his condition was recent; my guess was the disease had confined him to the bed for a while.

Mr. Ziggler held up his hands in his defense. "I was against it, but some of the pack tried it and said it made their abilities stronger. We wanted to see if we couldn't spark his regeneration abilities. He's been battling cancer for a decade. Even with his healing, it's just too much now."

I nodded, disappointed we didn't have a heavy hitting alpha to take on the other wolf pack, but I was also glad that we didn't have to deal with another raging alpha.

I turned back to Mr. Ziggler, who now seemed like my best bet to organize the pack. "Their target is Stewart, and the alpha coming for him is powerful."

"Not a fucking chance," Mr. Ziggler growled. "We have almost fifty in the pack, and they can only get through one at a time."

His words were answered with the grating and groaning of metal being torn back the way we had come.

"You just had to put those words out into the universe, didn't you?" Scarlett sighed. "Sounds like you are about to be proven wrong."

I hurried back to the entrance of the bunker. Wolves were gathered and growing in number at the top of the concrete tube. Chad was there in his massive, grotesque werewolf form. His hands were more like backhoes as he tore apart the top of the entrance.

"Holy shit. What happened to him?" Scarlett was seeing his warped alpha werewolf for the first time.

"I'd like to know that too," I muttered. It was more than just the drug. That ritual dagger he had used to cut Brent's heart seemed off. It wasn't something that fit with his personality.

Chad's hulking werewolf form moved back from view, leaving room for smaller werewolves to jump down one by one. They landed with a crunch of broken legs—it wasn't a small drop. Without using the ladder to control our descent, we could have ended up in a very similar position.

Mr. Ziggler's pack didn't need any encouragement. They rushed forward to try to take out the newly arrived werewolves.

But in doing so, they created a new problem. Chad's pack was still jumping down, and now they were using the bodies of the werewolves clashing at the bottom to soften their landing, keeping their legs intact.

Soon the bottom of the shaft became a dog pile, although wolf pile was probably more accurate. The packs fought viciously, sometimes not knowing the difference between friend and foe in a gruesome display of sheer savagery.

Scarlett and I stood back, watching the display, unable to participate.

"Any ideas?" I asked. My own gun would hit friendly as likely as the enemy, and I wasn't about to join that dog pile.

Before she could reply, one of the grotesque wolves pulled itself from the dogpile, its injuries healing as it lumbered forward like it already had Scarlett cornered.

I went to move to protect her, but my badass kitsune surprised it, jerking left with an illusion while the real Scarlett came in from the right.

The wolf went cross-eyed for a second before swiping at the wrong target. I was there by then, grabbing its big paws while Scarlett pulled out a military knife and punched it into the wolf's skull repeatedly. The wolf sagged, probably from the lack of brain matter as Scarlett finished it, severing its head as it shrank back to a forty-year-old man.

"Damn. I'll make sure not to piss you off."

"Kind of cathartic in its own way." Scarlett blew a raspberry at me. It would have been more innocent looking if she hadn't been holding a bloody knife and looking deadly.

We fought alongside each other at the edge of the mass of wolves, working to contain them from being able to spread throughout the bunker. I used my strength to hold them while Scarlett went to work like a butcher.

"So. About earlier," Scarlett started as she finished another wolf.

"Is now really the time to talk about this?" I couldn't believe she was bringing it up then.

She shrugged after she dropped the dead wolf. "Maybe it's because my blood is pumping, or maybe it's because it might not matter now that it's easier to talk about it."

I grabbed another wolf coming out of the pile and held him still as Scarlett jumped on his back and went to work on his spine. "You know, talking about our relationship while you dismember someone is a little scary."

"Good." She punctuated that with a stab to the base of the wolf's skull, dropping it like a sack of potatoes. "So, as you could tell, I got a little upset. But I think I'm mostly upset that she's already coming for you. I just got you."

Chad roared up above, apparently done sending down his little minions. He began to dig out the rest of the shaft.

"See, he agrees," Scarlett joked, and I couldn't help but wish she'd take it all a little more seriously. We were holding our own, but at some point, we'd be overrun.

She just continued on, though. "I know that you'll have other women eventually—you're a 'you know what', after all. Is it too much for me to have some time alone with you?"

Not wanting to get too deep into it and being okay with it despite a part of me not wanting to commit, I replied, "Deal."

"Wait, really?"

"Sure. I really like you, Scarlett. My beast won't hold out forever, but I think it can live with it being a little further out. You're worth that."

She hopped over the dead wolf in front of her and grabbed my head, getting blood on me as she pulled me in for a quick, passionate kiss. "Thank you. I know it won't last forever."

Nodding, I turned her back towards the battle. "Now focus." I smacked her ass playfully, but my attention was solely focused behind her. Chad's massive frame tore through the ground at a remarkable speed.

CHAPTER 29

As I stood, preparing to square off against a massive alpha wolf hyped up on drugs and magic, I once again questioned the choices I'd made to reach that moment.

The fucker was huge. Chad tore through the last of the shaft. Blood seeped from where his skin tore and stretched too far as he worked his mouth. I squinted at the massive monster; he seemed even bigger than the last time.

"Get out of the shaft," I yelled, knowing it was about to become the site of a carnage.

But the wolves just continued fighting; none of them listened to me. And they paid the price. Chad's giant body landed on top of many of them, and those he hadn't hit he tore through with no concern for what side they were on. It was gore on the level of some twisted horror film.

I knew my gun wouldn't put a dent in him, and I doubted Scarlett's knife would go deep enough to do any actual damage. We were limited in our options to slow him down and keep him from the other alpha.

The best tool I had was my breath, and I had to hope it wouldn't fail me at that moment.

I focused, feeling the heat build in my chest, and I smiled. It would come when I called it. But before I could do anything, a crash came from behind me as another huge alpha wolf stumbled drunkenly through the bunker, tangled up in wires and dragging medical equipment as it thrashed, ripping the wires off. He sagged low, his eyes burning with determination.

Chad didn't seem to consider the alpha much of a threat, his lupine grin growing wider. He charged, completely ignoring Scarlett and me as he slammed into the wolf I assumed was Stewart. Both of them went down in a mess.

The two of them, both titans of power on their own. But, together, they destroyed the bunker, reducing the cinder block walls to dust every time they collided.

I couldn't unleash my fire breath without killing them both, so I held it. Spitting a curse, I pulled out my gun and squeezed off several rounds into Chad, hoping to weaken him at least slightly. But they were nothing more than gnats from the way he ignored them.

It took little time before Stewart was pinned to the ground and Chad went to town, flaying the other werewolf's chest. I realized he was probably trying to get his heart like he had Brent's. I had to stop it, and I no longer had a reason to hold back my fire.

Stepping forward, I pulled Scarlett behind me. "Stay back."

I focused on the pent-up fire in my chest, and I let it loose. Fire streamed out of my mouth and quickly blossomed in the air, billowing into a cloud of raging flames. The flames consumed both werewolves, but my breath only lasted a few seconds before it petered out.

Luckily, it was long enough to do some serious damage.

As the flames and smoke cleared, all I could see was a dark, still lump on the floor. The noise of the surrounding werewolves went silent for a moment. The wolves at the bottom of the shaft had stopped fighting and watched for their alpha. To see if they had survived.

The black lump moved, and Chad's grotesquely large head rose, pushing a blackened and charred body off of it. My heart fell, he had rolled Stewart into the brunt of the heat, protecting himself.

But it hadn't been a total loss. One of Chad's arms ended in a black stump at his elbow. It must have been the one he used to hold the other alpha ahead of him. I'd blackened much of Chad's skin, but it was all surface level damage that was healing before my eyes.

I breathed deep, gathering more heat into my chest. Or at least, I tried to, but that heat felt dry and empty. I didn't have a continuous stream, and it looked like I'd used what I had.

"Zach, what's happening? Why aren't you finishing this?" Scarlett said, hiding behind me.

"Can't." It came out in a quiet growl. I was mad at my body, but I stared Chad down, not wanting him to see weakness.

The gesture might have been enough, because fear entered Chad's eyes, and he bolted on three legs for the exit, tearing through the wolves again as he broke into the open air. He just needed time to heal. Then I knew he'd be back.

I looked around. Stewart's pack was in shambles, and their alpha was dead. I'd cooked him thoroughly, and luckily destroyed the heart I assumed Chad had been after. There was no reason for Chad to stay.

The rest of Chad's pack followed his lead, but they struggled to get out of the shaft without the size advantage that Chad had.

I couldn't let Chad get away. He'd just target another pack, and we might not be there in time to stop the next one. Taking a deep breath, I filled my nose with his scent, which still lingered throughout the bunker.

Looking at all the wolves on the ladder, I tried to figure out how to get myself out of the bunker. Deciding to try out an idea, I turned to Scarlett.

"Hold on to me."

Bending over slightly, she jumped and latched onto my back, her arms wrapping around my shoulders. "What are we doing now?" She sounded a little scared.

I ran at the werewolves, but before I got too close, I bent at the knees like loaded springs and used all my enhanced strength to launch myself up and out of the collapsed shaft. My strength and for once my lower mass didn't let me down; it was like flying briefly as I shot into the air, clearing the werewolves and landing outside the massive, freshly dug hole.

"Wow," Scarlett said, jumping off my back. I smiled, but I wasn't done yet. Rain misted down as a storm rolled in, followed by flashes of lightning and booms of thunder, as the scene grew even more grisly.

"I'm going after Chad, Scarlett. He can't get away again; not this time." I pushed off the ground with a loping stride. Pushing my legs further, my next step cleared several meters, the one after that moving me even further.

"Hey, wait up," Scarlett shouted behind me, and she raced after me, but there was no time. I had Chad's scent, and I was going to chase him down and end it all.

Each leaping stride ate up ground faster than any pace my human legs could have ever gone.

Bounding through the woods, I closed in on Chad, his scent growing stronger. Eventually, I was close enough to hear him crashing through the woods ahead. He was injured, and it was slowing him down.

Something about the thought of a weakened prey woke up the primal part of me that wanted to hunt.

Chad was cutting a jagged path through the woods, eventually ending up under an overpass. It was the middle of the night, so not many cars were on the road. He came to a stop in the shadows of the overpass.

Stooping down, Chad cradled where his arm had burned away. I watched as he shifted back into Chad, the starting quarterback. His eyes were bloodshot and ghostly pale around the edges. He didn't look right.

Chad saw me and stumbled back under the overpass, like he was going to keep running. Rain was running off the highway, making a curtain of streams between us. I took a step forward, my foot splashing on the muddy ground.

I pulled to breathe fire again, but it was a slowly building fire, one that wasn't ready yet. Knowing I needed to buy some time, I stalled. "Chad. It's over. The council knows you are here. They are encircling you even now."

In the deeper shadows of the overpass, all I could make out were his glowing eyes in the darkness as he turned to me. "You don't understand. No one understands."

"Then help me understand, Chad. We found something to reverse the drug. We could undo all of this and save those other werewolves." And I meant it. If we could cure Chad, it would help all the other wolves. For that, I would hold back on finishing this with him. It may come back to bite me in the ass later, but it was worth all the lives saved.

Chad's breathing was deep and ragged. I began to wonder what was going on in the darkness. It seemed like more than a wounded arm. "The pressure. So much pressure to be the best. Always the best. And even then, it wasn't enough. I had to be better and better until no one could dare think of trying to be my equal. Do you understand that sort of pressure?" Chad sounded unhinged, but I could understand what he was saying.

I'd experienced pressure, just like anybody, but I'd also had a pretty wonderful support system most of my life. I wondered what had led Chad to crack. Was he really destined to be a beta from the beginning, and this resulted from pushing himself too far to be an alpha?

"Okay, so what do we do, Chad? How do we take away the pressure?" I tried to keep him engaged. The fire was building back up inside of me, and I just needed a little longer.

Howls pierced the night, and heavy gunfire followed. It sounded like the wolves were out of the bunker and the sirens had arrived. I hoped they had gotten enough of the cleansing potion made to save the wolves.

"He offered. He gave me a way out, to become better than ever and consume the other alphas."

I paused, processing what he'd just said. I'd known deep down it had felt like more than Chad was capable of, but I hated that it all went deeper.

"He who, Chad? Who did this?" I guessed that person was likely also responsible for the drug. "Chad, who gave you the dagger?" I stepped forward, eager to know.

Lightning lit up the sky, illuminating everything around us. In the light, I saw Chad crouching, ready to pounce, the obsidian dagger in his hands.

The runoff from the highway splashed as he erupted from his crouch, and I barely grabbed onto his wrist before the dagger touched me. I knew little about the dagger, but I had a feeling letting it touch me would be a mistake.

Twisting, I rolled him over, splashing the two of us into a muddy puddle and pushing his hand further away from me.

"Who gave this to you?" I shouted over the storm.

I had him pinned down, but I felt something approaching behind me. Rolling off Chad, I narrowly avoided a werewolf passing through the space I'd just been in.

I could hear the splashing of many paws. Another peal of lighting lit up the night sky, confirming that I was surrounded by dozens of werewolves.

"Maybe I'll tell you after I kill you." Chad wiped at his mouth as he rose out of the puddle covered in mud. "You are strong. I don't know what you are, but you are close enough to a shifter that I think this'll work on you too." He flashed the sinister dagger at me.

I was surrounded, with a homicidal maniac pointing a magic dagger at me, but my mind had still caught on one thing he'd said. "You think I'm close enough to be considered a shifter?"

Chad paused, pulling up short, clearly confused at where I was going. The surrounding wolves howled in frustration at the pause.

"I challenge you for your alpha position," I projected my voice, hoping I'd done it properly.

Wolves all around me started howling into the sky, growling and barking as they backed up, making a large ring for us to fight in. I was glad that the drugs hadn't numbed their brains to where they would ignore their traditions.

Chad's face went slack. He hadn't been expecting that, and I could see fear taking root inside of him. The same insecurities that had caused him to go down this path were exactly what I was bringing forward. One on one, he didn't have the security of the pack behind him.

Chad immediately shifted, but this time he didn't shift to the massive monstrosity. It was closer to when we'd fought on campus. I hadn't realized he'd be able to still shift to that form.

His arms sprouted fur, and his one remaining hand turned to wicked claws. He leaned forward as his back elongated, hunched with muscles. His feet and legs became a hairy mess, but his legs remained human instead of the digitigrade legs of a werewolf.

It was a show of his skill that he was able to manage such a partial transformation. I imagined this form would also be far quicker than if he were a big, hulking brute.

It made sense. Chad was concerned about my fire. Remaining light and nimble enough to have a chance to get out of the way when it came was a safer bet.

I at least had to give him a nod of respect for using his brains, but I'd have to find a way to torch him, regardless. It was my best bet at winning.

"You'll regret this." Chad put down the dagger to the side, surprising me. I figured he'd use it, but maybe weapons weren't allowed in an alpha challenge.

Chad began circling around, and I watched him. But he moved faster than I expected, his claws catching my shirt before I could lean back, tearing the front wide open and scoring shallow red lines across my chest.

"You sure about that?" I brought my hands up and came at him, throwing punch after punch at him, pushing forward. Unfortunately, his legs seemed like giant springs as he bounced backwards effortlessly.

The wolves around us howled like a stadium full of spectators watching their favorite blood sport. There was something terribly macabre about cheers taking the form of howls.

Chad lashed forward with his singular arm again, but this time I blocked it, stepping forward with a direct punch to his chest. He sprang back with my punch, and I knew it didn't connect solidly enough to do anything to the werewolf.

The fight continued on like that. Chad kept dancing around me, taking small, calculating swings. He hadn't gone for any killing blows; he was trying to wear me down.

I had fully expected Chad to be all brute force and no brains; he was proving me wrong. Chad was more strategic than I'd given him credit for, and I was still early in my training with Morgana.

Chad's claws raked across my body, destroying my jacket and dyeing my shirt red. With the help of the rain, the crimson color quickly bled down through to my pants. The muddy ground beneath us was getting slicker by the second as rain poured off the highway and our feet mixed it into the ground.

I ducked his next probing attack, realizing his strategy was working. He was wearing me down. I decided it was time to play dirty.

Grabbing a hunk of mud in my left hand, I came up, slinging it in his face. He hadn't expected it, instinctively moving to try to dodge it. I used his movement to my advantage. My right hand came around in a hook he didn't see coming, and I got a clean hit to the side of his head. He staggered back; I'd got him good.

Pressing forward, I got in several more solid jabs before I caught his chin and he fumbled backwards. I only needed to keep him still long enough to finish this.

"I was never that weak. Alpha wolves can't be that weak," Chad's voice came up next to us. I did a double take, but then I realized with my dragon eye, it wasn't a physical body, but one of Scarlett's illusions.

The real Chad screamed in rage and clawed at the illusion, dispelling it in a puff and completely losing his cool. I silently thanked Scarlett. It had put him over the edge, and his scrappy fighting was turning into a berserk rampage that I could handle. He clawed at the wolf behind the illusion, and it whimpered, backing up.

All the wolves backed up but started making more noise. Howls and growls picked up, and I realized Chad's loss of faculties was affecting this pack.

"Think you can get rid of your failure so easily? What a joke." Another Chad illusion popped up.

This time Chad shifted into his hulking, grotesque werewolf and dove into the surrounding ring of wolves, killing several as he tried to charge away from the illusions. I took advantage and jumped on his back, grabbing his fur to hold on, even as it fell off in tufts.

I was worried the rain would dissipate my fire, but I didn't have that worry now.

Getting the best grip that I could, I saw his massive head rear back and stare at me. There was a look in his eye; he knew it was the end of it. Breathing deeply, I breathed fire right between his shoulder blades.

Bright orange flames washed over Chad and me, the rain and the water exploding in a cloud of steam that hid us in our own little world as my dragon fire torched through Chad's back, consuming all that he was in just seconds.

I rode what was left of his body to the ground as it splashed messily into the mud.

"Zach?" Scarlett's voice called outside the steam. Wolves were howling, mourning notes, and I heard heavy engines in the background just before rapid gunfire ripped through the gathering.

Rolling to the ground, I did my best to stay low and get away, ducking under the underpass. "Stop firing! Chad is dead," I yelled at the top of my lungs, but through all the wolves and gunfire, no one heard me.

A round seared my shoulder as it nicked me. I was pissed, and the beast bubbled up inside of me until it came out in a deafening roar that rose above all else and blew away the steam cloud.

Everything stopped, paused, and turned to me.

"Chad is dead. I won in the alpha challenge. Wolves, stand down." My tone brooked no argument, and wolves curled in on themselves, their tails tucking under them, and many shifted back into naked humans.

It looked like we'd just finished a very violent orgy in the woods.

"Get them potions and clean this up. Oh, and someone get me something to hold that." I pointed to the obsidian and bone dagger with a look of disgust. I didn't even want to touch it, but I wanted to keep an eye on it. The dagger was dangerous. I hoped it could either help lead us to the leader, but if not, it needed to just get buried deep in the ground somewhere. Morgana would know what to do.

Sirens jumped off the Jeeps, and together with a group of elves, they carried crates around and started offering the potions to the werewolves.

One of the sirens jogged up to me and looked down at the dagger, starting to reach for it. I grabbed him by their collar and jerked him away.

"Don't even touch it. Get someone who knows enough not to do something stupid with it. I want it contained and given to me."

"O-of course," he stuttered.

I realized that, covered in blood and gore, mixed with my roar, I'd become something deathly terrifying to him.

"Zach." Scarlett bounded into me, and I let the siren go. "Oh, thank god."

At least Scarlett didn't fear me. I kissed her, finally relaxing ever so slightly with her in my arms. I was relieved she was safe.

Picking her up by her thighs and holding her to me, I savored being alive and the feeling of her lips as I threw myself into the kiss, ignoring the mess around us for another day.

***

It all seemed to be a blur after that. Or maybe that was just the result of me coming off the largest adrenaline high of my life.

I was sitting on the back of one of the dozen or so Jeeps they were providing support out of. They had given me one of those crinkling foil blankets, like I was going to go into shock.

Scarlett was coordinating much of the efforts to get the wolves back on their feet, though she had insisted that I rest. My two attempts to get up and help had been rebuffed, and so I found myself back on the bumper of a Jeep.

"Oh my god. Zach." Jadelyn came around the Jeep and her head snapped to me.

"You should see the other guy," I joked. My chin pointed to the burnt-out husk that used to be Chad.

Jadelyn's wide eyes followed my gesture. "He's gone? For good?"

"He won't bother you anymore. Not to mention that you don't have to marry him and deal with that whole drama."

She threw herself onto me, wrapping her arms around my neck like I was a life raft in turbulent seas. "Thank you. Thank you so much. If you ever need anything, all you have to do is ask."

I thought that maybe I had heard a slight suggestion in there, but that thought was washed away as she sagged and started crying into my shoulder.

Of course, this caught Scarlett's attention, who gave me a squinty-eyed look full of scrutiny before she nodded with a smile and kept on working. It was beyond complicated, and tonight wasn't the night to deal with any of it.

So when I heard the peel of tires spraying dirt up against the other side of the Jeep, I wasn't surprised when Morgana appeared around the side and froze, watching me holding Jadelyn.

She clearly didn't know what to do, but I waved her over around Jadelyn's hug. "Morgana. Good to see you. As you can see, I more than handled this."

Her eyes looked up from me, and she seemed to notice the carnage for the first time. "Yes. I can see that. Very draconian justice you dealt out here." She winked.

It rang true. What I'd done out here tonight had been... right. The beast and I agreed on that. We had served out justice for all those that Chad had harmed. But what surprised me was how much that meant to the beast, it would seem there was more to him than a savage need to fight and fuck. "I have a favor: there's a creepy dagger right over by him. I don't even want to touch it. Can you help me bring it back?" I wanted to horde it and hide it from the world. As if, I had a responsibility to keep it locked up.

Morgana strolled over to the dagger that had been abandoned since I had nearly throttled that siren.

"Yes, I don't think it's a problem to touch, but I understand your caution." She poked at it a few times before getting up and coming back with a gun case, stuffing it inside. "Best to be careful with it though."

"Hi, Morg." Jadelyn let out the last of her sniffles and greeted the vampire.

"Busy night." Morgana smiled back. "I hope this lays to rest your worries, but we both know your father is just going to find you another."

Jadelyn looked up at me through her eyelashes. "I hope I can sway his target at least."

This was not the time to get into this. "I hope you get what you want, Jade. But for now, let's just get out of here. I'm tired and starving."

Chapter 30

The past week had been a blur following Chad's death. The council had swooped in immediately, and the media spun up stories about a drug that was causing people to go wild. In low doses, it was said to have caused hallucinations and had proven to have made its way into the city's water supply.

That story was plastered over the front of every newspaper in the city and was on constant replay on every television station.

And then, a few days later, it became old news, pushed to the bottom of forums as the next news cycle took over and talked about what some politician had said. It proved what Morgana had been telling me.

I'd expected some sort of giant reaction, but nobody seemed to believe that the monsters they'd seen with their own eyes had been real. There were a few that had, but not enough for public opinion to believe them.

I was shocked at just how successful the council had been in suppressing everything. But I'd gotten used to it.

As I sat having lunch with Scarlett at Bumps in the Night, I looked around at the paranormal dining openly, understanding that, while they often lived their lives in the corners and shadows of the real world, they had also found ways to be in the world safely.

My phone buzzed, and it was Kelly. I turned it over, ignoring the call and the mess that had become the two wolf packs. Brent's pack had become omegas, and the council was hard-pressed to support almost two hundred new omegas in Philly.

The college pack was still active, though the bonds hadn't been cemented yet and now they were jostling for a new alpha. Hence, me ignoring Kelly's call. After my duel with Chad, the waters were a little murky there. I wasn't a werewolf, but that wasn't stopping Kelly from pushing me to take responsibility for her pack.

"Zach, focus. You missed three classes, and you need to prepare for the test." Scarlett rolled her eyes at me.

I just grinned at her. "Okay, geek out on me. What did I miss?" It was cute watching Scarlett go on about science. She'd get super passionate and, once in a while, a fox ear would pop out of her hair.

Listening to what she was trying to teach me, I enjoyed the moment. She was one of the best things to come from entering the paranormal world, and she'd become a pretty integral part of my life. Normally, that would make me insecure, but I could tell the feeling was mutual. She'd been clear she wasn't going anywhere.

We just fit together, like two pieces of a puzzle. Our lives had already become inseparably intertwined.

"Excuse me." Detective Fox approached. "I hate to interrupt my daughter when she actually studies"—he gave her a fatherly look—"but I have something for your friend." He refused to call me Scarlett's boyfriend, even though we were using those terms now.

"It's fine. She can listen to it too."

The detective scowled only for a moment before putting down two file folders. One was an old, faded blue, and the other a crisp new green. "I managed to track down that report your parents filed when your supposed birth parents dropped by their house. But I have another question. The reports we make for our... discreet activities take a while. I just got it today, and I have a few questions for you first."

He pulled back the faded blue folder and instead pushed the green one out and flipped it open. I was a little annoyed that he held back my parents' report, but I understood the man was still skeptical of me.

I looked at what he was showing me. "Yeah, that's the second drug location we found. It looked like they were just drying a solution into a powder though." I passed back the photos of the manufacturing area.

"We figured as much, but as the drug is coming off the streets, we think they are done making it. No, I had a question here. You found the girls in this room?" He pulled out several photos of the freezer that Jadelyn and Kelly had been locked up in.

"Yep. Killed two wolves and a human in there," I answered, seeing the warped metal racks and feeling a phantom pain in my back just remembering the struggle.

"This human?" Detective Fox flipped to a photo. It was the drug dealer, but the image was very wrong. Instead of a body, it looked like... like a flesh suit. Like someone had skinned the guy cleanly from top to bottom with a single cut that went from his hairline to his crotch. It resembled a human skin onesie. A shudder ran through me just thinking about it.

"Gross." Scarlett wrinkled her nose. "What did that?"

"That's what we'd like to find out." Detective Fox tapped the photo. "I'm assuming you didn't do that?"

"No. I was able to see that he was about to use magic for something, so I killed him. Snapped his neck. What is that?"

"Very dark magic. The kind we kill for. There's no such thing as a skin walker, at least not a naturally existing one in the paranormal world. However, there are witches and warlocks who use foul magic. It would seem one of them was in town."

I nodded, understanding where he was going with his questioning. "You think this witch was behind all of this, don't you? We both know Chad wasn't smart enough to make this drug, and that dagger wasn't something he could have come by naturally. All this points to someone being involved in this that had just that sort of understanding and dark magic." I pointed to the picture.

"I'd feel more confident in that if you'd let us see the dagger." Detective Fox was not pleased that we had been withholding evidence, but he hadn't found a way to get it from us yet. I wasn't going to let that thing back out into the world, no matter how much he asked.

"No." I wouldn't entertain the question. I knew enough to know the dagger was dangerous and needed it to stay where it was. I'd made sure, along with Morgana's help, that it wouldn't see the light of day.

She'd also made me what she called my hoard room using her magic. The knife and half a brick of gold, along with the gold my adoptive father and I had panned, were the totality of my current hoard, but it was enough for me at the moment.

Detective Fox didn't like my answer, but we had had the same argument before, and it seemed he didn't want to go at it again. "Fine. Thank you for your time." He stood up and left the blue folder on the table.

I stared at the folder for a moment in hesitation before Scarlett picked it up and opened it herself. "Oh, there isn't much here besides a name and a physical description of them."

"What are their names?"

"Arthur and Marie Smith," she said, frowning. "I feel like that last name is a lie."

"Me too. It isn't much to go on." I had hoped for more. I got up and leaned over her shoulder, disappointment setting in at the limited details.

They had insisted on seeing me, but my adoptive parents had stood firm that they didn't want to confuse me. My parents had made their choice, and they were going to have to deal with the consequences. It sounded like Arthur was on the edge of violence before my dad had called the cops.

"It is something. You know they existed, and they wanted to get in touch with you. And they're likely still out there somewhere," Scarlett reminded me. "Something is better than nothing."

I took the file as I sat back down in my seat, feeling like it would likely wind up in my hoard room later. It was just as important as a brick of gold for me. "Just sucks. What now?"

"We get you back to studying so you can pass chemistry. Things aren't usually as crazy as they were last week. We just need to catch you up." She nudged my book closer to me, clearly wanting me to focus on it.

But my hands found her thigh and started tracing soft symbols on it.

"You are distracting me," she said, looking at me up through her eyelashes with a breathy look. "We already gave into temptation this morning."

"Sorry, you know what I am." I smirked.

And, not only that, I had learned the past week how fleeting life could be. I had come out on the winning side with the fight with Simon and Chad, but I had no doubt there would be more. I fully planned to grab what I wanted out of life and make sure I filled my cup. A bit of selfishness wasn't bad; it was healthy.

I flagged down Morgana, seeing her in the main room. "Can we get half a dozen filets for lunch?

Scarlett lowered her head and whispered, "Zach, that's pricey."

"Zach eats for free here," Morgana's Swiss accent confirmed.

"One's for you too," I offered.

Scarlett buried her face in her hands. "That's even worse—you are going to eat Morgana into bankruptcy."

The drow vampiress simply shook her head. "It's not a problem. I offered it. It's a perk of his new job." She smiled. I hadn't gone back to work with the EMT service. Instead, I was still taking jobs with Morgana. Though they were far less exciting than the last one.

I smiled up at Scarlett. I knew the meat would fill my beast the best, and in turn could do more to help others like I had the week before. It was like on an airplane and they told you to put your mask on first before helping others.

With Morgana, I had no doubt there were more fights and challenges to come that could use my help. There were definitely things in the world that went bump in the night. I may have thought them to be a myth once, but now I knew better.

And I was one of the more powerful paranormals, even if I had a lot more training to go to realize that potential. I needed to prepare to take the monsters on. Something told me there was more riding on me than I even realized. It would seem that danger lurked even deeper in this new world that I had become a part of.

Afterword

I had an absolute blast writing this book. As those who follow me know, I'm still learning about writing with each book. This series was a self study in humor for me. Simply, I had too much fun with a snarky, sarcastic main character.

Obviously for those of you who enjoy haremlit, this book is certainly going that direction. The characters and everything going on in the story, it just felt right to take it a little slower. I kept this book to a single main romance plotline and just really tried to dig in to create memorable characters. Have no fear, we'll get another girl next book. I don't think Scarlett is going to be able to handle him on her own, and the beast certainly won't let Zach settle for just one woman.

What's next? Well, I have a minor interruption in the form of a baby boy. So Mana 4 had to have its editing pushed back. I plan to have the preorder for it out October 9th with the book due to release November 9th. Then I'll try to get back on the book-a-month train with Dao 3 on December 9th. The goal is a book a month, but I'm sure the reality is more like 10 a year with a couple of opportunities to skip a month and refresh the creative juices. I have plenty of stories still to tell. I'm super excited about this book and hope it lays the runway for a long series.

If you enjoyed Zach and want more, the best ways you can get it is by leaving a review below or simply telling others how much you enjoyed it. I want to write a lot more of Zach's snarky humor.

Leave a Review

If you want to follow my progress for future books I do monthly updates on my mailing list and Facebook page.

Mailing List Sign Up

Author Bruce Sentar on Facebook

Patreon

Also By

Legendary Rule:
Ajax Demos finds himself lost in society. Graduating shortly after artificial intelligence is allowed to enter the workforce; he can't get his career off the ground. But when one opportunity closes, another opens. Ajax gets a chance to play a brand new Immersive Reality game. Things aren't as they seem. Mega Corps hover over what appears to be a simple game. However, what he does in the game seems to affect his body outside.
But that isn't going to make Ajax pause when he finally might just get that shot at becoming a professional gamer. Join Ajax and Company as they enter the world of Legendary Rule.

Series Page

A Mage's Cultivation – Complete Series
In a world where mages and monster grow from cultivating mana. Isaac joins the class of humans known as mages who absorb mana to grow more powerful. To become a mage he must bind a mana beast to himself to access and control mana. But when his mana beast is far more human than he expected; Isaac struggles with the budding relationship between the two of them as he prepares to enter his first dungeon.
Unfortunately for Isaac, he doesn't have time to ponder the questions of his relationship with Aurora. Because his sleepy town of Lock-springs is in for a rude awakening, and he has to decide which side of the war he is going to stand on.

Series Page

The First Immortal – Complete Series

Darius Yigg was a wanderer, someone who's never quite found his place in the world, but maybe he's not supposed to be here...Ripped from our world, Dar finds himself in his past life's world, where his destiny was cut short. Reignited, the wick of Dar's destiny burns again with the hope of him saving Grandterra.

To do that, he'll have to do something no other human of Grandterra has done before, walk the dao path. That path requires mastering and controlling attributes of the world and merging them to greater and greater entities. In theory, if he progressed far enough, he could control all of reality and rival a god.

He won't be in this alone. As a beacon of hope for the world, those from the ancient races will rally around Dar to stave off the growing Devil horde.

Series Page

Saving Supervillains – Complete Series

A former villain is living a quiet life, hidden among the masses. Miles has one big secret: he might just be the most powerful super in existence.

Those days are behind him. But when a wounded young lady unable to control her superpower needs his help, she shatters his boring life, pulling him into the one place he least expected to be—the Bureau of Superheroes.

Now Miles has an opportunity to change the place he has always criticized as women flock to him, creating both opportunity and disaster. He is about to do the strangest thing a Deputy Director of the Bureau has ever done: start saving Supervillains.

Series Page

Dragon's Justice

Have you ever felt like there was something inside of you pushing your actions? A dormant beast, so to speak. I know it sounds crazy.

But, that's the best way I could describe how I've felt for a long time. I thought it was normal, some animal part of the human brain that lingered from evolution. But this is the story of how I learned I wasn't exactly human, and there was a world underneath our own where all the things that go bump in the night live. And that my beast was very real indeed.

Of course, my first steps into this new unknown world are full of problems. I didn't know the rules, landing me on the wrong side of a werewolf pack and in a duel to the death with a smug elf.
But, at least, I have a few new friends in the form of a dark elf vampiress and a kitsune assassin as I try to figure out just what I am and, more importantly, learn to control it.

Series Page

Dungeon Diving

The Dungeon is a place of magic and mystery, a vast branching, underground labyrinth that has changed the world and the people who dare to enter its depths. Those who brave its challenges are rewarded with wealth, fame, and powerful classes that set them apart from the rest.
Ken was determined to follow the footsteps of his family and become one of the greatest adventurers the world has ever known. He knows that the only way to do that is to get into one of the esteemed Dungeon colleges, where the most promising young adventurers gather.
Despite doing fantastic on the entrance exam, when his class is revealed, everyone turns their backs on him, all except for one.
The most powerful adventurer, Crimson, invites him to the one college he never thought he'd enter. Haylon, an all girls college.
Ken sets out to put together a party and master the skills he'll need to brave the Dungeon's endless dangers. But he soon discovers that the path ahead is far more perilous than he could have ever imagined.

Series Page

There are of course a number of communities where you can find similar books.
https://www.facebook.com/groups/haremlit
https://www.facebook.com/groups/HaremGamelit
And other non-harem specific communities for Cultivation and LitRPG.
https://www.facebook.com/groups/WesternWuxia
https://www.facebook.com/groups/LitRPGsociety
https://www.facebook.com/groups/cultivationnovels